# BROTHERHOOD OF WAR

The magnificent *New York Times* bestselling saga that made Griffin a superstar of military fiction—the epic story of the U.S. Army, from the privates to the generals, in the world's most harrowing wars . . .

"Griffin is a storyteller in the grand tradition, probably the best man around for describing the military community. BROTHERHOOD OF WAR . . . is an American epic."
—Tom Clancy, bestselling author of *The Sum of All Fears*

"Extremely well-done . . . First-rate."
—*The Washington Post*

"Absorbing . . . fascinating descriptions of weapons, tactics, Army life and battle."
—*The New York Times*

"A major work . . . magnificent . . . powerful."
—William Bradford Huie, author of *The Execution of Private Slovik*

"A crackling good story. It gets into the hearts and minds of those who . . . fight our nation's wars."
—William R. Corson, Lt. Col. (Ret.) U.S.M.C., author of *The Betrayal* and *The Armies of Ignorance*

# W.E.B. GRIFFIN

# THE ASSASSIN

### FIFTH IN THE <u>BADGE OF HONOR</u> SERIES

JOVE BOOKS, NEW YORK

BADGE OF HONOR: THE ASSASSIN

A Jove Book / published by arrangement with
the author

PRINTING HISTORY
Jove edition / May 1993

ISBN: 0-515-11113-9

Jove Books are published by The Berkley Publishing Group,
200 Madison Avenue, New York, New York 10016.
The name "JOVE" and the "J" logo
are trademarks belonging to Jove Publications, Inc.

PRINTED IN THE UNITED STATES OF AMERICA

10  9  8  7  6  5  4  3  2  1

*For Sergeant Zebulon V. Casey*
    *Internal Affairs Division*
*Police Department, Retired, the City of Philadelphia.*
    *He knows why.*

# ONE

Marion Claude Wheatley, who was thirty-three years of age, stood just under six feet tall, weighed 165 pounds, and was just starting to lose his hair, had no idea why God wanted to kill the Vice President of the United States, any more than he did why God had selected him to carry out His will in this regard, together with the promise that if he did so, he would be made an angel, and would live forever in the presence of the Lord, experiencing the peace that passeth all understanding.

He had, of course, thought a good deal about it. After all, he had a good education (BA, Swarthmore, cum laude; MBA, Pennsylvania) and as a market analyst (petrochemicals) for First Pennsylvania Bank & Trust, his brain had been trained to first determine the facts and then to draw reasonable inferences from them.

The first fact was that God was all powerful, which Marion accepted without question. But that raised the question why didn't God, figuratively speaking, of course, just snap his fingers and cause the Vice President to disappear? Or blow up, which is how the Lord had told him He wished the Vice President to die?

1

Since He had the power to disintegrate the Vice President without any mortal assistance, but had chosen instead to make Marion the instrument of His will, the only conclusion that could be reasonably drawn was that the Lord had his reasons, which naturally he had not elected to share with a simple mortal.

Perhaps, Marion reasoned, later, after he had proven himself worthy by unquestioningly carrying out the Lord's will, the Lord might graciously tell him why He had chosen the course of action He had.

And if that happened, Marion reasoned, it would seem to follow that God might even tell him how the Vice President of the United States had offended the Lord Most High.

There were a thousand ways the Vice President might have caused offense. He was of course a politician, and one did not need divine insight to understand how much evil they caused each and every day.

Marion suspected that whatever the Vice President's offense, it was a case of either one really terrible thing, in the eyes of God, or a series of relatively minor offenses against the Lord's will, the cumulative effect of which equaled one really terrible sin.

When the Lord had spoken with Marion, the subject of repentance and forgiveness vis-à-vis the Vice President had never even come up. Marion, of course, would not have had the presumption to raise the question himself, but certainly, if God wanted the Vice President to repent, to straighten up and fly right, so to speak, it would seem logical to expect that He would have said something along those lines. It was thus reasonable to assume that whatever the Vice President had done to offend the Lord was unforgivable.

But this was not, Marion had decided while having lunch at the Reading Terminal Market, the same thing as saying that the Vice President could not, or should not, make an effort to get himself right with the Lord. If the Lord was merciful, as Marion devoutly believed Him to be, He just might change His mind if the Vice President, figuratively or literally, went to Him on his knees and begged forgiveness.

It was even possible, if unlikely, Marion had concluded, that the Vice President was unaware of how, or to what degree, he had offended the Lord. But if that was the case, it would certainly be a Christian act of compassion, of Christian love, for Marion to let the Vice President know that he was in trouble with the Lord.

The question then became how to do so in such a way that he

would not draw attention to himself. Obviously, he could not call the Vice President on the telephone. There would be several layers of people in place to protect the Vice President from every Tom, Dick, and Harry who wanted to talk to him.

The only way to do it, Marion concluded, was to write him a letter. And that was not quite as simple as it sounded. He would have to be careful to make sure the Secret Service, who protected the Vice President, did not find out who he was. Since the Secret Service would have no way of knowing that he was not some kind of nut, rather than working at the specific direction of the Lord, if they found out he had mailed the Vice President a letter telling him that he was about to be blown up, they would come and arrest him.

Going to prison, or a lunatic asylum, was a price Marion was willing to pay for doing the Lord's work, but only *after* he had done it. If he was in prison, obviously, he could not blow the Vice President up.

And from what Marion had seen on television, and read in books, the Secret Service was very skilled in what they did. They would obviously make a great effort to locate him, once the Vice President showed them the letter. He was going to have to strive for anonymity.

On the way back to the office from the Reading Terminal, he went to the Post Office Annex and bought two stamped envelopes. Then he went into one of the discount stores on Market Street and bought a thin pad of typing paper.

He often worked late, so no one was suspicious when he stayed in his office after everyone else had gone home. When he was absolutely sure that there was no one in the office but him, he went to the typing pool and sat down at the first typist's desk. He opened the top drawer and found two spare disposable ribbons.

He took the plastic cover off the typewriter, then opened it, and removed the ribbon on the machine, carefully placing it on the desktop. Then he put in a new ribbon. He addressed the envelope:

The Hon. Vice President of the United States
Senate Office Building
Washington, D.C.

And then he took the envelope out and tore a sheet of paper from the typing paper pad and rolled that into the typewriter. He sat there drumming his fingers on the desk for a moment as he made up his

mind how to say what he wanted to say. Then he started to type. He
was a good typist, and when he was finished, there wasn't even one
strikeover, and Marion was pleased.

> Dear Mr. Vice President:

> You have offended the Lord, and He has de-
> cided, using me as His instrument, to disintegrate
> you using high explosives.

> It is never too late to ask God's forgiveness, and
> I respectfully suggest that you make your peace
> with God as soon as possible.

> Yours in Our Lord,

> A Christian.

Marion carefully folded the letter in thirds, slipped it into the envelope, and then licked the flap and sealed it. He put it into his
breast pocket.

Then he removed the ribbon from the typewriter, put the old one
back in, and closed the typewriter and covered it with its plastic
cover.

He tore off the section of ribbon that had the impressions of the
typewriter keys on it and put it into the second stamped envelope
he had purchased against the contingency that he would make an
error. He carried the envelope, the pad of typing paper, and the ribbon he had used and then removed from the typewriter back into
his office. He turned on his shredder and fed first the envelope with
the used ribbon inside into it, and then, half a dozen sheets at a
time, the typing paper. Next came the cardboard backing and cover
sheet of the typing paper pad. The only thing left was the almost intact unused plastic typewriter ribbon. It was too thick to get into the
mouth of the shredder, and moreover, he suspected that even if it
had fit into it, it probably would have jammed the mechanism.

He took the sterling silver Waterman's ballpoint pen that had
been the firm's gift to him at Christmas from his pocket, and held it
through the little plastic inside of the typewriter ribbon. Then he
fed the loose end of the ribbon into the shredder. The mechanism
drew the ribbon between the cutters. It took a long time for all of
the ribbon to be drawn into the shredder, but it was somehow fasci-

nating to watch the process, and he was a little disappointed when it was all gone.

He held the plastic center in his hand and left his office for the men's room. He went into a stall and flushed the plastic center down the toilet. Then he carefully washed his hands and left the office.

He bought a Philadelphia *Ledger* from the newsstand at 16th and Chestnut Streets, and grew warm with the knowledge that he had done the right thing and pleased God. There was a headline that said, VICE PRESIDENT TO VISIT.

The meeting in the commissioner's conference room on the third floor of the Police Administration Building, commonly called the Roundhouse, was convened, and presided over, by Arthur C. Marshall, deputy commissioner (Operations) of the Police Department of the City of Philadelphia.

The police commissioner of the City of Philadelphia is a political appointee who serves at the pleasure of the mayor. There are three deputy commissioners in the Philadelphia Police Department. They are the first deputy commissioner, who is the highest ranking member of the Department under Civil Service regulations, and the two deputy commissioners, Operations and Administration.

Under the deputy commissioner (Operations) are four Bureaus, each commanded by a chief inspector: the Patrol Bureau, the Special Patrol Bureau, the Detective Bureau, and the Command Inspections Bureau.

Present for the Roundhouse meeting were Chief Inspector Matt Lowenstein, of the Detective Bureau, and Chief Inspector Dennis V. Coughlin, of the Command Inspections Bureau, both of whom were subordinate to Deputy Commissioner Marshall. Also present were Chief Inspector Mario C. Delachessi, of the Internal Investigations Bureau; Chief Inspector Paul T. Easterbrook, of the Special Investigations Bureau; Staff Inspector Peter Wohl, commanding officer of the Special Operations Division; and Captain John M. "Jack" Duffy, special assistant to the commissioner for inter-agency liaison.

Internal Investigations, Special Investigations, and Special Operations in theory took their orders from the first deputy commissioner directly. In practice, however, First Deputy Commissioner Marshall and Chiefs Lowenstein and Coughlin exercised more than a little influence in their operations. There was no question in anyone's mind that Lowenstein and Coughlin were the most

influential of all the eleven chief inspectors in the Department, and
that both were considered ripe candidates for the next opening as a
deputy commissioner.

Part of this was because they were first-class police executives
and part was because they had long-running close relations with
the Honorable Jerry Carlucci, mayor of the City of Philadelphia.

Prior to running for mayor, in his first bid for elective office,
Jerry Carlucci had been the police commissioner. And prior to that,
the story went, he had held every rank in the Police Department except policewoman. As a result of this, Mayor Carlucci felt that he
knew as much, probably more, about the Police Department than
anyone else, and consequently was not at all bashful about offering
helpful suggestions concerning police operations.

"Okay," Commissioner Marshall said, "let's get this started."

He was a tall, very thin, sharp-featured man with bright, intelligent eyes.

There was a moment's silence broken only by the scratching of a
wooden match on the underside of the long, oblong conference table by Chief Lowenstein. The commissioner watched as
Lowenstein, a large, stocky, balding man, applied the flame carefully to a long, thin, black cigar.

"Is that all right with you, Matt?" the commissioner asked,
gently sarcastic. "Is your rope on fire? We can begin?"

"A woman is only a woman, but a good cigar is a smoke. Remember that, Art," Lowenstein said, unabashed. He and Commissioner Marshall went back a long way too. Lowenstein had been
one of Captain Marshall's lieutenants when Marshall had commanded the 19th District.

There were chuckles. Marshall shook his head, and began:

"We have a problem with the Bureau of Narcotics and Dangerous Drugs. . . ."

"So what else is new?" Chief Lowenstein said. He was a large,
nearly handsome man, with a full head of curly silver hair, wearing
a gray pin-striped suit.

"Let me talk, for Christ's sake, Matt," Marshall said.

"Sorry."

"They've come to Duffy. Officially. They say they have information that drugs, specifically heroin, are getting past the Airport
Unit."

"Did they give us the information?" Lowenstein asked.

Marshall shook his head, no.

"You said, 'getting past the Airport Unit,' " Chief Lowenstein said. "Was that an accusation?"

"Jack?" Marshall said.

"They stayed a hairbreadth away from making that an accusation, Chief," Captain Duffy, a florid-faced, nervous-appearing forty-five-year-old, said.

"Paul?" Marshall asked Chief Inspector Easterbrook, under whose Special Investigations Bureau were the Narcotics Unit, the Narcotics Strike Force, and Vice.

Easterbrook was just the near side of being fat. His collar looked too tight.

"Is heroin coming through the airport?" he asked rhetorically. "Sure it is. I haven't heard a word, though, that anybody in the Airport Unit is dirty."

Everyone looked at Chief Inspector Delachessi, a plump, short, natty forty-year-old, among whose Internal Investigations Bureau responsibilities were Internal Affairs, the Organized Crime Intelligence Unit, and the Staff Investigation Unit. Eighteen months before, he had been Staff Inspector Peter Wohl's boss.

"Neither have I," Delachessi said. "Not a whisper. And what is it now—two months ago?—when that Airport Unit corporal got himself killed coming home from the shore, the corporal who was his temporary replacement was one of my guys. He didn't come up with a thing. Having said that, is somebody out there dirty? Could be. I'll have another look."

"Hold off on that, Mario," Commissioner Marshall said.

"What, exactly, is the problem with Narcotics and Dangerous Drugs?" Chief Lowenstein asked. "You said there was a problem."

"They want to send somebody out there, undercover," Marshall said.

"*In* the Airport Unit?" Lowenstein asked incredulously. "As a *cop*?"

Marshall nodded.

"They've made it an official request," Captain Duffy said. "By letter."

"Tell them to go fuck themselves, by official letter," Lowenstein said.

"It's not that easy, Matt," Marshall said. "The commissioner says we'll have to come up with a good reason to turn them down."

"Why doesn't that surprise me?" Lowenstein replied. "There's no way some nice young agent of the Bureau of Narcotics and Dangerous Drugs can pass himself off to anyone in the Airport

Unit as a cop. And if there's dirty cops out there, we should catch them, not the feds. Do you think you could explain that to the commissioner?"

"Art and I had an idea, talking this over," Chief Coughlin said.

*Ah ha!* thought Staff Inspector Peter Wohl, a lithe, well-built, just under six feet tall thirty-five-year-old. *The mystery is about to be explained. This is not a conference. Whatever is going to be done has already been decided upon by Marshall and Coughlin. The rest of us are here to be told what the problem is, and what we are expected to do. I wonder what the hell I'm here for? None of this is any of my business.*

"I'll bet you did," Lowenstein said.

*Shame on you, Commissioner Marshall,* Wohl thought. *You broke the rules. You are not supposed to present Chief Lowenstein with a fait accompli. You are supposed to involve him in the decision-making process. Otherwise, he is very liable to piss on your sparkling idea.*

"Matt, of course, is right," Chief Coughlin went on. "There is no way a fed could go out to the Airport Unit and pass himself off as a cop. And, no offense, Mario, I personally would be very surprised if the people out there weren't very suspicious of the corporal you sent out there when their corporal got killed."

"He feels very strongly that no one suspected he worked for me," Chief Delachessi said.

"What did you expect him to say?" Lowenstein said, somewhat unpleasantly. " 'Boy, Chief, sending me out there was really dumb. They made me right away'?"

"So what we need out there is a real cop . . ." Coughlin said.

"Are you inferring, Denny, there's something wrong with the guy I sent out there?" Chief Delachessi interrupted.

"Come on, Mario, you know I didn't mean anything like that," Coughlin said placatingly.

"That's what it sounded like!"

"Then I apologize," Coughlin said, sounding genuinely contrite.

"What Chief Coughlin meant to say, I think," Commissioner Marshall said, "was that if we're to uncover anything dirty going on out there—and I'm *not* saying anything is—we need somebody out there who will (a) not make people suspicious and (b) who will be there for the long haul, not just a temporary assignment, like Mario's corporal."

*The rest of you guys might as well surrender,* Peter Wohl thought. *If Marshall and Coughlin have come up with this brilliant idea, whatever it is, there's only one guy who can shoot it down, and he's got a sign on his desk reading Mayor Jerry Carlucci.*

"Where are you going to get this guy?" Lowenstein asked.

"We think we have him," Coughlin said. "We wanted to get your input."

*Yeah, you did. As long as the input is "Jesus, what a great idea, why didn't I think of that?"*

"We need an officer out there," Commissioner Marshall said, "whose assignment will not make anybody suspicious, and an officer who is experienced in working undercover."

"You remember the two undercover officers, from Narcotics, who bagged the guy who shot Dutch Moffitt?" Chief Coughlin asked.

"Mutt and Jeff," Lowenstein said.

*Now I know why I was invited,* Peter Wohl thought.

The officers in question were Police Officers Charles McFadden and Jesus Martinez, who had been assigned to Narcotics right out of the Police Academy. McFadden was a very large Irish lad from South Philadelphia, in whom, Wohl was sure, Chief Coughlin saw a clone of himself. Martinez was very small, barely over departmental minimum height and weight requirements, of Puerto Rican ancestry. They were called "Mutt and Jeff" because of their size.

Staff Inspector Peter Wohl knew a good deal about both officers. They had been assigned to Special Operations after they had run to earth an Irish junkie from Northeast Philadelphia who had shot Captain Dutch Moffitt, then the Highway Patrol commander, to death, and thus blown their cover. Assigned, he now reminded himself, through the influence of Chief Inspector Dennis V. Coughlin.

"They now work for Peter," Coughlin said.

"Doing what, Peter?" Captain Delachessi asked.

"They're Highway Patrolmen," Wohl replied.

"They won't be for long," Coughlin said.

"Sir?" Wohl asked, surprised.

"We got the results of the detective exam today." Commissioner Marshall said. "Both of them passed in the top twenty."

"So, incidentally, Peter, did Matt Payne," Chief Coughlin added, "He was third."

Officer Matthew M. Payne was Peter Wohl's administrative assistant, another gift from Chief Dennis V. Coughlin.

"I thought he might squeeze past," Wohl replied. Matt Payne had graduated from the University of Pennsylvania cum laude.

Wohl didn't think he would have trouble with the detective's examination.

"Well, hold off on congratulating him," Coughlin said. "Any of them. The results of the examination are confidential until Civil Service people make the announcement. No word of who passed is to leave this room, if I have to say that."

"Let's try this scenario on for size," Commissioner Marshall said. "And see if it binds in the crotch. Martinez's name does not appear on the examination list as having passed. He is disappointed, maybe even a little bitter. And he asks for a transfer. They've been riding his ass in Highway, Denny tells me, because of his size. He doesn't seem to fit in. But he's still the guy who got the guy who killed Dutch Moffitt, and he deserves a little better than getting sent to some district to work school crossings or in a sector car. So Denny sends him out to the Airport Unit."

Both Commissioner Marshall and Chief Inspector Coughlin looked very pleased with themselves.

*If there's going to be an objection to this, it will have to come from Lowenstein. He's the only one who would be willing to stand up against these two.*

Chief Lowenstein leaned forward and tapped a three-quarter-inch ash into an ashtray.

"That'd work," he said. "Martinez is a mean little fucker. Not too dumb, either."

*From you, Chief Lowenstein, that is indeed praise of the highest order.*

"Do you think he would be willing, Chief?" Wohl asked.

"Yeah, I think so," Coughlin said. "I already had a little talk with him. No specifics. Just would he take an interesting undercover assignment?"

*You sonofabitch, Denny Coughlin! You did that, went directly to one of my men, with something like this, without saying a word to me?*

"What we would like from you gentlemen," Commissioner Marshall said, "is to play devil's advocate."

"Will the commissioner hold still for this?" Lowenstien said.

"No problem," Commissioner Marshall said.

*The translation of that is that there was a third party, by the name of Carlucci, involved in this brainstorm. The commissioner either knows that, or will shortly be told, and will then devoutly believe the idea was divinely inspired.*

"What we thought," Coughlin went on, "is that Peter can serve as the connection. We don't want anyone to connect Martinez with Internal Affairs, or Organized Crime, or Narcotics. If Martinez comes up with something for them, or vice versa, they'll pass it through Peter. You see any problems with that, Peter?"

"No, sir."

"Anyone else got anything?" Commissioner Marshall asked.

There was nothing.

"Then all that remains to be done," Coughlin said, "is to get with Martinez and drop the other shoe. What I suggest, Peter, is that you have Martinez meet us here."

"Yes, sir. When?"

"Now's as good a time as any, wouldn't you say?"

Officer Matthew M. Payne, a pleasant-looking young man of twenty-two, who looked far more like a University of Pennsylvania student, which eighteen months before he had been, than what comes to mind when the words "cop" or "police officer" are used, was waiting near the elevators, with the other "drivers" of those attending the first deputy commissioner's meeting. They were all in civilian clothing.

Technically, Officer Payne not a "driver," for drivers are a privilege accorded only to chief inspectors or better, and his boss was only a staff inspector. His official title was administrative assistant.

There is a military analogy. There is a military rank structure within the Police Department. On the very rare occasions when Peter Wohl wore a uniform, it carried on its epaulets gold oak leaves, essentially identical to those worn by majors in the armed forces. Inspectors wore silver oak leaves, like those of lieutenant colonels, and chief inspectors, an eagle, like those worn by colonels.

Drivers functioned very much like aides-de-camp to general officers in the armed forces. They relieved the man they worked for of annoying details, served as chauffeurs, and performed other services. And, like their counterparts in the armed forces, they were chosen as much for their potential use to the Department down the line as they were for their ability to perform their current duties. It was presumed that they were learning how the Department worked at the upper echelons by observing their bosses in action.

Most of the other drivers waiting for the meeting to end were sergeants. One, Chief Lowenstein's driver, was a police officer.

Matt Payne was both the youngest of the drivers and, as a police officer, held the lowest rank in the Department.

There was a hissing sound, and one of the drivers gestured to the corridor toward what was in effect the executive suite of the Police Administration Building. The meeting was over, the bosses were coming out.

Chief Delachessi came first, gestured to his driver, and got on the elevator. Next came Chief Coughlin, who walked up to his driver, a young Irish sergeant named Tom Mahon.

"Meet me outside Shank & Evelyn's in an hour and a half," he ordered. "I'll catch a ride with Inspector Wohl."

Shank & Evelyn's was a restaurant in the Italian section of South Philadelphia.

"Yes, sir," Sergeant Mahon said.

Then Chief Coughlin walked to Officer Payne and shook his hand.

"Nice suit, Matty," he said.

"Thank you."

For all of his life, Officer Payne had called Chief Coughlin "Uncle Denny," and still did when they were alone.

Staff Inspector Wohl walked up to them.

"Officer Martinez is on his way to meet me in the parking lot," he said to Officer Payne. "You meet him, give him the keys to my car, and tell him that Chief Coughlin and I will be down in a couple of minutes. You catch a ride in the Highway car back to the Schoolhouse. I'll be there in a couple of hours. I'll be, if someone really has to get to me, at Shank & Evelyn's."

"Yes, sir," Officer Payne said.

Chief Coughlin and Inspector Wohl went back down the corridor toward the office of the police commissioner and his deputies. Sergeant Mahon and Officer Payne got on the elevator and rode to the lobby.

"What the hell is that all about?" Mahon asked.

"I think Coughlin and Wohl are being nice guys," Matt Payne said. "The results of the detective exam are back. Martinez didn't pass it."

"Oh, shit. He wanted it bad?"

"Real bad."

"You saw the list?"

"I respectfully decline to answer on the grounds that it may tend to incriminate me," Matt Payne said.

Mahon chuckled.

"How'd you do?"

"Third."

"Hey, congratulations!"

"If you quote me, I'll deny it. But thank you."

Matt Payne had to wait only a minute or two on the concrete ramp outside the rear door of the Roundhouse before a Highway Patrol RPC pulled up to the curb.

He went the rest of the way down the ramp to meet it. The driver, a lean, athletic-looking man in his early thirties, who he knew by sight, but not by name, rolled down the window as Highway Patrolman Jesus Martinez got out of the passenger side.

"How goes it, Hay-zus?" Payne called.

Martinez nodded, but did not reply. Or smile.

"We had a call to meet the inspector, Payne," the driver said. While the reverse was not true, just about everybody in Highway and Special Operations knew the inspector's "administrative assistant" by name and sight.

Payne squatted beside the car. "He'll be down in a minute," he said. "I'm to give Hay-zus the keys to his car; you're supposed to give me a ride to the Schoolhouse."

The driver nodded.

*I wish to hell I was better about names.*

Payne stood up, fished the car keys from his pocket, and tossed them to Martinez.

"Back row, Hay-zus," he said, and pointed. "I'd bring it over here. If anyone asks, tell them you're waiting for Chief Coughlin."

Martinez nodded, but didn't say anything.

*I am not one of Officer Martinez's favorite people. And now that he busted the detective exam, and Charley and I passed it, that's going to get worse. Well, fuck it, there's nothing I can do about it.*

He walked around the front of the car and got in the front seat. Martinez walked away, toward the rear of the parking lot. The driver put the car in gear and drove away.

"You have to get right out to the Schoolhouse?" Matt asked.

"No."

"You had lunch?"

"No. You want to stop someplace?"

"Good idea. Johnny's Hots okay with you?"

"Fine."

"You have an idea where McFadden's riding?"

"Thirteen, I think," the driver said.

Matt checked the controls of the radio to make sure the frequency was set to that of the Highway Patrol, then picked up the microphone.

"Highway Thirteen, Highway Nine."

"Thirteen," a voice immediately replied. Matt recognized it as Charley McFadden's.

"Thirteen, can you meet us at Johnny's Hots?"

"On the way," McFadden's voice said. "Highway Thirteen. Let me have lunch at Delaware and Penn Street."

"Okay, Thirteen," the J-band radio operator said. J-band, the city-wide band, is the frequency Highway units usually listen to. It gives them the opportunity to go in on any interesting call anywhere in the city.

"Highway Nine. Hold us out to lunch at the same location."

Matt dropped the microphone onto the seat.

"I guess you and McFadden are buying, huh?" the driver asked.

"Why should we do that?"

"You both passed the exam, didn't you?"

"You heard that, did you?"

"I also heard that Martinez didn't."

"I think that's what the business at the Roundhouse is all about. The inspector and Chief Coughlin are going to break it to him easy."

"I tried the corporal's exam three years ago and didn't make it," the driver said. "Then I figured, fuck it, I'd rather be doing this than working in an office anyhow."

*Was that simply a conversational interchange, or have I just been zinged?*

"I'm surprised Hay-zus didn't make it," Matt said.

"Yeah, I was too. But I guess some people can pass exams, and some people can't."

"You're right. You think McFadden knows we passed?"

"He told me this morning at roll call."

"So that means Martinez knows too, I guess?"

"Yeah, I'm sure he knows."

*Was that why Hay-zus cut me cold, or was that on general principles?*

# TWO

Detective Matthew M. Payne, of East Detectives, pulled his unmarked car to the curb just beyond the intersection of 12th and Butler Streets in the Tioga section of Philadelphia.

There was a three-year-old Ford station wagon parked at the curb. Payne reached over and picked up a clipboard from the passenger seat, and examined the Hot Sheet. It was a sheet of eight-and-a-half-by-eleven-inch paper, printed on both sides, which listed the tag numbers of stolen vehicles in alphanumeric order.

There were three categories of stolen vehicles. If a double asterisk followed the number, this was a warning to police officers that if persons were seen in the stolen vehicle they were to be regarded as armed and dangerous. A single asterisk meant that if and when the car was recovered, it was to be guarded until technicians could examine it for fingerprints. No asterisks meant that it was an ordinary run-of-the-mill hot car that nobody but its owner really gave a damn about.

The license number recorded on the Hot Sheet corresponded with the license plate on the Ford station, which had been reported stolen twenty-eight hours previously. There were no asterisks following the listing. Two hours previously, Radio Patrol Car 2517, of the 25th Police District, on routine patrol had noticed the Ford station wagon, and upon inquiry had determined that it had been reported as a stolen car.

The reason, obviously, that this Ford station wagon had attracted the attention of the guys in the blue-and-white was not hard for someone of Detective Payne's vast experience—he had been a detective for three whole weeks—to deduce. The wheels and tires had been removed from the vehicle, and the hood was open, suggesting that other items of value on the resale market had been removed from the engine compartment.

The officer who had found the stolen car had then filled out Philadelphia Police Department Form 75-48, on which was listed the location, the time the car had been found, the tag number and the VIN (Vehicle Identification Number), and the condition (if it had been burned, stripped, or was reasonably intact).

If he had recovered the vehicle intact, that is to say drivable, he would have disabled it by removing the coil wire or letting the air out of one or more tires. It is very embarrassing to the police for them to triumphantly inform a citizen that his stolen car has been recovered at, say, 12th and Butler, and then to have the car stolen again before the citizen can get to 12th and Butler.

The officer who had found the car had turned in Form 75-48 to one of the trainees in the Operations Room of the 25th District, at Front and Westmoreland Streets, because the corporal in charge was otherwise occupied. The term "trainee" is somewhat misleading. It suggests someone who is learning a job and, by inference, someone young. One of the trainees in the Operations Room of the 25th District had in fact been on the job longer than Detective Payne was old, and had been working as a trainee for eleven years.

The trainee did not feel it necessary to ask the corporal for guidance as to what should be done with the Form 75-48. The corporal, in fact, would have been surprised, even shocked, if he had.

If the car had been stolen inside the city limits of Philadelphia, the trainee would have simply notified the owner, and, in the name of the district, canceled the listing on the Hot Sheet. But this Ford had been stolen from a citizen of Jenkintown, Pennsylvania, just north of Philadelphia. It thus became an OJ, for Other Jurisdiction.

First, he assigned a DC (for District Control) Number to it. In this case it was 74-25-004765. Seventy-four was the year, twenty-five stood for the 25th District, and 004765 meant that it was the four thousandth seven hundredth sixty-fifth incident of this nature occurring since the first of the year.

Then the trainee carried the paperwork upstairs in the building, where EDD (East Detective Division) maintained their offices, and turned it over to the EDD desk man, who then assigned the case an EDD Control Number, much like the DC Number.

The EDD desk man then placed the report before Sergeant Aloysius J. Sutton, who then assigned the investigation of the recovered stolen vehicle to Detective Matthew M. Payne, the newest member of his squad.

Theoretically, the investigation should have been assigned to the detective "next up on the Wheel." "The Wheel" was a figure of speech; actually, it was a sheet of lined paper on a pad, on which the names of all the detectives of the squad available for duty were written. As jobs came into East Detectives, they were assigned in turn, according to the list. The idea was that the workload would thus be equally shared.

In practice, however, especially when there was a brand-new detective on the squad, the Wheel was ignored. Sergeant Sutton was not about to assign, say, an armed robbery job to a detective who had completed Promotional Training at the Police Academy the week, or three weeks, before. Neither, with an armed robbery job to deal with, was Sergeant Sutton about to assign a recovered stolen vehicle investigation to a detective who had been on the job for ten or twelve years, especially if there was a rookie available to do it.

Since he had reported for duty at East Detectives, Detective Payne had investigated eight recovered stolen vehicles. During that time, nine had been reported to East Detectives for appropriate action.

Actually, Detective Payne knew more about auto theft than all but one of the detectives who had passed the most recent examination and gone to Promotional Training with him. In his previous assignment, he had had occasion to discuss at some length auto theft with Lieutenant Jack Malone, who had at one time headed the Auto Theft Squad in the Major Crimes Division of the Philadelphia Police Department.

Lieutenant Malone had recently received some attention in the press for an investigation he had conducted that had resulted in the Grand Jury indictment of Robert L. Holland, a prominent Delaware Valley automobile dealer, on 106 counts of trafficking in stolen automobiles, falsification of registration documents, and other auto-theft-related charges.

Detective Payne had learned a great deal from Lieutenant Malone about big-time auto theft. He knew how chop-shops operated; how Vehicle Identification Number tags could be forged; how authentic-looking bills of sale and title could be obtained; and he even had a rather detailed knowledge of how stolen vehicles could be illegally exported through the Port of Philadelphia for sale in Latin and South American countries.

None of this knowledge, unfortunately, was of any value whatever in the investigation Detective Payne was now charged with conducting.

Detective Payne had also learned from Lieutenant Malone that the great majority of vehicular thefts could be divided into two categories: those cars stolen by joyriders, kids who found the keys in a car and went riding in it for a couple of hours; and those stolen by sort of amateur, apprentice choppers. These thieves had neither the knowledge of the trade nor the premises or equipment to actually break a car down into component pieces for resale. They did, however, know people who would purchase wheels and tires, generators, air-conditioning compressors, batteries, carburetors, radios, and other readily detachable parts, no questions asked.

Very few thieves in either category were ever brought before the bench of the Common Pleas Court. Only a few joyriders were ever caught, usually when they ran into something, such as a bridge abutment or a station wagon full of nuns, and these thieves were almost always juveniles, who were treated as wayward children, and instead of going to jail entered a program intended to turn them into productive, law-abiding adults.

Very few strippers were ever caught, either, because they were skilled enough to strip a car of everything worth a couple of dollars in less than half an hour. They waited for the local RPC to drive past, in other words, and then stripped the car they had boosted secure in the knowledge that the RPC wouldn't be back in under an hour.

But under the law, it was felony theft and had to be investigated with the same degree of thoroughness as, say, a liquor store burglary.

In practice, Detective Payne had learned, such investigations were assigned to detectives such as himself, in the belief that not only did it save experienced detectives for more important jobs, but also might, in time, teach rookies to be able to really find their asses with both hands.

Carrying the clipboard with him, Detective Payne got out of his car and walked to the station wagon. He was not surprised when he put his head into the window to see that the radio was gone from the dash, and that the keys were still in the ignition.

Moreover, these thieves had been inconsiderate. If they had been considerate, they would have dumped this car by a deserted lot, or in Fairmount Park or someplace not surrounded by occupied dwellings. Now he would have to go knock on doors and ask people if they had seen anyone taking the tires and wheels off the Ford station wagon down the street, and if so, what did they look like.

An hour later, he finished conducting the neighborhood survey. Surprising him not at all, none of the six people he interviewed had seen anything at all.

He got back in the unmarked car and drove back to East Detectives. Not without difficulty, he found a place to park the car in the tiny parking lot, went inside, found an empty desk and a typewriter not in use, and began to complete the paperwork. Once completed, he knew, it would be carefully filed and would never be seen by human eyes again.

At five minutes to four, when his eight-to-four tour would be over, Detective Payne became aware that someone was standing behind him. He turned from the typewriter and looked over his shoulder. Sergeant Aloysius J. Sutton, a ruddy-faced, red-haired, stocky man in his late thirties, his boss, was smiling at him.

"I wish I could type that fast," Sergeant Sutton said admiringly.

"You should see me on a typewriter built after 1929," Payne replied.

Sutton chuckled. "You got time for a beer when we quit?"

"Sure."

The invitation surprised him. Having a beer with his newest rookie detective did not seem to be Sutton's style. But it was obviously a command performance. Rookie detectives did not refuse an invitation from their sergeant.

"Tom & Frieda's, you know it?"

Matt Payne nodded. It was a bar at Lee and Westmoreland, fifty yards from East Detectives.

"See you there."

Sergeant Sutton walked away, back to his desk just outside Captain Eames's office, and started cleaning up the stuff on the desk.

*What the hell is this all about? Jesus Christ, have I fucked up somehow? Broken some unwritten rule? It has to be something like that. I am about to get a word-to-the-wise. But what about?*

• • •

At five past four, Matt Payne left the squad room of East Detectives and walked down the street to Tom & Frieda's. Sergeant Sutton was not in the bar and grill when he got there, and for a moment, Matt was afraid that he had been there, grown tired of waiting, and left. Left more than a little annoyed with Detective Payne.

But then Sutton, who had apparently been in the gentlemen's rest facility, touched his arm.

"I'm sorry I'm late, Sergeant."

"In here, you can call me Al. We're . . . more or less . . . off duty."

"Okay. Thank you."

"Ortlieb's from the tap all right?"

"Fine."

"What you have to do is find a bar where they sell a lot of beer, so what they give you is fresh. Most draft beer tastes like horse piss because it's been sitting around forever."

*He is making conversation. He did not bring me here because he likes me, or to deliver a lecture on the merits of fresh beer on draft. I wish to hell he would get to it.*

"You got anything going that won't hold for three days?" Sergeant Al Sutton asked as he signaled the bartender.

Matt thought that over briefly. "No."

"Good. As of tomorrow, you're on three days special assignment at the Roundhouse. Report to Sergeant McElroy in Chief Lowenstein's office."

Matt looked at Sutton for amplification. None came.

"Can you tell me what this is all about?" Matt asked.

Sutton looked at him carefully. "I thought maybe you could tell me," he said, finally.

Matt shook his head from side to side.

"I'll tell you what I know," Sutton said. "Harry McElroy . . . you know who he is?"

"I know him."

"Harry called down for Captain Eames, and I took the call because he wasn't there. He said the chief wants you down there starting tomorrow morning, for three days, maybe four, and the fewer people know about it, the better."

Matt shrugged again. That had told him nothing.

"So I asked him, what was it all about, and Harry said if anybody asked, they needed somebody to help out with paperwork, that you were good at that."

Matt grunted.

"So if anybody asks, that's the story," Sutton said.

"I know what it is," Matt said. "Based on my brilliant record as the recovered car expert of East Detectives, they're going to transfer me to Homicide."

Sutton looked at him, and after a moment laughed.

"It's a dirty job, kid," he said, "but somebody has to do it."

"Well, it can't be worse, whatever it is, than recovered cars," Matt said.

"I got to get home. We have to go to a wake. Jerry Sullivan, retired as a lieutenant out of the 9th District a year ago. Just dropped dead."

"I didn't know him."

"They had just sold their house; they were going to move to Wildwood," Sutton said.

He pushed himself off the bar stool, picked up his change, nodded at Matt, and walked out of the bar.

Detective Matthew M. Payne lived in a very small apartment on the top floor of a brownstone mansion on Rittenhouse Square, in what is known in Philadelphia as Center City. The three main floors of the mansion had three years before been converted to office space, all of which had been leased to the Delaware Valley Cancer Society.

It had never entered the owner's mind when he had authorized the expense of converting the attic, not suitable for use as offices, into an apartment that it would house a policeman. He thought that he could earn a small rent by renting the tiny rooms to an elderly couple, or a widow or widower, someone of limited means who worked downtown, perhaps in the Franklin Institute or the Free Public Library, and who would be willing to put up with the inconvenience of access and the slanting walls and limited space because it was convenient and, possibly more important, because the building was protected around the clock by the rent-a-cops of the Holmes Security Service. Downtown Philadelphia was not a very safe place at night for people getting on in years.

Neither, at the time of the attic's conversion, had it ever entered the owner's mind that his son, then a senior at the University of Pennsylvania, would become a policeman. Brewster Cortland Payne II had then believed, with reason, that Matt, after a three-year tour of duty as a Marine officer, would go to law school and join the law firm of Mawson, Payne, Stockton, McAdoo & Lester, of which he was a founding partner.

Matt's precommissioning physical, however, had found something wrong with his eyes. Nothing serious, but sufficient to deny him his commission. Brewster Payne had been privately relieved. He understood what a blow it was to a twenty-one-year-old's ego to be informed that you don't measure up to Marine Corps standards, but Matt was an unusually bright kid, and time would heal that wound. In the meantime, a word in the right ear would see Matt accepted in whatever law school he wanted to attend.

Despite a life at Pennsylvania that seemed to Brewster C. Payne to have been devoted primarily to drinking beer and lifting skirts, Matt had graduated cum laude.

And then Captain Richard C. "Dutch" Moffitt, commanding officer of the Highway Patrol of the Pennsylvania Police Department, had been shot to death while trying to stop an armed robbery.

It was the second death in the line of duty for the Moffitt family. Twenty-two years before, his brother, Sergeant John Xavier Moffitt, had been shot to death answering a silent alarm call. Six months after his death, Sergeant Moffitt's widow had given birth to their son.

Four months after that, having spent the last trimester of her pregnancy learning to type, and the four months since her son had been born learning shorthand, Sergeant Moffitt's widow had found employment as a typist trainee with the law firm of Lowerie, Tant, Foster, Pedigill & Payne.

There was a police pension, of course, and there had been some insurance, but Patricia Moffitt had known that it would not be enough to give her son all that she wanted to give him.

On a Sunday afternoon two months after entering the employ of Lowerie, Tant, Foster, Pedigill & Payne, while pushing her son in a stroller near the Franklin Institute, Patricia Moffitt ran into Brewster Cortland Payne II, whom she recognized as the heir apparent to Lowerie, Tant, Foster, Pedigill & Payne. She had been informed that Young Mr. Payne was not only the son of the presiding partner of the firm, but the grandson of one of the founding partners.

Despite this distinguished lineage, Brewster Cortland Payne II was obviously in waters beyond his depth outside the Franklin Institute. He was pushing a stroller, carrying a two-year-old boy, and leading a four-and-half-year-old girl on what looked like a dog harness and leash.

As Mrs. Moffitt and Mr. Payne exchanged brief greetings (she had twice typed letters for him) the girl announced somewhat self-righteously that "Foster has poo-pooed his pants and Daddy didn't bring a diaper."

Mrs. Moffitt took pity on Mr. Payne and took the boy into a rest room in the Franklin Institute and diapered him. When she returned, Mr. Payne told her, he was "rather much in the same situation as yourself, Mrs. Moffitt."

Specifically, he told her that Mrs. Brewster Cortland Payne II had died in a traffic accident eight months before, returning from their country place in the Poconos.

Three months after that, Mrs. Moffitt and Mr. Payne had shocked and/or enraged the Payne family, the Moffitt family, and assorted friends and relatives on both sides by driving themselves and their children to Bethesda, Maryland, on Friday after work and getting married.

Six months after their marriage, Brewster had adopted Patricia's son, in the process changing Matthew Mark Moffitt's name to Payne.

When, the day after Captain Dutch Moffitt had been laid to rest in the cemetery of St. Monica's Roman Catholic Church, Matt Payne had joined the Philadelphia Police Department, Brewster Payne did not have to hear the professional psychiatric opinion of his daughter, Amelia Payne, M.D., that Matt had done so to prove that he was a man, to overcome the psychological castration of his rejection by the Marines. He had figured that out himself.

And so had Chief Inspector Dennis V. Coughlin of the Philadelphia Police Department. Denny Coughlin had been Sergeant John X. Moffitt's best friend, and over the years had become quite close to Brewster Payne, as they dealt with the problem of Mother Moffitt, Matt's grandmother, a bellicose German-Irish woman who sincerely believed that Brewster Cortland Payne II would burn in hell for seducing her son's widow into abandoning Holy Mother Church for Protestantism, and raising her grandson as a heathen.

Over more whiskey than was probably good for them in the bar at the Union League, Denny Coughlin and Brewster Payne had agreed that Matt's idea that he wanted to be cop was understandable, but once he found out how things were, he would come to his senses. A couple of weeks, no more than a month, in the Police Academy would open his eyes to what he had let himself in for, and he would resign.

Matt did not resign. On his graduation, Denny Coughlin used his influence to have him assigned to clerical duties in the newly formed Special Operations Division. He had knocked on Patricia Moffitt's door to tell her that her husband had been killed in the line of duty. He had no intention of knocking on Patricia M. Payne's door to tell her her son had been killed.

He had explained the situation to the commanding officer of the Special Operations Division, Staff Inspector Peter Wohl. Coughlin believed, with some reason, that Peter Wohl was the smartest cop in the Department. Peter Wohl had been a homicide detective, the youngest sergeant ever in Highway Patrol, and had been the youngest ever staff inspector working in Internal Affairs when the mayor had set up Special Operations and put him in charge. Wohl's father was Chief Inspector Augustus Wohl, retired, for whom both Denny Coughlin and Jerry Carlucci had worked early on in their careers.

Peter Wohl understood the situation even better than Denny Coughlin thought. He understood that Matt Payne was the son Denny Coughlin had never had. And his father had told him that Denny Coughlin had been waiting a suitable period of time before proposing marriage to John X. Moffitt's widow when she surprised everybody by marrying the Main Line lawyer.

Inspector Wohl decided it would pose no major problem to keep Officer Matthew M. Payne gainfully, and safely, employed shuffling paper until the kid came to his senses, resigned, and went to law school, where he belonged.

That hadn't worked out as planned, either. Ninety-five percent of police officers complete their careers without ever once having drawn and fired their service revolver in anger. In the nineteen months Officer Payne had been assigned to Special Operations, he had shot to death two armed felons.

Both incidents, certainly, were unusual happenstances. In the first, Wohl had loaned Young Payne to veteran Homicide detective Jason Washington as a gofer. Washington was working the Northwest Philadelphia serial rapist job, where a looney tune who had started out assaulting women in their apartments had graduated to carrying them off in his van and then cutting various portions of their bodies off. Washington needed someone to make telephone calls for him, run errands, do whatever was necessary to free his time and mind to run the rapist/murderer down.

Officer Payne had been involved in nothing more adventurous, or life-threatening, than reporting to Inspector Wohl that Detective Washington had secured plaster casts of the doer's van's tires, and that he had just delivered said casts to the Forensic Laboratory when he happened upon the van. The very first time that Officer Payne had ever identified himself to a member of the public as a police officer, the citizen he attempted to speak with had tried to run him over with his van.

Payne emptied his revolver at the van, and one bullet had entered the cranial cavity of his assailant, causing his instant death. In the back of the van, under a canvas tarpaulin, was his next intended victim, naked, gagged, and tied up with lamp cord.

The second incident occurred during the early morning roundup of a group of armed robbers who elected to call themselves the Islamic Liberation Army. Officer Payne's intended role in this operation was to accompany Mr. Mickey O'Hara, a police reporter for the Philadelphia *Bulletin*. His orders were to deter Mr. O'Hara, by sitting on him if necessary, from entering the premises until the person to be arrested was safely in the custody of Homicide detectives and officers of the Special Operations Division.

The person whom it was intended to arrest quietly somehow learned what was going on, suddenly appeared in the alley where Officer Payne was waiting with Mr. O'Hara for the arrest to be completed, and started shooting. One of his .45 ACP caliber bullets ricocheted off a brick wall before striking Officer Payne in the leg, and another caused brick splinters to open Officer Payne's forehead and make it bleed profusely. Despite his wounds, Payne got his pistol in action and got off five shots at this assailant, two of which hit him and caused fatal wounds.

The circumstances didn't matter. What mattered was that Payne had blown the serial murderer/rapist's brains all over the windshield of his van, thus saving a naked woman from being raped and dismembered, and that he had been photographed by Mr. O'Hara as he stood, blood streaming down his face, over the scumbag who had opened fire on him with his .45 and lost the shootout.

Denny Coughlin had been spared having to tell Patricia Moffitt Payne that her son had just been shot in the line of duty only because Brewster Payne had answered the phone.

There had been another long conversation over a good many drinks in the Union League between Denny Coughlin and Brewster C. Payne about the results of the most recent examination for promotion to detective. There had been no way that Officer Payne, who had the requisite time on the job, could be kept from taking the examination. And neither Chief Coughlin nor Mr. Payne doubted he would pass.

It was obvious to both of them that Matt was not going to resign from the Department. And within a matter of a month or so, perhaps within a couple of weeks, he would be promoted to detective. He had never issued a traffic ticket, been called upon to settle a domestic dispute, manned the barricades against an assault by brick-throwing citizens exercising their constitutional right to peaceably demonstrate against whatever governmental outrage it was currently chic to oppose, worked a sector car, or done any of the things that normally a rookie cop would do in his first couple of years on the job.

"The East Detective captain is a friend of mine, Brewster," Denny Coughlin said, finally. "I think Personnel will send Matt there. He'll have a chance to work with some good people, really learn the trade. He needs the experience, and they'll keep an eye out for him."

Brewster Payne knew Denny Coughlin well enough to understand that if he said he thought Personnel would send Matt somewhere, it was already arranged, and with the understanding that Chief Inspector Dennis V. Coughlin would be keeping an eye on the people keeping an eye on Matt.

"Thank you, Denny," Brewster Cortland Payne II had said.

When Matt drove the Bug into the parking garage beneath the Delaware Valley Cancer Building (and the buildings to the right and left of it) he found that someone was in his reserved parking spot. Ordinarily, this would have caused him to use foul language, but he recognized the Cadillac Fleetwood. He knew it was registered to Brewster C. Payne, Providence Road, Wallingford.

When he had moved into the apartment, his father had told him that he had reserved two parking spaces in the underground garage for the resident of the attic apartment, primarily as a token of his affection, of course, and only incidentally because it would also provide a parking space for his mother, or other family members, when they had business around Rittenhouse Square.

Until three weeks before it had never posed a problem, because Matt had kept only one car in the garage. Not the battered twelve-year-old Volkswagen Beetle he was now driving, but a glistening, year-old, silver Porsche 911. It had been his graduation present from his father. From the time he had been given the Porsche, the Bug—which had also been a present from his father, six years before, when he had gotten his driver's license—had sat, rotted actually, in the garage in Wallingford. He had for some reason been reluctant to sell it.

Three weeks before, as he sat taking his promotion physical, he had realized that not selling it had been one of the few wise decisions he had made in his lifetime.

One of the dumber things he had ever done, when assigned to Special Operations out of the Police Academy, was to drive to work in the Porsche. It had immediately identified him as the rich kid from the Main Line who was playing at being a cop. He would not make that same mistake when reporting to East Detectives as a rookie detective.

The battery had been dead, understandably, when he rode out to Wallingford with his father to claim the car, but once he'd put the charger on it, it had jumped to life. He'd changed the oil, replaced two tires, and the Bug was ready to provide sensible, appropriate transportation for him back and forth to work.

The Porsche was sitting in the parking spot closest to the elevator, beside the Cadillac, which meant that he had no place to park the Bug, since his mother had chosen to exercise her right to the "extra" parking space. He was sure it was his mother, because his father commuted to Philadelphia by train.

There were several empty parking spaces, and after a moment's indecision, he pulled the Bug into the one reserved for the executive director. With a little bit of luck, Matt reasoned, that gentleman would have exercised his right to quit for the day whenever he wanted to, and would no longer require his space.

He walked up the stairs to the first floor, however, found the rent-a-cop, and handed him the keys to the Bug.

"I had to park my Bug in the executive director's slot; my mother's in mine."

"Your *father*," the rent-a-cop said. He was a retired police officer. "He said if I saw you, to tell you he wants to see you. He'll be in the Rittenhouse Club until six. I stuck a note under your door."

"Thank you," Matt said.

"I'll take care of the car, don't worry about it. I think he's gone for the day."

"Thank you," Matt said, and got on the elevator and rode up to the third floor, wondering what was going on. He had a premonition, not that the sky was falling in, but that something was about to happen that he was not going to like.

He unlocked the door to the stairway, opened it, and picked up the envelope on the floor.

4:20 P.M.

Matt:

If this comes to hand after six, when I will have left the Rittenhouse, please call me at home no matter what the hour. This is rather important.

Dad.

He jammed the note in his pocket and went up the stairs. The red light on his answering machine was blinking. There were two messages. The first was from someone who wished to sell him burglar bars at a special, one-time reduced rate, and the second was a familiar voice:

"I tried to call you at work, but you had already left. Your dad and I are going to have a drink in the Rittenhouse Club. You need to be there. If you don't get this until after six, call him or me when you finally do."

The caller had not identified himself. Chief Inspector Dennis V. Coughlin did not like to waste words, and he correctly assumed that his voice would be recognized.

*And,* Matt thought, *there had been something in his voice suggesting there was something wrong in a new detective having gone off shift at the called-for time.*

*What the hell is going on?*

Matt picked up the telephone and dialed a number from memory.

"Yeah?" Detective Charley McFadden was not about to win an award for telephone courtesy.

"This is Sears Roebuck. We're running a sale on previously owned wedding gowns."

Detective McFadden was not amused. "Hi, Matt, what's up?"

"I don't know, but I'm not going to be able to meet you at six. You going to be home later?"

"How much later?"

"Maybe six-thirty, quarter to seven?"

"Call me at McGee's. I'll probably still be there."

"Sorry, Charley."

"Yeah, well, what the hell. We'll see what happens. Maybe I'll get lucky without you."

Matt hung up, looked at his watch, and then quickly left his apartment.

● ● ●

Matt walked up the stairs of the Rittenhouse Club, pushed open the heavy door, and went into the foyer. He looked up at the board behind the porter's counter, on which the names of all the members were listed, together with a sliding indicator that told whether or not they were in the club.

"Your father's in the lounge, Mr. Payne," the porter said to him.

"Thank you," Matt said.

Brewster Cortland Payne II, a tall, angular, distinguished-looking man who was actually far wittier than his appearance suggested, saw him the moment he entered the lounge and raised his hand. Chief Inspector Dennis V. Coughlin, a heavyset, ruddy-faced man in a well-fitting pin-striped suit, turned to look, and then smiled. They were sitting in rather small leather-upholstered armchairs between which sat a small table. There were squat whiskey glasses, small glass water pitchers, a silver bowl full of mixed nuts, and a battered, but well-shined, brass ashtray with a box of wooden matches in a holder on it on the table.

"Good," Brewster Payne said, smiling and rising from his chair to touch Matt softly and affectionately on the arm. "We caught you."

"Dad. Uncle Denny."

"Matty, I tried to call you at East Detectives," Coughlin said, sitting back down. "You had already gone."

"I left at five *after* four, Uncle Denny. The City got their full measure of my flesh for their day's pay."

An elderly waiter in a white jacket appeared.

"Denny's drinking Irish and the power of suggestion got to me," Brewster Payne said. "But have what you'd like."

"Irish is fine with me."

"All around, please, Philip," Brewster Payne said.

*I have just had a premonition: I am not going to like whatever is going to happen. Whatever this is all about, it is* not *"let's call Good Ol' Matt and buy him a drink at the Rittenhouse Club."*

# THREE

"Are we celebrating something, or is this boys' night out?" Matt asked.

Coughlin chuckled.

"Well, more or less, we're celebrating something," Brewster Payne said. "Penny's coming home."

"Is she really?" Matt said, and the moment the words were out of his mouth, he realized that not only had he been making noise, rather than responding, but that his disinterest had not only been apparent to his father, but had annoyed him, perhaps hurt him, as well.

Penny was Miss Penelope Alice Detweiler of Chestnut Hill. Matt now recalled hearing from someone, probably his sister Amy, that she had been moved from The Institute of Living, a psychiatric hospital in Connecticut, to another funny farm out west somewhere. Arizona, Nevada, someplace like that.

Matt had known Penny Detweiler all his life. Penny's father and his had been schoolmates at Episcopal Academy and Princeton, and one of the major—almost certainly the most lucrative—clients of Mawson, Payne, Stockton, McAdoo & Lester, his father's law firm, was Nesfoods International, Philadelphia's largest employer, H. Richard Detweiler, president and chief executive officer.

After a somewhat pained silence, Brewster Payne said, "I was under the impression that you were fond of Penny."

"I am," Matt said quickly.

*I'm not at all sure that's true. I am not, now that I think about it, at all fond of Penny. She's just been around forever, like the walls. I've never even thought of her as a girl, really.*

He corrected himself: *There was that incident when we were four or five when I talked her into showing me hers and her mother caught us at it, and had hysterically shrieked at me that I was a filthy little boy, an opinion of me I strongly suspect she still holds.*

*But fond? No. The cold truth is that I now regard Precious Penny (to use her father's somewhat nauseating appellation) very much as I would regard a run-over dog. I am dismayed and repelled by what she did.*

"You certainly managed to conceal your joy at the news they feel she can leave The Lindens."

The Lindens, Matt recalled, *is the name of the new funny farm. And it's in* Nevada, *not Arizona. She's been there what? Five months? Six?*

There was another of what Matt thought of as "Dad's Significant Silences." He dreaded them. His father did not correct or chastise him. He just looked at the worm before him until the worm, squirming, figured out himself the error, or the bad manners, he had just manifested to God and Brewster Cortland Payne II.

Finally, Brewster Payne went on: "According to Amy, and according to the people at The Lindens, the problem of her physical addiction to narcotics is pretty much under control."

Matt kept his mouth shut, but in looking away from his father, to keep him from seeing Matt's reaction to that on his face, Matt found himself looking at Dennis V. Coughlin, who just perceptibly shook his head. The meaning was clear: *You and I don't believe that, we know that no more than one junkie in fifty ever gets the problem under control, but this is not the time or place to say so.*

"I'm really glad to hear that," Matt said.

"Which is not to say that her problems are over," Brewster Payne went on. "There is specifically the problem of the notoriety that went with this whole unfortunate business."

The newspapers in Philadelphia, in the correct belief that their

readers would be interested, indeed, fascinated, had reported in
great detail that the good-looking blonde who had been wounded
when her boyfriend—a gentleman named Anthony J. "Tony the
Zee" DeZego, whom it was alleged had connections to organized
crime—had been assassinated in a downtown parking garage was
none other than Miss Penelope Detweiler, only child of the Chestnut Hill/Nesfoods International Detweilers.

"That's yesterday's news," Matt said. "That was seven months
ago."

"Dick Detweiler doesn't think so," Brewster Payne said. "That's
where this whole thing started."

"Excuse me?"

"Dick Detweiler didn't want Penny to get off the airliner and
find herself facing a mob of reporters shoving cameras in her face."

"Why doesn't he send the company airplane after her?" Matt
wondered aloud. "Have it land at Northeast Philadelphia?"

"That was the original idea, but Amy said that she considered it
important that Penny not think that her return home was nothing
more than a continuation of her hospitalization."

"I'm lost, Dad."

"I don't completely understand Amy's reasoning either, frankly,
but I think the general idea is that Penny should feel, when she
leaves The Lindens, that she is closing the door on her hospitalization and returning to a normal life. Hence, no company plane.
Equally important, no nurse, not even Amy, to accompany her,
which would carry with it the suggestion that she's still under
care."

"Amy just wants to turn her loose in Nevada?" Matt asked incredulously. "How far is the funny farm from Las Vegas?"

Brewster Payne's face tightened.

"I don't at all like your choice of words, Matt. That was not only
uncalled for, it was despicable!" he said icily.

"Christ, Matty!" Dennis V. Coughlin said, seemingly torn between disgust and anger.

"I'm sorry," Matt said, genuinely contrite. "That just . . . came
out. But just turning her loose, alone, *that's* insane."

"It would, everyone agrees, be *ill-advised*," Brewster Payne
said. "That's where you come in, Matt."

"I beg your pardon?"

"Amy's reasoning here, and in this I am in complete agreement, is that you are the ideal person to go out there and bring her
home . . ."

"No. Absolutely not!"

" . . . for these reasons," Brewster Payne went on, ignoring him. "For one thing, Penny thinks of you as her brother. . . ."

"She thinks of me as the guy who pinned the tail on her," Matt said. "If it weren't for me, no one would have known she's a junkie."

"I don't like that term, either, Matt, but that's Amy's point. If you appear out there, in a nonjudgmental role, as her friend, welcoming her back to her life . . ."

"I can't believe you're going along with this," Matt said. "For one thing, Penny does not think of me as her brother. I'm just a guy she's known for a long time who betrayed her, turned her in. If I had been locked up out there for six months in that funny farm, I would really hate me."

"The reason Amy, and the people at The Lindens, feel that Penny is ready to resume her life is because, in her counseling, they have caused her to see things as they really are. To see you, specifically, as someone who was trying to help, not hurt her."

*I just don't believe this bullshit, and I especially don't believe my dad going along with it.*

"Dad, this is so much bullshit."

"Amy said that would probably be your reaction," Brewster Payne said. "I can see she was right."

"Anyway, it's a moot point. I couldn't go out there if I wanted to," Matt said. "Uncle Denny, tell him that I just can't call up my sergeant and tell him that I won't be in for a couple of days. . . ."

"I'm disappointed in you, Matty," Chief Coughlin said. "I thought by now you would have put two and two together."

*I'm a little disappointed in me myself, now that the mystery of my temporary assignment, report to Sergeant McElroy, has been cleared up.*

"What did Detweiler do, call you?"

"He called the mayor," Coughlin said. "And the mayor called Chief Lowenstein and me."

"I don't think it entered Dick Detweiler's mind, it certainly never entered mine, that you would have any reservations at all about helping Penny in any way you could," Brewster Payne said. Matt looked across the table at him. "But if you feel this strongly about it, I'll call Amy and . . ."

Matt held up both hands. "I surrender."

"I'm not sure that's the attitude we're all looking for."

Matt met his father's eyes.

"I'll do whatever I can to help Penny," he said.

There was another Significant Silence, and then Brewster C. Payne reached in his breast pocket and took out an envelope.

"These are the tickets. You're on American Airlines Flight 485 tomorrow morning at eight-fifteen. A car will meet you at the airport in Las Vegas. You will spend the night there . . ."

"At The Lindens?"

"Presumably. And return the next morning."

Shortly afterward, after having concluded their business with Detective Payne, Chief Coughlin and Brewster C. Payne went their respective ways.

Matt spent the balance of the evening in McGee's Saloon, in the company of Detective Charley McFadden of Northwest Detectives.

Perhaps naturally, their conversation dealt with their professional duties. Detective McFadden, who had been seven places below Matt on the detective examination listing, told Matt what he was doing in Northwest Detectives.

Charley had been an undercover Narc right out of the Police Academy, before he'd gone to Special Operations where he and Matt had become friends. On his very first assignment as a rookie detective, he found that his lieutenant was a supervisor (then a sergeant) he'd worked under in Narcotics, and who treated him like a detective, not a rookie detective. His interesting case of the day had been the investigation of a shooting of a numbers runner by a client who felt that he had cheated.

Matt had not felt that Detective McFadden would be thrilled to hear of his specialization in investigating recovered stolen automobiles, and spared him a recounting. Neither had he been fascinated with Detective McFadden's report on the plans for his upcoming wedding, and the ritual litany of his intended's many virtues.

The result of this was that Matt had a lot to drink, and woke up with a hangover and just enough time to dress, throw some clothes in a bag, and catch a cab to the airport, but not to have any breakfast.

At the very last minute, specifically at 7:40 A.M., as he handed his small suitcase to the attendant at the American Airlines counter, Detective Payne realized that he had, as either a Pavlovian reflex, or because he was more than a little hung over, picked up his

Chief's Special revolver and its holster from the mantelpiece and clipped it to his waistband before leaving his apartment.

Carrying a pistol aboard an airliner was in conflict with federal law, which prohibited any passenger, cop or not, to go armed except on official business, with written permission.

"Hold it, please," Officer Payne said to the counter attendant. She looked at him with annoyance, and then with wide-eyed interest as he took out his pistol, opened the cylinder, and ejected the cartridges.

"Sir, what are you doing?"

"Putting this in my suitcase," he said, and then added, when he saw the look on her face, "I'm a police officer."

That, to judge from the look on her face, was either an unsatisfactory reply, or one she was not willing to accept. He found his badge and photo ID and showed her that. She gave him a wan smile and quickly walked away. A moment later someone higher in the American Airlines hierarchy appeared.

"Sir, I understand you've placed a weapon in your luggage," he said.

"I'm a police officer," Matt said, and produced his ID again.

"We have to inspect the weapon to make sure it is unloaded," the American Airlines man said.

"I just unloaded it," Matt said, and offered the handful of cartridges as proof.

"We do not permit passengers to possess ammunition in the passenger cabins of our aircraft," the American Airlines man said.

Matt opened the suitcase again, handed the Chief's Special to the man, who accepted it as if it were obviously soaked in leper suppuration, and finally handed it back. Matt returned it to the suitcase and dumped the cartridges in an interior pocket.

By then, the American Airlines man had a form for Matt to sign, swearing that the firearm he had in his luggage was unloaded. When he had signed it, the man from American Airlines affixed a red tag to the suitcase handle reading UNLOADED FIREARM.

*If I were a thief,* Detective Payne thought, *and looking for something to steal, I think I'd make my best shot at a suitcase advertising that it contained a gun. You can get a lot more from a fence for a gun than you can get for three sets of worn underwear.*

"Thank you, sir," the man from American Airlines said. "Have a pleasant flight."

• • •

A stewardess squatted in the aisle beside him.

"May I get you something before we take off, sir?"

"How about a Bloody Mary?"

"Certainly, sir," she said, but managed to make it clear that any-one who needed a Bloody Mary at eight o'clock in the morning was at least an alcoholic, and most probably was going to cause trouble on the flight for the *nice* passengers in first class.

The Bloody Mary he had on the ground before they took off had made him feel a little better, and the Bloody Mary he had once they were in the air made him feel even better. It also helped him doze off. He became aware of this when a painful pressure in his ears woke him and alerted him to the fact that the airliner was making its descent to Las Vegas. The stewardess, obviously, had decided that someone who drank a Bloody Mary and a half at eight A.M., and then passed out, had no interest in breakfast.

Primarily to make sure that he still had it, he took the envelope containing the tickets from his pocket. There was something, a smaller, banknote-sized envelope, in the *NESFOODS INTERNA-TIONAL Office of the President* envelope he had not noticed be-fore.

He tore it open. There were five crisp one-hundred-dollar bills, obviously expense money, and a note:

Dear Matt:

I am not much good at saying "Thank You," but I want you to know that Grace and I will always have you in our hearts and in our prayers for your selfless, loving support of Penny in her trou-bles. Our family is truly blessed to have a friend like you.

Dick

"Oh, shit," Matt moaned.

"Please put your chair in the upright position and fasten your seat belt," the stewardess said.

There was a man wearing a chauffeur's cap holding a sign for MR. PAYNE when Matt stepped out of the airway into the terminal.

"I'm Matt Payne."

"If you'll give me your baggage checks, Mr. Payne, I'll take care of the luggage. The car is parked just outside Baggage Claim. A cream Cadillac."

"If you don't mind," Matt said, "I'll just tag along with you."

"Whatever you say, sir."

Matt looked around the terminal with interest. It was his first visit to Las Vegas. He saw that it was true that there were slot machines all over. There was also a clock on the wall. It said it was 10:15, and it was probably working, for he could see the second hand jerk, although his wristwatch told him it was 1:15.

It took him a moment to understand. He had been in the air four and a half or five hours. It was 1:15 in Philadelphia, which meant that he had missed lunch as well as breakfast. But they had changed time zones.

His bag was the very last bag to show up on the carousel, and the red UNLOADED FIREARM tag on it attracted the attention of a muscular young man with closely cropped hair, who was wearing blue jeans and a baggy sweater worn outside the jeans. He looked at the chauffeur, and then at Matt, when he saw he was with the chauffeur, with great interest, and then followed them out of the baggage room and watched them get into the cream-colored Cadillac limousine.

*Clever fellow that I am,* Matt thought, *I will offer odds of three to one that the guy in the crew cut is a plainclothesman on the airport detail. He is professionally curious why a nice, clean-cut young man such as myself is arriving in Las Vegas with an UNLOADED FIRE-ARM in his luggage.*

The chauffeur installed Matt, whose stomach was now giving audible notice that it hadn't been fed in some time, in the back seat and then drove away from the airport.

*I'm going to have to get something to eat, and right now.*

He pushed himself off the seat, and with some difficulty found the switch that lowered the glass divider.

"How far is this place? I've got to get something to eat."

"The Lindens, sir, or the Flamingo?"

"What about the Flamingo?"

"My instructions are to take you to the Flamingo, sir, and then pick you up there at seven-fifteen tomorrow morning and take you out to The Lindens."

"Oh."

"They have very nice restaurants in the Flamingo, sir. It's about fifteen, twenty minutes. But I can stop . . ."

The Flamingo, Matt recalled, was a world-famous den of iniquity, a gambling hall where Frank Sinatra, Dean Martin, and other people of that ilk entertained the suckers while they were being parted from their money at the roulette and blackjack tables. He also recalled hearing that the world's best-looking hookers plied their trade in the better Las Vegas dens of iniquity.

"No. That's fine. I can wait."

There was a basket of fruit and a bottle of champagne in a cooler in Suite 9012, which consisted of a sitting room overlooking what Matt decided was The Strip of fame and legend, and a bedroom with the largest bed, with a mirrored headboard, Matt had ever seen.

The bellman also showed him a small bar, stocked with miniature bottles of liquor, and a refrigerator that held wine and beer. As soon as he had tipped the bellman, he headed for the refrigerator and opened a bottle of Tuborg, and drank deeply from it.

A moment later he felt a little dizzy.

*Christ, I haven't had anything to eat since that cheese-steak in McGee's. No wonder the beer's making me dizzy.*

He ripped the cellophane off the basket of fruit and peeled a banana. And noticed that there was an envelope in the basket.

### *Flamingo Hotel & Casino*

Dear Mr. Payne:

Welcome to the Flamingo! It is always a pleasure to have a guest of Mr. Detweiler in the house.

A $10,000 line of credit has been established for you. Should you wish to test Lady Luck at our tables, simply present yourself at the cashier's window and you will be allowed to draw chips up to that amount.

If there is any way I can help to make your stay more enjoyable, please call me.

Good luck!

James Crawford
General Manager

It took Matt only a second or two to conclude that Mr. James Crawford had made a serious error. Dick and Grace Detweiler might feel themselves blessed to have a friend like him, and they might really have him in their prayers, but there was no way they were going to give him ten thousand dollars to gamble with.

*Detweiler probably entertains major clients out here, and the general manager made the natural mistake of thinking I'm one of them, someone in a position to buy a trainload of tomato soup or fifty tons of canned chicken.*

*The possibilities boggle the mind, but what this nice, young, nongambling police officer is going to do is find someplace to eat and then come back up here and crap out in that polo-field-sized bed.*

To get to the restaurant from the lobby, it was necessary to walk past what he estimated to be at least a thousand slot machines, followed by a formidable array of craps tables, blackjack tables, and roulette tables.

He felt rather naive. As far as gambling was concerned, he had lost his fair share, and then some, of money playing both blackjack and poker, but he really had no idea how one actually shot craps, and roulette looked like something you saw in an old movie, with men in dinner jackets and women in low-cut dresses betting the ancestral estates in some Eastern European principality on where the ball would fall into the hole.

The restaurant surprised and pleased him. The menu was enormous. He broke his unintended fast with a filet mignon, hash-brown potatoes, two eggs sunny side up, and two glasses of milk. It was first rate, and it was surprisingly cheap.

He started to pay for it, but then decided to hell with it, and signed the bill with his room number.

*Why should I spend my money when I'm out here doing an unpleasant errand for Dick Detweiler?*

He walked past the blackjack, craps, and roulette tables and was almost past the slot machines when he decided that it would really be foolish to have been out here in Las Vegas, in one of the most famous gambling dens of them all, without having once played a slot machine.

He looked in his wallet and found that he had a single dollar bill and several twenties. There were also, he knew, two fifties, folded as small as possible, hidden in a recess of the wallet, against the possibility that some girl would get fresh and he would have to walk home.

He took one of the twenties and gave it to a young woman in a very short shirt who had a bus driver's change machine strapped around her waist.

She handed him a short, squat stack of what looked like coins, but what, on examination, turned out to be one-dollar slugs.

He found a slot machine and dropped one of the slugs in and pulled the handle. He did this again seventeen times with no result, except that the oranges and lemons and cherries spun around. On the nineteenth pull, however, the machine made a noise he had not heard before, and then began noisily spitting out a stream of slugs into a sort of a shelf on the bottom of the machine.

"Jesus Christ!"

There were more slugs than he could hold in both hands. But the purpose of the waxed paper bucket he had noticed between his machine and the next now became apparent. Successful gamblers such as himself put their winnings in them.

*And wise successful gamblers such as myself know when to quit. I will take all these slugs—Jesus, there must be two hundred of them—to the cashier and turn them in for real money.*

He didn't make it to the cashier's cage. His route took him past a roulette table, and he stopped to look. After a minute or two he decided that it wasn't quite as exotic or complicated as it looked in the movies about the Man Who Broke the Bank at Monte Carlo.

There were thirty-six numbers, plus 0 and 00, for a total of thirty-eight. The guy with the stick—the *croupier*, he recalled somewhat smugly—paid thirty-six to one if your number came up. Since there were thirty-eight numbers, that gave the house a one-in-nineteen advantage, roughly five percent.

That didn't seem too unfair. And in another minute or two he had figured out that you could make other bets, one through twelve, for example, or thirteen to twenty-four, or odd or even, or red or black, that gave you a greater chance of winning, but paid lower odds.

Since 0 and 00 were neither odd or even, and were green, rather than black or red, the house, Matt decided, got its five percent no matter how the suckers bet.

And he also decided that since he had already made the mental decision to throw twenty dollars away, so that he could say he had gambled in Las Vegas, there was no reason to change simply because the slot machine had paid off.

He would now be able to say, he thought, as he put five of the slot machine slugs on EVEN that he had lost his shirt at roulette. That sounded better than having lost his shirt at the slot machines.

Six came up.

The croupier looked at him.

"Pennies or nickels?"

*What the hell does that mean?*

"Nickels," Matt said.

The croupier took his slot machine slugs and laid two chips in their place.

*Obviously, a "nickel" means that chip is the equivalent of five slot machine slugs.*

Matt let his two-nickel bet ride. Twenty-six came up. The croupier added two chips to the two on the board. Matt decided it was time to quit, since he was ahead. He picked up the four chips, and felt rather wise when the ball fell into a slot marked with a seven.

He waited until the wheel had been spun again, odd again, and then placed another five slot machine slugs on the green felt, this time on One to Twelve.

Nine came up. The croupier took the slot machine slugs and replaced them with three nickel chips.

"Sir, would you like me to exchange your coins for you?"

Obviously, it was for some reason impolite to play roulette with slot machine slugs.

"Please," Matt said, and pushed the waxed paper bucket to the croupier.

"All nickels?"

"Nickels and dimes," Matt said.

Two small stacks of chips were pushed across the table to him.

Matt yawned, and then again.

*Jesus, what's the matter with me? I was just going to get something to eat and then crap out. How long have I been doing this?*

His watch said that it was quarter to six.

*Time to quit.*

He watched the ball circle the wheel and then bounce around the slots before finally dropping in one.

*Obviously, it is time to quit. I have been betting on 00 every fourth or fifth bet since I have been here, and that's the first time I ever won.*

As the croupier counted out chips to place beside the chip he had laid on 00, Matt said, "Quit when you're ahead, I always say."

"You want to cash in, sir?"

"Please," Matt said, and pushed the stacks of chips, nickels, dimes, and quarters in front of him to the croupier.

He wondered where the cashier kept the real money to cash him out. There was no money, no cash box, in sight.

The croupier put all the chips in neat little stacks, and then said "Cash out." A man in a suit who had been hovering around in the background came up behind the croupier, looked, nodded, wrote something on a clipboard, and then smiled at Matt.

The croupier pushed a stack of chips, including some oblong ones Matt hadn't noticed before, across the felt to him.

"What do I do with these?" he wondered aloud.

"Take them to the cashier, sir," the croupier said.

Matt reclaimed his waxed paper bucket, and as he dumped the chips into it, he recalled that the polite thing to do was tip the croupier. He pushed one of the oblong chips across the table to the croupier.

"Thank you very much, sir," the croupier said. It was the first time, Matt noticed, that he had sounded at all friendly.

He walked to the cashier's cage and pushed the waxed paper bucket through what looked like a bank teller's window to a gray-haired, middle-aged woman.

She put all the chips in neat little stacks and then counted to herself, moving her lips. She looked at him.

"Would you like me to draw a check, sir?"

*What the hell would I do with a check? I couldn't cash a check out here.*

"I'd rather have the cash, if that would be all right."

The gray-haired woman took a stack of bills from a drawer and started counting them out. Matt was surprised to see that the bills were hundred-dollar bills, and then astonished to see how many of them she was counting out into thousand-dollar stacks. When she was finished there were four one-thousand-dollar stacks, one stack with six hundred-dollar bills in it, and a sixth stack with eighty-five dollars in it, four twenties and a five.

"Four thousand six hundred eighty-five," the gray-haired woman said.

"Thank you very much."

"Thank *you*, sir."

*I don't believe this.*

Matt divided the money into two wads, put one in each pocket, and walked out of the casino.

● ● ●

The first thing Matt Payne experienced when he woke up was annoyance. He had fallen asleep with his clothes on. And then he remembered the money and sat up abruptly. It was still there on the bed. No longer in the one thick wad into which he had counted it, three or four times, but there.

He counted it again. $4,685.

*Jesus H. Christ!*

He put the stack of bills in the drawer of the bedside table, then undressed and took a shower. He wrapped himself in a terry-cloth robe, went back into the bedroom, sat on the enormous bed, took the money from the bedside table, and counted it again.

Then he laid on the bed with his hands laced behind his head and thought about it.

The first thing he thought was that he was a natural-born gambler, that his quick mind gave him an edge over people who lost at roulette. He knew when to bet and when not to bet.

*That's so much bullshit! You were just incredibly lucky, that's all. Dumb beginner's luck. Period. If you go back down there and try to do that again, you will lose very dime of that, plus the two fifties mad money.*

*The thing to do is put that money someplace safe and forget about it.*

He figured that he might as well round it off, to forty-five hundred, keeping one hundred eight-five to play with, and then he changed that to rounding it off to four thousand even, which left him six hundred eight-five to play with, which meant lose.

He took out his toilet kit, and with some effort managed to cram forty hundred-dollar bills into the chrome soap dish.

He looked at his watch. It was quarter after three. That was Philadelphia time. It was only a little after midnight here, but it explained why he was hungry again.

With his luck, the restaurants would be closed at this hour. He would be denied another meal.

*That's not true. With* my *luck, the restaurant will not only be open, but the headwaiter will show me to my table with a flourish of trumpets.*

The headwaiter made him wait for a table, as the restaurant was even more crowded at midnight, Las Vegas time, than it had been when he'd had lunch, or breakfast, or whatever meal that had been. He had a martini, a shrimp cocktail, and another filet mignon, and then went back to the casino.

He went to the same roulette table and gave the croupier one hundred eight-five dollars, specifying nickels, and promptly lost it all.

He moved away from the table and decided he would see if he could figure out how one bet at a craps table, as he had figured out how one bet at roulette.

There was a man at the head of the table rolling dice. He looked like a gambler, Matt decided. He had gold rings on both hands, and a long-collared shirt unbuttoned nearly to his navel, so as to display his hairy chest and a large gold medallion. And he had, one on each side of him, a pair of what Matt decided must be Las Vegas hookers of fame and legend.

Matt moved to what he hoped was an unobtrusive distance from the gambler and tried to figure out what was going on. Ten minutes later, the only thing he was fairly sure of was that the gambler was a fellow Philadelphian. The accent was unmistakable.

"Sir, if you are not going to wager, would you mind stepping aside and making room for someone who would like to play?"

"Sorry," Matt said, and pulled his wad of hundred-dollar bills from his pocket and laid one somewhere, anywhere, on the felt of the craps table. The gambler threw the dice. The hooker on his left said "ooooh" and the one on his right kissed him and gave him a little hug.

The croupier picked up Matt's one-hundred-dollar bill . . .

*I lost. Why did I bet a hundred?*

. . . and held a handful of chips over it.

"Quarters all right, sir?"

*I won. I'll be goddamned. What did I bet on?*

"Quarters are fine, thank you."

He picked up the stack of quarters, there were twelve of them, and walked away from the table.

*If you have no idea what you're betting on, you have no business betting.*

"Stick around," the gambler said. "I'm on a roll."

The temptation was nearly irresistible. The hooker on the left was smiling at him with invitation in her eyes. He had never been with a hooker.

*Was this the time and place?*

*Get thee behind me, Satan! Back to the roulette table.*

The Lindens was a forty-five-minute drive from the Flamingo. Matt was sorry that he had let himself be ushered into the back seat of the limousine. He certainly could have seen more of Las Vegas and the desert upfront than he could see from the back seat, through the deeply tinted windows.

But he had been more than a little groggy when he left the Flamingo. He had lost the seven hundred dollars he had walked away from the craps table with, gone to bed, woken up, and—absolute insanity—decided he could take a chance with another five hundred, and then had compounded that insanity by taking a thousand dollars, not five hundred, from the soap dish and going back to the casino with it.

When he'd finally left the table, at quarter past six, Las Vegas time, he had worked the thousand up to thirty-seven hundred. Since that obviously wouldn't fit into the soap dish, and he didn't want to have that much money in his pockets, or put it in the suitcase, he told the man in the cashier's cage to give him a check for his winnings.

By the time they had made out the check, and he'd taken another quick shower, they had called from the desk and told him his limousine was waiting for him.

There was nothing he could see for miles around The Lindens, which turned out to be a rambling, vaguely Spanish-looking collection of connected buildings built on a barren mountainside. There was a private road, a mile and a half long, from a secondary highway.

There was no fence around the place. Probably, he decided, because you would have to be out of your mind to try to walk away from The Lindens. There was nothing but desert.

In front of the main building, in an improbably lush patch of grass, were six trees. Lindens, he decided, as in Unter den Linden.

A hefty, middle-aged man in a blazer with retired cop written all over him saw him get out of the limousine and unlocked a double door as Matt walked up to it.

"Mr. Payne?"

"Right?"

"Dr. Newberry is expecting you, sir. Will you follow me, please?"

He locked the door again before he headed inside the building.

Dr. Newberry was a woman in a white coat who looked very much like the cashier in the Flamingo.

"You look very much like your sister," Dr. Newberry greeted him cordially. Matt did not think he should inform her that that must be a genetic anomaly, because he and Amy shared no genes. He nodded politely.

"It was very good of you to come out to be with Penelope on her trip home."

"Not at all."

"We believe, as I'm sure Dr. Payne has told you, that we've done all we can for Penelope here. We've talked her through her problems, and of course, we believe that her physical addiction is under control."

"Yes, ma'am."

"We've tried to convince her that the best thing she can do is put what happened behind her, that she's not the only young woman who has had difficulty like this in her life, and that she will not be the only one to overcome it."

"Yes, ma'am."

"What I'm trying to get across is that I hope you can behave in a natural manner toward Penelope. While neither you nor she can deny that she has had problems, or has spent this time with us, the less you dwell upon it, the better. Do you understand?"

"Yes, ma'am. I think so."

Dr. Newberry got up and smiled.

"Well, let's go get her. She's been waiting for you."

She led him through a series of wide corridors furnished with simple, heavy furniture and finally to a wide door. She pushed it open.

Penny was sitting on a chair. Her shoulder-length blond hair was parted in the middle. She was wearing a skirt and two sweaters. A single strand of pearls hung around her neck. There was a suitcase beside the chair.

It was a fairly large room with a wall of narrow, ceiling-high windows providing a view of the desert and mountains. Matt saw the windows were not wide enough for anyone to climb out.

"Your friend is here, dear," Dr. Newberry said.

Penny got to her feet.

"Hello, Matt," she said, and walked to him.

*Christ, she expects me to kiss her.*

He put his hands on her arms and kissed her cheek. He could smell her perfume. Or maybe it was soap. A female smell, anyway.

"How goes it, Penny?"

"I'm sorry you had to come out here," she said.

"Ah, hell, don't be silly."

"Shall I have someone come for your bag?"

"I can handle the bag," Matt said.

"Well, then, Penelope, you're all ready to go. I'll say good-bye to you now, dear."

"Thank you, Dr. Newberry, for everything."

"It's been my pleasure," Dr. Newberry said, smiled at Matt, and walked out of the room.

Penny looked at Matt.

"God, I hate that woman!" she said.

He could think of no reply to make.

"Have you got any money?" she asked.

"Why?"

"Some people have been nice to me. I'd like to give them something."

*What did they do, smuggle you junk?*

"I don't think you're supposed to tip nurses and people like that."

"For god's sake, Matt, let me have some money. You know you'll get it back."

"When you get home, you can write them a check," Matt said.

"What are you thinking, that I'm going to take the money and run?"

*As a matter of fact, perhaps subconsciously, that is just what I was thinking.*

"I don't know what to think, Penny. But I'm not going to give you any money."

"Fuck you, Matt!"

He wondered if she had used language like that before she had met Tony the Zee DeZego, or whether she had learned it from him.

She picked up her bag and marched out of her room. He followed her. The rent-a-cop in the blue blazer, who, Matt thought, probably had a title like director of Internal Security Services, was at the front door. He unlocked it.

"Good-bye, Miss Detweiler," he said. "Good luck."

Penny didn't reply.

Matt got in the back seat of the limousine with her.

"Well, so how was the food?"

"Fuck you, Matt," Penny said again.

# FOUR

It is accepted almost as an article of faith by police officers assigned to McCarran International Air Field, Las Vegas—which does not mean that it is true—that the decision to have a large number of plainclothes officers, as opposed to uniformed officers, patrolling the passenger terminal was based on the experience of a very senior Las Vegas police officer in the French Quarter of New Orleans, Louisiana.

The legend has it that the senior officer (three names are bandied about) was relaxing at a Bourbon Street bar after a hard day's work at the National Convention of the International Association of Chiefs of Police when an unshaven sleaze-ball in greasy jeans and leather vest approached him and very politely said, "Excuse me, sir, I believe this is yours."

He thereupon handed the senior police officer his wallet. (In some versions of the story, the sleaze-ball handed him his wallet, his ID folder, his wristwatch, and his diamond-studded Masonic ring.) It came out that the sleaze-ball was a plainclothes cop who had been watching the dip (pickpocket) ply his trade. (In some versions of the story, the dip was a stunning blond transvestite with whom the senior police officer had just been dancing.)

In any event, the senior police officer returned to Las Vegas with the notion, which he had the authority to turn into policy, that the way to protect the tourists moving through McCarran was the way the cops in New Orleans protected the tourists moving down Bourbon Street, with plainclothes people.

They could, the senior police said, protect the public without giving the public the idea that Las Vegas was so crime-ridden a place that you needed police officers stationed every fifty yards along the way from the airway to the limo and taxi stands to keep the local critters from separating them from their worldly goods before the casino operators got a shot at them.

And so it came to pass that Officer Frank J. Oakes, an ex-paratrooper who had been on the job for almost six years, was standing on the sidewalk outside the American Airlines terminal in plainclothes when the white Cadillac limo pulled up. Oakes was wearing sports clothes and carrying a plastic bag bearing the logotype of the Marina Motel & Casino. The bag held his walkie-talkie.

The white Cadillac limo attracted his attention. Even before he took a look at the license plate to make sure, he was sure that it was a *real* limo, as he thought of it, as opposed to one of the livery limos, or one operated by one of the casinos to make the high rollers feel good. For one thing, it wasn't beat up. For another, it did not have a TV antenna on the trunk. Most important, it wasn't a stretch limo, large enough to transport all of a rock-and-roll band and their lady friends. It looked to him like a real, rich people's private limo, an analysis that seemed to be confirmed when the chauffeur got out wearing a neat suit and white shirt and chauffeur's cap and quickly walked around the front to open the curbside door.

The first person to get out was a female Caucasian, early twenties, five feet three, 115 pounds. She wore her shoulder-length blond hair parted in the middle, a light blue linen skirt, a pullover sweater, and a jacket-type sweater unbuttoned. There was a single strand of pearls around her neck. She did not have a spectacular breastworks, but Officer Oakes found her hips and tail attractive.

A male Caucasian, early twenties, maybe 165, right at six feet, followed her out of the limo. He was wearing a tweed coat, a tieless white shirt, gray flannel slacks, and loafers. Oakes thought that the two of them sort of fit the limo, that something about them smelled of money and position.

The chauffeur took a couple of bags from the limo trunk and

handed them to the American Airlines guy. Then he went to the young guy, who handed him the tickets. Then the young guy looked at Officer Oakes, first casually, then gave him a closer look. Then he smiled and winked.

It was ten to one that he wasn't a fag, so the only thing that was left was that he had made Oakes as a cop. Oakes didn't like to be made, and he wondered how this guy had made him.

The chauffeur got the tickets back from the American Airlines guy, handed them to the young guy, and then tipped his hat. The blonde went to the chauffeur and smiled at him and shook his hand. No tip, which confirmed Oakes's belief that it was a private limo.

The chauffeur got behind the wheel and drove off. The blonde and the well-dressed young guy walked into the terminal. The more he thought about it, Oakes was sure that he was right. The guy had made him as a cop on the job.

Another limo, this one a sort of pink-colored livery limo that looked like it was maybe five thousand miles away from the salvage yard, pulled into the space left by the real limo.

A real gonzo got out of it, a white male Caucasian in his late twenties or early thirties, maybe five-ten and 170, swarthy skin with facial scars, probably acne. He was wearing a maroon shirt with long collar points, unbuttoned halfway down to expose his hairy chest and a gold chain with some kind of medal. He had on a pair of yellow pants and white patent-leather loafers with a chain across the instep. He had a gold wristwatch and a diamond ring on one hand, and a couple of gold bracelets around the wrist of the other.

He got out and looked around as if he had just bought the place, made a big deal of checking the time, so everybody would see the gold watch, and then waited for the limo driver to get his bags from the trunk. Cheap luggage. He waited until the guy had carried his bags to the American Airlines counter, then pulled out a thick wad of bills, hundreds outside, and then counted out four twenties.

"Here you go, my man," the gonzo said.

A limo, no matter at what hotel you were staying, was no more than fifty bucks, so the last of the big spenders was laying a large tip on the driver. The gonzo had apparently done well at the tables.

The Las Vegas Chamber of Commerce, Oakes knew, would be happy. There was no better advertisement than some gonzo like this going home and telling the other gonzos what a killing he'd made in Vegas.

Officer Oakes's attention was diverted from the gonzo by the sound of a strident female voice, offering her anything but flattering opinion of the gentleman with her. Drunk probably, Oakes decided.

He stepped into a doorway, unzipped his Marina Hotel & Casino plastic bag and took out the radio and called for a uniformed officer to deal with the disturbance at American Airlines Arrival.

By the time the uniforms, two of them, got there, the female Caucasian, five-three, maybe 135, 140, brown hair, had warmed to the subject of what a despicable, untrustworthy sonofabitch the gentleman with her was, and Officer Oakes put the blonde with the nice ass, the gonzo, and the good-looking young guy he was sure had made him as a cop from his mind.

Matt caught up with Penny as she marched through the airport and took her arm.

"Is that really necessary?"

"I've got to make a phone call," he said.

He guided her to a row of pay telephones, took a dime from his pocket, dropped it in the slot, gave the operator a number, told her it was collect, that his name was Matthew Payne, and that he would speak with anyone.

"Who are you calling?" Penny asked, almost civilly.

"My father."

"Why?"

"Because I was told to call when I was sure the plane was leaving on schedule," Matt Payne replied, and then turned his attention to the telephone.

"Hello, Mrs. Craig. Would you please tell that slave driver you work for that American Airlines Flight 6766 is leaving on schedule?"

There was brief pause and then he went on:

"Everything's fine. Aside from the fact that I lost my car and next year's salary at the craps tables."

There was a reply, and he chuckled and hung up.

"Why did you call your father?" Penny asked.

"Because I thought he would be better able to deal with a collect call than yours," Matt Payne replied, then took her arm again. "There's what I have been looking for."

He led her to a cocktail lounge and set her down at a tiny table in a relatively uncrowded part of the room.

A waitress almost immediately came to the table.

"Have you got any Tuborg?" Matt Payne asked.

The waitress nodded.

"Penny?" he asked.

"I think a 7UP, please."

"Sprite okay?"

"Yes, thank you," Penny said. Then, turning to Matt: "You were kidding, right, about losing a lot of money gambling?"

"As a matter of fact, I made so much money, I don't believe it."

"Really?"

He took the Flamingo's check for $3,700 from his pocket and showed it to her.

"My God!"

"And that's not all of it," he said.

"What were you playing?"

"Roulette."

"Roulette? What do you know about playing roulette?"

"Absolutely nothing, that's why I won," Matt said.

She smiled. The anger seemed to be gone. He had a policeman's cynical thought. *Is she charming me?*

"When did you get here?" Penny asked.

"A little after ten yesterday morning."

"Then why didn't you come get me yesterday?"

"Because I was told to get you this morning," he said. "Mine not to reason why, et cetera, et cetera."

"So instead you went gambling."

"Right. I quit half an hour before the limousine came back for me." When he saw the look on her face, he went on solemnly, "Las Vegas never sleeps, you know. They don't even have clocks."

"I really wouldn't know. I didn't get to go to town."

He did not respond.

"You really gambled all night?" she asked.

"I took a couple of naps and a shower, but yes, I guess I did."

"Well, I'm glad you had fun."

"Thank you."

"You were the last person I expected to see," Penny said.

"You could have been knocked over with a fender, right?"

She smiled dutifully.

"What are you doing out here, Matt? I mean, why you?"

The waitress appeared with their drinks. Matt handed her a credit card and waited for her to leave before replying.

"My father called me up and asked me to have a drink at the Rittenhouse. When I got there, Chief Coughlin was with him . . ."

"That's the man you call 'Uncle Denny'?"

"Right. My father told me it had been decided by your father and Amy that I was the obvious choice to come out here and bring you home. I told him that while the thought of being able to be of some small service to you naturally thrilled me, I would have to regretfully decline, as I had to work. Then Denny Coughlin told me your father had talked to the mayor, and that was no problem. So here I am."

"You're still a . . ." Penny asked, stopped just in time from saying "cop," and finished, ". . . policeman?"

"No, Precious Penny," Matt said. "I am no longer a simple police officer. You have the great privilege of sitting here with one of Philadelphia's newest detectives. M. M. Payne, East Detective Division, at your service, ma'am. Just the facts, please."

She smiled dutifully again.

He smiled back and took a healthy swallow of his beer.

Matt Payne felt nowhere near as bright and clever as he was trying to appear. As a matter of fact, he could recall few times in his twenty-two years when he had been more uncomfortable.

"Then congratulations, Matt," Penny said.

"Thank you, ma'am," he said.

"But that doesn't answer why you? Out here, I mean?"

"I think the idea, I think *Amy's* idea, is that I am the best person to be with you as you begin your passage back into the real world. Amy, I hope you know, is calling the shots."

"She's been coming out here," Penny said.

"Yeah, I know," Payne said. "For whatever the hell it's worth, Penny, even if she is my sister, the word on the street is that she's a pretty good shrink."

That was the truth: Amelia Payne, M.D., *was* a highly regarded psychiatrist.

" 'The word on the street'?" Penny asked, gently mocking him.

"The consensus is," he corrected himself.

"I don't understand . . ." Penny said.

"Neither do I," he said, "but to coin a phrase, 'mine not to reason why, mine but to ride into the valley of the hustlers' . . ."

"Well, thanks anyway for coming out here, even if you didn't want to."

"Better me than Madame D, right?"

Matt Payne had been calling Grace (Mrs. H. Richard) Detweiler "Madame D" since he had been about twelve, primarily because he knew it greatly annoyed her.

Penny laughed.

"Oh, God, I don't think I could have handled my mother out here."

"You better prepare yourself, she'll be at the airport."

"And then what?"

"Jesus Christ, Penny, I don't know. Knowing her as I do, I suspect she'll be a pain in the ass."

"I've always liked your tact and charm, Matt," Penny said, and then, "God, that beer looks good."

"You want one?"

"I'm a *substance abuser*," Penny said. "Don't tell me you haven't heard."

"You're a . . . you *were* a junkie, not a drunk."

"Alcohol is a drug," Penny said, as if reciting something she had memorized.

"So is aspirin," Matt said, and pushed his beer glass to her.

She met his eyes, and looked into them, and it was only with a good deal of effort that he could keep himself from looking away.

Then she picked up his glass and took a swallow.

"If you're going to start throwing things, or taking your clothes off, or whatever, try to give me a little notice, will you?" Matt said.

"Go to hell, Matt," Penny said, then almost immediately, first touching his hand, added, "I don't mean that. My God, I was so glad to see you this morning!"

"You were always a tough little girl, Penny," Matt said after a moment. "I think you're going to be all right."

*Did I mean that, or did I just say it to be kind?*

"I wish I was sure you meant that," Penny said.

He shrugged, and then looked around for the waitress and, when he had caught her eye, signaled for another beer.

"On the way to the airplane, we're going to have to get you some Sen-Sen or something. I don't want Amy or your mother to smell booze on your breath."

"Did they tell you to make sure I didn't get . . . anything I wasn't supposed to have?"

"They knew I wouldn't give you, or let you get, anything to suck up your nose."

"Detective Payne, right?"

He nodded.

"And what did they say about talking to me about . . . about what happened?"

"About what, what happened?"

"You know what I mean," she said, somewhat snappishly. "About *who* I mean. Anthony."

The waitress delivered the beer.

"Get me the bill, please," Matt said.

Penny waited until the waitress was out of earshot.

"I loved him, Matt."

"Jesus Christ!" he said disgustedly.

"I'd hoped you would understand. I guess I should have known better."

"DeZego, Anthony J., 'Tony the Zee,' " Matt recited bitterly, "truck driver, soldier in the Savarese family. I'm not even sure that he had made his bones. And incidentally, loving husband and beloved father of three."

"You're a sonofabitch!"

"For Christ's sake, Penny. He's dead. Let it go at that! Be glad, for Christ's sake!"

She glowered at him. He picked up his beer glass and as he drank from it met her eyes. After a moment she averted hers.

"I don't know what that means," she said softly, after a moment, "what you said about bones."

"In order to be a real mobster, you have to kill somebody," Matt said evenly. "They call it 'making your bones.' "

"In other words, you really think he was a gangster?"

"Mobster. There's a difference. He was a low-level mobster. We can't even find out why they hit him."

"And the people who did it? They're just going to get away with it?"

He looked at her for a long moment before deciding to answer her.

"The bodies of two people with reputations as hit men, almost certainly the people who hit your boyfriend, have turned up, one in Detroit and one in Chicago. The mob doesn't like it when innocent civilians, especially rich ones with powerful fathers like you, get hurt when they're hitting people."

"They're dead?" she asked.

He nodded.

"Good!"

Something between contempt and pity flashed in Matt's eyes. He stood up and looked around impatiently for the waitress. When she came to the table, he quickly signed the bill and reclaimed his credit card.

"I haven't finished my beer," Penny said coldly.

"You can have another on the airplane," he said, as coldly. "Let's go."

"Yes, sir, Mr. Detective, sir," Penny said. The waitress gave the both of them a confused look.

"You're in luck, Mr. Lanza," the not-too-bad-looking ticket clerk at the American counter said. "This is the last first-class seat on 6766."

"When you're on a roll, you're on a roll," Vito Joseph Lanza said with a smile. He pulled the wad of bills with the hundreds on the outside from the side pocket of his yellow slacks, flicked it open, and waited for her to tell him how much it was going to cost him to upgrade the return portion of his thirty-days-in-advance, tourist-class, round-trip ticket to first class. Then he counted out what she told him.

She made change, handed him the upgraded ticket and a boarding pass, and said, "Gate 28. They're probably just about to board. Thank you, Mr. Lanza."

"Yeah. Right. Sure," Vito said, stuffed the wad back in his trousers, and looked around for directions to Gate 28.

They were not yet boarding Flight 6766, non-stop service to Philadelphia, when he reached Gate 28. He leaned against the wall and lit a Pall Mall with the gold Dunhill lighter he'd bought in the casino gift shop just before going to bed about three that morning.

*I probably could have picked up another couple of grand, if I'd have stuck around,* he thought, *but the cards had started to run against me, and the one thing a good gambler has to know is when to quit. I certainly wouldn't have lost it all back, but I would probably have lost some, and quitting the way I did, I sort of have the Dunhill to show for quitting when that was the smart thing to do.*

He had taken only a couple of puffs when the ticket lady got on the loudspeaker and announced that they were preboarding. Women with small children, people who needed assistance in boarding, and of course passengers holding first-class tickets, who could board at their leisure.

Vito had to wait until a couple of old people on canes and what looked like a real Indian-Indian lady with three kids got on, but he was the first passenger in the first-class cabin. He checked his boarding pass, and then found his seat, on the aisle, on the left, right against the bulkhead that separated the first-class compartment from the tourist-class section.

As soon as he'd dug the seat belt out from where someone had stuffed it between the seats, a stewardess appeared, squatted in the aisle, and asked if she could get him something to drink before they took off.

*They don't do that in the back of the airplane*, he thought.

"Scotch, rocks," Vito said.

She smiled and went forward and returned almost immediately with his drink. Two things surprised him, first that it came in a plastic cup—*Jesus, for what they charge you to sit up here, you'd think they'd at least give you a real glass*—and that she didn't hold her hand out for any money. First he thought that they maybe ran a tab, but then he remembered that drinks in first class were on the house.

He examined his surroundings.

*Class,* he decided. *The seats are wide and comfortable, and real leather. This is the way to travel.*

He reached up and touched the back of the seat in front of him. That was real leather too.

He watched the other passengers get on. A lot of them looked, he noticed, at the only passenger in first class. He wondered for a moment if the ticket counter had been handing him a line about being lucky to get the only remaining seat in first class, but then some other first-class passengers got on and he decided that maybe she had been telling him the truth.

A good-looking blonde came into the cabin. *Nice ass,* Vito thought. For some reason she looked familiar. *Not a movie or TV star,* he decided. *She isn't good-looking enough for that. But I'm almost sure I seen her someplace.*

A Main Line type came on behind her, wearing a tweed jacket and a dress shirt with no tie. He had the boarding pass stubs in his hand. He glanced at them and stopped the blonde at the second row of seats from the front on the right, asked her did she want the aisle or the window. As she was getting in to sit in the window seat, the young guy looked around the cabin and smiled and nodded at Vito.

*I remember him. He was at the craps table in the Flamingo when I was really hot. She wasn't there. I would have remembered her. Neither of them is wearing a wedding ring. She doesn't look like the kind of girl who would go off to Vegas with some guy she isn't married to for a couple of days. Maybe they're brother and sister.*

He watched as the stewardess took their order, and then came back with a couple of cans of beer.

*Jesus, if it's free booze up here, why drink beer?*

Vito Lanza woke up when his ears hurt because they were coming down to land. His mouth was dry. He remembered—*what the hell, it was free*—that he'd had a lot to drink before they served dinner, and wine with the dinner, and he remembered that they had started to show the movie, and decided that he had fallen asleep during the movie.

Ten minutes later, the airplane landed. Vito was a little disappointed, for they had not flown over Philadelphia. The wind was blowing the wrong way or something, and all he could see out the window was Delaware and the oil refineries around Chester.

When they finally taxied up to the terminal building, Vito looked out the window and saw something that caught his attention. There was an Airport Unit Jeep and a limousine and what looked like an unmarked detective's car sitting down there, with the baggage carts and the other airport equipment.

*What the hell is that all about?*

"Ladies and gentlemen," the stewardess said over the public address system, "the captain has not yet turned off the FASTEN SEAT BELTS sign. Please remain in your seats until he does."

When the stewardess finally got the door open, a stocky, red-faced man wearing the uniform of a lieutenant of the Philadelphia Police Department stepped into the cabin and looked around. Vito knew who he was, Lieutenant Paul Ardell of the Airport Unit.

Ardell looked around the first-class cabin, did a double take when he saw Vito, and then looked down at the Main Line type in the second row. He said something to him—Vito couldn't hear what—and the Main Line type got up, backed up a little in the aisle to let the blonde with the nice ass out, and then they both followed Ardell out the door.

A moment later Vito saw the two of them walking toward the limousine. The door opened and a gray-haired guy got out and put his arms around the blonde and hugged her. Then she got into the limousine and the gray-haired guy shook the Main Line type's hand and then gave him a little hug.

The Main Line type then walked out of Vito's sight, under the airplane. Vito guessed, correctly, that he was going to intercept their luggage before it got from the airplane to the baggage conveyor, but he didn't get to see this. The FASTEN SEAT BELTS sign went off, and the stewardess gave her little speech about how happy American Airlines was that they had chosen American, and hoped they would do so again in the future, and people started getting off.

Joe Marchessi, and the new guy, the little Spic, was working the baggage claim room when Vito got there. Until somebody who transferred into the Airport Unit got to know his way around, they paired him with somebody with experience.

The Airport Unit was different. In other areas you could move a cop from one district to another, and just about put him right to work. But things were different at the Airport; it was a whole new ballgame. You had to learn what to look for, and what you looked for at the Airport was not what you looked for in an ordinary district.

Airport Unit cops were something special. For one thing, they were sworn in as officers both in Philadelphia and Tinnicum Township, which is in Delaware County. Some parts of the runways and their approaches are in Tinnicum Township, and they need the authority to operate there too.

The mob, over the years, had found the Tinnicum Marshes a good place to dump bodies. But aside from that, there was not much violent crime at the Airport.

Most of what you had to deal with was people stealing luggage, and they were most often professional thieves, not some kid who saw something he decided he could get away with stealing and stole it. Or keeping thieves, professional and amateur, from helping themselves to the air freight in "Cargo City."

Then there was smuggling, but that was handled by the feds, the Immigration and Naturalization Service, and the Customs Service, and sometimes the Bureau of Narcotics and Dangerous Drugs, and they usually made the arrest, and all the Airport Unit had to do was arrange for the prisoners to be transported.

All things considered, working the job in the Airport Unit was a pretty good job. Most of the time you got to stay inside the terminal, instead of either freezing your balls or getting a heat stroke outside.

Vito didn't think much of Marchessi: He had been on the job ten, twelve years, never even thought about taking the examination for corporal or detective and bettering himself, just wanted to put in his eight hours a day doing as little as possible, inside where it was warm, until he was old enough to retire and get a job as a rent-a-cop or something.

And Officer Marchessi did not, in Vito's opinion, treat him with the respect to which he was entitled as a corporal.

Vito walked up to them. "Whaddaya say, Marchessi?"

"How's it going, Lanza?"

It should have been "Corporal," but Vito let it ride.

"You're Martinez, right?"

"That's right, Corporal."

"Well, what do you think of Airport?"

"So far, I like it."

"It'll get worse, you can bet on that," Lanza said.

*At least he calls me "Corporal." He's got the right attitude. I wonder what makes a little fuck like him want to be a cop?*

"You were in Las Vegas, somebody said?" Marchessi asked. "Win any money?"

Vito pulled the wad of bills from his pocket and let Marchessi have a look.

"Can't complain. Can't complain a goddamn bit," Vito said. He saw the little Spic's eyes widen when he saw his roll.

Vito stuffed the money back in his pocket.

"What was going on just now on the ramp?" he asked.

From the looks on their faces, it was apparent to Corporal Vito Lanza that neither Officer Joseph Marchessi nor Officer Whatsisname Martinez had a fucking clue what he was talking about.

"Lieutenant Ardell come on the plane, American from Vegas, Gate 23, and took a good-looking blonde and some Main Line asshole off it," Lanza explained. "There was a limousine, one of our cars, and a detective car on the ramp."

"Oh," Marchessi said. "Yeah. That must have been the—Whatsername?—*Detweiler* girl. You remember, three, four months ago, when the mob hit Tony the Zee DeZego in the parking garage downtown?"

Vito remembered. DeZego had been taken down with a shotgun in a mob hit. The word on the street was that the doers were a couple of pros, from Chicago or someplace.

"So?"

"She got wounded or something when that happened. She's been in a hospital out west. They didn't want the press getting at her."

"Who's they?"

"Chief Lowenstein himself was down here a couple of hours ago," Marchessi said.

Vito knew who Chief Lowenstein was. Of all the chief inspectors, it was six one way and half a dozen the other if Lowenstein or Chief Inspector Dennis V. Coughlin had the most clout. It was unusual that Lowenstein would personally concern himself with seeing that some young woman was not bothered with the press.

"How come the special treatment?"

Marchessi said, more than a little sarcastically, "I guess if your father runs and maybe owns a big piece of Nesfoods, you get a little special treatment."

The bell rang, signaling that the luggage conveyor was about to start moving. Vito nodded at Marchessi and Martinez and walked to the conveyor and waited until his luggage appeared. He grabbed it, then went back into the terminal and walked through it to the Airport Unit office. He walked past without going in, and went to the parking area reserved for police officers either working the Airport Unit or visiting it, where he had left his car.

His car, a five-year-old Buick coupe, gave him a hard time starting. He had about given up on it when it finally gasped into life.

"Piece of shit!" he said aloud, and then had a pleasant thought: When he was finished work tomorrow, he would get rid of the sonofabitch. What he would like to have was a four-door Cadillac. He could probably make a good deal on one a year, eighteen months old. That would mean only twelve, fifteen thousand miles. A Caddy is just starting to get broken in with a lousy fifteen thousand miles on the clock, and you save a bunch of money.

*Just because you did all right at the tables,* Vito Lanza thought, *is no reason to throw money away on a new car. Most people can't tell the fucking difference between a new one and one a year, eighteen months old, anyway.*

Corporal Vito Lanza lived with his widowed mother, Magdelana, a tiny, intense, silver-haired woman of sixty-six in the house in which he had grown up. She managed to remind him at least once a day that the row house in the 400 block of Ritner Street in South Philadelphia was in her name, and that he was living there, rent free, only out of the goodness of her heart.

When he finally found a place to park the goddamned Buick and walked up to the house, Magdelana Lanza was sitting on a folding aluminum and plastic webbing lawn chair on the sidewalk, in the company of Mrs. D'Angelo (two houses down toward South Broad Street) and Mrs. Marino (the house next door, toward the Delaware River). She had an aluminum collander in her lap, into which she was breaking green beans from a paper bag on the sidewalk beside her.

Vito nodded at Mrs. D'Angelo and Mrs. Marino and kissed his mother and said, "Hi, Ma" and handed her a two-pound box of Italian chocolates he had bought for her in the gift shop at the Flamingo in Vegas.

She nodded her head, but that was all the thanks he got.

"The toilet's running again," Mrs. Lanza said. "And there's rust in the hot water. You either got to fix it, or give me the money to call the plumber."

"I'll look at it," Vito said, and went into the house.

To the right was the living room, a long, dark room full of heavy furniture. A lithograph of Jesus Christ with his arms held out in front of him hung on the wall. Immediately in front of him was the narrow stairway to the second floor, and the equally narrow passageway that led to the kitchen in the rear of the house. Off the kitchen was the small dark dining room furnished with a table, six chairs, and a china cabinet.

He went up the stairs and a few steps down the corridor to his room. It was furnished with a single bed, a dresser, a small desk, and a floor lamp. There were pictures on the wall, showing Vito when he made his first communion at Our Lady of Mount Carmel Church, his graduation class at Mount Carmel Parochial School, Vito in his graduation gown and tasseled hat at Bishop John Newmann High School, and Vito in police uniform and his father the day he graduated from the Philadelphia Police Academy. There was also an eighteen-inch-long plaster representation of Jesus Christ on his crucifix.

Vito tossed his bags on the bed and went down the corridor to the bathroom. He voided his bladder, flushed the toilet, and waited to see if the toilet was indeed running.

It was, and he took the top off the water box and looked at the mechanism.

He didn't know what the fuck was wrong with it. He jiggled the works, and it stopped running. Then he ran the hot water in the sink, letting it fill the bowl. When he had, he couldn't even see the fucking drain in the bottom.

*Sonofabitch!*

The simplest thing to do would be to give his mother the money and tell her to call the plumber. But if he did that, there was certain to be some crack about his father, May He Rest In Peace, never having once in all the years they were married calling a plumber.

*After work tomorrow,* Vito decided, *I'll go by Sears and get one of those goddamned repair kits. And see what they want to replace the fucking hot water heater.*

# FIVE

"Mayor Carlucci's residence," Violetta Forchetti said, clearly but with a distinct Neapolitan accent when she picked up the telephone.

Violetta was thirty-five but looked older. She was slight of build, and somewhat sharp-faced. She had come to the United States from Naples seventeen years before to marry Salvatore Forchetti, who was twenty-five and had himself immigrated four years previously.

There had just been time for them to get married, and for Violetta to become with child when, crossing 9th and Mifflin Streets in South Philadelphia, they were both struck by a hit-and-run driver. Salvatore died instantly, and Violetta, who lost the child, had spent four months in St. Agnes's Hospital.

The then commander of the 6th District of the Philadelphia Police Department, Captain Jerry Carlucci, had taken the incident personally. He was himself of Neapolitan heritage, had known Sal, who had found work as a butcher, and been a guest at their wedding.

He had suggested to his wife that it might be a nice thing for her to go to St. Agnes's Hospital, see what the poor woman needed, and tell her she had his word that he would find the hit-and-run driver and see that he got what was coming to him.

Angeline Carlucci, who looked something like Violetta Forchetti, returned from the hospital and told him things were even worse than they looked. Violetta's parents were dead. The relatives who had arranged for her to come to America and marry Salvatore didn't want her back in Naples. She was penniless, a widow in a strange country.

When Violetta got out of the hospital, she moved in temporarily with Captain and Mrs. Carlucci, Jerry's idea being that when he caught the sonofabitch who had run them down, he would get enough money out of the bastard's insurance company to take care of Violetta, to make her look like a desirable wife to some other hard-working young man.

They never found the sonofabitch who had been driving the car. So when Jerry and Angeline, right after he'd made inspector, moved out of their house on South Rosewood Street in South Philly to the new house (actually it was thirty years old) on Crefield Street, Violetta went with them. She was good with the kids, the kids loved her, and Angeline needed a little help around the house.

A number of young, hard-working, respectable men were introduced to Violetta, but she just wasn't interested in any of them. She had found her place in life, working for the Carluccis, almost a member of the family.

When, as police commissioner, Jerry bought the big house in Chestnut Hill, and did it over, they turned three rooms in the attic into an apartment for Violetta, and she just about took over running the place, the things that Angeline no longer had the time to do herself.

It was said, and it was probably true, that Violetta would kill for the Carlucci family. It was true that Violetta did a better job of working the mayor's phone than any secretary he'd ever had in the Roundhouse or City Hall. When she handed him the phone, he knew that it was somebody he should talk to, not some nut or ding-a-ling.

"Matt Lowenstein, Violetta," the caller said. "How are you?"

"Just a minute, Chief," Violetta said. Chief Inspector Lowenstein was one of the very few people who got to talk to the mayor whenever he called, even in the middle of the night, when she had to put her robe on and go downstairs and wake him up.

The Honorable Jerry Carlucci, who was fifty-one years old and had an almost massive body and dark brown hair and eyes, was wearing an apron with CHIEF COOK painted on it when Violetta went into the kitchen of the Chestnut Hill mansion. He was in the act of examining with great interest one of two chicken halves he had been marinating for the past two hours, and which, when he had concluded they had been soaked enough, he planned to broil on a charcoal stove for himself and Angeline.

"Excellence, it is Chief Lowenstein," Violetta said.

Violetta had firm Italianate ideas about the social structure of the world. Jerry had never been able to get her to call him "Mister." It had at first been "Captain," which was obviously more prestigious than "Mister," then "Inspector" as he had worked his way up the hierarchy from staff inspector through inspector to chief inspector, and then "Excellence" from the time he'd been made a deputy commissioner.

He joked with Angeline that Violetta had run out of titles with "Excellence." There were only two more prestigious: "Your Majesty" and "Your Holiness," plus maybe "Your Grace," none of which, obviously, fit.

"*Grazie,*" he said and went to the wall-mounted telephone by the door.

"How's my favorite Hebrew?" the mayor said.

He and Matt Lowenstein went way back. And he was fully aware that behind his back, Matt Lowenstein referred to him as "The Dago."

"The package from Las Vegas, Mr. Mayor, arrived safely at the airport, and two minutes ago passed through the gates in Chestnut Hill."

"No press?"

"Ardell—Paul Ardell, the Airport lieutenant?—"

"I know who he is."

"He said he didn't see any press. We probably attracted more attention taking her off the plane that way than if we'd just let Payne walk her through the terminal."

"Yeah, maybe. But this way, Matt, we did Detweiler a favor. And if Payne had walked her into the airport and there had been a dozen assholes from the TV and the newspapers . . ."

"You're right, of course."

"I'm always right, you should remember that."

"Yes, sir, Mr. Mayor."

"You free for lunch tomorrow?"

*That's* cant, Matt Lowenstein thought, having recently discovered that cant without the apostrophe meant that what was said was deceitful or hypocritical. *What Jerry Carlucci was really saying was, "If you had something you wanted to do for lunch tomorrow, forget it."*

"Yeah, sure."

"Probably the Union League at twelve-thirty. If there's a change, I'll have my driver call yours."

"Okay. Anything special?"

"Czernich called an hour or so ago," the mayor said. "The Secret Service told him what I already knew. The Vice President's going to honor Philadelphia with his presence."

Taddeus Czernich was police commissioner of the City of Philadelphia.

"It was in the papers."

"Maybe Czernich's driver was too busy to read the papers to him," the mayor said.

Jerry Carlucci was not saying unkind things behind Commissioner Czernich's back. He regularly got that sort of abuse in person. Matt Lowenstein had long ago decided that Carlucci not only really did not like Czernich, but held him in a great deal of contempt.

But Lowenstein had also long ago figured out that Czernich would probably be around as commissioner as long as Carlucci was the mayor. His loyalty to Carlucci was unquestioned, almost certainly because he very much liked being the police commissioner, and was very much aware that he served at Carlucci's pleasure.

"Half past twelve at the Union League," Lowenstein said. "I'll look forward to it."

Carlucci laughed.

"Don't bullshit a bullshitter, Matt," he said, and then added, "I just had an idea about Payne too."

"Excuse me?"

"I'm still thinking about it. I'll tell you tomorrow. You call—Whatsisname?—At the airport?"

"Paul Ardell?"

"Yeah, right. And tell him I said thanks for a job well done."

"Yes, sir."

"Good night, Matt. Thank you."
"Good night, Mr. Mayor."

Marion Claude Wheatley made pork chops, green beans, apple sauce, and mashed potatoes for his supper. He liked to cook, was good at it, and when he made his own supper not only was it almost certainly going to be better than what he could get at one of the neighborhood restaurants, but it spared him both having to eat alone in public and from anything unpleasant that might happen on the way home from the restaurant.

Marion lived in the house in which he had grown up, in the 5000 block of Beaumont Street, just a few blocks off Baltimore Avenue and not far from the 49th Street Station. There was no point in pretending that the neighborhood was not deteriorating, but that didn't mean his house was deteriorating. He took a justifiable pride in knowing that he was just as conscientious about taking care of the house as his father had been.

If something needed painting, it got painted. If one of the faucets started dripping, he went to the workshop in the basement and got the proper tools and parts and fixed it.

About the only difference in the house between now and when Mom and Dad had been alive was the burglar bars and the burglar alarm system. Marion had had to have a contractor install the burglar bars, which were actually rather attractive, he thought, wrought iron. The burglar alarm system he had installed himself.

Marion had been taught about electrical circuits in the Army. He could almost certainly have avoided service by staying in college, but that would have been dishonorable. His father had served in World War II as a major with the 28th Division. He would have been shamed if his son had avoided service when his country called upon him.

He had taken Basic Training at Fort Dix, and then gone to Fort Riley for Officer Candidate School, and been commissioned into the Ordnance Corps. He had been trained as an ammunition supply officer, and then they had asked him if he would be interested in volunteering to become an Explosive Ordnance Disposal officer before he went to Vietnam. Marion hadn't even known what that meant when they asked him. They told him that EOD officers commanded small detachments of specialists who were charged with disposing of enemy and our own ordnance, which he understood to mean artillery and mortar shells, primarily, which had been fired but which for some reason hadn't exploded when they landed.

Sometimes shells and rockets could be disarmed, which meant that their detonating mechanisms were rendered inoperative, but sometimes that wasn't possible, and the explosive ordnance had to be "blown in place."

That meant that Explosive Ordnance Disposal people had to be trained in explosives, even though, as an officer, he wouldn't be expected to do the work himself, but instead would supervise the enlisted specialists.

That training had included quite a bit about electrical circuits, about which Marion had previously known absolutely nothing.

But what he had learned in the Army was more than enough for him to easily install the burglar alarm. Actually, it was plural. Alarms. There was one system that detected intrusion of the house on the first floor. If the alarm system was active, and any window, or outside door, on the first floor was opened, that set off one warning buzzer and a light on the control panel Marion had set up in what had been Mom and Dad's bedroom, but was now his.

The second system did the same thing for windows on the second floor and the two dormer windows in the attic. The third system protected the powder magazine only. The powder magazine was in the basement. It had originally been a larder where Mom had stored tomatoes mostly, but beans too, and chow-chow and things like that. Marion liked cooking, but he wasn't about to start canning things the way Mom had. It wasn't worth it.

The first time he had put something in the powder magazine, it was still a larder. That was when he had come from Vietnam on emergency leave when Mom had gotten so sick. At the time, he had wondered why it was so important that he knew he had to bring twenty-seven pounds of Czechoslovakian *plastique* and two dozen detonators home with him. Now, of course, he knew. It was all part of God's plan.

If God hadn't wanted him to bring the *plastique* home, then when the MPs at Tan Son Nhut had randomly inspected outbound transient luggage, they would have selected his to inspect, and taken it away from him.

Marion hadn't then yet learned that when something odd or out of the ordinary happens, that he didn't have to worry about it, because it was invariably God's plan, and sooner or later, he would come to understand what the Lord had had in mind.

When he'd come home, Mom was already in University Hospital, but there was a colored lady taking care of the house, and he didn't want her hurting herself in any way, so he had put the *plastique* and the detonators in the larder and put a padlock on the door.

God had put off taking Mom into Heaven until they had had a chance to say good-bye, but not much more than that. He had been home seventy-two hours when the Lord called her home. And then he'd had those embarrassing weeping sessions whenever he thought of Mom or Dad or all the kids (he thought of them as kids, although they weren't much younger than he was) who'd fouled up, or been unlucky and been disintegrated, and they hadn't sent him back to Vietnam, but instead to Fort Eustis, Virginia, as an instructor in demolitions to young officers in the Engineer Basic Officer School.

They used mostly Composition C-4 at Eustis, which wasn't as good as the Czechoslovakian *plastique* the Viet Cong used, and sometimes just ordinary dynamite, and when he was setting up the demonstrations, he often slipped a little Composition C-4, or a stick of dynamite, or a length of primer cord, in his field jacket pocket and then brought it to Philadelphia and put it in the larder when he came home on weekends.

God, of course, had been making him do that, even though at the time he hadn't understood it.

One of the first things he did when he was released from active duty was to turn the larder into a proper powder magazine. This meant not only reinforcing the door with steel bars and installing some really good locks, but also installing a small exhaust fan for ventilation that turned on automatically for five minutes every hour, and, after a good deal of experimentation and consulting a humidity gauge, one 100-watt and one 40-watt bulb that burned all the time and kept the humidity down below twenty percent.

After Marion had his supper, he put the leftover green beans in the refrigerator, and the leftover mashed potatoes and the pork chop bones in the garbage, and then washed his dishes.

He then went to watch the CBS Evening News, to see if there would be anything on it about the Vice President coming to Philadelphia. There was not, but it had been in the newspapers, and therefore it was true.

He turned the television off, and then went down the stairs to the cellar. He took the keys to the powder magazine from their hiding place, on top of the second from the left rafter, and unlocked the door.

Everything seemed to be in good shape. The humidity gauge said there was twelve percent humidity and that it was fifty-nine degrees Fahrenheit in the magazines. That was well within the recommended parameters for humidity and temperature. He carefully locked the door again, put the keys back in their hiding place, and went back upstairs and turned the television back on.

Maybe he would be lucky, and there would be a decent program for him to watch. Everything these days seemed to be what they called T&A. For Teats and Ass. He thought that was a funny phrase. He knew the T&A offended God, but he thought that God would not be offended because he thought T&A was funny. He had learned words like that in the Army, and he wouldn't have been in the Army if God hadn't wanted him to be.

Vito Lanza went back to his room and emptied his pockets, tossing everything on the bed. Everything included the wad of bills he had left over after he'd had the Flamingo cashier give him a check for most of the money he'd won. There was almost five hundred dollars, two hundreds, two fifties, and a bunch of twenties and tens, plus some singles.

It sure looked good.

He unpacked his luggage, dividing the clothing into two piles, the underwear and socks and shirts his mother would wash, and the good shirts and trousers and jackets that would have to go to the dry cleaners.

The money looked good. He collected it all together and made a little wad of it, with the hundreds outside, and stuck them in his pocket.

*The one goddamned thing I don't want to do is stick around here and have Ma give me that crap about not understanding why I have to go somewhere to relax.*

He made a bundle of the clothing that had to go to the dry cleaners, and then picked up one of the jackets on the bed and put that on. He went to the upper right-hand drawer of the dresser and took out his Colt snubnose, and his badge and photo ID. From the drawer underneath, he took out a clip holster and six .38 Special cartridges. He loaded the Colt, put it in the holster, and then clipped the holster to his belt.

"You just got home," his mother said when he went out of the house, "where are you going?"

"To the dry cleaners, and then I got some stuff to do."

He decided to walk. He had found a place to park the goddamned Buick, and if he took it now, sure as Christ made little apples, there would be no parking place for blocks when he came back.

Vito dropped the clothes off at the Martinizer place on South Broad Street and then headed for Terry's Bar & Grill. Then he changed his mind. He wasn't in the mood for Terry's. It was a neighborhood joint, and Vito was still in a Flamingo Hotel & Casino mood.

He stepped off the curb and looked down South Broad in the direction of the navy yard until he could flag a cab. He got in and told the driver to take him to the Warwick Hotel. There was usually some gash in the nightclub in the Warwick, provided you had the money—and he did—to spring for expensive drinks.

The cab dropped him off at the Warwick right outside the bar. The hotel bar is on the right side of the building, off the lobby. The nightclub is a large area on the left side of the building, past the desk and the drugstore. Vito decided he would check out the hotel bar, maybe there would be something interesting in there, and then go to the nightclub.

He found a seat at the bar, ordered a Johnnie Walker on the rocks, and laid one of the fifty-dollar bills on the bar to pay for it.

Francesco Guttermo, who was seated at a small table near the door to the street in the Warwick Bar, leaned forward in his chair, then motioned for Ricco Baltazari to move his head closer, so that others would not hear what he had to say.

"The guy what just come in, at the end of the bar, he's got a gun," Mr. Guttermo, who was known as "Frankie the Gut," said. The appellation had been his since high school, when even then he had been portly with a large stomach.

Mr. Baltazari, who was listed in the records of the City of Philadelphia as the owner of Ristorante Alfredo, one of Center City's best Italian restaurants (northern Italian cuisine, no spaghetti with marinara sauce or crap like that), was expensively and rather tastefully dressed. He nodded his head to signify that he had understood what Frankie the Gut had said, and then relaxed back into his chair, taking the opportunity to let his hand graze across the knee of the young woman beside him.

She was a rather spectacularly bosomed blonde, whose name was Antoinette, but who preferred to be called "Tony." She slapped his hand, but didn't seem to be offended.

After a moment Mr. Baltazari turned his head just far enough to be able to look at the man with the gun, his backside and, in the bar's mirror, his face.

Then he leaned forward again toward Mr. Guttermo, who moved to meet him.

"He's probably a cop," Mr. Baltazari said.

"He paid for the drink with a fifty from a wad," Mr. Guttermo said.

"Maybe he hit his number," Mr. Baltazari said with a smile. "Maybe that's your fifty he's blowing."

It was generally believed by, among others, the Intelligence Unit and the Chief Inspector's Vice Squad of the Philadelphia Police Department that Mr. Guttermo, who had no other visible means of support, was engaged in the operation of a Numbers Book.

"You don't think he's interested in us?" Frankie the Gut asked.

"We're not doing anything wrong," Mr. Baltazari said. "Why should he be interested in us? You're a worrier, Frankie."

"You say so," Frankie the Gut replied.

"All we're doing is having a couple of drinks, right, Tony?" Mr. Baltazari said, touching her knee again.

"You said it, baby," Tony replied.

But Mr. Baltazari, who hadn't gotten where he was by being careless, nevertheless kept an eye on the guy with a gun who was probably a cop, and when the guy finished his drink and picked up his change and walked out of the bar, a slight frown of concern crossed his face.

"Go see where he went, Tony," he said.

"Huh?"

"You heard me. Go see where that guy went."

Tony got up and walked out of the bar into the hotel lobby.

"What are you thinking, Ricco?" Frankie the Gut asked. "That cops don't buy drinks with fifties?"

"Some cops don't," Mr. Baltazari said.

Tony came back and sat down and turned to face Mr. Baltazari.

"He went into The Palms," she said.

Mr. Baltazari was silent for a long moment. It was evident that he was thinking.

"I would like to know more about him," he said, finally.

"You think he was interested in us?" Frankie the Gut said.

"I said I would like to know more about him," Mr. Baltazari said.

"How are you going to do that, baby?" Tony asked.

"You're going to do it for me," Mr. Baltazari said.

"What do you mean?" Tony asked suspiciously.

Mr. Baltazari reached in his pocket and took out a wad of crisp bills. He found a ten, and handed it to Tony.

"I want you to go in there, I think it's five bucks to get in, find him, and be friendly," he said.

"Aaaah, Ricco," Tony protested.

"When you are friendly with people, they tell you things," Mr. Baltazari observed. "Be friendly, Tony. We'll wait for you."

"Do I really have to?"

"Do it, Tony," Mr. Baltazari said.

Tony was gone almost half an hour.

"Let's get out of here," she said, "I told him I had to go to the ladies'."

"What did you find out?" Mr. Baltazari asked.

"Can't we leave? What if he comes looking for me?"

"What did you find out?"

"He's a cop. He's a corporal. He just made a killing in Vegas."

"Did he say where he worked?"

"At the airport."

"Did he say how much of a killing?"

"Enough to buy a Caddy. He said he's going out and buy a Cadillac tomorrow."

Mr. Baltazari thought that over, long enough for Tony to find the courage to repeat her request that they leave before the cop came looking for her.

"No," Mr. Baltazari said. "No. What I want you to do, Tony, is go back in there and give him this."

He took a finely bound leather notebook from the monogrammed pocket of his white-on-white shirt, wrote something on it, tore the page out, and handed it to her.

"What's this?"

"Joe Fierello is your uncle. He's going to give your friend a deal on a Cadillac."

"You're kidding me, right?"

"No, I'm not. You go back in there and be nice to him, and tell him you think your Uncle Joe will give him a deal on a Caddy."

"You mean *stay* with him?"

"I gotta go home now anyway, my wife's been on my ass."

"Jesus, Ricco!" Tony protested.

Mr. Baltazari took out his wad of bills again, found a fifty, and handed it to Tony.

"Buy yourself an ice-cream cone or something," he said.

Tony looked indecisive for a moment, then took the bill and folded it and stuffed it into her brassiere.

"I thought we were going to my place," she said.

"I'll make it up to you, baby," Mr. Baltazari said.

Detective Payne had fallen asleep in his arm chair watching Fred Astaire and Ginger Rogers gracefully swooping around what was supposed to be the terrace of a New York City penthouse on WCAU-TV's Million Dollar Movie.

He woke up with a dry mouth, a sore neck, a left leg that had apparently been asleep so long it was nearly gangrenous, and a growling hunger in his stomach. He looked at the clock on the fireplace mantel. It was quarter to eight. That meant it was probably the worst time of the day to seek sustenance in his neighborhood. The hole-in-the-wall greasy spoons that catered to the office breakfast and lunch crowd had closed for the day.

That left the real restaurants, including the one in the Rittenhouse Club, which was the closest. That attracted his interest for a moment, as they did a very nice London broil, but then his interest waned as he realized he would have to put on a jacket and tie, then stand in line to be seated, and then eat alone.

The jacket-and-tie and eating-alone considerations also ruled out the other nice restaurants in the vicinity. Without much hope, he checked his cupboard. It was, as he was afraid it would be, nearly bare and, in the case of two eggs, three remaining slices of bread, and a carton of milk, more than likely dangerous. He nearly gagged disposing of the milk, eggs, and green bread down the Disposall.

He had a sudden, literally mouth-watering image of a large glass of cold milk to wash down a western omelette. And there was no question that his mother would be delighted to prepare such an omelette for him.

He went into his bedroom, pulled a baggy sweater over his head, and headed for the door, stopping only long enough to take his pistol, a Smith & Wesson .38 Special caliber "Chief's Special" and the leather folder that held his badge and photo ID from the mantelpiece. The holster had a clip, which allowed him to carry the weapon inside his waistband. If he remembered not to take his sweater off, his mother wouldn't even see the pistol.

He went down the narrow stairway to the third floor of the building, then rode the elevator to the basement, and after a moment's hesitation made the mature decision to drive the Bug to Wallingford. It would have been much nicer to drive the Porsche but the Bug had been sitting for two days, and unless it was driven, the battery would likely be dead in the morning when he had to drive it to work.

As he drove out Baltimore Avenue, which he always thought of as The Chester Pike, he made another mature decision. He drove past an Acme Supermarket, noticed idly that the parking lot was nearly empty, and then did a quick U-turn and went back.

He could make a quick stop, no more than five minutes, pick up a half gallon of milk, a dozen eggs, a loaf of bread, and a package of Taylor Ham, maybe even some orange juice, and be prepared to make his own breakfast in the morning. He would be, as he had learned in the Boy Scouts to be, prepared.

The store was, as he had cleverly deduced from the near-empty parking lot, nearly deserted. There were probably no more than twenty people in the place.

He was halfway down the far-side aisle, bread and Taylor Ham already in the shopping cart, moving toward the eggs-and-milk section, when he ran into Mrs. Glover.

"Hi!" he said cheerfully.

It was obvious from the hesitant smile on her face that Mrs. Glover was having trouble placing him. That was certainly understandable. While Mrs. Glover, who presided over the Special Collections desk at the U of P library had attracted the rapt attention of just about every heterosexual male student because of her habitual costume of white translucent blouse and skirt, it did not logically follow that she would remember any particular one of her hundreds of admirers.

"Matt Payne. Pre-Constitutional Law," he said. He had had occasion to partake of Mrs. Glover's professional services frequently when he was writing a term paper on what had happened, and who had been responsible for it, when the fledgling united colonies had been adapting British common law to American use.

"Oh, yes, of course," she said, and he thought her smile reflected not only relief that he was not putting the make on her, but genuine pleasure at seeing him. "How are you, Matt?"

"Very well, thank you," Matt said. "It's nice to see you, Mrs. Glover."

"Nice to see you too," she said, and pushed her cart past him.

She was wearing a sweater over her blouse, Matt Payne noticed, but the blouse was still translucent and her breastworks were as spectacular as he remembered them.

"This is the police," an electronically amplified voice announced. "Drop your weapons and put your hands on your head!"

"Oh, shit!" Matt Payne said.

There was the sound of firearms. First a couple of loud pops, and then the deep booming of a shotgun. There was a moment's silence, and then the sound of breaking glass.

Matt turned and ran and caught up with Mrs. Glover, and put his hands on her shoulders.

"Get on the floor!" he ordered.

She looked at him with terror in her eyes, and let him push her first to her knees and then flat on her stomach.

As he pushed his sweater aside to get at his pistol, and then fumbled to find his badge, he saw her looking at him with shock in her eyes.

There was the sound of another handgun firing twice.

"Motherfucker!" a male voice shouted angrily, and there was another double booming of a shotgun being fired twice. A moment later there was the sound of a car crash.

"Everybody all right?" a voice of authority demanded loudly.

A moment later the same voice, now electronically amplified, went on: "This is the police. It's all over. There is no danger. Please stay right where you are until a police officer tells you what to do."

Matt got to his feet, and holding his badge in front of him walked toward the front of the store.

As he reached the end of the aisle, he called out, "Three six nine, three six nine," and held the badge out as he carefully stepped into the checkout area.

"Who the hell are you?" a lieutenant holding a shotgun in one hand and a portable loudspeaker in the other demanded. He and three other cops in sight were wearing the peculiar uniform, including bulletproof vests, Stakeout wore on the job.

"Payne, East Detectives, sir."

"What are you doing in here?"

"I came in to get milk and eggs," Matt said.

"You see what happened?"

"I didn't see anything," Matt said truthfully.

There were flashing lights, and the sound of dying sirens, and Matt looked through the shattered plate-glass window and saw the first of a line of police vehicles pull up to the door.

The lieutenant made a vague gesture toward the last checkout counter. Matt saw a pair of feet extending into the aisle, and a puddle of blood.

"One there and another outside, in his car," the lieutenant said. "They had their chance to drop their guns and surrender, but they probably thought it would be like the movies. Jesus Christ!"

There was more contempt for the critters he had dropped than compassion, Matt thought.

*That's the way it is. Not like the movies, either, where the cops are paralyzed with regret for having had to drop somebody. The bad dreams I have had about my shootings have been about those assholes getting me, not the other way around.*

Matt looked through the hole where the plate-glass window had been. Three uniforms were in the act of pulling a man from his car. The car-crashing noise he had heard had apparently come when the doer, trying to flee, had crashed into one of the cars parked in the lot.

Matt had twice gone through the interviews conducted by the Homicide shooting team of officers involved in a fatal shooting. He blurted what popped into his mind.

"You'll spend the next six hours in Homicide."

The lieutenant's eyebrows rose.

"You been through this?" he asked.

"It goes on for goddamned ever," Matt said, and then added, "Christ, I'll be there all night too, and I didn't even see what happened."

The lieutenant met his eyes.

"You want to go, get out of here, now."

Matt had a quick mental image of Mrs. Glover, who looked to be on the edge of hysteria, getting carried down to the Homicide Bureau, in the Roundhouse, in a district wagon and then sitting around until one of the Homicide detectives had time to take her statement.

"I'm with somebody," Matt said. "A woman."

"Get out of here now, then," the lieutenant repeated. "Homicide, or the brass, will be coming in on this any minute."

"I owe you one," Matt said, and trotted back to where he had left Mrs. Glover lying on the floor.

She was still lying on the floor.

"It's all right," he said, and reached down and helped her to her feet. "Did you see anything? Anything at all?"

She shook her head, no.

"I told them you're with me," he said.

There was confusion in her eyes.

"We can go. Otherwise, you'll be taken to the Roundhouse and be there for hours."

"Are you a policeman or something?" she asked incredulously.

"I'm a detective," he said. "You all right? Can you walk?"

"I'm all right," she said. "What do we do about the groceries?"

"Leave them," he said, and took Mrs. Glover's arm and led her out the front of the store.

"Oh, my God!" Mrs. Glover said. "That's my car!"

And then she was clinging to him, whimpering. She had looked at the ground beside her car, where the second robber Stakeout had taken down was on his back in the middle of a spreading pool of blood. He had taken a load, Matt decided, maybe two loads, of double aught buckshot.

*Well, that blows any chance we had to get away from here. Shit!*

# SIX

"My car's over there," Matt said, and started to lead Mrs. Glover toward it.

Mrs. Glover seemed to want the reassurance of his arm around her, and stayed close to him. He was very much aware of her body against his.

He put her in the car.

"Listen," he said. "We can't leave now. Let me go talk to the lieutenant, and I'll come back."

The lieutenant told him there was nothing he could do now but wait for Homicide and the brass to show up.

*That means instead of Mother's western omelette, I will have to find sustenance in a cup of coffee in a paper cup, and if I'm lucky, a stale doughnut.*

The first Homicide detective to arrive at the crime scene was Detective Joe D'Amata. Matt knew him. He waited until D'Amata had taken a quick look around inside, and then gone to the body in the parking lot, and then walked up to him.

"Hey, Joe."

"Matthew, my boy," D'Amata said, smiling. "Don't tell me you did this."

"I came in to get a dozen eggs."

"You see what happened?"

"No. But I know who owns this car, the one he ran into."

"Oh?"

"She's a librarian at U of P. Nice lady. She saw the body and she's nearly hysterical."

"I would be too," D'Amata said. "Do you think she saw anything?"

"She saw what I saw, zilch. We were in the back of the store."

"We'll need your statements," D'Amata said. "But I don't see why you couldn't take her to the Roundhouse before the mob gets there. I'll let them know you're coming."

"I owe you one, Joe."

"Yeah. Don't forget."

Matt went back to his Bug and got behind the wheel and turned to Mrs. Glover.

"What happens now?" she asked.

"I know one of the Homicide detectives. He's fixed it so that we can go to the Roundhouse now, before the crowd gets there, and make our statements."

"But I didn't see anything."

"That's your statement. And they'll want to know about your car."

"What am I going to do about my car?"

"They'll want to take pictures of it. Maybe, if we're lucky, we can get them to turn it loose when they're finished. We can ask."

"What would have happened if you weren't here?"

"They'd have taken you, when they got around to it, to the Roundhouse in a car."

"What's this 'Roundhouse' you keep talking about?"

"The Police Administration Building. At 8th and Race. That's where Homicide is." He paused. "You all right, Mrs. Glover?"

"I'll be all right," she said.

He started the Bug and drove downtown to the Roundhouse.

It was quarter to twelve when they left. Captain Quaire, the commanding officer of Homicide, had come in, and he authorized the release of Mrs. Glover's car to her when the Mobile Crime Lab was through with it.

When they got back to the Acme parking lot, they were told that it would be at least an hour before the car could be released.

"I'm sorry," Matt told Mrs. Glover. "But that's the way it is. I'll take you home and then bring you back in an hour."

"You're sweet, Matt. I appreciate all this," Mrs. Glover said, and touched his arm.

He started the car and asked her where she lived. She gave him an address in Upper Darby Township.

"It's not far," Mrs. Glover said. "But I appreciate the offer to take me back there."

"I'll take your husband back," Matt said. "What you should do is make yourself a stiff drink, and then go to bed, and forget this whole thing."

He saw they had crossed into Upper Darby Township. "You're going to have to start giving me directions."

It was a fairly nice ranch house in a subdivision, the sort of house he would have expected people like the Glovers to have. He remembered hearing that Mr. Glover, probably *Doctor* Glover, was some sort of professor. There was a light on in the carport, and there were lights in the living room, behind the curtain that covered the picture window.

"I don't see a car," Matt said. "It looks like Dr. Glover's not home."

"Not here, he's not," Mrs. Glover said, more than a little bitterly.

*Oh!*

"Could you use one of those stiff drinks you recommended for me?" Mrs. Glover asked. "Or are you on duty?"

"Yes, ma'am."

"Well, you're going to have to watch while I have one, I'm afraid. I'm shaking like a leaf."

"I meant that 'no drinking on duty' business is only in the movies, or on TV cop shows. And anyway I'm not. On duty, I mean."

She got out of the car and went to the door that opened off the carport into the kitchen. He followed her inside. She snapped on fluorescent lights and pulled open a cabinet over the sink.

"I'm not much of a drinker," she said, taking out four bottles. "But this is an occasion, isn't it?" She turned to him. "What do you recommend?"

There was a bottle of gin, a bottle of blended whiskey, a bottle of Southern Comfort, and, surprisingly, an unopened bottle of Martel cognac.

"The cognac, if that would be all right," Matt said.

"I've even got the glasses for it," she said. "They're probably a little dusty."

She went farther into the house and returned with two snifters that were, in fact, dusty. She wiped them with a paper towel and set them on the kitchen counter.

"Do you need a corkscrew?"

"No, I don't think so," he said, and twisted the metal foil off the neck. The bottle was closed with a cork, but the kind that can be pulled loose.

He poured cognac in both glasses, and handed her one.

"You don't mix it with anything?"

"My father says it's a sin to do that," Matt said. "But my mother drinks hers with soda water."

"I've got ginger ale. Would that be all right?"

"That would be a sin," he said.

"I think I'll be a sinner," she said, and went into the refrigerator and took out a bottle of ginger ale, and poured some into her glass. Then she held the glass out to touch his.

"I'm glad you were there, Matt," she said. "This whole experience has been horrible. I would have hated to have had to go through it alone."

He smiled and took a sip from his glass. She took a tentative sip of hers. She smiled. "That's not so bad."

He took another swallow and felt the warmth course through his body.

"Funny," Mrs. Glover said, "you don't look like a detective."

"Probably because I've only been a detective a couple of weeks."

"Or a policeman," she said. "I thought you were one of those who was going in the Marines?"

He was surprised that she had paid enough attention to him to have known that.

"I flunked the physical," he said.

"Oh," she said. "And do you like being a policeman?"

"Most of the time," he said. "Not tonight."

She hugged herself, which caused the material of her blouse to draw taut over her bosom.

"That warms you, doesn't it?" she said.

"Yes, it does."

"My husband's father gave him that when he was promoted."

"Oh."

"I was tempted to throw it out when he left, but I decided that would be a waste, that sooner or later, I'd need it. For an occasion. I didn't have something like this in mind."

"Well, it's over," Matt said. "Put it out of your mind."

"I'm not letting you get on with whatever you were about to do when this happened."

"Don't worry about it."

"Where do you live?"

"In Center City. I was driving past the Acme, saw the parking lot was pretty empty, and thought it would be a good time to get a dozen eggs and a loaf of bread."

"Me too," she said, and upended her brandy snifter and drained it. "I went there to get something for my supper. Have you eaten?"

He shook his head, no.

"The least I can do is feed you," she said. "There should be something in the freezer."

She found two Swanson Frozen Turkey Breast Dinners and put them in the oven.

"It'll take thirty-five minutes," she said. "Is that going to make you terribly late where you were going?"

"I just won't go," he said. "It wasn't important."

She made herself another cognac and ginger ale and extended the bottle to him.

"Well, we'll eat the leathery turkey, and then you can drive me back there."

"Fine."

"I'm now going to do something else I rarely do," Mrs. Glover said. "I'm going to smoke a cigarette."

"I'm sorry, I don't have any."

"I've got some somewhere," she said, and went farther into the house again. She immediately returned. "I'm sorry. Why are we in the kitchen? Come on in the living room."

An hour later, they drove back to the Acme Supermarket. Her car was gone, and so had just about everybody else. There was a uniformed cop by the shattered plate-glass window.

Matt showed him his badge.

"Where's the car, the victim's car the doer ran into?"

The uniformed cop shrugged. "I guess they took it to an impound area. Maybe at the district."

Matt returned to the Bug and told Mrs. Glover that the authority they had to reclaim her car was useless. It was somewhat in limbo, and there was nothing that could be done until the morning.

"What do I do now?" Mrs. Glover asked. "Can you take me home again?"

"Of course."

She wanted an explanation of where in "limbo" her car actually was, so it seemed perfectly natural that he follow her into the house again and have another cognac.

"I was thinking," Mrs. Glover said an hour later, dipping her index finger into her cognac snifter to stir the ginger ale into the cognac, "I mean it's just an idea. But if you stayed here, there's a guest room, you could drive me down to the Roundhouse in the morning."

*She is not making a pass at me. She is at least thirty years old, maybe thirty-five, and . . .*

"And the truth of the matter seems to be that we've both had more of this cognac than is good for us," she added.

"Well, if it wouldn't inconvenience you."

"Don't be silly," she said. "I'll just get sheets and make up the spare bed."

"I'm sorry I don't have any pajamas to offer you," Mrs. Glover said at the door to the spare bedroom.

"I don't wear them anyway. I'll be all right."

"If you need anything, just ask," she said, and gave him her hand. "And thank you for everything."

"I didn't do anything," he said.

She smiled at him and pulled the door closed.

He looked around the room, and then went and sat on the bed and took his clothing off. He rummaged in the bedside table and came up with a year-old copy of *Scientific American.* He propped the pillows up and flipped through it.

He could hear the sound of a shower running, and had an interesting mental image of Mrs. Glover at her ablutions.

"Shit," he said aloud, turned the light off, and rearranged the pillow.

He had a profound thought: *No good deed goes unpunished.*

The sound of the shower stopped after a couple of minutes. He had an interesting mental image of Mrs. Glover toweling her bosom.

A moment later he heard the bedroom door open.

"Matt, are you asleep?"

"No."

He sensed rather than heard her approach the bed. When she sat on it, he could smell soap and perfume.

*Maybe perfumed soap?*

She found his face with her hand.

"I've been separated from my husband for eleven months," Mrs. Glover said. "I haven't been near a man in all that time. Not until now."

He reached up and touched her hand. She caught his hand, locked fingers with him, and then moved his hand to the opening of her robe, directed it inside, and then let go.

His fingers found her breast and her nipple, which was erect. She put her hand to the back of his head and pulled his face to her breast.

When he tried to pull her down onto the bed, she resisted, then stood up.

"Not here," Mrs. Glover said throatily. "In my bed."

At quarter to seven the next morning, Detective Matt Payne drove into the garage beneath the Delaware Valley Cancer Society Building, and turned to look at Mrs. Glover, whose Christian name, he had learned two hours before, was Evelyn.

"What is this?" she asked.

"This is where I live. Where I have to change clothes."

"The signs says this is the Cancer Society."

"There's an attic apartment," he said.

"Oh."

"Come on up. It won't take me a minute."

"I'm not so sure that's a good idea."

"You mean, you don't want to see my etchings?"

"What happened last night was obviously insane. Maybe we better leave it at that."

"I like what happened last night."

"You should be running around with girls your own age, not having an affair with someone my age. And vice versa."

"I don't seem to have much in common with girls my own age," Matt said. "And I don't think that was the first time in the recorded history of mankind that . . ."

"A woman my age took a man your age into her bed?"

"Right."

"Go change your clothes, Matt. I'll wait here."

"You don't want to do that."

"Yes, I do."

"Whatever you say," Matt said, and got out of the Bug and went to the elevator.

When he reached the top step of the narrow stairway leading into his apartment, he saw the red light blinking on his telephone answering machine. He pulled his sweater over his head, tossed it onto the couch, went to the answering machine, and pushed the PLAY MESSAGES switch.

"Matt, I know you're there, pick up the damned telephone."

That was Amelia Payne, M.D. He wondered what the hell she wanted, and then realized she probably wanted a report on Penny Detweiler's trip home.

Then Brewster Cortland Payne II's voice: "Matt, Amy insisted I try to get you to call her. She's positive you're there and just not picking up. She wants to talk to you about Penny. Will you call her, please? Whenever you get home?"

The next voice was Charley McFadden's: "Matt, Charley. Give me a call as soon as you can. I gotta talk to you about something. Oh. How was Las Vegas?"

*Something's wrong. I wonder what? Well, it'll have to wait.*

"Matt, this is Penny. I just wanted to say 'thank you' for coming out there to get me. I forgot to thank you at the airport. When you have a minute, call me, and I'll buy you an ice-cream cone or lunch or something. Ciao."

*Oh, Christ, I don't want to get sucked into that!*

"Matt, this is Joe D'Amato. They took your lady friend's car to the Plymouth place in Upper Darby. I called her house, and there was no answer. If we'd left it at the scene, there would be nothing left but the ignition switch."

*Jesus, why didn't I think about just calling Joe from her house? Because you were thinking with your dick, again, Matthew!*

"Payne, this is Al Sutton. If you were thinking of coming to work this morning, don't. They want you in Chief Lowenstein's office at half past one."

*Now, what the hell is that about? Something to do with last night?*

He pushed the REWIND button and went into his bedroom and laid out fresh clothes on his bed. He picked a light brown suit, since he was possibly going to see Chief Lowenstein and did not want to look like Joe College. Then he took his clothing off.

The doorbell rang.

He searched for and found his bathrobe and went to the intercom.

"Yeah?"

"You were right, I don't want to wait down there," Mrs. Glover said. "May I come up?"

He pushed the door release button and heard it open. She came up the stairs.

"That wasn't exactly true," she said. "Curiosity got the best of me."

"They took your car to the Plymouth place in Upper Darby," Matt said. "There was a message on the machine. Let me grab a shower, and I'll take you out there."

"They don't open until nine-thirty," she said.

"Well, we'll just have to wait."

He smiled uneasily at her, and then walked back in the apartment toward his bedroom.

"Matt . . ."

He turned.

"Was that true, what you said, about you don't have much in common with girls your own age?"

"Yes, it was."

"You're a really nice guy. Be patient. Someone will come along."

"I hope so," he said, and turned again and went and had his shower.

When he came out, he sensed movement in his kitchen. He cracked the door open. Mrs. Glover was leaning against the refrigerator. She had a cheese glass in one hand, and a bottle of his cognac in the other.

"I hope you don't mind."

"Of course not."

"You want one?"

"No. I don't want to smell of booze when I go to work."

"When do you have to be at work? Is taking me back to Upper Darby going to make you late?"

"No. I've got until half past one."

She looked at him, and then away, and then drained the cheese glass.

"What I said before," she said, "was what my father told me when Ken and I broke up. That I was a nice girl, that I should be patient, that someone would come along."

*What the hell is she leading up to? Am I the someone?*
"I'm sure he's right."
"Now, you and I are obviously not right for each other . . ."
*Damn!*
". . . but what I've been thinking, very possibly because I've had
more to drink in the last twelve hours than I've had in the last six
months, is that, until someone comes along for you, and someone
comes along for me . . ."
"The sky wouldn't fall? There will not be a bolt of lightning to
punish the sinners?"
She raised her head and met his eyes.
"What do you think?"
"I think I know how we can kill the time until the Plymouth
place opens."
"I'll bet you do," she said, and set the cheese glass and the bottle
of cognac on the sink and then started to unbutton her blouse.

As Matt Payne was climbing the stairs to his apartment at quarter to seven, across town, in Chestnut Hill, Peter Wohl stepped out
of the shower in his apartment and started to towel himself dry.
The chimes activated by his doorbell button went off. They
played "Be It Ever So Humble, There's No Place Like Home." One
of what Wohl thought of as the "xylophone bars" was out of
whack, so the musical rendition was discordant. He had no idea
how to fix it, and privately, he hated chimes generally and "Be It
Ever So Humble" specifically, but there was nothing he could do
about the chimes. They had been a gift from his mother, and installed by his father.
He said a word that he would not have liked to have his mother
hear, wrapped the towel around his middle, and left the bathroom.
He went through his bedroom, and then through his living room,
the most prominent furnishings of which were a white leather
couch, a plate-glass coffee table, a massive, Victorian mahogany
service bar, and a very large oil painting of a Rubenesque naked
lady resting on her side, one arm cocked coyly behind her head.
The ultrachic white leather couch and plate-glass coffee table
were the sole remnants of a romantic involvement Peter Wohl had
once had with an interior decorator, now a young suburban matron
married to a lawyer. The bar and the painting of the naked lady he
had acquired at an auction of the furnishings of a Center City men's
club that had gone belly up.

He unlatched the door and pulled it open. A very neat, very wholesome-looking young man in a blue suit stood on the landing.

"Good morning, Inspector," the young man said. His name was Paul T. (for Thomas) O'Mara, and he was a police officer of the Philadelphia Police Department. Specifically, he was Wohl's new administrative assistant.

*Telling him,* Peter Wohl thought, *that when I say between seven and seven-fifteen, I don't mean quarter to seven, would be like kicking a Labrador puppy who has just retrieved his first tennis ball.*

"Good morning, Paul," Wohl said. "Come on in. There's coffee in the kitchen."

"Thank you, sir."

Officer O'Mara was a recent addition to Peter Wohl's staff. Like Peter Wohl, he was from a police family. His father was a captain, who commanded the 17th District. His brother was a sergeant in Civil Affairs. His grandfather, like Peter Wohl's father and grandfather, had retired from the Philadelphia Police Department.

More important, his father was a friend of both Chief Inspector Dennis V. Coughlin and Chief Inspector (Retired) Augustus Wohl. When Officer O'Mara, who had five years on the job in the Traffic Division, had failed, for the second time, to pass the examination for corporal, both Chief Coughlin and Chief Wohl had had a private word with Inspector Wohl.

They had pointed out to him that just because someone has a little trouble with promotion examinations doesn't mean he's not a good cop, with potential. It just means that he has trouble passing examinations.

*Not like you, Peter,* the inference had been. *You're not really all that smart, you're just good at taking examinations.*

One or the other or both of them had suggested that what Officer O'Mara needed was a little broader experience than he was getting in the Traffic Division, such as he might get if it could be arranged to have him assigned to Special Operations as your administrative assistant.

"Now that you've lost Young Payne . . ." his father had said.

"Now that Matt's gone to East Detectives . . ." Chief Coughlin had said.

In chorus: "You're going to need someone to replace him. And you know what a good guy, and a good cop, his father is."

And so Officer O'Mara had taken off his uniform, with the distinctive white Traffic Division brimmed cap, and donned a trio of suits Inspector Wohl somewhat unkindly suspected were left over from his high school graduation and/or obtained from the Final Clearance rack at Sears Roebuck and come to work for Special Operations.

Peter Wohl was sitting on his bed, pulling his socks on when Officer O'Mara walked in with a cup of coffee.

"I couldn't find any cream, Inspector, but I put one spoon of sugar in there. Is that okay?"

Inspector Wohl decided that telling Officer O'Mara that he always took his coffee black would be both unkind and fruitless: He had told him the same thing ten or fifteen times in the office.

"Thank you," he said.

"Stakeout got two critters at the Acme on Baltimore Avenue last night. It was on TV," Officer O'Mara said.

" 'Got two critters'?"

"Blew them away," O'Mara said, admiration in his voice.

"Any police or civilians get hurt?"

"They didn't say anything on TV."

Wohl noticed that Officer O'Mara did not have any coffee.

"Aren't you having any coffee, Paul?"

"I thought you just told me to get you some," O'Mara said.

"Help yourself, Paul. Have you had breakfast?"

"I had a doughnut."

"Well, we're going to the Roundhouse. We can get some breakfast on the way."

"Yes, sir," O'Mara said, and walked out of the bedroom.

Peter Wohl walked to his closet and after a moment's hesitation selected a gray flannel suit. He added to it a light blue button-down collar shirt and a regimentally striped tie.

*Clothes make the man,* he thought somewhat cynically. *First impressions are important. Particularly when one is summoned to meet with the commissioner, and one doesn't have a clue what the sonofabitch wants.*

There was no parking space in the parking lot behind the Police Administration Building reserved for the commanding officer, Special Operations, as there were for the chief inspectors of Patrol Bureau (North), Patrol Bureau (South), Command Inspections Bureau, Administration, Internal Affairs, Detective Bureau, and even the Community Relations Bureau.

Neither could Paul O'Mara park Peter Wohl's official nearly new Ford sedan in spots reserved for CHIEF INSPECTORS AND INSPEC-

TORS ONLY, because Wohl was only a staff inspector, one rank below inspector. The senior brass of the Police Department were jealous of the prerogatives of their ranks and titles and would have been offended to see a lowly staff inspector taking privileges that were not rightly his.

Wohl suspected that if a poll were taken, anonymously, of the deputy commissioners, chief inspectors, and inspectors, the consensus would be that his appointment as commanding officer, Special Operations Division, reporting directly to the deputy commissioner, Operations, had been a major mistake, acting to the detriment of overall departmental efficiency, not to mention what harm it had done to the morale of officers senior to Staff Inspector Wohl, who had naturally felt themselves to be in line for the job.

If, however, he also suspected, asked to identify themselves before replying to the same question, to a man they would say that it was a splendid idea, and that there was no better man in the Department for the job.

They all knew that the Hon. Frank Carlucci, mayor of the City of Philadelphia, had suggested to Police Commissioner Taddeus Czernich that Wohl be given the job. And they all knew that Mayor Carlucci sincerely—and not without reason—believed himself to know more about what was good for the Police Department than anybody else in Philadelphia.

A "suggestion" from Mayor Carlucci to Commissioner Czernich regarding what he should do in the exercise of his office was the equivalent of an announcement on faith and morals issued by the pope, ex cathedra. It was not open for discussion, much less debate.

Peter Wohl had not wanted the job. He had been the youngest, ever, of the fourteen staff inspectors of the Staff Investigations Unit, and had liked very much what he was doing. The penal system of the Commonwealth of Pennsylvania was now housing more than thirty former judges, city commissioners, and other high-level bureaucrats and political office holders whom Peter Wohl had caught with their hands either in the public treasury or outstretched to accept contributions from the citizenry in exchange for special treatment.

He had even thought about passing up the opportunity to take the examination for inspector. There had been little question in his mind that he could pass the examination and be promoted, but he suspected that if he did, with only a couple of years as a staff inspector behind him, with the promotion would come an assignment to duties he would rather not have, for example, as commanding officer of the Traffic Division, or the Civil Affairs Division, or even the Juvenile Division.

Department politics would, he had believed, keep him from getting an assignment as an inspector he would really like, which would have included commanding one of the nine Police Divisions (under which were all the police districts) or one of the two Detective Field Divisions (under which were the seven Detective Divisions) or the Tactical Division, under which were Highway Patrol, the Airport, Stakeout, Ordnance Disposal, the police boats in the Marine Unit, the dogs of the Canine Unit, and a unit whose function he did not fully understand called Special Operations.

And then Mayor Carlucci had a little chat with Commissioner Czernich. There was a chance for the Philadelphia Police Department to get its hands on some federal money, from the Justice Department. Some Washington bureaucrat had decided that the way to fight crime was to overwhelm the criminal element by sheer numbers. Under the acronym ACT, for Anti-Crime Team, federal money would allow local police departments to dispatch to heavy crime areas large numbers of policemen.

Philadelphia already was trying the same tactic, more or less, with the Highway Patrol, an elite, specially uniformed, two-men-in-a-car unit who normally practiced fighting crime by going to heavy crime areas. But they were, of course, paying for it themselves.

There was a way, Mayor Carlucci suggested, to enlist the financial support of the federal government in the never-ending war against crime. The Philadelphia Police Department would form an ACT unit. It would be placed in the already existing Special Operations Unit. And since Highway Patrol was already doing the same sort of thing, so would Highway Patrol be placed in the Special Operations Division. And Special Operations, the mayor suggested, would be taken out from under the control of the Special Investigations Bureau, made a division, and placed under the direct command of the police commissioner himself.

And the mayor suggested that they needed somebody who was really bright to head up the new division, and what did the commissioner think of Peter Wohl?

The police commissioner knew that as Mayor Carlucci had worked his way up through the ranks of the Police Department, his rabbi had been Chief Inspector Augustus Wohl, retired. And he know that Peter Wohl had just done a hell of a fine job putting Superior Court Judge Moses Findermann into the long-term custody of the state penal system. But most important, he understood that when His Honor the Mayor gave a hint like that, it well behooved him to act on it, and he did.

Paul O'Mara, on his second trip through the parking lot, finally found a place, against the rear fence, to park the Ford. He and Staff Inspector Wohl got out of the car and walked to what had been designed as the rear door, but was now the only functioning door, of the Police Administration Building.

A corporal sitting behind a thick plastic window recognized Inspector Wohl and activated the solenoid that unlocked the door to the main lobby. Officer O'Mara pushed it open and held it for Staff Inspector Wohl, an action that made Wohl feel just a bit uncomfortable. Officer Payne had not hovered over him. He was willing to admit he missed Officer Payne.

They rode the curved elevator to the third (actually the fourth) floor of the Roundhouse and walked down the corridor to where a uniformed police officer sat at a counter guarding access to what amounted to the executive suite. Officer O'Mara announced, somewhat triumphantly, their business: "Inspector Wohl to see the commissioner."

The commissioner, Peter Wohl was not surprised to learn, was tied up but would be with him shortly.

The door to the commissioner's conference room was open, and Wohl saw Captain Henry C. Quaire, the head of the Homicide Division, whom he liked, leaning on the conference table, sipping a cup of coffee.

He walked in, and was immediately sorry he had, for Captain Quaire was not alone in the room. Inspector J. Howard Porter, commanding officer of the Tactical Division, was with him.

Inspector Porter had, when word of the federal money and the upgrading of Special Operations had spread through the Department, naturally considered himself a, perhaps the, prime candidate for the command of Special Operations. He not only had the appropriate rank, but his Tactical Division included Highway Patrol.

He had not been given the Special Operations Division, and Highway Patrol had been taken away from Tactical and given to Special Operations. Peter Wohl did not think he could include Inspector Porter in his legion of admirers.

"Good morning, Inspector," Wohl said politely.

"Wohl."

"Hello, Henry."

"Inspector."

"Do you know Paul O'Mara?"

"I know your dad," Quaire said, offering O'Mara his hand.

Inspector Porter nodded at Officer O'Mara but said nothing, and did not offer to shake hands.

*What is that,* Wohl thought, *guilt by association? Or is shaking hands with a lowly police officer beneath your dignity?*

He glanced at Quaire, and their eyes met for a moment.

*I don't think Quaire likes Porter any more than I do.*

"I saw your predecessor last night," Captain Quaire said, as much to Wohl as to O'Mara. "You heard about what happened at the Acme on Baltimore Avenue?"

"I didn't hear Payne shot them," Wohl said without thinking about it.

Quaire laughed. "Not this time, Peter. He was just a spectator."

"I'm glad to hear that."

"That's why we're here," Quaire said. "The commissioner wants to be absolutely sure the shooting was justified."

"Was there a question?"

"Hell no. Both of the doers fired first."

The commissioner's secretary appeared in the conference room door.

"The commissioner will see you now, Inspector," she said, and then realized there were two men answering to that title in the room, and added, ". . . Wohl."

"Thank you," Peter Wohl said.

*If I needed one more nail in my coffin, that was it. Porter knows I just walked in here. And I get to enter the throne room first.*

# SEVEN

"Good morning, Peter," Commissioner Czernich said, smiling broadly. He was a large, stocky, well-tailored man with a full head of silver hair. "Sit down."

"Good morning, sir."

"Would you like some coffee?"

"Please."

"Black, right?"

"Yes, sir."

*I don't think I am about to have my head handed to me on a platter. But on the other hand, I don't think he called me in here to express his appreciation for my all-around splendid performance of duty. And nothing has gone wrong in Special Operations, or I would have heard about it.*

"How's your dad?"

"Fine, thank you. I had dinner with him on Monday."

"Give him my regards, the next time you see him."

"I'll do that, thank you."

"You see the Overnights, Peter?"

The Overnights were a summary of major crimes, and/or significant events affecting the Police Department that were compiled from reports from the districts, the Detective Divisions, and major Bureaus, and then distributed to senior commanders.

"No, sir. I came here first thing."

*Obviously, I've missed something, and I am about to hear what it is, and why it is my fault.*

"Stakeout took down two critters at an Acme on the Baltimore Pike," Czernich said. "It's almost a sure thing these were the characters we've been looking for. If it was a good shooting, we're home free."

"I did hear about that, sir. And from what I heard, I think it was a good shooting."

"Every once in a while, Peter, we do do something right, don't we?"

*I'll be damned. I didn't do anything wrong.*

"Yes, sir, we do."

"The Vice President's coming to town."

"I saw it in the newspaper."

"He's coming by airplane. He's going to do something at Independence Hall. Then he wants to make a triumphal march up Market Street to 30th Street Station, and get on a train."

" 'March,' sir?"

"Figure of speech. What do they call it, 'motorcade'?"

"Yes, sir."

"I talked to the Secret Service guy. He really wants a Highway escort. On wheels, I mean. I think he thinks, or at least the Vice President does, that that makes them look good on the TV."

"Well, there's nothing I know of, sir, that would keep us from giving Dignitary Protection all the wheels they want."

Highway Patrol, as its name suggested, had been formed before World War II, as "The Bandit Chasers." That had evolved into the "Motor Bandit Patrol" and finally into the Highway Patrol. It had originally been equipped with motorcycles ("wheels") only, and its members authorized a special uniform suitable for motorcyclists, breeches, leather boots, leather jackets, and billed caps with an unstiffened crown.

It had evolved over the years into an elite unit that, although it patrolled the Schuylkill Expressway and the interstate highways, spent most of its effort patrolling high-crime areas in two-man RPCs. Other RPCs in the Department were manned by only one police officer, and patrolled only in the district to which they were assigned.

The evolution had begun when command of Highway had been given to Captain Jerry Carlucci, and had continued under his benevolent, and growing, influence as he rose through the ranks to commissioner, and continued now that he was mayor.

Applying for, being selected for, and then serving a tour in Highway was considered an almost essential career step for officers who had ambition for higher rank. Peter Wohl had been a Highway sergeant before his promotion to lieutenant and assignment to the Organized Crime Intelligence Unit.

Highway still had its wheels, and every man in Highway was a graduate of the Motorcycle Training Program (known as "Wheel School"), and continued to wear, although months often passed between times that a Highway Patrolman actually straddled a motorcycle, the special Highway uniform.

Dignitary Protection was ordinarily an inactive function; a sergeant or a lieutenant in the Intelligence Division of the Detective Bureau performed the function and answered that phone number in addition to his other duties.

When a dignitary showed up who needed protection, a more senior officer, sometimes, depending on the dignitary, even a chief inspector, took over and coordinated and commanded whatever police units and personnel were considered necessary.

"What I've been thinking, Peter," Commissioner Czernich said, "is that Dignitary Protection should really be under you. I mean, really, it's a special function, a special operation, am I right? And you have Special Operations."

*Carlucci strikes again,* Peter Wohl thought. *Czernich might even have come by himself to the conclusion that Dignitary Protection should come under Special Operations, but he would have kept that conclusion to himself. He would not have done anything about it himself, or even suggested it to the mayor, because the mayor might not like the idea, or come to the conclusion that Czernich was getting a little too big for his britches.*

"Yes, I'm sure you're right," Wohl said. "Dignitary Protection is a special function, a special operation."

"And there's something else," Czernich went on. "I don't think it would be a bad idea at all to show the feds where all that ACT money is going."

"Yes, sir."

"What I thought I'd do, Peter . . . Do you know Sergeant Henkels?"

"No, sir. I don't think so."

"He's the man in Chief Lowenstein's office who handles Dignitary Protection. I thought I'd ask Lowenstein to get the paperwork going and transfer him and his paperwork out to the Schoolhouse."

When the Special Operations Division had been formed from the Special Operations Unit, there had been no thought given to providing a place for it to exist. Since there was no other place to go, Peter Wohl had set up his first office in what had been the Highway Patrol captain's office in a building Highway shared with the 7th District at Bustleton Avenue and Bowler Street in Northeast Philadelphia.

There really had not been room in the building for both the District and Highway, and the addition of the ever-growing Special Operations staff made things impossible. His complaints had fallen on deaf ears for a long time, but then, somewhat triumphantly, he had been told that the City was willing to transfer a building at Frankford and Castor Avenues from the Board of Education to the Police Department, and Special Operations could have it for their very own.

There was a slight problem. The reason the Board of Education was being so generous was that the Board of Health had determined that the Frankford Grammar School (built A.D. 1892) posed a health threat to its faculty and student population, and had ordered it abandoned. There were, of course, no funds available in the Police Department budget for repairs or rehabilitation.

But since a building had been provided for Special Operations, Staff Inspector Wohl was soon led to understand, it would be considered impolite for him to complain that he was no better off than he had been. It was also pointed out that the health standards that applied to students and teachers did not apply to policemen.

And then Staff Inspector Wohl's administrative assistant, Officer M. M. Payne, who apparently had nothing more pressing to do at the time, read the fine print in the documents that outlined how the ACT funds could be spent. Up to $250,000 of the federal government's money could be expended for emergency *repairs* to, but not *replacement* of, equipment and facilities. He brought this to Wohl's attention, and Wohl, although he was not of the Roman Catholic persuasion, decided that it was time to adopt a Jesuit attitude to his problem: *The end justifies the means.*

*Replacing* broken *windowpanes* was obviously proscribed, and could not be done. But emergency *repairs* to windows (which incidentally might involve replacing a couple of panes here and there) were permissible. Similarly, *replacing* shingles on the roof was proscribed, but *repairing* the roof was permissible. *Repairing* the walls, floor, and plumbing system as a necessary emergency measure similarly posed no insurmountable legal or moral problems vis-à-vis the terms of the federal grant.

But the building's heating system posed a major problem. The existing coal-fired furnaces, after seventy-odd years of service, were beyond repair. In what he seriously regarded as the most dishonest act of his life, Peter Wohl chose not to notice that the *repairs* to the "heating system" consisted of "removing malfunctioning components" (the coal furnaces) and "installing replacement components" (gas-fired devices that provided both heat and air-conditioning).

He had also circumvented the City's bureaucracy in the matter of awarding the various contracts. On one hand, his experience as a staff inspector had left him convinced that kickbacks were standard procedure when the City awarded contracts. The price quoted for services to be rendered to the City included the amount of the kickback. On the other hand, he knew that the law required every contract over $10,000 to be awarded on the basis of the lowest bid. He was, in fact, consciously breaking the law.

He had come to understand, further, that it wasn't a question of if he would be caught, but when. He didn't think there would be an attempt to indict him, but there had been a very good chance that he would either be fired, or asked to resign, or, at a minimum, relieved of his new command when the Department of Public Property finally found out what he had done.

That hadn't happened. The mayor had visited the Schoolhouse and liked what he found. And from a source Peter Wohl had in the Department of Public Property, Peter learned that the mayor had shortly thereafter visited the Department of Public Property and made it clear to the commissioner that he didn't want to hear any complaints, to him, or to the newspapers, about how the old Frankford Grammar School building had been *repaired*.

There were several reasons, Wohl had concluded, why the mayor could have chosen to do that. For one thing, it would have been politically embarrassing for him had there been a fuss in the newspapers. He had appointed Wohl to command Special Operations, and look what happened!

Another possibility was that it was repayment of a debt of honor.

Peter didn't know all the details, or even many of them, but he had heard enough veiled references to be sure that when Jerry Carlucci had been an up-and-coming lieutenant and captain and inspector, Chief Inspector Augustus Wohl had gone out on the limb a number of times to save Carlucci's ass.

Another obvious possibility was that since Carlucci had saved his ass, he was now deeply in Carlucci's debt.

The last possibility was the nicest to consider, that the mayor understood that while Peter was bending, even breaking, the law he was not doing it for himself, but for the betterment of the Department. Peter didn't like to accept this possibility; it let him off the hook too easily.

*The road to hell, or more precisely to the Commonwealth of Pennsylvania's penal system, was paved,* his experience had taught him, *if not entirely with good intentions, then with good intentions and the rationalization you aren't doing something really crooked, but rather something that other people do all the time and get away with.*

"Is that all there is, Commissioner, one sergeant?"

"He just holds down the desk until there's a dignitary to protect," Czernich said. "You didn't know?"

"No, sir. I didn't."

"You don't have any objections to this, Peter, do you?"

"No, sir. If you think this makes sense, I'll give it my best shot."

"If you run into problems, Peter, you know my door is always open."

"Yes, sir. I know that, and I appreciate it, Commissioner."

The commissioner stood up and offered his hand.

"Always good to see you, Peter," he said. "Ask my girl to send Inspector Porter and Captain Quaire in, will you?"

"Yes, sir."

There was a Plymouth station wagon in the driveway of Evelyn Glover's ranch house in Upper Darby when Matt turned into it in the Porsche.

"You've got a visitor," he said.

Evelyn tried to make a joke of it. "That's no visitor, that's my husband."

As Matt stopped the car, a man, forty years old, tall, skinny, tweedy, whom Matt vaguely remembered having seen somewhere before, and who had apparently been peering into the kitchen door, came down the driveway.

Evelyn fumbled around until she found the tiny door latch, opened the door, and got out.

Matt felt a strong urge to shove the stick in reverse and get the hell out of here, but that, obviously, was something he could not do. He opened his door and got out.

He heard the tail end of what Evelyn's husband was saying: ". . . so I called the library, and when they said they had no idea where you were, I got worried and came here."

He looked at Matt with unabashed curiosity.

"Mr. Payne," Evelyn said, "this is my husband. He saw my car at Darby Plymouth."

Professor Glover offered his hand to Matt.

"Harry, this is Detective Payne," Evelyn said. "He's been helping me. We just came from Darby Plymouth."

"How do you do?" Professor Glover said, and then blurted what was on his mind: "That's quite a police car."

"It's my car," Matt said. "I'm off duty."

"Oh," Professor Glover said.

"Well, if there's nothing else I can do for you, Mrs. Glover . . ."

"You've already done more for me than I had any right to expect," Evelyn said, and offered him her hand. "I don't know how to thank you."

"Don't mention it," Matt said. "Sorry you had the trouble. Nice to meet you, Professor."

"Yes," Professor Glover said.

*Jesus Christ, he knows!*

Matt got back in the Porsche, and backed out of the driveway. He glanced at the house and saw Professor Glover following his wife into the house.

Officer Paul O'Mara dropped Staff Inspector Wohl at a door over which was carved in stone, GIRLS' ENTRANCE, at the former Frankford Grammar School, and then drove around to the cracked cement now covering what at one time had been the lawn in front of the building and parked the Ford.

Captain Michael Sabara, a swarthy, acne-scarred, stocky man in his forties, who was wearing a white civilian shirt and yellow V-neck sweater, and Captain David Pekach, a slight, fair-skinned man of thirty-six, who was wearing the special Highway Patrol uniform, were both waiting for Wohl when he walked into his (formerly the principal's) office.

Captain Mike Sabara was Wohl's deputy. He had been the senior lieutenant in Highway, and awaiting promotion to captain when Captain Dutch Moffitt had been killed. He had naturally expected to step into Moffitt's shoes. Dave Pekach, who had been in Narcotics, had just been promoted to captain, and transferred to Special Operations.

Enraging many of the people in Highway, including, Wohl was sure, Mike Sabara, he had named Sabara his deputy and given Highway to Pekach. But that had been almost a year ago, and it had worked out well. It had probably taken Sabara, Wohl thought, no more than a week to realize that the alternative to his being named Wohl's deputy was a transfer elsewhere in the Department, and probably another month to believe what Wohl had told him when he took over Special Operations, that he would be of greater usefulness to the Department as his deputy than he would have been commanding Highway.

Wohl understood the Highway mystique. He still had in his closet his Highway sergeant's leather jacket and soft-crowned billed cap, unable to bring himself to sell, or even give them away, although there was absolutely no way he would ever wear either again. But it had been time for Sabara to take off his Highway breeches, and for Pekach, who had worn a pigtail in his plainclothes Narcotics assignment, to get back in uniform.

"Good morning, Inspector," they said, almost in chorus.

Wohl smiled and motioned for them to follow him into his office.

"I hope you brought your notebooks," he said. "I have just come from the Fountain of All Knowledge."

"I don't like the sound of that," Sabara said.

Pekach closed the office door behind him.

"What did the Polack want, Peter?" he asked.

Wohl did not respond directly.

"Is Jack Malone around?" he asked. "I'd rather go through this just once."

"He went over to the garage," Sabara said, stepping to Wohl's desk as he spoke and picking up a telephone. "Have you got a location on Lieutenant Malone?" He put the phone back in its cradle. "He just drove in the gate."

Wohl sat down at his desk and took the Overnight from his IN box. He read it. He raised his eyes to Pekach.

"We have anybody in on the shooting at the Acme?"

"One car, plus a sergeant who was in the area."

"Did you talk to them? Was it a good shooting?"

"It looks that way. They shot first. The lieutenant—what the hell is his name?—"

Wohl and Sabara shrugged their shoulders.

"—not only identified himself as a police officer, but used an electronic megaphone to do it. One of the doers *then* shot at him and another Stakeout guy. When he was down, the other doer started shooting. It looks to me like it was clearly justified."

"The commissioner seemed a little unsure," Wohl said. "Open the door, Dave, and see if O'Mara's out there. If he is, have him lasso Jack."

"I'll tell you who was also at the Acme, Peter, in case you haven't heard. Matt Payne."

"I heard. I saw Henry Quaire in the Roundhouse."

"This time he was a spectator," Sabara said.

Pekach came back into the office, followed by a uniformed lieutenant, John J. "Jack" Malone, who showed signs of entering middle age. His hairline was starting to recede; there was the suggestion of forming jowls, and he was getting a little thick around the middle.

"Good morning, sir," he said.

"Close the door, Jack, please," Wohl said. "Gentlemen, I don't believe you've met the new commanding officer of Dignitary Protection?"

Malone misinterpreted what Wohl had intended as a little witticism. The smile vanished from his face. It grew more than sad, bitter.

"When did that happen, sir?" he asked.

Wohl saw that his little joke had laid an egg, and he was furious with himself for trying to be clever. Malone thought he was being told, kindly, that he was being transferred out of Special Operations. And with that came the inference that he had been found wanting.

"About ten minutes ago, Jack," Wohl said, "which is ten minutes after the commissioner told me we now have Dignitary Protection. Have you got something against taking it over?"

"Not here," Malone said, visibly relieved. "I thought I was being sent to the Roundhouse."

*Well, that's flattering. He likes it here.*

"Do you know a sergeant by the name of Henkels?"

"Yes, sir, I know him."

"There is something in your tone that suggests that you are not especially impressed with the sergeant."

"There used to be a Sergeant Henkels in Central Cell Room," Pekach volunteered. "If it's the same guy, he has a room temperature IQ."

"That's him, Captain. I guess they moved him upstairs," Malone said.

The Central Cell Room was in the Police Administration Building.

"Well, Sergeant Henkels and his Dignitary Protection files are about to be transferred out here. Into your capable command, Lieutenant Malone."

"Oh, God. He's a real dummy, Inspector. God only knows how he got to be a sergeant."

"Well, I'm sure you will find a way to keep the sergeant usefully occupied."

"How about sending him to Wheel School and praying he breaks his neck?" Malone suggested.

"I don't think there will be time to do that before the Vice President comes to town," Wohl said.

"I saw that in the papers," Malone said. "We're going to have that? There's not a hell of a lot of time . . ."

"We'll have to manage somehow."

"Who are they going to move into command?" Malone asked. "Did the commissioner say?"

Wohl shook his head, no. He was more than a little embarrassed that he hadn't considered that.

"One of the chiefs probably," Mike Sabara said. "It's the Vice President."

"They're not going to move anybody in," Peter Wohl said, softly but firmly. "If this is a Special Operations responsibility, we'll be responsible."

"You'd be putting your neck on the line, Peter," Mike Sabara said. "Let them send somebody in, somebody who's familiar with this sort of operation."

"Let them send someone in here with the authority to tell our people what to do?" Wohl replied. "No way, Mike. We'll do it. Discussion closed."

Corporal Vito Lanza had not been the star pupil in Bishop John Newmann High School's Basic, Intermediate, and Advanced Typing courses, but he had tried hard enough not to get kicked out of the class. Being dropped from Typing would have meant assignment as a library monitor (putting books back on shelves), or as a laboratory monitor (washing all that shit out of test tubes and Ehrlenmayer flasks), neither of which had great appeal to him.

Almost despite himself, he had become a fairly competent typist, a skill he thought he would never use in real life after graduation, and certainly not as a cop, chasing criminals down the street on his Highway Patrol Harley-Davidson motorcycle.

There was a two-and-a-half-year period after graduation from Bishop Newmann High, until he turned twenty-one and could apply for the cops, during which Vito had had a number of jobs. He worked in three different service stations, worked in a taxi garage, and got a job cleaning Eastern airliners between flights at the airport. He hated all of them, and prayed after he took the Civil Service Examination for the cops that he would not be found wanting.

Officer Lanza had quickly learned that being a cop was not what he thought it would be. Right out of the Academy, he had been assigned to the 18th District at 55th and Pine Streets. He spent eight months riding around the district in a battered Ford van, with another rookie police officer. Hauling prisoners (a great many of whom were drunks, not even guys who'd done a stickup) from where they had been arrested to the holding cells in the District Station was not exactly what he'd had in mind when he had become a law enforcement officer. Neither was hauling sick people from their houses to a hospital.

(Philadelphia Police, unlike the police of other major American cities, respond to every call for help. The citizens of Philadelphia have learned over the years that what one does when Junior falls off the porch and cracks his head open, or Grandma falls on an icy sidewalk, or Mama scalds herself with boiling water on the stove, is to call the cops.)

And Vito learned that while it was certainly possible that he could become a Highway Patrolman and race around the streets on a Harley, or in one of the antennae-festooned special Highway Radio Patrol Cars, fighting crime, that would have to be some time in the future. *After* he had four, five, six *good* years on the job, he could *apply* for Highway. It was police folklore—which is not always accurate—that unless you had done something spectacular, like personally catch a bank robber, or unless you knew somebody in Highway, or had a rabbi, some white shirt who liked you, your chances of getting in Highway were about as good as they were to win the Irish Sweepstakes.

But one night, after he had been pushing the van for eight

months, the sergeant at roll call had asked, "Does anybody know how to type good?"

Vito had always thought that typing was something girls did, and was reluctant to publicly confess that he could do that sort of thing, but maybe it would get him out of the fucking van for the night.

"Over here, Sergeant," Officer Lanza had said, raising his hand.

"Okay," the sergeant had said. "See the corporal. Sweitzer, you take his place in the van."

"Shit," Officer Sweitzer said.

The district was behind in its paperwork, the corporal told Officer Lanza, and the captain was on his ass, because the inspector was on his ass.

It had not taken Officer Lanza long to figure out that (a) while he was not a really good typist, compared to anybody in the district he was a world fucking champion and (b) that sitting behind a desk in the district building pushing a typewriter was way ahead of staggering around in the ice and slush loading a fat lady into the back of a van.

That particular typing job had taken three days. Over the next two years, Officer Lanza had spent more and more time behind a typewriter in the office than he had spent in an emergency patrol wagon, in an RPC, or walking a beat.

When he had almost three years on the job, he had taken the examinations for both detective and corporal. He hadn't expected to pass either first time out—he just wanted to see what the fuck the examinations were like—and he didn't. He found that the detective examination was tougher than the corporal examination. Probably, he deduced, because he had been doing so much paperwork, which is what corporals did, that he had come to understand a lot of it.

Two years later, when there was another examination for both detective and corporal, he figured fuck the detective, I think I'd rather be a corporal anyhow, detectives spend a lot of time standing around in the mud and snow.

He passed the corporal's examination, way down on the numerical list, so it was another year almost before he actually got promoted. He did four months working the desk in the Central Cell Room in the Roundhouse, and then they transferred him upstairs to the Traffic Division, where he had met Lieutenant Schnair, who was a pretty good guy for a Jew, and was supposed to have Chief Inspector Matt Lowenstein, the chief inspector of the Detective Division, for a rabbi.

Obviously, pushing a typewriter for the Traffic Division in the

Roundhouse was a lot better than standing in the snow and blowing your whistle at tractor trailers at some accident scene for the Traffic Division, and Vito tried hard to please Lieutenant Schnair.

When Schnair got promoted to captain, and they gave him the Airport Unit (which, so far as Vito was concerned, proved Chief Lowenstein *was* his rabbi), he arranged for Corporal Lanza to be transferred to Airport too, after one of the corporals there got himself killed driving home from the shore.

It was a good job. All he had to do was keep on top of the paperwork, and everybody left him alone. The lieutenants and the sergeants and the other corporals knew how good he got along with Captain Schnair. If he came in a little late, or left a little early, no one said anything to him.

It never entered Corporal Vito Lanza's mind to ask permission to leave his desk in the Airport Unit office at 11:15. He simply *told* the lieutenant on duty, Lieutenant Ardell, that he was going to lunch.

He would get back when he got back. He was going to have a real lunch, not a sandwich or a hot dog, which meant getting out of the airport, where they charged crazy fucking prices. Just because he had a bundle of Las Vegas money was no excuse to pay five dollars for something worth two-fifty.

The Buick surprised him by starting right off. Now that he was going to dump the sonofabitch, it had decided to turn reliable. It was like when you went to the dentist, your teeth stopped hurting.

Thinking of dumping the Buick reminded him that he was supposed to meet Antoinette after work and go see her uncle, who had a car lot. He'd told her, of course, that he'd had a little luck in Vegas and was going to look around for a Caddy, and she told him her uncle had a car lot with a lot of Caddys on it.

He hadn't been sure then whether she had been trying to be nice to him, or just steering her uncle some business. After she'd taken him to her apartment, he decided that she really did like him, and maybe this thing with her uncle would turn out all right.

It also made him feel like a fool for slipping that bimbo in Vegas two hundred dollars. He didn't really have to pay for it, and now he couldn't understand why he had. Except, of course, that he was on a high from what had happened at the tables.

Antoinette had told him her uncle's car lot was one of those in the "Auto Mall" at 67th Street and Essington Avenue. Just past the ballpark on South Broad, he decided that it wouldn't hurt to just drive past the uncle's car lot, it wasn't far, to see what he had. If he was some sleaze-ball with a dozen cars or so, that would mean that Antoinette was trying to push some business his way, and when he saw her after work, he would tell her he had made other arrangements. Tell her nice. The last thing in the world he wanted to do was piss her off. She was really much better in the sack than the bimbo in Vegas he'd given the two hundred dollars to.

Fierello's Fine Cars, on Essington Avenue, was no sleaze operation. Vito thought there must be a hundred, maybe a hundred fifty cars on the lot, which was paved and had lights and everything and even a little office building that was a real building, not just a trailer. And there were at least twenty Caddys, and they all looked like nearly new.

He drove past it twice, and then started back to the airport. He didn't get the real lunch he started out to get—he stopped at Oregon Steaks at Oregon Avenue and Juniper Street and had a sausage and peppers sandwich and a beer—but he was in a good mood and it didn't bother him. Not only was he probably going to drive home tonight in a new Caddy, but on the way, the odds were that he might spend some time in Antoinette's apartment.

He was still on a roll, no question about it.

Marion Claude Wheatley, the Hon. Jerry Carlucci, and Detective M. M. Payne all had lunch at the Union League Club on South Broad Street, but not together.

Mr. Wheatley was the guest of Mr. D. Logan Hammersmith, Jr., who was a vice president and senior trust officer of the First Pennsylvania Bank & Trust Company and who, like Mr. Wheatley, held an MBA from the University of Pennsylvania.

Mr. Hammersmith did not really know what to think of Mr. Wheatley beyond the obvious, which was that he was one hell of an analyst; not only was his knowledge of the petrochemical industry encyclopedic, but he had demonstrated over the years a remarkable ability to predict upturns and downturns. Acting on Mr. Wheatley's recommendations, Mr. Hammersmith had been able to make a lot of money for the trusts under his control, and he was perfectly willing to admit that this success had been a factor, indeed a major factor, in his recent promotion to senior trust officer, which carried with it the titular promotion to vice president.

(While he was willing to concede that it was true that First Philadelphia dispensed titular promotions instead of salary increases, it was, nevertheless, rather nice to have the bronze name plate reading D. LOGAN HAMMERSMITH, JR. VICE PRESIDENT sitting on his desk.)

Logan Hammersmith was not the only one around First Philadelphia who had noticed that M. C. Wheatley had never married. But there never had been any talk that he was perhaps light on his feet. For one thing, the contents of his personnel file, although they were supposed to be confidential, were well known. One is not prone to jump to the conclusion that someone who has served, with great distinction, was twice wounded and three times decorated, as an Army officer in Vietnam is a fag simply because he has not marched to the marriage altar.

And he didn't have effeminate mannerisms, either. He drank his whiskey straight and sometimes smoked cigars. Hammersmith's final, best guess was that Wheatley was either very shy, and incapable of pursuing women, or, more likely, asexual.

And, of course, for all that anybody really *knew*, Marion Claude Wheatley might be carrying on, discreetly, with a married woman, or for that matter with a belly dancer in Atlantic City. He had a country place, a farm, or what had years before been a farm, acquired by inheritance, in that area of New Jersey known as the Pine Barrens. He spent many of his weekends there, and presumably his summer vacations.

Hammersmith, over the years, had had Marion C. Wheatley out to the house in Bryn Mawr a number of times for dinner. His behavior had been impeccable. He'd brought the right sort of wine as a gift, and he didn't get plastered, or try to grope some shapely knee under the table. But he was not a brilliant, or even mediocre, conversationalist. He was, as Bootsie (Mrs. D. Logan, Jr.) Hammersmith had put it, a crashing bore.

It had been, Hammersmith thought, as he handed the menu back and told the waiter he'd have the Boston scrod, well over a year since Wheatley had been out to the house. He would have to do something about that.

"I think the same for me, please," Marion C. Wheatley said.

"Do you think the building would fall down if we walked back in reeking of gin?" Hammersmith asked.

Employees of First Philadelphia were expected not to take alcohol at lunch. *Officers* were under no such unwritten proscription.

"I think a martini would be a splendid idea," Marion said with a smile.

Hammersmith held up two fingers to the waiter, and then his eyes fell on a familiar face.

"We are in the presence of the mayor," he said, and discreetly nodded his head in the mayor's direction.

After a moment Marion C. Wheatley looked.

"Is he a member, do you think?"

"I think ex-officio," Hammersmith said. "For the obvious reasons. Speaking of the upper crust, Bootsie and I were invited to the Peebles wedding."

Marion C. Wheatley looked at him curiously.

"Peebles," Hammersmith repeated. "As in Tamaqua Mining."

"Oh," Wheatley said.

*That rang a bell,* Hammersmith thought. *I thought it would. Tamaqua Mining owned somewhere between ten and twelve percent of the known anthracite reserves of the United States. Anthracite coal was still an important part of petrochemicals, and according to Marion Claude Wheatley it would grow in financial importance. Miss Martha Peebles owned all of the outstanding shares of Tamaqua Mining, and Wheatley would know that.*

After a moment Marion Claude Wheatley asked, "Is that in a trust?"

"No. She manages it herself. With Mawson, Payne, Stockton, McAdoo & Lester's assistance of course."

"You know her, then?" Wheatley asked.

Hammersmith was pleased they had found something to talk about. Making conversation with Wheatley was often difficult. Or impossible.

"No. I know the brother. Alexander Peebles, Jr."

Wheatley's face showed that he didn't understand.

"When the old man died, he, in the classic phrase, cut the boy off without a dime. There is an unpleasant story that the son, how should I phrase this delicately?"

"He's a fairy," Marion Claude Wheatley said. "Now that you mention it, I've heard that."

*I don't think he would have used that word if he was queer himself.*

"Not from me," Hammersmith said. "Anyway, he left everything to the daughter. There was a nasty law suit but he was up against Mawson, Payne, Stockton, McAdoo & Lester, and he lost. Then the sister set up a trust fund for him. With us. Specifically with me. We couldn't have Alexander Peebles, Jr., sleeping in the subway."

"And he invited you?"

"I don't know. I guess he's been told to show up and behave at the wedding. Brewster Payne's going to give her away, and I suspect he was responsible for the invitation."

"Who is she marrying?"

"The story gets curiouser and curiouser," Hammersmith said. "A cop."

"A *cop*?"

"Well, a captain. A fellow named Pekach. He's the head of Highway Patrol."

"Where did she meet him?"

"The story as I understand it is that her place in Chestnut Hill kept getting burglarized. She complained to the mayor, or Payne complained to the mayor for her, and the mayor sent the Highway Patrol. . . ."

"Carlucci's Commandos," Wheatley interrupted. "That's what the *Ledger* calls the Highway Patrol."

"Right. So, as the story goes, His Honor the Mayor sent the head commando, this Captain Pekach, to calm the lady down, and it was love at first sight."

"What does this lady look like?"

"Actually, she's rather attractive."

"Then why didn't you arrange for me to meet her?"

"You don't have a motorcycle and a large pistol. The lady probably wouldn't have been interested in you."

"I could have gone out and bought them," Marion Claude Wheatley said. "In a good cause."

He smiled at Hammersmith and Hammersmith smiled back. He was pleased that he had decided to take Wheatley to lunch. There was no longer a gnawing suspicion that Wheatley was queer. It could have been awkward at First Philadelphia if that had come out. Everyone knew that he relied heavily on Wheatley's advice, and there would have been talk if something embarrassing had developed.

# EIGHT

Detective Matthew M. Payne was the guest of Brewster C. Payne for lunch at the Union League. On the way into Philadelphia from Upper Darby, while pumping gas into the Porsche, he had seen a pay telephone and remembered that his father had left a message on the answering machine to which he had not responded. He'd called him, and been invited to lunch.

He had hung up the phone thinking that virtue *was* its own reward. He had nobly been the dutiful son, and only in the middle of the conversation realized that his father would have the solution to what he should do with his Las Vegas winnings.

Brewster Payne arrived first and was asked by the headwaiter how many would be in his party.

"Just my son, Charley."

"Then you wouldn't mind sitting at a small table?"

"Not at all."

One of the prerogatives of being a member of the Board of Governors was being able to walk into the dining room anytime

112

before twelve-thirty without a reservation and finding a good four-place table with a RESERVED sign on it was available to you.

Brewster Payne had just been served, without having to ask for it, a Famous Grouse with an equal amount of water and just a little ice, when he saw his son stop at the entrance and look around for him.

He thought, as he very often did, *it is incredible that that well-dressed, very nice young man is a policeman with a gun concealed somewhere on his person. A gun, even more incredibly, with which he has killed two people.*

Matt spotted him and smiled and walked across the room. Brewster Payne got to his feet and extended his hand. At the last moment, he moved his hand to his son's shoulders and gave him a brief hug.

"I didn't know how long I would have to wait, so I ordered a drink."

"I am ninety seconds late, just for the record."

A waiter appeared.

"I'll have a Tuborg, please," Matt ordered.

"Your sister is annoyed with you."

"Anything else new?"

"Have you called her?"

"No."

"I think you should have. She wanted to know how things went in Las Vegas."

"Vis-à-vis Precious Penny, more smoothly than I would have thought," Matt said. "She only said 'Fuck you, Matt' twice."

"What was that about?"

"Idle conversation," Matt said. "She left a message on the machine, very sweetly thanking me for going out there and fetching her home. I don't really have anything to tell Amy; that's why I didn't call her."

"That you had nothing to report would have been useful in itself."

"Okay, I'll call her."

"You don't have to now. She went out to Chestnut Hill this morning and saw her."

"Great," Matt said. "Then that's over. Ask me what else happened in Las Vegas."

"What else happened in Las Vegas?"

Matt reached in his pocket and handed his father the $3,700 check from the Flamingo.

"And I have another three thousand in cash," Matt said as soon as he saw his father's eyebrows raise in surprise.

Brewster Payne looked at him.

"Three thousand more in cash?"

Matt nodded. "What do I do with it?"

"What were you playing?"

"Roulette."

"I didn't know you knew how to play roulette."

"Now you do. I think I have found my niche in life." He saw the look in his father's eyes and added: "Hey, I'm kidding."

"I hope so. How did this happen?"

"I started out to lose twenty dollars and got lucky and lost my mind."

"Lost your mind?"

"If I had been thinking clearly, I would have quit when I was four thousand odd ahead. But I didn't, and went back to the tables and won another twenty-seven hundred."

"Then you were smart enough to quit?"

"Then it was time to go get Penny."

Brewster Payne shook his head and tapped the check with a long, thin finger.

"The first thing you do is put enough of this in escrow to pay your taxes."

"What taxes?"

"Income taxes. Gambling winnings are taxable."

"That's outrageous!"

Brewster Payne smiled at his son's righteous indignation.

" 'The law is an ass,' right?"

"That sums it up nicely," Matt said. And then he had a thought. "How does the IRS know I won? Or how much I won?"

Brewster Payne held the check up.

"You'll notice your social security number is on here. They're required to inform the IRS, and they do."

"What about the three thousand in cash?"

"An unethical lawyer might suggest to you that you could probably conceal that from the IRS and get away with it. I am not an unethical lawyer, and *you* are an officer of the law."

"Jesus H. Christ!"

"Pay the two dollars, Matt. Sleep easy."

"It's not *two* dollars!"

"You're a big boy. Do what you like."

"So what do I do with it?"

"My advice would be to put it in tax-free municipals. You've already got a good deal of money in them. If you'd like, I'll take care of it for you."

Matt's indignation had not run completely down.

"You win, we get our pound of flesh. You *lose*, tough luck, right?"

"Essentially," Brewster Payne said. "And if you would like some additional advice?"

"Sure."

"I would not tell your mother about this. Right now she thinks of you as her saintly son who went out to the desert to help a sick girl. I would rather have her think that than to have a mental picture of you at the Las Vegas craps tables . . ."

"Roulette."

". . . *roulette tables*, surrounded by scantily dressed chorus girls."

"It's true."

"What's true?"

"They have some really good-looking hookers out there."

"But you, being virtuous, had nothing to do with them, and were rewarded by good luck at the roulette tables?"

"Absolutely. I have the strength of ten because in my heart, I'm pure."

"When do you go back to work?"

"Tomorrow, probably. I've got to go to Chief Lowenstein's office at half past one. I suspect that someone is going to tell me that when I go back to work, I say I was doing paperwork in the Roundhouse, not running out to Vegas to fetch Precious Penny."

The waiter appeared and interrupted the conversation to take their order.

"Have you plans for tonight?"

"No, sir."

"I think your mother would like to have you for dinner. She's making a leg of lamb."

"Thank you."

"Amy will be there."

"I have just been sandbagged."

"Yes," Brewster Payne said. "I had that in mind when I mentioned the lamb." He handed Matt the Flamingo check. "Take this, and the cash, to the bank. Cash this, and have them give you a cashier's check for the entire amount of money, payable to First Philadelphia. Give it to me tonight, and I'll take care of it from there."

Matt nodded, and took the check back.

"How much in taxes are they going to get?"

"You don't really want to know. It would ruin your lunch."

"I'll have the vegetable soup and the calves' liver, please," Chief Inspector Matt Lowenstein told the waiter.

"Shrimp cocktail and the luncheon steak, pink in the middle," the Honorable Jerry Carlucci ordered.

When the waiter had gone, the mayor said, "You should have had the shrimp and steak. I'm buying."

"Most of the time when you say you're buying I wind up with the check. Besides, I like the way they do liver in here."

"I had a call from H. Richard Detweiler this morning," the mayor said.

"And?"

"And he said he wanted me to know he was very grateful for our letting the Payne kid go out there and bring his daughter home, and if there was ever anything he could for me I should not hesitate to let him know."

"You should hold off calling that marker in until you're running for governor or the Senate. Or the White House."

"All I want to do is be mayor of Philadelphia."

"Isn't that what you said when they appointed you police commissioner? That all you wanted to be was commissioner?"

"What is this, Beat Up On Jerry Carlucci Day?"

"You want a straight answer to that?"

"No, lie to me."

"I sent word to Payne to meet me in my office at half past one. I'm going to tell him, when he goes back on the job, that what he was doing was paperwork in the Roundhouse, not running out to Las Vegas, for Christ's sake, baby-sitting Detweiler's daughter. He's going to have a hard enough time proving himself over at East as it is . . ."

"I've been in a detective division. Right there in East Detectives, as a matter of fact. You don't have to tell me about detective divisions."

". . . . without us pulling him out of there every time somebody like Detweiler wants a favor from you," Lowenstein finished.

"I'm not as dumb as I look, Matt," the mayor said. "I'm even one or two steps ahead of you."

"Are you?"

"Yes, I am. I thought you and Denny Coughlin did a dumb thing when you sent him to East Detectives in the first place."

"He made detective. What you do with new detectives is send them to out to the Academy to learn the new forms, and then to a division, to learn how to *be* a detective. You tell me, why is that dumb?"

"Because he is who he is."

"You tell me, who is he?"

"He's the guy who took down the Northwest Philadelphia serial rapist, and the guy who shot it out with that Islamic Liberation Army jackass and won. That makes him different, without the other things. Like I said, I've been in a detective division. They're really going to stay on his ass to remind him he's a rookie, until he proves himself."

"He's a good kid. He can handle that."

"Sure he can, and what have we got then? I'll tell you what we'll have—one more detective who can probably work a crime scene about as good as any other detective."

"I don't know what the hell you're talking about."

"The Good of the Department is what I'm talking about."

"Then you have lost me somewhere along the way."

"Do you know how many college graduates have applied for the Department in the last year?"

"No."

"Fifty-three."

"So?"

"Do you know how many college graduates applied, in the three years previous to this one?"

"I have no idea."

"Seventeen. Not each year. Total."

"Now I'm really lost."

"Public relations," the mayor said significantly.

"What does that mean?"

"That a lot of young men, fifty-three young men, with college degrees, with the potential to become really good cops, saw Payne's picture in the newspapers and decided they might like being a cop themselves."

"Do you know that? Or just think that?"

"I checked it out," the mayor said.

"So what are you saying, Jerry? That we should put Payne on recruiting duty?"

"I'm saying you and Coughlin should have left him right where he was, in Special Operations."

"A," Lowenstein said, "you always transfer people who get promoted. B, there are no detectives in Special Operations."

"A, that 'transfer people when they get promoted' didn't come off the mountain with Moses, engraved on stone, and B, as of today there are two detectives assigned to Special Operations."

"Two detectives who should have been sent back to Homicide where they belong," Lowenstein said.

"If you mean Jason Washington, he's a sergeant now. He got promoted, and he didn't get transferred out of Special Operations. I said two *detectives*. One of whom is Tony Harris, who would probably go back to being a drunk if we sent him back to Homicide."

Lowenstein took a deep swallow of his Jack Daniel's and water. He was impressed again with Jerry Carlucci's intimate knowledge of what was going on in the Department.

Detectives Jason Washington and Tony Harris, in Lowenstein's judgment the two best Homicide detectives, had been "temporarily" assigned to the then newly formed Special Operations Division when Mayor Carlucci had taken away the Northwest serial rapist job from Northwest Detectives and given it to Peter Wohl.

Other special jobs had come up, and they had never gone back to Homicide, which had been a continuing source of annoyance to Matt Lowenstein. The only good thing about it was that Tony Harris seemed to have gotten his bottle problem under control working for Wohl. Until just now, Matt Lowenstein had believed that Harris's boozing was known to only a few people, not including the mayor.

"You said 'two detectives,' " Lowenstein said, finally. "The other one's name is Payne, right?"

"You're a clever fellow. Maybe you should be a detective or something," Jerry Carlucci said.

Lowenstein did not reply.

"He can learn as much watching Washington and Harris as he could have learned in East Detectives, and probably quicker," Carlucci said. "And he'll be available, without a lot of bullshit and resentment, the next time the Department needs to do somebody who can do the Department a lot of good a favor."

"Oh, shit," Matt Lowenstein said.

"You don't like it?" the mayor said. There was just a hint of coldness in his voice.

"What I don't like is that you're right," Lowenstein said. "It wasn't fair to either East Detectives or Payne to send him there. I don't know if he'll stay on the job or not, but if he does, it wouldn't be at East Detectives."

"I thought about that too," Carlucci said. "Whether he would stay. I decided he would. He's been around long enough, done enough, to have it get in his blood."

"You make it sound like syphilis," Lowenstein said.

Mr. Ricco Baltazari had his luncheon, a dozen cherrystone clams, a double thick lamb chop, medium rare, with mint sauce, and a sliced tomato with olive oil and vinegar in his place of business, the Ristorante Alfredo, in Center City, Philadelphia, three blocks east of the Union League.

A table in the rear of the establishment had been especially laid for the occasion, for Mr. Gian-Carlo Rosselli had called Mr. Baltazari with the announcement that Mr. S. thought he would like to have a little fish for his lunch and was that going to pose any problems?

Mr. Baltazari had told Mr. Rosselli that it would be no problem at all, and what time was Mr. S. thinking of having his lunch?

"Twelve-thirty, one," Mr. Rosselli had replied and then hung up without saying another word.

Mr. Baltazari had personally inspected the table after it was set, to make sure there wasn't any grease or lipstick or whatever the dishwasher had missed; that there were no chips on the dishes or glasses; and that there were no spots on the tablecloth or napkins the laundry hadn't washed out. Then he went into the kitchen and personally first selected the slice of swordfish that would be served to Mr. S., and then the wines he thought Mr. S. might like. After a moment's thought, he added a third bottle, of sparkling wine, to his original selections and had it put into the refrigerator to cool. Sometimes Mr. S. liked sparkling wine.

As a final preparation, Mr. Baltazari walked two blocks farther east, toward the Delaware River, where he had a shave and a trim and had his shoes shined.

Mr. S., whose full name was Vincenzo Carlos Savarese, was more than just a customer. Despite what it said on Ristorante Alfredo's restaurant and liquor licenses, that Ricco Baltazari was the owner and licensee, it was really owned by Mr. Savarese. Mr. Baltazari operated it for him, it being understood between them that no matter what it said on the books about salary and profits, that Mr. S. was to be paid, in cash, once a month, fifty percent of gross receipts less the cost of food, liquor, rent, salaries, and laundry.

Out of his fifty percent, Mr. Baltazari was expected to pay all other expenses. Anything left over after that was his.

There was no written agreement. They were men of honor, and it was understood between them that if it ever came to Mr. S.'s attention that Mr. Baltazari had been fucking with the books, taking cash out of the register, or in any other way, no matter how, depriving Mr. S. of his full return on his investment, Mr. Baltazari could expect to find himself floating facedown in the Delaware River, or stuffed into the trunk of his Cadillac with twenty-dollar bills inserted into his nostrils and other cranial cavities.

Mr. Savarese, a slightly built, silver-haired, superbly tailored and shod man in his early sixties, arrived at Ristorante Alfredo at five minutes to one. He took great pride in his personal appearance, believing that a businessman, such as himself, should look the part.

He had, ten years before, arranged the immigration from Rome of a journeyman gentlemen's tailor and set him up in business in a downtown office building. At Mr. S.'s recommendation, a number of his business associates had begun to patronize the tailor, and he had found financial security and a good life in the new world. It was understood between the tailor and Mr. Savarese that the tailor would not offer to cut a suit for anyone else from a bolt of cloth from which he had cut a suit for Mr. Savarese.

Shoes were something else. Mr. Savarese was a good enough businessman to understand there was not a sufficient market in Philadelphia to support a custom bootmaker, no matter how skilled, so he had his shoes made in Palermo on a last carved there for him on a visit he had made years before attending the funeral of a great-aunt.

Mr. Savarese did not own an automobile, and rarely drove himself, although he took pains to make sure his driver's license did not lapse. The Lincoln sedan in which he arrived at Ristorante Alfredo was owned by Classic Livery, which supplied limousines to the funeral trade, and which was owned, in much the same sort of arrangement as that which Mr. Savarese had with Mr. Baltazari vis-à-vis Ristorante Alfredo, by Mr. Paulo Cassandro. Mr. Cassandro, as now, habitually assigned his brother, Pietro, to drive the automobile he made available for Mr. Savarese's use.

Mr. Savarese, as now, was habitually accompanied by Mr. Gian-Carlo Rosselli, a tall, heavyset gentleman in his middle thirties.

When the Lincoln pulled to the curb before the marquee of

Ristorante Alfredo, Mr. Rosselli, who was riding in the front seat, got out of the car and walked around the front to the sidewalk. He glanced up and down the street, and then nodded at Mr. Cassandro. Mr. Cassandro then got from behind the wheel and opened the rear door for Mr. Savarese.

By the time Mr. Savarese reached the door of the restaurant, Mr. Rosselli had pulled the door open for him. He stepped inside, where Mr. Baltazari was waiting for him. They shook hands. Mr. Baltazari was always very careful when shaking hands with Mr. Savarese, for his hands were very large and strong, and Mr. Savarese's rather delicate. Mr. Savarese played the violin and the violoncello, primarily for his own pleasure, but sometimes for friends, say at a wedding or an anniversary celebration. It was considered a great honor to have him play at such gatherings.

Mr. Baltazari led Mr. Savarese and Mr. Rosselli to the table, where the maître d'hôtel was standing behind the chair in which Mr. Savarese would sit, and a waiter (not the wine steward; that sonofabitch having this day, of all goddamned days, with Mr. S. coming in, called in sick) stood before two wine coolers on legs.

Mr. Savarese sat down, and the headwaiter pushed his chair in for him. He looked up at Mr. Rosselli, who was obviously waiting for direction, and made a little gesture with his hand, signaling that Mr. Rosselli should sit down.

"What are you going to feed me, Ricco?" Mr. Savarese asked with a smile.

"I thought some cherrystones," Mr. Baltazari said. "And there is some very nice swordfish?"

"I leave myself in your hands."

"I have a nice white wine . . ."

"Anything you think . . ."

"And some nice Fiore e Fiore sparkling . . ."

"The sparkling. It always goes so well with the clams, I think."

Mr. Baltazari snapped his fingers and the waiter who was standing in for the goddamned wine steward who'd chosen today to fuck off twisted the wire holding the cork in the sparkling wine off, popped the cork, and poured a little in a champagne glass whose stem was hollow to the bottom and cost a fucking fortune and was only taken out of the cabinet when Mr. S. was in the place.

Mr. Savarese tasted the sparkling wine.

"That's very nice, Ricco," he said.

"Thank you," Mr. Baltazari said, beaming, and then added, to the headwaiter, "Put a case of that in Mr. S.'s car."

"You're very kind," Mr. Savarese said.

The waiter filled Mr. Savarese's glass with the Fiore e Fiore, and then poured some in Mr. Baltazari's and Mr. Rosselli's glasses.

Mr. Baltazari then raised his glass, and Mr. Rosselli followed suit.

"Health and long life," Mr. Baltazari said.

Mr. Savarese smiled.

"What is it the Irish say? 'May the sun'—or is it the wind?—'always be at your back.' I like that."

"I think 'the wind,' Mr. S.," Mr. Rosselli said.

"I think it's the sun," Mr. Savarese said.

"Now that I think about it, I'm sure you're right," Mr. Rosselli said.

"It doesn't matter, either way," Mr. Savarese said graciously.

"The cherrystones and the swordfish for Mr. Savarese, right?" the maître d'hôtel asked. "And for you, sir?"

"What are you eating, Ricco?" Mr. Rosselli asked.

"Lamb chops."

"Same for me," Mr. Rosselli said. "Sometimes swordfish don't agree with me."

"How would you like them cooked, sir?"

"Pink in the middle."

The clams, on a bed of ice, were served. While they were eating them, Mr. Savarese inquired as to the health of Mr. Baltazari's wife and children, and Mr. Baltazari asked Mr. Savarese to pass on his best respects to Mr. Savarese's wife and mother.

The clams were cleared away, and the entree served.

Mr. Baltazari made a gesture, and a folding screen was put in place, screening the table from the view of anyone in the front part of the restaurant.

"Open another bottle of the Fiore e Fiore," Mr. Baltazari ordered, "and then leave us alone."

Mr. Savarese delicately placed a piece of the swordfish into his mouth, chewed, and nodded.

"This is very nice, Ricco," he said.

"I'm glad you're pleased, Mr. S."

"It has to be fresh," Mr. Savarese said. "Otherwise, when it's been on ice too long, it gets mushy."

"That was swimming in the Gulf of Mexico two days ago, Mr. S."

"Tell me why you told Joe Fierello to make the police officer a good deal," Mr. Savarese said as he placed another piece of swordfish into his mouth. "Tell me about the police officer, is what I want."

"I was going to call you this morning, but then Carlo called and said you was coming, and I figured it could wait until I could tell you in person."

Mr. Savarese nodded, and then gestured with his fork for Mr. Baltazari to continue.

"I try to keep my eyes open," Mr. Baltazari said. "So when I saw this cop flashing a wad in the Warwick . . ."

"How did you know he was a police officer?" Mr. Savarese interrupted.

"I can tell a cop, Mr. S.," Mr. Baltazari said, a bit smugly. "So I checked him out."

"How?"

"I happened to be with a lady," Mr. Baltazari said, just a little uneasily. "I had her do it for me."

"Can this lady be trusted?"

"She's a divorced lady, Mr. S. With a kid. She has a hard time making out on what they pay her at the phone company, so I help her out from time to time."

Mr. Savarese nodded, and Mr. Baltazari went on.

"She struck up a conversation with this guy, like I told her, and come back and told me he's a corporal, working at the airport, and that he just come home from Vegas, where he won a lot of money . . ."

"How much?"

"I don't know exactly, but he was talking about buying a Caddy, so I figure fifteen, twenty big ones, maybe a little more."

Mr. Savarese nodded his understanding again.

"So I figured this was one of those times when you have to do something right away, or forget it," Mr. Baltazari went on. "So I sent the lady back to the cop and told her to tell him she has an uncle who has a car lot who would give him a good deal."

"Is this police officer married?" Mr. Savarese asked.

"I don't *know*, Mr. S. He told Antoinette he's a bachelor."

"It would be better, if he was married," Mr. Savarese said.

"I'll find out for sure and let you know, Mr. S. Anyway, I figured if this wasn't such a hot idea, no harm. So I called Joe, and told him. . . ."

"What you should have done, Ricco," Mr. Savarese said, "was call me and let me talk to Joe."

"I wasn't sure if you would have time to talk with me today, Mr. S."

"Joe called me," Mr. Savarese said, "and asked exactly what was going on. I didn't know, and that was very embarrassing. So I told him I would talk to you and get back to him."

"If I stepped out of line, Mr. S., I'm really sorry. But like I said, I figured no harm . . ."

Mr. Savarese interrupted Mr. Baltazari by holding up the hand with the fork in it.

"Gian-Carlo," he said. "Get on the phone to Joe. Tell him there was a slight misunderstanding. Tell him I have absolute faith in Ricco's judgment."

Mr. Rosselli laid down his knife and fork and pushed himself away from the table.

"There's a pay station in the candy store on the corner," Mr. Savarese said.

"Right, Mr. S.," Mr. Rosselli said.

When he had gone, Mr. Savarese laid his hand on that of Mr. Baltazari.

"Ricco," he said. "This may be more important than you know. This police officer works at the airport? You're sure of that?"

"That's what he told Antoinette."

"Do you recall reading, or seeing on the television, two months back, about the police officer who was killed in an auto accident on the way from the shore?"

"I seem to remember something about that, Mr. S."

"He was a friend of ours, Ricco."

"I didn't know that, Mr. S."

"And he worked at the airport. And now that he's gone, we don't have a friend at the airport. That's posing certain problems for us. Serious problems, right now."

"Oh."

"This police officer you found could be very useful to us, Ricco."

"I understand."

"Whatever is done with him has to be done very carefully, you understand. But at the same time, so long as we don't have a friend at the airport, the problems we are having there are not going to go away."

"I understand," Mr. Baltazari said, although he had no idea what Mr. S. had going at the airport.

"I want you to let me know what goes on, when it happens,

Ricco. And while I trust your judgment, whenever there is any question at all in your mind about what to do, I want you to call me and we'll decide what to do together. You understand me, Ricco?"

"Absolutely, Mr. S."

"Why don't you go get us some coffee, Ricco?"

"Certainly, Mr. S."

Marion Claude Wheatley did not own an automobile, and had not for several years. He suspected, and then had proved by putting all the figures down on paper, that it was much cheaper, considering the price of automobiles and their required maintenance, and especially the price of insurance, to rent a car when he needed one.

And the inconveniences—particularly that of getting groceries from the supermarket checkout counter to the house—were overwhelmed by the elimination of annoyances not owning an automobile provided.

Paying his automobile insurance had especially annoyed him. There were, he was quite sure, actuarial reasons for the insurance company's classifications of people they insured. They were, after all, a business, not a charitable organization. Statistically, it could be proved that an unmarried male between twenty-one and thirty-five living in Philadelphia could be expected to cost the insurance company far more in settling claims than a thirty-six-year-old who was married and lived, say, in New Hope or Paoli. But there was an exception to every rule, and they should have acknowledged that.

He had never had a traffic violation in his life, had never been involved in an accident, and did not use his automobile to commute to work. He drove it back and forth to the supermarket and every month to New Jersey to check on the farm. Sometimes, on rare occasions, such as when Hammersmith, or someone like him, felt obliged to have him to dinner, he drove it at night out to Bryn Mawr, or someplace.

But most of the time the car had sat in the garage, letting its battery discharge.

He had tried to make this point to his insurance broker, who had not only been unsympathetic to his reasoning but had practically laughed at him.

He had solved both problems by selling the car and changing insurance brokers. Marion believed that when you know something is right, you do it.

And he had learned that while renting a car wasn't as cheap as the rental companies advertising would have one believe, it was possible, by carefully reading the advertisements and taking advantage of discounts of one kind or another, to rent a car at perfectly reasonable figures.

When he returned to his office from having lunch with Hammersmith at the Union League, he spent the next forty-five minutes calling around and arranging a car for the weekend. The best price was offered, this time, by Hertz. If he picked up the car at the airport, not downtown, after six-thirty on Friday, and returned it not later than eleven-thirty on Saturday, they would charge him for only one twenty-four-hour day, providing he did not add more than two hundred miles to the odometer. They would also provide him a "standard" size car, for the price of a "compact."

It averaged between 178.8 and 192.4 miles, round trip (he didn't really understand why there should be a difference, unless the odometers themselves were inaccurate) from the airport to the farm, so he would be within the 200-mile limitation. And since he was getting a standard-sized car, that meant he could conceal the equipment he was taking to the farm in the trunk.

Marion Claude Wheatley knew enough about explosives to know that the greater distance one can put between detonators and explosives the better. He didn't think the Lord would cause an accident now, but it was better to be safe than sorry. Marion knew that the Lord would probably not be at all forgiving, if through his own carelessness he had an accident, and hurt—or disintegrated—himself while having a test run of the demolition program for the Vice President at the farm.

The only risky part would be getting from the house to the airport in the taxicab to pick up the car. He would have to have the detonators, half a dozen of them, in his suit jacket breast pocket. They were getting pretty old now, and with age came instability. There were half a dozen ways in which they could be inadvertently set off. He would carry the Composition C-4 in his attaché case, as usual. The cabdriver might look askance if he asked to put the attaché case in the trunk, with the suitcases, particularly if it was a small taxi, and there would not be a lot of room.

The risk was that something would set off one of the detonators. If that happened, it was a certainty that the other five detonators would also detonate. The technical phrase was "sympathetic detonation." If one detonator went off, and then, microseconds later, the other five, it was a possibility, even a likelihood, that the Composition C-4 would detonate sympathetically.

It was a risk that would have to be taken. The more he thought about it, the less worried he became. If something happened in the taxicab, the Lord, who knew everything, would understand that he had been doing the best he knew how. And if he permitted Marion to be disintegrated, who would be available to disintegrate the Vice President?

# NINE

Joe Fierello did not like Paulo Cassandro. The sonofabitch had always been arrogant, long before he'd made his bones and become a made man, and now he was fucking insufferable. Joe didn't really understand why they had made the sonofabitch a made man.

But that didn't matter. What was was, and you don't let a made man know that you think he's really an ignorant asshole.

"Paulo!" Joe called happily when, around half past two, Paulo got out of the back seat of his Jaguar sedan and walked up to the office. "How are you, pal? What can I do for you?"

"A mutual friend wanted to make sure that nothing goes wrong when your niece comes in later."

"Nothing will, Paulo. I talked with Gian-Carlo not more than an hour ago."

"I just talked with Mr. S., and he suggested I come down here and explain exactly what has to be done."

Joe Fierello was more than a little curious about that. When Gian-Carlo Rosselli said something, you knew it was direct from Mr. S. So what was Paulo Cassandro doing here?

"Let me know what I can do," Joe said.

"You know this guy coming is a cop?"

Joe nodded.

"What Mr. S. wants you to do is sell him a really nice car . . ."

"I was going to."

". . . at a special price. Like a thousand, fifteen hundred under Blue Book loan."

The Blue Book was a small, shirt-pocket-size listing of recent automobile transactions, published for the automotive trade. It listed the average retail sale price of an automobile, the average amount of money a bank or finance company had loaned for an installment purchase, and the average price dealers had paid as a trade-in.

"You got it."

"And he wants you to pay him at least a grand more for his trade-in than it's worth."

"Any friend of Mr. S.'s . . ."

"Don't be a wiseass, Joe. This is business."

"Sorry."

"Yeah. You got a Xerox machine, right?"

"Sure."

"We're going to make up a little file on this cop. In it will be copies of this week's Blue Book showing what his trade is worth, and what the car you're going to sell him is worth. And then, on Tuesday, when you run his trade-in through the auction, where you will give it away, we want a Xerox of that too."

"This has all been explained to me, Paulo," Joe said.

"Yeah, well, Mr. S. obviously figured somebody better explain it again, so there would be no mistakes, which is why I'm here, okay?"

"Absolutely."

"And in addition to everything else you're going to do nice for this cop," Paulo went on, "you're going to give him this."

He handed him a printed form. Joe looked at it without understanding. It bore the logotype of the Oaks and Pines Resort Lodge in the Poconos, and it said that the Bearer was entitled to have a room and all meals, plus unlimited free tennis and two rounds of golf.

"What is this?"

"It's what they call a comp," Paulo explained. "This place is owned by a friend of Mr. S.'s. Let's say, for example, they buy a case of soap to wash the dishes. Or two cases, something worth a couple of hundred bucks. Instead of paying them cash, the lodge people give them one of these. *Retail*, it's worth more than the two hundred. *Cost-wise* maybe a hundred. So the guy who came up with the soap gets more than the soap is worth, and the lodge people get the soap for less than the guy wanted. *Capisce?*"

"I seen a comp coupon before, Paulo," Joe said. "What I was asking was, is this cop gonna be a tennis player? Or a golf player?"

"He gets to take the girl to a hotel," Paulo said. "He don't give a fuck about golf."

Joe still looked confused, and Paulo took pity on him.

"There's a story going around, I personally don't know if it's true or not, that in some of these lodge places in the Poconos you can gamble in the back room."

Joe now nodded his understanding.

"You tell this guy you shoot a little craps at this place from time to time, and they sent you the comp coupon, and you can't use it, so he can have it."

"Right."

"Don't fuck this up, Joe. Mr. S. is personally interested in this."

"You tell Mr. S. not to worry."

"He's not worrying. I'm not worrying. You should be the one that's worrying."

Antoinette Marie Wolinski Schermer had moved back in with her parents when Eddie, that sonofabitch, had moved out on her and Brian, which was all she could do, suspecting correctly that getting child support out of Eddie was going to be like pulling teeth.

That hadn't worked out. Her mother, especially, and her father were Catholic and didn't believe in divorce no matter what a sonofabitch you were married to, no matter if he slapped you around whenever he had two beers in him. What they expected her to do was go to work, save her money, and wait around the house for the time when she could straighten things out with Eddie.

No going out, in other words.

She had met Ricco Baltazari in the Reading Terminal Market on Market Street. She had gone there for lunch, and so had he. She decided later, when she found out that he owned Ristorante Alfredo, which was before she found out that he was connected with the Mob, that he had probably got bored with the fancy food in his restaurant and wanted a hot Italian sausage with onions and peppers, which was what she was having when she saw him looking at her.

She had noticed him too, saw that he was a really good-looking guy, that he was dressed real nice, and that when he paid for his sausage and pepper and onions, he had a wad of fifties and hundreds as thick as his thumb.

It probably had something to do, too, with what people said about opposites attracting. She was blonde (she only had to touch it up to keep it light, not dye it, the way most blondes had to) and fair-skinned, and he was sort of dark olive-skinned with really black hair.

The first time she noticed him, she wondered what it would be like doing it with him, never suspecting that she would find out that same night.

The first night, he picked her up outside work in his Cadillac and they went first to a real nice restaurant in Jersey, outside Cherry Hill, where everybody seemed to know him, and the manager or whatever sent a bottle of champagne to the table. Ricco told her right out that he was married, but didn't get along with his old lady, but couldn't divorce her because his mother was old and a Catholic, and you know how Catholics feel about divorce.

After dinner, they went to a motel, not one of the el cheapos that lined Admiral Wilson Boulevard, but to the Cherry Hill Inn, which was real nice, and had in the bathroom the first whatchamacallit that Antoinette had ever seen. She had to ask Ricco what it was for.

The truth of the matter was that when he was driving her back to her parents' house she thought that she had blown it, that she had been too easy to pick up, that she had gone to the motel with him on the First Date, and that once there, she had been a little too enthusiastic. She hadn't been with anybody in months, and the two whiskey sours and then the champagne and then the two Amaretto liqueurs afterward had put her more than a little into the bag.

Antoinette figured, in other words, that Ricco had got what he wanted (probably more than he expected) and that was the last she would ever see of him. She could have played it smarter, she supposed, but the vice versa was also true. She had got what she wanted too, a nice dinner, a nice ride in a Caddy, and then what happened in the motel, which she had needed and wanted from the moment she first saw him trying to look down her blouse.

But then a week later, when she walked out of the building after work, there he was at the curb, looking real nice, and smiling at her, and holding the door of his Caddy open for her.

He told her that he would have called her sooner, but his wife was being a bitch, and he couldn't arrange it. She told him that she understood, she had been married to someone like that herself, a real bastard.

He told her he would like to show her his restaurant, but that she understood why he couldn't do that, with his wife and all, and she told him she understood. The second night, they had gone to the bar in the Warwick Hotel, and then across the street to a bar that had a piano player, and then back across the street to the Warwick, to a nice hotel suite he said a business associate kept all the time so he could use it when he was in town.

When she went home that night, her father and mother were waiting up for her like she was sixteen or seventeen, instead of a woman who was twenty-three and had a kid, and said she looked like a whore and smelled like a drunk and they weren't going to put up with that. And who was the Guinea in the Cadillac, some gangster?

The next time she saw Ricco, three days later, she told him what had happened, and that if they were going to do anything, they would have to do it early, so she wouldn't get hell when she got home.

He asked her why she still lived at home, and she told him about Eddie and Brian, and how Eddie, that sonofabitch, wasn't paying child support. He told her maybe something could be worked out; he would look into it.

The first thing that happened was that Eddie, out of the goddamned blue, sent a Western Union money order for four hundred bucks, which wasn't all he owed, of course, but was four hundred Antoinette didn't expect to get.

And then she heard from her mother that she had heard from Eddie's mother that Eddie had gotten mugged going home from work, that two white guys had done a real job on him, knocked out a couple of teeth, and broken his glasses and a couple of ribs, and taken all his money.

Antoinette wasn't stupid. She knew that the last thing Eddie would have done if he had got mugged and they took all his money would suddenly decide to send child support. And three days after the Western Union money order came, there was one from the Post Office, what he owed for two weeks child support, plus twenty dollars on account.

The only way Eddie would suddenly decide to start doing what was right was because somebody had convinced him that he better do right, and Antoinette suspected that Ricco was that somebody.

Ricco wouldn't admit it, of course, but what he said was that bastards who won't support their own children deserve whatever happens to them, like losing a couple of teeth.

The second thing that happened was that Ricco said he knew where she could get a nice apartment, a couple of blocks from the Warwick, the only problem being she couldn't have a kid in there. Antoinette told him it didn't matter whether she could have Brian or not, on what the phone company was paying her, she couldn't afford it. He said he would be happy to help out with the whole thing.

Her mother and father threw a fit when she said she was moving out, and her father said he knew it had something to do with that Guinea gangster with the shiny Cadillac, and her mother said she was making the mistake of her life, because Eddie was straightening himself out, like for example paying the child support for one thing. But she moved out anyway, and came to believe that her mother and father were really glad she had, because that way, except when she saw him on weekends, they had Brian all to themselves.

The apartment was nice, and Ricco not only picked up the rent, but was always slipping her a fifty or a hundred and telling her to buy herself something. She knew that she was kidding herself whenever she thought about maybe getting him to marry her. He was going to stay married to his Guinea princess for ever.

The only thing that had ever really bothered her was the first time he told her that he had a friend from Chicago that was coming to town and he wanted her to be very nice to him, and she knew what very nice meant. That made her feel like a hooker, but she had just moved into the apartment, and couldn't just move back home again, so she did it. It wasn't as bad as she thought, the guy was nicer than she thought he would be, and to tell the truth, he was pretty good between the sheets, and when he went back to Chicago, Ricco handed her four fifties and told her to buy herself a cheese-steak or something.

And it didn't happen often, maybe two, three, four times a year. It wasn't as if he was telling her to go stand on a sidewalk someplace and wink at strange men, just be very nice to people who were important to Ricco. That didn't seem to be, considering, all that much for him to ask of her.

This Vito Lanza the cop was something else. This was the first time something like this had happened. But if Ricco wanted her to do it, it was important. And what the hell, the truth was Vito was kind of cute, and not too bad in the bedroom department, either. It wasn't as if he made her want to throw up, like that.

Ricco told her he wanted her to be very nice to Vito the cop until he told her different. He said the cop was in a position to be useful to some business associates of his, and part of that meant getting him to figure that he owed her something.

It was pretty clear to Antoinette that it had something to with his being a cop at the airport. They wanted him to be looking the other way when something happened, something like that. It wasn't as if they were *after* Vito, anything like that. If they were after him, the same thing that had happened to Eddie would already have happened to him.

Vito was waiting for her outside the apartment in his Buick when she got home from work. He acted like he wanted to go up to the apartment with her, and then go see her Uncle Joe, but she told him that her uncle expected them now, before he had to go home, and they could come back to the apartment later.

Take care of business first. Antoinette had learned that from Ricco. Ricco was always saying that.

Marion reached the farm about quarter to nine. There had been no cars on the highway when he turned off onto the dirt county road, and he encountered no cars on the dirt road as he drove to the farm.

There are approximately 1,200,000 acres in that portion of southern New Jersey known as the Pine Barrens. Statistically speaking, the built-up portions of southern New Jersey represent a very small fraction of the total land area. The term "Pine Barrens," Marion had learned, had been applied to the area from the earliest days of colonization. "Barrens" meant the area was barren, except for stunted pine trees.

There were some exceptions of course. Some people had acquired title to land within the Barrens with the intention of farming it. Some had succeeded, including, for a time, some of Marion's maternal ancestors. It was a mystery to Marion how they had managed to eke a living out of their double section (1,280 acres, more or less, as the deed described it) but there was no question that they had, from the early 1800s for almost a century.

The house, as closely as he had been able to determine, had been built circa 1810, and the farm had been in use until just before World War I. He had no idea why it had not been sold, but it hadn't, and it had come to him via inheritance.

For a long time, he had thought that the reason he had not sold it was because no one wanted it. The house was 6.3 miles from the nearest paved road. There was a well, but the water was foul-tasting, and while Marion did not pretend to understand things like this, he suspected it was somehow contaminated. The taxes were negligible, and he had simply kept the farm.

Now he knew, of course, that it hadn't been his decision at all, but the Lord's. The Lord had had plans for the farm all along.

The fences, except for vestiges here and there, had long ago disappeared, as had the wooden portions of the farmhouse, and the barns and other outlying structures. What was left was a three-room building, partly constructed from field stone and partly from crude brick.

Marion's father had replaced the windows in the building, and installed a tin roof when Marion was a little boy. Marion now understood that his father had had some half-baked idea of making the farmhouse into some sort of vacation cabin, but that idea had sort of petered out. Marion's mother had not liked driving into the Pine Barrens to spend the weekend cooking on a camping stove and using an outside privy. There was absolutely nothing to do at the farm but sit around and talk and look out at stunted pine trees.

She had, he now understood, tried. She had planted various kinds of flowers and bushes, most of which had died, but some of which, roses and some bushes the names of which he had never known, had survived and even flourished. You couldn't see the farmhouse, behind the vegetation, until you were within a hundred yards.

There were unpaved roads running along the south and north property lines, maintained as little as possible by the county, who showed up once a year with road scrapers. There were two roads, more properly described as paths, leading from the unpaved roads. One of them led to the farmhouse, and the other, nothing more than earth beaten into two tracks, simply crossed between the two unpaved county roads.

When Marion reached the house, he parked the car behind the house, and then, using a flashlight to light his way, walked around to the front, unlocked the padlock, removed it from the hasp, and let himself in.

He flashed the light around the room. There were no signs of intruders. Standing the flashlight on its end, he took a Coleman lantern from a shelf, filled the tank from a gallon can of Coleman Fluid, pumped it up and got it going. Then he extinguished the flashlight, and carried the Coleman lantern and the can of Coleman Fluid into the bedroom, where he repeated the fueling and lighting procedure for a second Coleman lantern.

He then returned to the front room, where he refueled a Coleman stove with Coleman liquid. Unless properly handled, the Coleman lanterns and stoves were dangerous. Marion could not understand why people were blind to that. The newspapers were always full of stories of people who were burned when they tried to refuel lanterns and stoves while they were still hot.

He then went out to the rental car and brought the six detonators into the house. He carefully placed them in a drawer of the dresser in the bedroom, lying them on a bed of work shirts and underwear, for a cushion under them, and then carefully placed more work shirts and underwear on top of them. Marion knew that there was no such thing as being too careful with detonators.

Then he returned to the car again, took his suitcase out of it, and carefully locked it. In the interests of safety, it was better to leave the Composition C-4 right where it was, in the car.

He went into the bedroom, and changed out of his suit and dress shirt into what he thought of as his farm clothes, a flannel shirt, denim overalls, and ankle-high work shoes.

Then he made another trip out to the car, unlocked it, took out the groceries he'd bought just outside of Camden, locked the car again, and carried the groceries into the house.

He pumped up the Coleman stove, got it going, and cooked his supper, a hamburger steak with onions, instant mashed potatoes, lima beans, and coffee. For dessert he had ice cream. It was cold, but no longer frozen, but that couldn't be helped. It was just too much of a nuisance to carry ice to the farm.

After he finished eating, he washed the dishes and the pots and pans and put the garbage into one of the grocery bags. He would take it to the garbage dump in the morning.

If, he thought, making a wry little joke with himself, if there was still any place to dump garbage in his garbage dump.

The problem with the farm, Marion often thought, was exactly opposite from the problem he had with the house in Philadelphia. In the city, people were always trying—and often succeeding—in taking away things that belonged to him. At the farm, people were always giving him things he hadn't asked for and didn't want. Such as worn-out automobile tires, refrigerators, mattresses, and bed springs.

He didn't like it, of course. No civilized person could be anything but annoyed with the transformation of one's private property into a public dump. But he understood why it had happened, and why the police couldn't do much about it.

While the land was mostly flat, there were two depressions, each more than two acres in size, both of them touching the road that cut across the property from one county road to the other. The garbage dumpers simply backed their trucks up to the edge of the depressions and unloaded their worn-out mattresses, rusty bed springs, old tires, and broken refrigerators.

Marion had from time to time complained to the authorities about the unauthorized dumping, but to no avail. They told him that if he, or they, caught someone dumping, they would of course deal with the matter. But since there was no one living in the area, police patrols seldom visited it, their presence being required elsewhere.

His only solution, they told him, was to both fence and post the property. Fencing 1,280 acres was of course for financial reasons out of the question. And when he had put up PRIVATE PROPERTY—TRESPASSERS WILL BE PROSECUTED signs where the paths began at the county roads, the only response had been that the garbage dumpers, or someone else, had used them for target practice. It had been a waste of money.

Four months before, on one of his monthly weekends at the farm, he had taken the canvas tarpaulin off the old Fordson tractor his father had bought years before, jump-started it with jumper cables from his rented Chevrolet, and driven it around the farm on what he thought of as his quarterly inspection of the property.

This time there had been something new in the larger of the two garbage dumps. Lockers. They appeared to have been in a fire. There were approximately fifty of them, each about three feet square. They were painted green, and they were constructed in units of three.

Curiosity had overcome his disgust and annoyance, and he'd gotten off the Fordson, leaving it running, and gone down in the depression and opened them. It was only then, when he found keys in most of them, that he recognized them for what they were. They were the lockers one found in railroad stations, where travelers stored their suitcases. You put a quarter in the slot, which allowed you to withdraw the key. When you returned to the locker for your belongings and put the key back in the lock, the door could be opened, but the mechanism now seized the key and would hold it until another quarter was deposited.

Marion had happened to have two quarters in his pocket, and tested two of the lockers. They were operable.

He had then regretted having thrown the fifty cents away, and climbed out of the depression and got back on the Fordson and drove back to the farmhouse. He had made his supper, and then got on his knees and prayed for the souls of those of his men whom the Lord had chosen to take unto Him in 'Nam.

He would have thought that he would have given no further thought to the lockers than he had to the refrigerators and worn-out tires or the other garbage, but they stayed in his mind. Where had they come from? He thought he would have heard if there had been a fire in a railroad station. Why, since some of them had hardly been damaged, had they been discarded?

He had thought of the lockers not only during that weekend on the farm, but often afterward. There had been no answers until he had read in *The Philadelphia Inquirer* that the Vice President was going to arrive in Philadelphia and depart from Philadelphia by train, at the 30th Street Station.

Then, of course, it had all become quite clear. The reason the lockers had been dumped on the farm was because the Lord wanted him to have the lockers to use when he disintegrated the Vice President.

The moment this had popped into his mind, Marion knew that it was true. There was no need to get on his knees and beg the Lord for a sign. The Lord had already given him a sign, back in 'Nam. Marion had personally gone to the locker room of the Hotel de Indochine to investigate the explosion that had taken the lives of twenty-six American civilian technicians. The Vietcong had set off explosives, almost certainly Composition C-4, in half a dozen lockers. He thought that each charge had probably been a half pound of C-4, around which chain had been wrapped. Each charge had functioned like an oversize fragmentation hand grenade. The American civilians had literally been disintegrated.

The lockers in the Hotel de Indochine were not identical to the ones that had been dumped in the depression—they had been eighteen inches by five feet, not three feet square. But that was a detail that didn't seem to matter.

There were rows of lockers like the ones that had been dumped all over 30th Street Station. All he was going to have to do was install a device in one locker in each of the rows. And then be in a position to see the Vice President, so that he could detonate the explosive device that would disintegrate him.

It was possible, even probable, Marion knew, that people who had not offended the Lord would also be disintegrated. But there were two ways to look at that. It couldn't be helped, for one thing, and certainly the Lord would somehow compensate in Heaven those whose premature deaths had been made necessary in order to carry out His will.

Marion had realized that it was becoming more and more clear why the Lord had chosen him as His instrument to carry out His will. There were not that many people around with his level of expertise in making lethal devices from readily available material. And there were not very many people around with access to a testing area. You can't cause an explosion in very many places without causing a good deal of curiosity. The farm, in the middle of the Pine Barrens, was one of the very few places where an explosion would not be heard.

After Marion had put the garbage from the meal into the paper bag from the grocery store, he turned off the Coleman lantern in the kitchen and went into the bedroom.

He made the bed, laid out fresh underwear and socks for the morning, took off his clothes, and then turned off the other Coleman lantern. He dropped to his knees by the side of the bed, and prayed the Lord's grace on himself as he began to carry out His will, and then for the souls of the boys who the Lord had taken into Heaven from Vietnam, and then he got in bed and was almost instantly asleep.

Marion woke at first light. He changed into the linen he had laid out the night before, and then made his breakfast. Bacon, two fried eggs, fried "toast," coffee, and a small can of tomato juice. After he ate he washed the dishes and pots and pans, and added the refuse to the garbage from supper.

He then began to lay out on the table everything he would need to make the devices. There were two large rolls of duct tape, approximately thirty feet of one-inch link chain, the shortwave receivers from Radio Shack, and an assortment of tools, including a large bolt cutter. Then he went out to the car and brought in the Composition C-4.

The basic device would be two quarter-pound blocks of Composition C-4, which looked not unlike sticks of butter, except of course they were gray in color, and had a hole to accommodate the detonator. He didn't have as many detonators as he would have liked to have had, so for the testing, he would use one detonator per device. The devices he would install in the lockers in 30th Street Station would have two detonators per device. Redundancy was the term. The chances of two detonators failing to function were infinitesimal.

First he taped a dozen blocks of Composition C-4 together, two blocks to a unit. Then he wound chain around one of the double blocks, as tightly as he could, twisting the links so that they sort of doubled up on each other. Then, holding the last link carefully in his hand, he unwound the chain. He took the bolt cutter and cut the link he had held in his hand.

Then he measured off five more lengths of chain, using the first length as a template. He then wound the chain around the six double blocks of Composition C-4, and then wound that with the duct tape.

That was all that he felt he should do, in the interests of safety, in the house. The rest he would do on site.

He put the partially constructed devices into a canvas satchel, and carried that outside to where the Fordson sat under its tarpaulin. He removed the tarpaulin, and checked to see that there was sufficient fuel in the tank. Then from a small, two-wheel trailer attached to the rear of the tractor, he took a set of jumper cables.

He then started the rental car, drove it to the tractor, opened the hood, and connected the jumper cables. The tractor started almost immediately, which Marion interpreted as a good omen. He set the throttle at fast idle.

He then put the satchel with the partially constructed devices in the utility trailer, and then, in four trips into the house, took the garbage, the shortwave equipment from Radio Shack, and most of the tools from the table and loaded it into the trailer. Finally he went into the bedroom and took the detonators from the dresser. He wrapped each very carefully in two socks, one outside the other, and then put the padded detonators in a tin Saltines box.

He took two pillows from the bed, and carried them and the Saltines tin box with the detonators to the trailer, where he carefully laid the Saltines box on one pillow, covered it with the second pillow, and then put the bricks on the upper pillow to keep it in place.

Then he disconnected the jumper cables from the tractor, got on it, and drove off between the stunted pines. He drove very carefully, so there would be no great risk of somehow, despite all his precautions, setting off one of the detonators.

When he reached the garbage dump, he decided that the first order of business was making sure the shortwave transmitter and the receivers worked. He had tested them in Philadelphia, but electronic equipment didn't like to be bounced around and it was better to be sure.

He dug out the Saltines box from between the pillows, and carried it carefully two hundred yards into the pines as a safety precaution. Then he returned to the garbage dump and carefully rigged the test setup.

When he pressed the key on the transmitter, the capacitors that he had installed in the receiver where the speaker had been began to accumulate electrical energy and then discharged. The 15-watt 110-volt refrigerator bulb Marion had installed where the detonator would ultimately be glowed brightly for a moment. There would be more than enough juice to fire the detonator.

He disconnected everything, in the interest of safety, walked back into the pines, and took one detonator from the Saltine box. He went back to the garbage dump and carefully slipped the detonator into one of the double blocks of Composition C-4. He taped this, except for the leads, into place with duct tape.

Then he carried this down into the garbage dump, to one of the lockers, and propped the door open with his shoulder as he inserted the device, then hooked the receiver up to the exposed leads.

He then closed the locker door, put a quarter in the slot, removed the key, and climbed up out of the garbage dump. He got back on the tractor and drove what he estimated to be two hundred yards away, and then stopped. Carrying the transmitter with him, he walked fifty feet from the tractor and then turned on the Radio Shack transmitter.

He depressed the key. Nothing happened.

*Kaboom!*

Marion smiled.

# TEN

Staff Inspector Peter Wohl, wearing a faded green polo shirt and somewhat frayed khaki trousers, both liberally stained with oil spots and various colors of paint was in the process of filling a stainless-steel thermos bottle with coffee when his door buzzer went off.

He went quickly to it and pulled it open. A slight, olive-skinned twenty-four-year-old was standing there, dressed in a somewhat flashy suit and obviously fresh from the barber.

"Hello, Hay-zus," Wohl said. "Come on in."

"Good morning, sir," Martinez said.

"You pulled your car in the garage?"

"Yes, sir."

"I just made coffee. Will you have some?"

"Thank you, please."

Wohl gestured for Martinez to have a seat on the couch under the oil painting of the naked Rubenesque lady, took two mugs from a kitchen cabinet, carried them to the coffee table, fetched the thermos, and sat down beside Martinez on the couch.

"So how are things at the airport?" Wohl asked with a smile.

The question had been intended to put Martinez at ease. It had, Wohl saw, almost the opposite reaction. Martinez was almost visibly uncomfortable.

"I'm not pushing you, Hay-zus," Wohl said. "You've only been out there a couple of weeks. I don't think anybody expected you to learn very much in that short a time."

"Yes, sir," Jesus said, then blurted: "I think I figured out how I would get drugs, or for that matter anything else, out of there."

"How?"

"For little packages, anyway. Coke. Heroin. Are they still trying to smuggle diamonds, jewels, into this country?"

*I really don't know,* Wohl thought. *That's the first time jewelry has come up.*

"All the Bureau of Narcotics and Dangerous Drugs mentioned was drugs," Wohl said. "You think someone is smuggling diamonds, gemstones, through the airport?"

"The way it works, on international flights, is that the plane lands and comes up to the terminal. The baggage handlers come out, they open doors in the bottom of the airplane. On the big airplanes, one guy, maybe two guys, actually get in the baggage compartment. Nobody can see them from the ground. If they knew which suitcase had the stuff, they could open it, take out a small package, packages, conceal it on their person, and then send the luggage onto the conveyor belt over to the customs area."

"Hay-zus," Wohl said. "I want to show you something."

He got up and walked to his desk, unlocked a drawer and took out a vinyl-covered loose-leaf notebook. On it was stamped:

## BUREAU OF NARCOTICS AND DANGEROUS DRUGS
### Investigator's Manual
### FOR INTERNAL USE ONLY

Martinez looked at the cover, then opened the manual and flipped through it, and then looked at Wohl for an explanation.

"They sent that over, they thought it would be helpful."

Martinez nodded.

"I took a look at it," Wohl said. "They refer to what you just described as a common means of smuggling."

"I guess it is," Martinez said. "I didn't exactly feel like Sherlock Holmes."

"Maybe not Sherlock Holmes," Wohl said. "But maybe Dick Tracy. It didn't take you long to figure that out."

That was intended, too, to put Martinez at ease. This time, Wohl saw in Martinez's face, it worked.

"When you leave, take this with you. I don't think I have to tell you not to let anybody see it."

"Yeah," Martinez said. "Thank you."

"Okay. So tell me what you've figured out about how someone, a baggage handler, or anyone else, would get a small package out of the airport."

"Well, there's all sorts of people keeping an eye on the baggage handlers. The airline has their security people. Customs is there, and the drug guys, and, of course, our guys. When the baggage handlers come to work, they change into uniforms, coveralls, or whatever, in their locker room. They change back into their regular clothes when they leave work. They have spot checks, they actually search them. What they're looking for is stuff they might have stolen, tools, stuff like that, but if the airlines security people should find a small package, they would damned sure know what it was."

"Unless they were part of the system," Wohl said thoughtfully.

"Yeah, but they're subject to the same sort of spot checks when *they* leave, and also, I think, when they're working. I thought about that. What they *could* do, once one of the baggage handlers had this stuff, is take it from them, and then move into the terminal and pass it to somebody, a passenger, for example. Once they got it into the terminal, that wouldn't be hard."

"You think that's the way it's being done?"

Martinez did not reply directly.

"Another way it could be done, which would not involve the airlines security people, I mean, them being in on it, would be to put the package in another piece of luggage, one being either unloaded off, or being put on, a domestic flight. They don't search domestic luggage."

"But they do have drug-sniffing dogs working domestic luggage."

"Not every place," Martinez argued. "Like for example, Allentown-Bethlehem-Easton. Or Harrisburg."

"Yeah," Wohl agreed.

"The risk the baggage handlers would run would be getting caught with this stuff before they could get rid of it. Which means they would have to know when the plane with the drugs was arriving, and when the plane for, say, Allentown was leaving. And then they would have to arrange it so they worked that plane too."

"How do you think it's being done? Or do you think it's being done?"

"It's being done, all right," Martinez said. "And I think we have a dirty cop involved in it."

"How?" Wohl asked.

"Nobody searches the cops. And nobody, except maybe the sergeant, or one of the lieutenants, asks a cop what he's doing. He's got keys to get onto the ramp, and keys to open the doors leading off the ramp onto the conveyors and into the terminal. I went onto the ramp and watched them unload arriving international airplanes, and nobody said beans to me. I could have been handed, say, three-, four-, even five-kilo bags of coke or heroin, and just walked away with it."

"Five kilos is ten, eleven pounds," Wohl said thoughtfully.

"Worth twenty, twenty-five thousand a K," Martinez said.

"How would you have gotten it out of the airport?"

"Passed it to somebody in the terminal. Put it in a locker, and passed the key to somebody. Or just put it in my car."

"Let me throw this at you," Wohl said. "Add this to the equation. I had a long talk with a BNDD agent. I got him to tell me something his boss didn't happen to mention. There have been two incidents of unclaimed luggage. Both about five weeks ago. Each piece had four Ks of heroin. That's why they're so sure it's coming into Philadelphia."

"The luggage is marked in some way, a name tag, probably with a phony name. If the baggage handler gets to take the stuff out of the bag, he also removes the tag. When the mule gets to the carousel, and sees his baggage, and the tag is still on it, he just doesn't pick it up."

*He didn't think about that before replying,* Wohl thought. *He'd already figured that out as a possibility. He's as smart as a whip.*

"That means giving up four Ks, a hundred thousand dollars worth of drugs."

"The cost of doing business," Martinez replied.

"I don't suppose you have any idea which cop is dirty?" Wohl asked.

"No," Martinez said.

*That was too quick,* Wohl thought.

"I'm not asking for an accusation," Wohl said. "Just a suspicion, a gut feeling. And nothing leaves this room."

"Nothing yet," Martinez said.

That was not the truth. The moment Jesus Martinez had laid eyes on Corporal Vito Lanza, he had had the feeling that something was not right about him. But you don't accuse a brother officer, or even admit you have suspicions about him, unless you have more to go on than the fact that he gambles big money in Las Vegas, and dresses and behaves like a Guinea gangster.

Wohl suspected that Martinez was concealing something from him, but realized he could not press him any more than he had.

One of the telephones in his bedroom rang. Wohl could tell by the sound of the ring that it was his personal, rather than his official, telephone.

*That makes it fairly certain,* he thought as he turned toward the bedroom, *that I am not to be informed that one of my stalwart Highway Patrolmen has just run though a red light into a station wagon full of nuns.*

He had used that for instance as the criteria for telephoning him at his home on weekends. Any catastrophe of less monumental proportions, he had ordered, should be referred to either Captain Michael Sabara, his deputy, or to Captain David Pekach, commanding officer of the Highway Patrol, for appropriate action.

"Excuse me," Wohl said, and went into his bedroom.

*The fact that this is on my personal line,* he thought as he sat down on his bed and reached for the telephone, *does not mean that I am not about to hear something I do not wish to hear, such as Mother reminding me that I have not been to Sunday dinner in a month, so how about tomorrow?*

"Hello?"

"From that tone of voice," his caller said, "what I think I should do is just hang up, but I hate it when people do that to me."

"Hello, Matt," Wohl said, smiling. "What's up?"

"I was wondering how welcome I would be if I drove over there."

*Not at all welcome, with Martinez here. And from the tone of your voice, Detective Payne, I think the smartest thing I could do is tell you, "Sorry, I was just walking out the door."*

"You would be very welcome. As a matter of fact, I was thinking of calling you. I am about to polish the Jaguar and I hate to do that alone. A weak mind and a strong back is just what I need."

"I'll be there in half an hour. Thank you," Detective Payne said, and hung up.

*It is possible,* Wohl thought, *that Matt is coming over here sim-*

*ply as a friend. The reason he sounds so insecure is that he's not sure of the tribal rites. Can a lowly detective and an exalted staff inspector be friends? The answer is sure, but he doesn't know that. And the truth of the matter is, I was glad to hear his voice and I miss him around the office.*

*But clever detective that I am, I don't think that a social visit is all he has in mind. His tone of voice and the "thank you" is not consistent with that.*

*Is he in trouble? Nothing serious, or I would have heard about it. And if he was in a jam, wouldn't he go first to Denny Coughlin?*

*There is a distinct possibility, now that I think about it, that Detective Payne has, now that he's been leading the exciting, romantic life of a real-life detective in the famous East Detective Division for two months, decided that law enforcement is not how he really wants to spend the rest of his life. Unless things have changed a hell of a lot, he has spent his time on recovered stolen vehicles, with maybe a few good burglary of autos thrown in for good measure.*

*If he did decide to quit, he would feel some sort of an obligation to tell me. That would be consistent with his polite asking if he could come over, and then saying "thank you."*

*So what will I do? Tell him to hang in there, things will get better? Or jump on the wise elders bandwagon with his father and Denny Coughlin, and tell him to go to law school?*

The telephone rang again.

"A Highway car ran the light at Broad and Olney, broadsided a station wagon full of nuns, and knocked it into a bus carrying the Philadelphia Rabbinical Council," his caller announced without any opening salutation.

Wohl chuckled. "Good morning, Captain Pekach," he said. "You better be kidding."

"Am I interrupting anything, boss?"

"No. What's up, Dave?"

"It's a beautiful day. Martha's got some shrimp and steaks and we're going to barbecue lunch. Mike and his wife are coming, and I thought maybe you'd be free?"

*Is he inviting me because he likes me, or because I am the boss? Why the hell are you so cynical? Dave is a good guy, and you like Martha. And they are friends. He is not sucking up to the boss.*

*Your cynicism just might have something to do with last night. When are you going to learn, Peter Wohl, that blond hair and splendid boobs do not a nice lady make?*

"I've got somebody coming over, Dave."

"Bring her, the more the merrier."

"It's a him. Specifically, Matt Payne."

"I thought maybe he'd be in touch . . ."

*What the hell does that mean?*

" . . . so bring him too. Martha likes him, and we've got plenty."

"I don't know what his plans are, but I'll be there. Thank you, Dave. When?"

"Noon. Anytime around there."

"Can I bring anything?"

"Nothing but an appetite."

Wohl walked back to his living room, where Martinez was reading the BNDD Investigator's Manual.

"That was Matt Payne," Wohl said. "The first call."

"How's he doing?"

"I understand he's become the East Detectives' specialist on recovered stolen cars," Wohl said, and then added: "He's coming over here."

Martinez closed the BNDD notebook and stood up.

"Then I better get going, huh?"

"I don't think it would be a good idea if he saw you here."

Martinez held up the notebook.

"How soon do you want this back?"

"Whenever you're finished with it. Take your time."

Martinez nodded.

"You're doing a good job, Hay-zus," Wohl said. "I think it's just a question of hanging in there with your eyes open."

"Yes, sir."

"Anytime you want to talk, Hay-zus, about anything at all, you have my personal number."

"Yes, sir."

Martinez stood up, looked at Wohl for a moment, long enough for Wohl to suspect that he was about to say something else, but then, as if he had changed his mind, nodded at Wohl.

"Good morning, sir."

Wohl walked to the door with him and touched his shoulder in a gesture of friendliness as Martinez opened it and stepped outside.

Wohl had just about finished carefully washing his Jaguar when Detective Payne drove onto the cobblestone driveway in his silver Porsche. It showed signs of just having gone through a car wash. The way Payne was dressed, Wohl thought, he looked like he was about to pose for an advertisement in *Esquire*—for either Porsche automobiles, twenty-five-year-old Ambassador Scotch, or Hart, Schaffner & Marx clothing.

Payne handed Wohl a paper bag.

"Present," he said.

"What is it?"

"The latest miracle automobile polish. It's supposed to go on and off with no perceptible effort, and last for a thousand years."

*I am not going to ask him what's on his mind. In his own time, he will tell me.*

"And you believe this?"

"Also in the tooth fairy. But hope springs eternal. I didn't think you would be willing to try it on the Jag, but I thought we could run a comparison test. I'll do mine with this stuff, and you do the Jag with your old-fashioned junk . . ."

"Which comes all the way from England and costs me five ninety-five a can . . ."

". . . and we'll see which lasts longer. You'll notice mine is also freshly washed."

"In a car wash," Wohl said. "I'm surprised you do that. Those brushes are supposed to be hell on a finish. They grind somebody else's dirt into your paint."

*He's looking at me as if I just told him I don't know how to read.*

"You don't believe that?" Wohl asked.

"You know the car wash on Germantown Avenue, right off Easton Road?"

Wohl nodded.

"For four ninety-five, they'll wash your car by hand."

"I didn't know that," Wohl confessed.

"They don't do a bad job, either," Matt said, gesturing toward the Porsche.

*Wisdom from the mouth of babes,* Wohl thought. *One is supposed to never be too old to learn.*

"So I see," Wohl said.

Payne took off his linen jacket, and then rolled up the sleeves of his light blue button-down collar shirt. Then he extended his can of car polish toward Wohl.

"You want to do a fender, or the hood, with this? Then you could really tell."

"The *bonnet*," Wohl said. "On a Jaguar the hood is the *bonnet*. And thank you, no."

Matt opened the hood of his rear-engined Porsche, which was of course the trunk, and took out a package of cheese cloth.

*Why don't I spend the two bucks? Instead of using old T-shirts? Except when I can't find an old T-shirt and have to use a towel that costs more than two bucks?*

"So how is life treating you, Matt?" Wohl asked.

"I thought you would never ask," Matt said. "The good news is that I won six thousand bucks, actually sixty-seven hundred, in Las Vegas, and the bad news is that the IRS gets their share."

*He is not pulling my leg. Jesus Christ, six thousand dollars! Nearer seven!*

"What were you doing in Las Vegas?"

"I was sent out there to bring Penny Detweiler home from the funny farm."

That was a surprising announcement, and Wohl wondered aloud: "How did you get time off?"

"Ostensibly, I was helping with the paperwork in Chief Lowenstein's office. That is the official version."

"Start from the beginning," Wohl said.

Payne examined a layer of polish he had just applied to the front of the Porsche before replying. Then he looked at Wohl.

"My father asked me to meet him for drinks. When I got there, Denny Coughlin was there. They asked me how I would like to go to Nevada and bring Penny home, and I said I would love that, but unfortunately, I couldn't get the time off. Then Uncle Denny said, 'That's been taken care of,' and Dad said, 'Here's your tickets.' "

*I wonder what Matt Lowenstein thought about that? Not to mention Matt's sergeant, lieutenant, and captain in EDD.*

"They won't hassle you in East Detectives, Matt, if that's what you're worrying about. That couldn't have happened without Chief Lowenstein knowing about it, ordering it. Your response should be the classic 'mine not to reason why, mine but to do what I'm told.' "

"I'm not worried about East Detectives. What I'm wondering about is how you feel about me coming back to Special Operations."

*Shit! That's disappointing. I didn't think he'd ask to get transferred back. I thought he was smart enough to know that would be a lousy idea, and I didn't think he would impose on our friendship for a favor. Helping him out of a jam is one thing, doing something for him that would be blatant special treatment is something en-*

*tirely different. But, on the other hand, the only thing he's known
since he's joined the Department is special treatment.*

"Matt," Wohl said carefully. "I think your coming back to Special Operations would be, at the very least, ill-advised. And let me clear the air between us. I'm a little disappointed that you can't see that, and even more disappointed that you would ask."

Wohl saw on Matt's face that what he had said had stung. He hated that. But he had said what had to be said.

Matt bent over the front of the Porsche and applied wax to another two square feet. Then he straightened and looked at Wohl again.

"Well, I suspected that I might not be welcomed like the prodigal returning to the fold, but just to clear the air between us, Inspector, I didn't ask to come back. You or anybody else. I was told to report to Chief Lowenstein's office at half past one yesterday, and when I got there, a sergeant told me to clean out my locker in East and report to Special Operations Monday morning."

"God*dammit*!" Wohl exploded.

"I could resign, I suppose. Suicide seems a bit more than the situation calls for," Matt said.

"You can knock off the 'Inspector' crap. I apologize for thinking what I was thinking. I should have known better."

"Yeah, you should have known better," Matt said. It was not the sort of thing a very junior detective should say, and it wasn't expressed in the tone of voice a junior detective should use to a staff inspector who was also his division commander. But Wohl was not offended.

*For one thing, I deserve it. For another, in a strange perverted way, that was a remark by one friend to another.*

"I wouldn't have said what I said, obviously, if I had known you were coming back," Wohl said. "This is the first I've heard of it."

"It was on the teletype," Matt said, and reached into the Porsche and handed Wohl a sheet of teletype paper. "Charley McFadden took that home from Northwest Detectives."

GENERAL: 1365 04/23/74 17:20 FROM COMMISSIONER
RECEIPT NO. 107
PAGE 1 OF 1

THE FOLLOWING TRANSFERS WILL BE EFFECTIVE 1201 AM
MON 04/23/74

| NAME | RANK | PAYROLL | FROM | TO |
|------|------|---------|------|-----|
| **** | **** | ******* | **** | ** |

ROBERT J. FODE   LT   108988   9TH DISTRICT   PLANS &
ANALYSIS

MATTHEW M. PAYNE   DET   126786   EAST DETECTIVE
SPECIAL OPERATIONS

TADDEUS CZERNICH
POLICE COMMISSIONER

"I wonder," Wohl said, and there was sarcasm and anger in his voice, "why no one thought I would be interested in this?"

"Maybe what you need is a good administrative assistant, to keep something like this from happening again," Matt said.

"No," Wohl said. "I've got an administrative assistant. Until I figure out what to do with you, you can work for Jason Washington."

Before the words were out of his mouth, Wohl had modified that quick decision. Matt would possibly wind up working for Jason somewhere down the line, he decided, but where he would go to work immediately was for Jack Malone.

Malone could use some help, certainly, in his new role in Dignitary Protection. And if Matt were working with him, he would not only learn something that would broaden his general education, but also just might keep Malone from doing something stupid. Malone was a good cop, but working with the feds was always risky.

Wohl decided this was not the time to tell Matt he had changed his mind. Instead, he changed the subject.

"We're invited to a party," he said.

"Oh?"

"Steak, you know, barbecue, at Martha Peebles's. Dave Pekach called up right after you did, invited me and, when I said you were coming over, said to bring you too."

"Fine," Matt said. "Maybe *he'll* glad to have me back."

"It is not nice to mock your superiors. Detective Payne. Make a note of that. Carve it in your forehead with a dull knife, for example."

Payne laughed, and Wohl smiled back at him.

*I am glad he's back.*

He remembered an insight he'd had about Matt Payne several months before, when Matt was still in Special Operations and had found himself in trouble not of his own making, and Wohl had jumped in with both feet in his defense before asking why. The reason, he had finally concluded, was that he thought of Matt as his younger brother.

"How is the Detweiler girl?" Wohl asked.

"She looks all right," Matt said.

"People do lick their drug problems, Matt."

"And I'll bet if you looked hard enough, you could find a pig who really can whistle."

"Is that a general feeling, or is there something specific?"

Matt looked at him and shrugged helplessly.

"She told me she was in love with Tony the Zee," Matt said.

"Have you considered that may be simple female insanity, not connected with narcotics?"

Matt laughed again.

"No," he said. "But isn't that a cheerful thought?"

Peter Wohl was not prepared to admit that Matt Payne's miracle auto polish was better in every way than his imported British wax, but there was no doubt that it went on and off faster, and with less effort.

For at least the last fifteen minutes, Detective Payne had been leaning on his gleaming Porsche, sucking on a bottle of beer and smiling smugly as he waited for Staff Inspector Wohl to finish waxing his Jaguar.

"Mine will last longer," Wohl said, when he had finally finished.

"We don't know that, do we?" Matt replied. "And you will notice that *I* am not sweating."

"No one loves a smartass."

"It is difficult for someone like myself to be humble," Matt said.

"I wonder what a contract on the mayor would cost?"

Matt picked up on that immediately.

"You think he was responsible for sending me back to Special Operations?"

Wohl put the galvanized steel bucket, the car polish, and the rags into the garage, came out again, closed the door, and motioned for Matt to follow him into his apartment before replying.

"Who else? Not only does it smell like one of his friendly suggestions for general improvement of departmental operations, but who else would dare challenge the collective wisdom of Lowenstein and Coughlin—and my dad, by the way—that the best place for you to learn how to be a detective was to send you to East Detectives?"

He turned on the stairs and looked back at Payne.

"I'd say five thousand dollars," Matt said. "I understand the price goes up if the guy to be hit is known to go around armed."

Mayor Carlucci was known to never feel completely dressed unless he had a Smith & Wesson Chief's Special .38 caliber snubnose on his hip.

"Maybe we could take up a collection," Wohl said. "Put a pickle jar in every district."

He pushed open the door to his apartment and went inside.

"I need a shower," he said. "If you haven't already drunk it all, help yourself to a beer, and then call the tour lieutenant and tell him I'll be at Pekach's . . . *Martha Peebles's*."

"Yes, sir," Matt said.

He sat down on the white leather couch and pulled the telephone to him. There were lipstick-stained cigarette butts in the ashtray.

"You forgot to conceal the evidence," he called. "How did you do with whoever likes Purple Passion lipstick?"

"And clean the ashtrays," Wohl called back. "And not that it's any of your business, but she told me she was not that kind of girl. She was deeply annoyed that I thought she would do that sort of thing on the fifth date."

Matt chuckled and dialed, from memory, the number of the lieutenant on duty at Special Operations.

"Special Operations, Lieutenant Wisser."

*Must be somebody new. I don't know that name.*

"Lieutenant, Inspector Wohl asked me to call in that until further notice, he'll be at the Peebles's residence in Chestnut Hill. The number's on the list under the glass on his desk."

"Who is this?"

"My name is Payne, sir. Detective Payne."

"I've been trying to reach the inspector. Is he with you?"

Matt could hear the sound of the shower.

"No, sir. But I can get a message to him in a couple of minutes."

"Tell him that Chief Wohl has been trying to get him. That he's to call. He said it was important."

"Yes, sir, I'll tell him."

"Do I know you, Payne?"

"I don't think so, sir."

The phone went dead in Matt's ear.

He replaced the telephone in its cradle, carried the ashtray into the kitchen, emptied it, took another Ortlieb's beer from the refrigerator, and sat on the couch with it and the current copy of *Playboy* until Wohl reappeared.

"Your dad wants you to call," Matt reported. "Lieutenant Wisser said he said it was important."

Wohl sat on the couch beside him and dialed the telephone.

Matt could only guess at what the conversation was, but there was no mistaking that Wohl's attitude changed from concern to annoyance, and then resignation.

"Okay, Dad. Six-thirty, maybe a little later. Okay. Six-thirty, *no later*," he concluded, and hung up, and turned to Matt: "If you can find the hit man, tell him the mayor will probably be at 8231 Rockwell Avenue from about half past six."

"Oh?"

"It may just be for a friendly evening with old friends, and then again, it may not be," Wohl said.

Matt waited for more of an explanation, but none was forthcoming.

# ELEVEN

There was a light-skinned black man in a white coat standing under the portico of the Peebles's turn-of-the-century mansion when Wohl drove up.

"Good afternoon, sir. I'll take care of your car. Miss Peebles is at the barbecue pit."

He gestured toward a brick path leading from the house to a grove of trees.

Peter Wohl did not permit anyone else to drive his car. He had spent three years and more money than he liked to remember rebuilding it from the frame up, and had no intention of having it damaged by someone else.

"I'll park it, thank you. Around the back?"

"Beside the carriage house, if you please, sir."

Matt, who had followed him to the estate, now followed him to the carriage house.

There were two cars already parked there. One, a nearly new Ford four-door sedan both Matt and Wohl recognized as the unmarked Department car assigned to Captain Mike Sabara, Wohl's deputy. The other was a four-year-old Chevrolet with a Fraternal Order of Police sticker in the rear windshield.

They each noticed the other looking at it, and then shrugged almost simultaneously, indicating that neither recognized it.

They walked across the cobblestones past the carriage house (now a four-car garage) to the brick walk and toward the barbecue pit. They were almost out of sight of the house when they heard another car arrive.

It was a Buick Roadmaster Estate Wagon, and at the moment Matt decided that it looked vaguely familiar, there was proof. The Buick wagon stopped at the portico of the mansion and Miss Penelope Detweiler got out.

"Shit," Matt said.

"Someone you know, I gather?" Wohl said.

"Precious Penny Detweiler," Matt said.

"Really?" Wohl sounded surprised.

"Before we send the hit man to the mayor's house, do you suppose he'd have time to do a job on Pekach's girlfriend?"

They reached the barbecue pit. It was a circular area perhaps fifty feet across, with brick benches, now covered with flowered cushions, at the perimeter. There were several cast-iron tables and matching chairs, each topped with a large umbrella. Each table had been set with place mats and a full set of silver and glassware.

A bar had been set up, and another black man in a white jacket stood behind that. A third black man, older and wearing a gray jacket, whom Matt recognized as Evans, Martha Peebles's butler, was, assisted by Captain Pekach, adjusting the rack over a large bed of charcoal in the grill itself, a brick structure in the center of the circle.

"God," Wohl said softly, "ain't getting back to simple nature wonderful?"

Martha Peebles came up to them when they stepped inside the circle.

"I'm so glad you could come," she said. "David is fixing the fire."

She gave her cheek to Matt, who kissed it, and then to Wohl, who followed suit.

"I think I should warn you, Martha," Matt said. "That when he's at work, we don't let the captain play with matches."

"Penny Detweiler's coming," Martha said. "She should be here any minute."

"She's here."

"I ran into her and her mother at the butcher's, and I asked them to join us. . . ."

Matt smiled insincerely.

"And Grace said she and Dick were tied up, but Penny . . ."

"Would just love to come, right?" Matt said.

"And I told Grace you would drive her home, afterward. Is that all right?"

The bartender approached them.

"Can I get you gentlemen something?"

"How are you fixed for strychnine?"

"I'm beginning to suspect that wasn't the smartest thing I've ever done," Martha said. "If I did the wrong thing, Matt, I'm sorry. It was just that I knew she is just home . . ."

"I don't think you're capable of doing the wrong thing, Martha," Matt said. "On the other hand, I'm famous for being ill-mannered. Sure, I'll take her home." He turned to the bartender: "I'll have a beer, please. Ortlieb's, if you have it."

"The same for me, please," Wohl said.

Officer Paul T. O'Mara, holding a bottle of Pabst, walked up. He was in civilian clothing, a sports coat, and slacks.

"Hello, Paul," Wohl said.

Matt decided Wohl was surprised and not entirely pleased to see whoever this guy was.

"Inspector, would you please call your father?"

"How old is that request?" Wohl asked.

"He called me at my dad's house about ten," O'Mara said. "He said he couldn't find you at your apartment. I called Captain Sabara . . ."

"And he said I'd probably be here?"

"Yes, sir."

"He got through to me," Wohl said. "But good job, Paul, running me down."

"Yes, sir. Miss Peebles asked me to stay . . ."

"How lucky for you."

"Captain Sabara said it would be all right."

"Paul, this is Matt Payne," Wohl said.

"Yes, sir, I know who he is." He put out his hand. "Nice to meet you, Payne."

"Paul took your job, Matt," Wohl said. "So far he's been doing a much better job than you ever did."

"Thanks a lot," Matt said.

Captain Mike Sabara, whose acne-scarred olive skin gave him a somewhat menacing appearance, walked up to them, trailed by his wife.

"How goes it, boss?" Sabara asked.

"Inspector," Mrs. Sabara said.

"Hello, Helen," Wohl said. "It's good to see you."

"How are you, Matt? How's things at East Detectives?"

"Take a note, O'Mara," Wohl said. "The inspector desires that supervisors read departmental teletypes."

Sabara looked confused and possibly a little worried, but before he could question the remark, Captain Dave Pekach came up.

"I'm glad you could come," he said. "Both of you. How's East Detectives, Matt?"

"O'Mara," Wohl said. "Take two notes. Same subject."

"Excuse me?" Pekach said.

"Gentlemen, permit me to introduce the latest addition to our happy little family. Detective Payne. The reason I know this is Detective Payne showed me the teletype transferring him. Which was nice, because it was apparently never sent to Special Operations, or if it was, nobody ever thought to tell me about it."

"Jesus, Peter, I didn't see it," Mike Sabara said.

"Me, either," Pekach confessed.

"Inspector, I did," O'Mara said. "I guess I should have told you, but I just thought you would know."

"I would have thought so too," Wohl said.

"Dammit," Dave Pekach said, and then stopped as Miss Penelope Detweiler walked up to them.

She took Matt's arm, leaned up and kissed his cheek, and then laid her head against his shoulder.

"Hi," she said. "I'm Penny."

"You know our hostess, of course," Matt said. "These delightful folks are Mrs. Mike Sabara, Captain Sabara, Captain Pekach, Officer O'Mara, and the boss, Inspector Wohl."

"How do you do, Miss Detweiler?" Mike Sabara said.

*From the look on your face, Mrs. Sabara,* Matt thought, *it is evident that you have just identified the sweet-looking blonde you thought was my girlfriend as the poor little rich girl who took dope, was involved with the Guinea gangster, and was just freed from the looney bin.*

"Couldn't you call me 'Penny'?" she asked plaintively.

"Hi, Penny," Wohl said. "Call me Peter."

"I'm Dave," Captain Pekach said.

"I like him, Martha," Penny said. "He's even nicer-looking than you told Mother."

"I like him too," Martha said, and kissed Captain Pekach on the cheek, an act that seemed to embarrass him.

"Please call me Helen," Mrs. Sabara said.

"My name is Tom," Officer O'Mara said.

"Hi, Tom," Penny said, and smiled at him.

*Officer O'Mara,* Matt thought, *looks as stunned as Madame Sabara. I think he has just fallen in love.*

"I think we're all here now," Martha said. "I thought we'd have some munchies and a drink or two to work up an appetite and then Dave will do the steaks."

"May I help in some way, Martha?" Penny asked.

"It's all been done, dear, thank you just the same."

*I wish to hell she would let go of my arm,* Matt thought. *As a matter of fact, I devoutly wish she weren't here at all.* And then he considered that for a moment. *You are really a prick, Matthew Payne. She isn't at all interested in you as a male. She is hanging on to you because she's scared to death. She's floating around all alone in strange waters, and you're the only life preserver in sight. You* are, *whether you like it or not, the closest thing she has to a brother, and you have a clear obligation to try to help her.*

"Nonsense," Matt said. "Put her to work. If nothing else, get her a broom and have her sweep the place up."

"Matt, that's terrible!" Martha said.

"No, it's not," Penny said. "I learned a long time ago that saying something rude is Matt's perverse way of showing affection."

She leaned up and kissed his cheek again.

"So go get a broom," Matt said.

"I won't get a broom, but I will pass the . . . what did you say, Martha, 'the munchies'?"

Matt glanced at Peter Wohl and found Wohl's thoughtful eyes already on him.

There was the muted sound of a telephone ringing, and Evans opened a small door in the low brick wall and took out a telephone.

"One moment, please, sir," he said, and covered the mouthpiece with his hand. "Are you available to take a call from a Lieutenant Malone, Inspector?"

"Sure," Wohl said, and got up and took the telephone from Evans.

"God," Pekach said. "I didn't think to ask him! Peter, let me talk to him when you're through."

"Hello, Mike," Wohl said. "What's up?" He paused. "Wait a minute, Captain Pekach wants to talk to you." He covered the microphone with his hand. "He says he needs to talk to me."

Pekach nodded, and took the phone.

"Mike, where are you? I've been trying to get you on the phone." There was a reply. "Okay, well, you come over here. No, you won't be intruding."

He handed the telephone back to Evans and turned to Wohl.

"He was over at your place. He'll be here in ten minutes. He say what was on his mind?"

Wohl shook his head no. "Thank you, David. I really didn't want to leave before the steak."

"I should have invited him, anyway. I don't know why I didn't."

"Probably for the same reason you don't read departmental teletypes," Wohl said. He saw on Pekach's face that he had stung him more than he intended, and quickly added: "You're in love. People in love are unreliable."

"I don't think I like that," Martha said in mock indignation.

Lieutenant Malone, in slacks and a cotton jacket, drove up the drive ten minutes later in his personal automobile, a battered Mustang that always made Peter Wohl wonder what Malone had on the State Certified Inspection Station garage that had certified it as safe for passage on the Commonwealth of Pennsylvania's public roads.

"I didn't mean to intrude," he said, when he came into the barbecue pit.

"You're not," Martha said. "David's been trying to get you on the phone ever since we decided to do this. Will what you have to tell Peter wait until after you've had a drink?"

"Unless one of Dave's cars has run into a station wagon full of nuns it will," Wohl said.

"Yes, thank you. Scotch, please."

Malone spotted Matt and smiled at him.

"Hello, Matt," he said.

"How are you, Lieutenant?"

Malone spotted Penelope Detweiler, looked hard to make sure it was she, and then looked away.

Wohl went to Penny, put his arm around her shoulders, and led her to Malone.

"Penny, I want you to meet the man who put one of your father's golf partners in jail," he said. "This is Lieutenant Jack Malone."

"One of Daddy's golf partners? Really? Who?"

"Bob Holland," Wohl said. "Philadelphia's Friendliest Car Dealer of Integrity."

"Oh, I heard about that!" Penny said. "He was stealing cars, wasn't he?"

"By the hundreds," Wohl said. "And Jack was the guy who caught him."

Malone looked torn between pleasure and embarrassment.

But he has also decided, Matt saw, that being somewhere with Penny Detweiler was no cause for being uncomfortable. If Peter Wohl had a friendly arm around her shoulders, she was all right.

*That was a goddammed nice thing for you to do, boss. And if it incidentally makes me feel like a shit, I deserve it.*

"Is what's on your mind going to take long, Jack?" Wohl asked.

"No, sir."

"Then why don't we take our drinks and wander off in the woods for a minute and get it over with? Will you excuse us, Penny?"

"Certainly," Penny said. "Nice to have met you, Lieutenant. I can't wait to tell my father."

When Wohl and Malone were out of earshot, Penny touched Matt's arm and when he looked at her, she said, "He's really nice, isn't he? I like your friends, Matt."

Wohl led Malone fifty yards away from the barbecue pit and then stopped.

"Okay, let's have it," he said.

"I had a call from the Secret Service this morning," Malone replied. "A guy named H. Charles Larkin. *Supervisory Special Agent* H. Charles Larkin."

"How did he get to you?"

"I told you that Dignitary Protection sergeant, Henkels, has a room temperature IQ. Larkin called him, and he gave him my number."

"What did this guy want?"

"He said that he was the guy in charge of the Vice President's security; that he was coming up here by train in the morning; and that I'm 'invited' to the Philly office of the Secret Service at nine-thirty to discuss the Vice President's visit."

"Tomorrow's Sunday," Wohl thought aloud, "and I can't believe this guy doesn't know he's supposed to go through Captain Whatsisname Duffy in the Roundhouse."

"*Jack* Duffy," Malone furnished. "Special assistant to the commissioner for inter-agency liaison."

Wohl looked at him and grunted. "What did you tell this guy?"

"That I would get back to him. And then I started looking for you."

"Have you got this guy's number?"

Malone nodded, and Wohl made a "follow me" gesture with his hand and led him back to the barbecue pit.

"Martha," he said. "I have to call Washington. May I use the phone? I'll have it billed to the Department, of course."

"Don't be silly. Just use the phone."

"Thank you," Wohl said, going to the cubicle in the brick wall where Evans had stored the telephone.

"Dave," he called. "I want you and Mike to hear this. And you too, Matt."

Pekach and Sabara walked over to him. Officer O'Mara, Matt thought, looked like he had just been told the Big Boys didn't want to play with him. And then Wohl saw the look on O'Mara's face too:

"And, of course, you too, O'Mara. You're supposed to be able to remind me of what I said."

"Yes, sir."

Wohl pointed to the phone. Malone took a notebook from his pocket, opened it, and found the number he had.

"Person to person, Jack," Wohl ordered.

The call went through very quickly. Malone put his hand over the microphone.

"They're ringing him."

Wohl took the telephone from Malone, and held it slightly away from his ear so the others would be able to hear both sides of the conversation.

"Larkin," a somewhat brusque voice said.

"Mr. Larkin, this is Inspector Peter Wohl of the Special Operations Division of the Philadelphia Police Department."

"What can I do for you, Inspector?"

"That's what I intended to ask you. You called one of my people, Lieutenant Malone, an hour or so ago."

"Oh, yeah. I asked him to come by our Philadelphia office in the morning. Is there a problem with that?"

"I'm afraid there is. I'm not free at that time."

"Is there sort of an inference in that that I should have called you, not this lieutenant?"

"That would have been nice. Dignitary Protection is under Special Operations. I run Special Operations."

"I thought it was run out of the commissioner's office."

"Not anymore."

"Oh, shit," Larkin said. "Okay, Inspector. You tell me. How do I make this right?"

"Are you open to suggestion?"

"Wide open."

"I was going to suggest . . . I understand you're coming by train?"

"Right. Arriving at 30th Street at nine-oh-five."

"I was going to suggest that I have one of my men, Detective Payne, pick you up at 30th Street and bring you by my office. By then, with a little luck, I can have my desk cleared for you."

There was a long pause before Larkin replied.

"That's very kind of you, Inspector," he said, finally.

"Detective Payne will be waiting for you at the information booth in the main waiting room," Wohl said.

"How will I know him? What does he look like?"

Wohl's mouth ran away with him: "Like a Brooks Brothers advertisement. What about you?"

Larkin chuckled. "Like a Brooks Brothers advertisement? Tell him to look for a bald fat man in a rumpled suit. Thanks for the call, Inspector."

There was a click on the line.

Wohl took the handset from his ear, held it in front of him, and looked at it for a moment before replacing it in its cradle.

"Tom," he said to Officer O'Mara as he tossed him a set of keys, "either tonight or first thing in the morning go get a car from the Schoolhouse, drop it at my apartment, and take my Department car. Pick Payne up at no later than eight-fifteen at his apartment. He lives on Rittenhouse Square, he'll tell you where."

"Yes, sir."

"Jack, I want you in uniform tomorrow."

"Yes, sir."

"And I would be grateful if you two," he said, nodding at Pekach and Sabara, "could just happen to drop by the Schoolhouse a little after nine. You in uniform, Dave."

Pekach nodded.

"And between now and nine tomorrow morning, I want the

more lurid graffiti removed from the men's room walls. *Supervisory Special Agent* Larkin may experience the call of nature, and we don't want to offend him."

"I'll drop by the Schoolhouse on my way home," Sabara said, "and be outraged at what I find on the toilet's walls."

"We are not about to start a guerrilla war against the Secret Service," Wohl said. "But on the other hand, I want to make sure that Larkin understands that Special Operations is a division of the Philadelphia Police Department, not of the Secret Service."

"I think you made that point, Peter," Sabara said.

Matt saw H. Richard Detweiler and Brewster C. Payne II sitting at a cast-iron table on the flagstone area outside the library of the Detweiler mansion, dressed in what Matt thought of as their drive-to-the-golf-club clothes when he drove up.

*There goes any chance I had of just dropping Penny off. Damn!*

"Your dad's here," Penny said.

"I saw them," Matt said, and turned the ignition off and got out of the car and started up the shallow flight of stairs to the front door.

Miss Penelope Detweiler waited in vain for Matt to open her door, finally opened it herself, got out, and walked after him.

Grace Detweiler came into the foyer as they entered. Behind her, in the "small" sitting room, he saw his mother, who saw him and waved cheerfully.

"Well, did you have a good time?" Grace Detweiler asked.

"Oh, yes!" Penny said enthusiastically.

"She especially liked the part where Dave Pekach bit the head off the rooster," Matt said.

"Matt!" Grace Detweiler said indignantly.

Matt saw his mother smiling. They shared a sense of humor. It was one of many reasons that he was extraordinarily fond of her.

"If you will excuse me, ladies, I will now go kiss my frail and aged mother."

"You can go to hell, Matthew Payne," Patricia Payne said, getting up and tilting her cheek to him for a kiss. " 'Frail and aged'!"

She took his arm and led him toward the door to the library.

"You look very nice," she said. "Was that for Penny's benefit?"

"I didn't even know she was going to be there. Madame D. and Martha Peebles sandbagged me with that."

His mother looked at him for a moment and then said, "Well,

thank you for not making that clear to Penny. Obviously, she had a good time, and that was good for her."

"I get a gold star to take home to Mommy, right?"

"Daddy," his mother replied. "He's with Penny's father out there." She made a gesture toward the veranda outside the library, then added, "Matt, it's always nice if you can make someone happy, particularly someone who needs, desperately, a little happiness."

She squeezed his arm, and then turned back toward the "small" sitting room. *The* sitting room of the Detweiler mansion was on the second floor, and Matt could never remember ever seeing anyone in it, except during parties.

H. Richard Detweiler got out of his chair and, beaming, offered Matt his hand.

"Hello, Matt," he said. "Sit down and help us finish the bottle."

*That's my gold star. Your usual greeting is a curt nod of the head. Until I became He-Upon-Whose-Strong-Shoulder-Precious-Penny-Leans, I was tolerated only because of Dad.*

"Hello, Mr. Detweiler."

"He's only being generous because he took all my money at the club," Brewster Payne said. "I couldn't stay out of the sandtraps."

"Or the water," Detweiler said. "Scotch all right, Matt?"

"Fine. Thank you."

Matt reached into his pocket and took out his wallet, and then five one-hundred-dollar bills. When Detweiler handed him the drink, Matt handed him the money.

"What's this?"

"The expense money. I didn't need it."

Detweiler took the money and held it for a moment before tucking it in the pocket of his open-collared plaid shirt.

"I didn't expect any back, and I was just about to say, 'Matt, go buy yourself something,' but you don't try to pay dear friends for an act of love, do you?"

*Oh, shit!*

Matt turned away in embarrassment, saw a cast-iron love seat, walked to it, and sat down.

"He doesn't need your money, Dick," Brewster C. Payne said. "He made a killing at the tables."

"Really?"

"More than six thousand," Brewster Payne said.

"I didn't know you were a gambler," Detweiler said.

"I'm not. That was my first time. Beginner's luck."

Detweiler, Matt thought, seemed relieved.

"You understand that the money I took from your father today," Detweiler went on, "is not really gambling."

"More beginner's luck?" Matt asked innocently.

His father laughed heartily.

"I meant, not really gambling. Gambling can get you in a lot of trouble in a hurry."

*That's why you give your guests at the Flamingo a ten-thousand-dollar line of credit, right? So they'll get in a lot of trouble in a hurry?*

"Yes, sir," Matt said. He took a sip of his Scotch. "Nice booze."

"It's a straight malt, whatever that means," Detweiler said. "it suggests there's a crooked malt."

Penny Detweiler, trailed by her mother and Mrs. Payne, came onto the veranda. She had a long-necked bottle of Ortlieb's and a glass in her hands.

"What's that?" Detweiler asked.

"It's what Matt's been drinking all afternoon," Penny said. "When did you start drinking whiskey?"

"As nearly as I can remember, when I was eleven or twelve."

"No, he didn't," Patricia Payne said.

"Yes, he did, dear," Brewster Payne said. "We just managed to keep it from you."

Penny sat beside Matt on the cast-iron love seat.

"What am I suppose to do with this?" she asked.

"You might try drinking it," Matt said.

"Penny . . ." Grace Detweiler said warningly.

"A glass of beer isn't going to hurt her," her father said. "She's with friends and family."

There was a moment's awkward silence, and then Penny put the glass on the flagstone floor and put the neck of the bottle to her mouth. Her mother looked very uncomfortable.

"Did you have a good time at Martha Peebles's, Precious?" Detweiler asked.

"Very nice," she said. "And her captain is just darling!"

"Polish, isn't he?" Detweiler said.

"Don't be a snob, Daddy," Penny said. "He's very nice, and they're very much in love."

"I'm happy for her," Patricia Payne said. "She's at the age where she should have a little romance in her life. And living in that big house all alone . . ."

"I would have bet she'd never get married," Detweiler said.

"Her father was one hell of a man. Alexander Peebles is a tough act to follow."

"I thought about that," Penny said. "And I think that it has a lot to do with Captain Pekach being a cop." She stopped and turned to Matt, and her hand dropped onto his leg. "Does that embarrass you, Matt?"

"Not at all. I thought everyone knew that women find cops irresistible."

"Good God!" his father said.

"I mean it," Penny went on. "I was talking with Matt's boss, Inspector Wohl, and he's darling too. . . ."

"Ex-boss," Brewster Payne interrupted.

"Please let me finish, Uncle Brew," Penny said.

"Sorry."

"I was talking to Inspector Wohl, and he moved, his jacket moved, and I could see that he was carrying a gun, and it occurred to me that every man in the barbecue pit, Martha's Captain Pekach, Captain Sabara, Lieutenant Malone, Matt, and even a young Irish boy who works for Inspector Wohl, was carrying a gun."

"They have to, I believe, Penny," Brewster C. Payne said. "Even off duty."

"Not here, I hope," Grace Detweiler said.

"Even here, Madame D.," Matt said.

"As I was saying," Penny went on, annoyance at being interrupted in her voice, "I realized that although they looked like ordinary people, they weren't."

*For one thing,* Matt thought, *they make a hell of a lot less money than the people you think of as ordinary do.*

He said, "We only bite the heads off roosters on special occasions, Penny. Barbecues. Wakes. Bar Mitzvahs. Things like that. We probably won't do it again for a month."

She turned to him again, and again her hand dropped to his leg.

"Will you stop?" she giggled. "I'm trying to say something flattering."

"Then, proceed, by all means."

"I realized that they were all—what was it you said about Mr. Peebles, Daddy?—'One hell of a man.' They're all special men. I can understand why Martha fell in love with Captain Pekach. He's one hell of a man."

*I am wholly convinced that your hand on my leg, Precious Penny, is absolutely innocent; you have always been one of those kiss-kiss, touch-touch airheads. Nevertheless, I wish you would take it off. You are about to give me a hard-on.*

Matt stood up and went to the table and splashed more Scotch into his glass. He did not return to the cast-iron love seat.

"You may very well be right, dear," Matt's mother said.

"Thank you," Penny said. She looked over at Matt. "You do work for Inspector Wohl, don't you, Matt?"

He nodded.

"Then what did you mean, Uncle Brew, when you said 'ex-boss'?"

"I've been transferred back to Special Operations, Dad," Matt said.

"When did that happen?"

"Yesterday."

"What are you going to do over there, as a detective?"

"Well, for one thing," Penny said proudly, "he's going to protect the Vice President when he comes to Philadelphia."

*Jesus, you have ears like a fox, don't you?*

"What I'm going to do," Matt said quickly, "is meet the *Secret Service guy* who is going to protect the Vice President at 30th Street Station."

*And that gives me my excuse to get out of here.*

"I don't understand," Brewster Payne said.

"He and Wohl are playing King of the Mountain," Matt said. "He wanted our guy to go to the Secret Service office. Wohl wanted him to come to his. Wohl won. I pick up this guy at 30th Street Station in the morning, and drive him to see Wohl." He looked at his watch. "Which means I have to leave now if I am to have a nice clean suit to wear to meet this guy."

"Oh, finish your drink," H. Richard Detweiler said. "And are you sure you don't want something to eat?"

"I had a steak an hour ago that must have weighed three pounds," Matt said. "Thank you, no."

He drained his drink and set it on the table.

"I know you're busy, dear," his mother said, "but if you could try to find time in your schedule to come see your frail and aged mother, I would be so grateful."

H. Richard Detweiler stood up and shook Matt's hand in both of his.

"Thank you, Matt. Don't be a stranger."

"Thank you, sir."

"I think I left my scarf in your car," Penny said. "I'll walk you out."

When they got to the Porsche, she said, "I didn't have a scarf. I just wanted to thank you for being so nice to me."

"No thanks necessary," he said, and then his mouth ran away with him. "Whenever I'm with a pretty blonde, I automatically shift into the seduce mode. Nothing personal."

She seemed startled for a moment, but only for a moment.

"Just to clear the air," Penny said. "It worked."

And her hand, ever so lightly, but obviously intentionally, grazed his crotch.

"I'd let you kiss me, but they're watching."

She stepped away from him, and said, loud enough for their parents to hear, "You heard what Daddy said, don't be a stranger."

He got quickly into the Porsche and drove away.

# TWELVE

Peter Wohl was only mildly surprised when he turned onto Rockwell Avenue and saw a gleaming black Cadillac limousine parked before the comfortable house in which he had grown up. He didn't have to look at the license plate to identify it as the official vehicle provided by the City of Philadelphia to transport its mayor; the trunk was festooned with shortwave antennae, and the driver, now leaning on the front fender conversing with two other similarly dressed, neat-appearing young men, was obviously a police officer. There were two other cars, almost identical to Wohl's, parked just beyond the Cadillac.

He didn't recognize the drivers, but there was little doubt in his mind that the cars were those assigned to Chief Inspectors Matt Lowenstein and Dennis V. Coughlin.

*I am about to get one of three things, good news, bad news, or a Dutch Uncle speech. I don't know of anything I've done, or anyone else in Special Operations has done, that should have me on the carpet, but that simply means I don't know about it, not that there is nothing. And the reverse is true. I can't think of a thing I've done that would cause the mayor to show up to tell me what a good job I've been doing.*

He pulled the Jaguar to the curb behind the limousine and got out.

The two drivers who had been leaning on the Cadillac pushed themselves erect.

"Good evening, Inspector."

"I guess the party can start now," Wohl said, smiling, "I'm here."

"They been in there the better part of an hour, Inspector," one of the drivers said.

That was immediately evident when his mother opened the door to his ring. There was hearty laughter from the living room, and when he walked in there, the faces of all four men were unnaturally, if slightly, flushed.

There were liquor and soft drink bottles and an insulated ice bucket on the coffee table, and the dining-room table was covered with cold cuts and bowls of potato salad.

"Well, here he is," Chief Inspector Augustus Wohl, retired, said. "As always, ten minutes late and a dollar short."

"Mr. Mayor," Wohl said, and then, nodding his head at Lowenstein and Coughlin in turn, said "Chief."

"Always the fashion plate, aren't you, Peter?" the mayor said as he shook Wohl's hand. "Even when you were a little boy."

"I've been out hobnobbing with the hoi polloi, Mr. Mayor."

"Which hoi polloi would that be?" the mayor asked, chuckling.

"Captain Pekach's fiancée."

"Oh, yes, Miss Peebles."

"And Miss Penelope Detweiler was there too," Wohl said.

"Is Pekach doing a little matchmaking?" the mayor said, and then went on without waiting for a reply. "You could do worse, Peter. It's about time you found a nice girl and settled down."

"Miss Peebles is doing the matchmaking, but her target, I think, is Detective Payne. The Detweiler girl is a little young for me."

"He was there too?"

"He was at my place when Dave Pekach called. He said to bring him along. He came to tell me he had been reassigned to Special Operations."

"Oh, yeah. That was one of the things I was going to mention to you. I heard the commissioner was thinking of sending him back over there."

*Do you really expect me to believe that was Czernich's idea, and you knew nothing about it?*

*And "one of the things" you were going to mention to me? What else, Mr. Mayor?*

Wohl's father handed him a drink.

"Thank you," Peter said, and took a sip.

"Jerry was just telling me that Neil Jasper's going to retire," Chief Wohl said.

It took a moment for Wohl to identify Neil Jasper as an inspector working somewhere in the Roundhouse bureaucracy.

*Christ, is he going to tell me "the commissioner is thinking" of making me Jasper's replacement?*

"A lot of people, Peter, including the commissioner," the mayor said, looking directly at him, "think Special Operations is getting too big to be commanded by a staff inspector."

"I'm sorry the Commissioner feels that way," Wohl said.

"Well, I'm afraid he's right," the mayor said.

*Oh, shit! I have just been told that I'm going to lose Special Operations. That's what this is all about. Jerry Carlucci is softening the blow by letting me know ahead of time, and is about to throw me a bone: Pick a job, Peter, any job. I owe your father.*

"Do I read you correctly, Peter? You don't want to work in the Roundhouse?"

"I would rather not work in the Roundhouse, Mr. Mayor."

"That's what I told Czernich," the mayor said. "That I didn't think you'd like that."

*So what does that leave? Back to Staff Investigations? Probably not. If Carlucci is throwing the dog a bone, and tells Czernich not to give me a job in the Roundhouse, there's not really much left for a staff inspector. Maybe as an assistant to Lowenstein in the Detective Bureau, or to Coughlin in Special Patrol. Why else would they be here?*

"May I ask who the commissioner's thinking of sending in to take over Special Operations?"

"That's pretty much up to you, Peter," the mayor replied.

*What the hell does he mean by that?*

"Unless, of course, you'd like to stay there," the mayor said.

"You just said that it had been decided Special Operations should have a full inspector. . . ."

"And so it should," the mayor said. "You were what, when you took the Inspector's exam."

"Seventh," Wohl replied, without thinking.

"And they promoted five people off the list, right? That's what Czernich said."

"I think that's right," Wohl replied.

*You know damned well it's right. Why are you being a hypocrite? You watched the promotions off the list like a hawk, until the two-year life of the list ran out and you knew you weren't going to get promoted from it.*

"Commissioner Czernich came to me with an idea," the mayor said. "He said that Marty Hornstein was number six, in other words next up, on the last Inspector's List, and said that it would be a pretty good idea if I could ask the Civil Service Board to extend the life of the list, so that Hornstein could be promoted and take Jasper's place."

Wohl was aware that the mayor was pleased with himself, and exchanging glances with Chiefs Wohl, Lowenstein and Coughlin.

*What the hell is that all about?*

"Now you have been around long enough, Peter, to know that I don't like to go to the Civil Service Board and ask them for a favor. They do something for you, you got to do something for them. But, on the other hand, I try to oblige commissioner Czernich whenever I can. So I thought it over, and what I decided was that if I had to go to all the trouble of going to the Board to ask them to extend the life of the Inspector's List so that we could promote one guy off it, why not promote two guys off it?"

*Jesus H. Christ!*

*The last board made it pretty clear to me that they didn't think I was old enough to be a captain, much less a staff inspector trying for inspector. I squeezed by that one only because they believed the list would be long expired before I got anywhere near the top of it, and that I would spend the next five years or so as a staff inspector investigator. If they had known I'd be given command of Special Operations after eighteen months, they would have found some reason to keep me off the list, or at least put me near, or at, the bottom.*

"If you can find time in your busy schedule, Peter," the mayor said. "Why don't you drop by the commissioner's office next Tuesday at say nine-thirty? Wear a nice suit. They'll probably want to take your picture. Yours and Hornstein's. But keep this under your hat until then."

*I have just been promoted. By mayoral edict, screw the established procedure.*

A massive arm went around his shoulders, and then Peter felt his father's stubbly cheek against his as he was wrapped in an affectionate embrace.

"You better have another drink, Peter," the mayor said. "You look as shocked as if you'd just been goosed by a nun."

The telephone was ringing when Matt climbed the narrow stairway to his apartment. He walked quickly to it, but at the last moment decided not to pick it up. On the fifth ring, there was a click, and then his voice, giving the *I'm Not Home* message. There was a beep, and then a click. His caller had elected not to leave a message.

The red *You Have Messages* light was blinking. He pushed the PLAY button. There were four buzz and click sounds, which meant that four other people had called, gotten his *I'm Not Home* message, and hung up.

*Evelyn,* he thought. *It has to be her.*

*Why are you so sure it's her? Because the gentle sex, contrary to popular opinion, does not have an exclusive monopoly on intuition, and also because everybody, anybody, else would have left a message.*

*If you call her back, there is a very good chance that you can wind up between, or on top of, the sheets with her, Why doesn't that fill you with joyous anticipation?*

The answer came with a sudden, very clear mental image of Professor Harry Glover outside the house in Upper Darby, specifically of the look in his eyes that said, *"I know you have been fooling around with my wife."*

*Jesus Christ, could it be him? "Stay away from my wife, you bastard!"*

*Conclusions: You did the right thing, Matthew, my boy, because God takes care of fools and drunks, and you qualify on both counts, in not picking up the telephone. You neither want to discuss with Professor Glover your relationship with his wife, or diddle the lady.*

*And why not? Because he knows? Or because Precious Penny has made it quite clear that she would be willing, indeed pleased, to roll around on the sheets with you?*

*Oh, shit!*

He turned on the television, sat down in his armchair, flicked through the channels, got up, and went to the refrigerator for a beer.

The telephone rang again.

He walked to the chair-side table, looked down at the telephone, and picked it up on the third ring.

"Payne."

"This is your friendly neighborhood FBI agent," a familiar voice said. "We have a report of a sexual deviate living at that address. Would you care to comment?"

"The word is 'athlete,' not 'deviate.' Guilty. What are you up to, Jack?"

Jack Matthews, a tall, muscular, fair-skinned man in his late twenties, was a special agent of the FBI. When Matt had been wounded by a member of the so-called Islamic Liberation Army, Jack had shown up to express the FBI's sympathy, and, Matt was sure, to find out what the Philadelphia Police knew about the Islamic Liberation Army and might not be telling the FBI. In addition, Lari Matsi, a nurse in the hospital who had raised Matt's temperature at least four degrees simply by handing him an aspirin, had suddenly found Matt invisible after a thirty-second look at the pride of the Justice Department.

Despite this, however, Matt liked Jack Matthews. He watched what he said about police activity when they were together, but they shared a sense of humor, and he had become convinced that there was a certain honest affection on Jack's part for him and Charley McFadden, whose fiancée and Lari Matsi were pals.

"I'm sitting at the FOP bar with a morose Irish detective," Jack said. "Who is threatening to sing, 'I'll take you home again, Kathleen.' McFadden wants you to come over here and sing harmony."

"You sound like you've been there for a while."

"Only since it opened," Jack said. "The girls are working."

"Did you call before, Jack?"

"No. Why?"

"No reason. Yeah, give me twenty minutes."

"Bring some of that Las Vegas money with you," Jack said, and hung up.

Matt went into his bedroom and changed into khakis and a sweatshirt. As he was reclaiming his pistol from the mantelpiece, the telephone rang again. He looked at it for a moment, and then went down the stairs.

Jack Matthews and Charley McFadden, a very large, pleasant-faced young man, were sitting at a table near the door of the bar in the basement of the Fraternal Order of Police Building on Spring Garden Street, just off North Broad Street, when Matt walked in.

There was a third man at the table, Jesus Martinez, in a suit Matt thought was predictably flashy, and whom he was surprised to see, although when he thought about it, he wondered why.

Charley McFadden and Jesus Martinez had been partners, working as undercover Narcs. When their anonymity had been destroyed when they ran to earth the junkie who had shot Captain Dutch Moffitt, they had been transferred to Special Operations. Charley and Martinez had been friends and, more important, partners, since before Matt had come on the job.

"How are you, Hay-zus?" Matt said, offering his hand and smiling at Officer Jesus Martinez of the Airport Unit.

"Whaddaya say, Payne?" Jesus replied.

*Both our smiles are forced,* Matt thought. *He doesn't like me, for no good reason that I can think of, and I am not especially fond of him. We are on our good behavior because Charley likes both of us, and we both like Charley.*

Matthews and McFadden were dressed much like Matt. Charley was wearing a zippered nylon jacket and blue jeans, and Matthews was wearing blue jeans and a sweatshirt with the legend PROPERTY OF THE SING-SING ATHLETIC DEPARTMENT. A loose-fitting upper garment of some sort is required to conceal revolvers.

They both had their feet up on chairs, and were watching the dancers on the floor, at least a half dozen of whom appeared to have their slacks and blouses painted on.

"We have a new rule," Jack said. "People who win a lot of money gambling have to buy the beer."

"Right," McFadden said.

*They're both plastered. I think Jack is here because he wants to be, not because the FBI told him to hang around the cops with his eyes and ears open.*

"Does that apply to guys who can tell certain females that their boyfriends spent Saturday night ogling the broads in the FOP bar?"

"You have a point, sir," Jack said. "I will buy the beer."

"Sit down," Matt said. "Ortlieb's, right? What are you drinking, Hay-zus?"

Martinez picked up a glass that almost certainly held straight 7UP.

"I'm okay. Thanks."

Matt crossed the room to the bar and picked up three bottles of Ortlieb's beer and a bottle of 7UP and returned to the table.

When he passed the 7UP to Jesus, Martinez snapped, "I told you I was okay."

"I'm the last of the big spenders, all right?" Matt countered, and then his annoyance overwhelmed him. "Drink it. Maybe it'll help you grow."

Martinez was instantly to his feet.

"I'm big enough to whip your ass anytime, hotshot."

"Don't fuck with me, Martinez, I've had a bad day."

"Shut up, Hay-zus," Charley said. "Shut up and sit down."

"Fuck him!" Martinez snarled. "Fucking hotshot!"

"Hey!" an authoritative voice called from somewhere in the large, dark, low-ceilinged room. "Watch the goddamned language. There's ladies in here, for Christ's sake."

Martinez turned on his heel and went quickly out the door. Matt could hear his shoes on the concrete stairs. They made a sort of metallic ringing sound.

"What was that all about?" Matthews asked.

"You shouldn't have made that crack about him growing, Matt," Charley said.

"All he had to do was say 'thank you' for the goddamn 7UP. Or say nothing. He didn't have to bite my ass. I don't have to put up with his shit. Or yours, either."

"Oh, boy," Matthews said. "I'm going to get to see a real barroom brawl."

"He never liked you for openers," Charley said, "and then you passed the exam, and he didn't."

"What am I supposed to do, apologize for passing the exam?"

"Just show a little consideration for his feelings is all," Charley said, almost plaintively.

Matt laughed and sat down.

"What's so funny?"

"Let it go, Charley," Matthews said.

"I want to know what he thinks is so funny!"

"Drink your beer, Charley," Matthews said.

"Jesus," Charley said, and sat down.

"I want to say something to you, Charley," Matt said.

"Yeah?" McFadden asked suspiciously. "What would that be?"

"I don't want you telling Mary, if she comes in here and finds you lying on the floor, that I held you down and poured booze down your throat."

McFadden glowered at him for a moment and then said, "Fuck you, Matt."

There was affection in his voice.

"And so what's new with you, Detective Payne?" Matthews asked. "Aside from you going back to Special Operations, I mean?"

"That upset Hay-zus too," Charley interrupted. "When he heard that you're going back out there. Sort of rubbing it in his face. With him flunking the exam."

"Loyalty, thy name is McFadden," Matt said.

"Something wrong with that?"

"Not a thing, pal. I admire it," Matt said, and then turned to Matthews. "How about the FBI? Arrested anybody interesting lately?"

"No, but I'm hot on the trail of a big-time gambler. Was he pulling my leg, or did you really win six thousand bucks out there?"

"Sixty-seven hundred, he tells you, in the interests of accuracy."

"And what if you had lost?"

"I was going to quit when I lost a hundred," Matt said. "But I didn't lose it."

"You went out there to bring the Detweiler girl home?"

"Right."

"How is she?"

"I don't know," Matt said. "She seems perfectly normal. As normal as she ever was."

The question and his response made him uncomfortable. He stood up.

"I need another beer."

He was surprised when Jack Matthews showed up at his elbow while he was waiting for his turn with the bartender.

"My turn to buy," Jack said.

*He wants something. How do I know that?*

"I thought you would never say that," Matt replied.

Matthews took money from his pocket.

"I understand Special Operations now runs Dignitary Protection," he said.

"I don't know. I haven't reported in yet. Why do you ask?"

"Oh, I've been assigned to liaise between the Bureau and the Secret Service for the Vice President's visit."

"What does that mean?"

"Well, for example, when the Secret Service big shot arrives at 30th Street Station from Washington tomorrow morning, I will be a member of the official welcoming party."

"You get to carry his bags? Boy, you are moving up in the FBI, aren't you?"

*Why am I unwilling to tell him,* "Whoopee, what a coincidence, me too!"

"Screw you, Matt," Matthews said, chuckling. "Look, if you can find out who's going to run this for the Police Department, it would be helpful to me. Okay?"

"Yeah, sure, Jack. I'll ask around."

At quarter to seven the next morning, half an hour early, Officer Tom O'Mara pulled Staff Inspector Peter Wohl's unmarked car to the curb in front of the Delaware Valley Cancer Society Building.

And then he didn't know what to do. It was an office building, and it was Sunday, and it was closed. Detective Payne had told him he lived on the top floor. That was a little strange to begin with. Who lived in an office building?

He got out of the car and walked to the plate-glass door and looked in. There was a deserted lobby, with a polishing machine next to a receptionist's desk, and nothing else. O'Mara walked to the edge of the sidewalk and looked up. He couldn't see anything. But then when he glanced back at the building, he saw a doorbell, mounted on the bricks next to the door where you could hardly see it.

He went to it and pushed it. He couldn't hear anything ringing. He decided the only thing he could do was just wait. He went to the car and leaned on the fender.

A minute or so later, a Holmes Service rent-a-cop appeared in the lobby and looked out curiously. O'Mara walked to the door as the rent-a-cop unlocked it.

"Can I help you?"

"I'm a police officer," O'Mara said.

"I never would have guessed," the rent-a-cop said, and then when he saw the look on O'Mara's face added, "I retired in 1965 out of the Third District."

"Does a detective named Payne live here?"

The rent-a-cop motioned him into the building and pointed at an elevator.

"Take a ride to the third floor. Payne lives up there. You'll see a doorway with an intercom."

"Thank you."

Matt Payne, obviously fresh from a shower, was buttoning his shirt when O'Mara climbed the flight of stairs from the third floor.

"I decided making coffee would be a waste of effort, sorry," he said.

"Nice apartment," O'Mara said.

"If you're a midget," Payne said. "Give me a minute to get my pants on."

"I'm early."

"You get the worm, then," Payne said as he walked to the rear of the apartment.

O'Mara looked around the apartment. There was an oil painting of a naked lady mounted to the bricks of the fireplace.

It would be nice, Officer O'Mara thought, to have a place like this to bring a girl to. He had thought of getting an apartment, but every time he brought the subject up, his mother had a fit. There would be enough time to get his own apartment later, when he was married. The thing he had to do now was learn to save his money, and renting an apartment when there was a perfectly good room for him to use at home would be like throwing money down the toilet.

He wondered if Payne brought the Detweiler girl here. She seemed to be a nice girl, even after what he'd heard about her being on drugs.

"I like your picture," O'Mara said. "The inspector's got one like it."

"Yeah, I know," Payne said. "Mrs. Washington gave me that one."

"Sergeant Washington's wife?"

"Yeah," Payne said, walking to the fireplace mantel and picking up his Chief's Special snub-nosed revolver and slipping it into a holster that fit inside his waistband.

"Is it hard to get through the qualification?" O'Mara asked.

"What?"

O'Mara pushed his coat aside to reveal his standard-issue Smith & Wesson Military and Police revolver, which had a six-inch barrel and was time and a half as large as the snubnose.

In order to carry anything but the issue revolver, it was necessary to go through a test—"the qualification"—at the range at the Police Academy.

"The Range guys make a big deal of it," Payne said. "It helps if you know one of them."

"I got a cousin works out there," O'Mara said.

"Then talk to him," Payne said as he shrugged into his jacket. "Where are you parked?"

"Out in front."

"I should have told you to come around the back, there's a garage in the basement. Sorry."

"No problem."

"How'd you get in?"

"I rang the doorbell. A rent-a-cop let me in."

"The guy who usually works the building on Sundays is a retired cop," Matt said.

"He told me."

The telephone rang.

O'Mara saw that Payne was reluctant to answer it, that he was really making up his mind whether or not he would, and he wondered what that was all about. Finally, Payne shrugged and picked it up.

"Hello."

"You sound grumpy," Evelyn said. "Did I wake you up?"

"Hi. No. As a matter of fact, I was just about to walk out the door." There was a silence, and then Matt added: "Hey, I mean that. I've got to work. Women work from sun to sun, a policeman's work is never done."

"I was going to ask you to dinner. Is that out of the question?"

"I'll have to call you. I don't know how long this will take."

"How long what will take? Or is it bad form to ask?"

"I've got to pick up a VIP at 30th Street Station and drive him to see my boss."

"Oh."

"I may be through at ten, ten-thirty, and I may not be through until five or six."

"Matt, it would be kinder, if you'd rather break this off, for you to come out and say so."

"There is nothing I would rather do than come out there right now," Matt said. "Don't be silly."

"You mean that, or you're being polite?"

"Of course, I mean it."

"Will you call me, please, when you know something?"

"As soon as I find out."

"I bought steaks yesterday," Evelyn said. "I thought you'd like a steak."

Then she hung up.

*You bought steaks, and then you went home and started calling me, apparently every half hour. Jesus!*

*Why the hell didn't you take the out she gave you?*

He put the handset in its cradle, and turned away from the table. The phone rang again.

*Jesus, now what does she want?*

"Hello."

"I just wanted to make sure you were out of bed," Peter Wohl said. "O'Mara should be there any minute."

"He's here now. We were just about to leave."

"No suggestion that either one of you is unreliable," Wohl said. "But things happen, and I didn't want the Secret Service standing around 30th Street feeling unloved."

"You want me to kiss him when he gets off the train?"

"That would be nice," Wohl said, and hung up.

Matt hung up again and looked at O'Mara.

"That was the boss. He wanted to be sure I was out of bed."

There are those that feel that Philadelphia's 30th Street Station is one of the world's most attractive railroad stations. It was built before World War II when the Pennsylvania Railroad was growing richer by the day, and the airplane was regarded as a novelty, not a threat for passenger business. And even after the airplane had killed the long-distance railroad passenger business in other areas, along the New York–Washington corridor, going by train remained quicker and more convenient.

There were a lot of people going in and out of the doors at the west exit of 30th Street Station when Tom O'Mara pulled up in a NO STANDING ZONE.

"If a white hat tries to run you off," Matt said. "Tell him you're waiting for Chief Coughlin."

"Chief Coughlin?" O'Mara asked.

"Everybody's afraid of Chief Coughlin," Matt said as he opened the door and got out.

He had almost reached the doors to the main waiting room when a voice called out, "Detective Payne?"

He turned and saw a Highway Patrol sergeant walking up to him. He was a good-looking young Irishman, and Matt now recalled seeing him with Pekach, but he couldn't come up with a name.

"Jerry O'Dowd," the sergeant said, putting out his hand. "I work for Captain Pekach."

"How are you, Jerry? What's up?"

"I got the captain's car. I was told to see if you showed up, and if not, to stand by the information booth and look for a bald fat man in a rumpled suit, named Supervisory Special Agent H. Charles Larkin, and then drive him to the Schoolhouse. You're here. What do you think I should do?"

"I think maybe you should stick around in case the battery in Wohl's car goes dead or something."

"Sure."

"Why don't you call in and say I'm here?"

"Captain Pekach said this guy's a Secret Service big shot?"

"That's all I know about him too."

"I'm across the street, you want me to pull up behind your car?"

"No. This guy's in the Secret Service, not a movie star."

Matt was standing beside the information booth in the center of the main waiting room at 9:05, his eyes fixed on the wide stairway that led down to the tracks below.

At 9:06, a crowd of people began to come up the stairway. After a moment, he had trouble seeing through them, and started to walk to the head of the stairs, but changed his mind. He had been told to be at the information booth.

At 9:08, a voice behind him said, "Excuse me, sir, but is that a Brooks Brothers suit?"

Matt turned and saw a man whose hair was thin, but who could not be called bald, who was heavyset, but could not be called fat, and whose suit appeared comfortable, but was not rumpled. He was surrounded by half a dozen neatly dressed men, one of whom was Special Agent Matthews of the FBI, and all of whom seemed baffled by the behavior of the man they had come to 30th Street Station to meet.

"Actually, it's from Tripler. Have I the privilege of addressing Mr. H. Charles Larkin?"

"Yes, you do," Larkin said, smiling conspiratorially at him.

"Welcome to Philadelphia, Mr. Larkin."

"Thank you very much. It's nice to be here."

Larkin turned to the men with him.

"I am going with this gentleman. I don't know where, but if you can't trust the Philadelphia Police Department, who can you trust?"

"Excuse me, sir?" one of the men standing behind him asked.

"Detective Payne, do you happen to know any of these gentlemen?"

"I have the privilege of Special Agent Matthews's acquaintance, sir. Good morning, Special Agent Matthews."

Jack Matthews looked embarrassed. Or annoyed. Or both. He nodded curtly at Matt but didn't say anything.

"How strange," Larkin said. "I was led to believe that the FBI and the Philadelphia Police Department were not on speaking terms."

"We talk to some of them, sir," Matt said.

"Well, shall we be on our way, Detective Payne?"

"The car is right outside, sir," Matt said, and pointed.

"I'll be in touch," Larkin said, and marched off toward the doors to the street. Matt walked quickly to catch up with him. Behind him, he heard one of the men left behind say, "Jesus *Christ!*"

O'Mara saw them coming and opened the rear door of the car. Larkin smiled at him, and then pulled open the front door and got in the front seat. Matt had no choice but to get in the back.

O'Mara walked quickly around the front of the car and got behind the wheel and drove off.

"Mr. Larkin, this is Officer O'Mara. Tom, this is Supervisory Special Agent Larkin of the Secret Service."

"Good morning," Larkin said, and then turned on the seat to face Matt. "I understand you're pretty close to Denny Coughlin."

The announcement surprised Matt.

"Yes, sir, I am."

"First chance you get, give him a call. I think he'll tell you I'm not the arrogant prick your boss apparently thinks I am. Not that Wohl has a reputation for being a shrinking violet himself."

"May I ask how you know Chief Coughlin, sir?"

"Ten, twelve, Christ, it must be fifteen years ago, there was a guy making funny money on Frankford Avenue. Wedding announcements in the daytime, funny money at night. First-class engraver. We had a hell of a time catching him. Denny was then working Major Crimes. Good arrest. We got indictments for twelve people, and ten convictions. He's a hell of a good cop."

"Yes, sir, he is."

"So am I," Larkin said. "Am I going to have to have Denny Coughlin tell Wohl that, or do you think we can make friends by ourselves?"

"Sir, I think that you and Inspector Wohl will have no trouble becoming friends. Sir, can I ask how you knew I know Chief Coughlin?"

"Our office here keeps files. One of them is on you. You're a very interesting young man, Payne."

Matt would have loved to have an amplification of that, but he suspected that none would be offered, and none was.

"Does Chief Coughlin know you're in town, sir?"

"No. I thought I would put that off until I met your Inspector Wohl," Larkin said, and then turned to O'Mara: "Are you speeding, son?"

O'Mara dropped his eyes quickly to the speedometer, before replying righteously, "No, sir."

"There's a Highway car following us," Larkin said. "If you're not speeding, what do you think he wants?"

Mat laughed. "He's there in case we get a flat or something," he said.

Larkin looked at him and smiled. "That's what the file said," he said. "Wohl is very careful, very thorough. And very bright."

"You have pretty good files, Mr. Larkin," Matt said.

"Yeah, we do," Larkin said.

# THIRTEEN

It took Vito Lanza several seconds to realize where he was when he woke up, several seconds more to reconstruct what had happened the night before, a few seconds more to realize that he was alone in the revolving circular bed, and a final second or two to grasp that the revolving bed was still revolving.

It didn't *spin* around, or anything like that, you really had to work at deciding it was really moving, but it did move, the proof of which was that he was now looking out the window, and the last he remembered, he had been facing toward the bathroom, waiting for Tony to come out.

The bed was also supposed to vibrate, but the switch for that was either busted, or they didn't know how to work it. They were both pretty blasted when they tried that.

He'd had too much to drink, *way* too much to drink, there was no question about that. He'd had a little trouble getting it up, *that* much to drink, and that hardly ever happened. And much too much to be doing any serious gambling, and he'd done that too.

It had started on the way up. Tony had said she hadn't had any-

187

thing for breakfast but toast and coffee and was getting a little hungry, so they stopped at a place just the Poconos side of Easton on US 611 for an early lunch. And he'd fed her a couple of drinks, and had a couple himself thinking it would probably put her in the mood for what he had in mind when they got to the Oaks and Pines Resort Lodge.

He had half expected the coupon Tony's Uncle Joe had given them for the Oaks and Pines Resort Lodge to be a gimmick; that when they got there there either wouldn't be a room for them, or there would be "service charges" or some bullshit like that that would add up to mean it wasn't going to be free at all.

But it hadn't been that way. They didn't get a free *room*, they got a free *suite*, on the top floor, a bedroom with the revolving bed and a mirror on the ceiling; a living room, or whatever it was called, complete to a bar and great big color TV, and a bathroom with a bathtub big enough for the both of them at once made out of tiles and shaped like a heart, and with water jets or whatever they were called you could turn on and make the water swirl around you.

And when they got to the room, there was a bottle of champagne in an ice bucket sitting on the bar, so they'd drunk that, and then tried out the bathtub, and that had really put Tony in the mood for what he had in mind.

And that was before they'd found out that the bed revolved.

After, they had gone down to the cocktail lounge, where the Oaks and Pines Resort Lodge had an old broad—not too bad-looking, nice teats, mostly showing—playing the piano, and they'd had a couple of drinks there.

That was when the assistant manager had come up to him and handed him a card.

"Just show this to the man at the door, Mr. Lanza," he said, nodding his head toward the rear of the cocktail lounge where there had been a door with no sign on it or anything, and a guy in a waiter suit standing by it. "He'll take care of you. Good luck."

They didn't go back there until after dinner. Whoever ran the place sent another bottle of champagne to the table, compliments of the house, and the dinner of course went with the coupon. Vito had clams and roast beef. Tony had a shrimp cocktail and a filet mignon with some kind of sauce on it. She gave him a little taste, and the steak was all right, but if he'd had a choice he would rather have had A-1 Sauce.

And then they had a couple of Benedictines and brandies, and danced a little, and he had tried to get her to go back to the room, but she said it was early, and it was going to be a long night, and he didn't push it.

Then he'd asked her if it would be all right if he went into the back room, and Tony said, sure, go ahead, she had to go to the room, and she would come down when she was done.

It wasn't Vegas behind the door. No slots, for one thing. And no roulette. But there was blackjack, two tables for that, and there was three tables where people were playing poker, with the house taking their cut out of each pot, and of course craps. Two tables. Pretty well crowded.

By the time Tony came down from the room, he had made maybe two hundred, maybe a little more, making five- and ten-dollar bets against the shooter. When she showed up, he didn't want to look like an amateur making five-dollar bets, so he started betting twenty-five, sometimes fifty, the same way, against the shooter.

When he decided it was time to quit, he had close to five thousand, over and above the thousand he had started with and was prepared to lose.

"You're going to quit, on a roll?" Tony had asked him, and he told her that was when smart people quit, when they were on a roll, and what he needed right now was a little nap.

So they'd had a little nap, and a couple of drinks, and that was when they fooled around with the switch Tony had found on the carpet when she'd fallen off the bed, and then they'd gotten dressed again and went back downstairs and to the room in the back.

And this time the dice had turned against him. He was sure it was that, not that he was blasted or anything. Sometimes, you just have lousy luck, and with him betting C-notes, and sometimes double C-notes, letting the bet ride, it hadn't taken long to go through the five big ones he'd won, plus the thousand he had brought with him.

That was when the pit boss told him that if he wanted, they would take his marker, that Mr. Fierello had vouched for him, said his markers were good.

So what the hell, he'd figured that as bad as his luck had been, it had to change, it was a question of probability, so he'd asked how much of a marker he could sign, and the guy said as much as he wanted, and he hadn't wanted to look like a piker in front of Tony, so he signed a marker for six big ones, what he was out, and they gave him the money, in hundreds.

When he lost that, he knew it was time to quit, so he quit. If he had really been blasted, he would have signed another marker, because his credit was good, and that would have been stupid. The way to look at it was that he had dropped seven big ones. That was a lot of money, sure, but he'd come home from Vegas with twenty-two big ones. So he was still ahead. He was still on a roll.

He had the Caddy, and about ten thousand in cash, and, of course, Tony. If that wasn't being on a roll, what was?

Vito focused his eyes on the mirror over the bed, and then pulled the sheet modestly over his groin.

Then he got out of bed and walked to the bathroom.

Tony was in the tub, and it was full of bubbles, a bubble bath. It was the first bubble bath Vito had ever seen, except of course in the movies.

"Jees, honey," Tony said, "I didn't wake you, did I? I tried to be quiet."

"Don't worry about it."

"How about this?" Tony said, splashing the bubbles, moving them just enough so that he could see her teats. "I found a bottle of bubble stuff on the dresser. You just pour it in, and turn on them squirter things, and—bubbles!"

"There still room in there for me?"

"Oh, I don't know. Maybe there is, maybe there isn't."

Vito walked to the edge of the tub, dropped his shorts, and got in with Tony.

"You know what I would like to do later?" Tony asked.

"I know what *I'd* like to do later. Or for that matter, right now."

"Behave yourself! What I would like to do is get one of them golf things. . . ."

"What golf things?"

"The buggies, or whatever."

"You mean a golf cart," he said.

"Yeah. Could we get one and just take a ride in it?"

He thought that over.

"Why the hell not?" he said, finally.

"You know what else I would like?"

"What?"

"Champagne."

"Christ, before breakfast?"

"Well, I figured champagne and bubble baths go together. You can eat breakfast anytime. How many times does a person get a chance to do something like this?"

"You want champagne," Vito said, and hoisted himself out of the tub, "you get champagne."

Marion Claude Wheatley had slept soundly and for almost twelve hours. That was, he decided, because no matter what else one could say about the Pine Barrens, it was quiet out here. No blaring horns, or sirens, no screeching tires, and one was not required to listen to other people's radios or televisions.

But on reflection, he thought as he got out of bed and started to fold the bedding to take back to Philadelphia with him, it was probably more than that. He had noticed, ever since he had understood what the Lord wanted him to do, and especially when he was actually involved in something to carry out the Lord's will, that he was peaceful. It probably wasn't the "Peace That Passeth All Understanding," to which the prayer book of the Protestant Episcopal Church referred so frequently, and which the Lord had promised he would experience in Heaven, but it was a peace of mind that he had never before experienced in his life.

It seemed perfectly logical that if one was experiencing such an extraordinary peace, one would be able to sleep like a log.

Before he made his breakfast, he put the bedding into a suitcase, turned the mattress, and then carried the suitcase out and put it in the trunk of the rental car.

He fired up the Coleman stove and made his breakfast. Bacon and eggs, sunny side up, basted with the bacon fat, the way Mother used to make them for him when he was a kid, served on top of a slice of toast. Mother had thought dipping toast into an egg yolk was rather vulgar; placing the egg on a slice of toast, so that when the yolk was cut, it ran onto the toast accomplished the same purpose and was more refined.

He didn't have toast, of course. There was no toaster. And if there had been, there was no electricity to power a toaster. He thought again of the pluses and minuses of getting a gasoline-powered generator and bringing it out here to the farm. There was a new generation of small, truly portable generators. He had spent the better part of an hour taking a close look at the ones Sears Roebuck now had.

The one he liked best advertised that it produced 110-volt alternating current at five amperes, and burned one-half gallon of unleaded gasoline per hour. The recommended load was up to 1,500 watts. That was more than enough to power a toaster. It was enough to power a small television. And it would pose no problem, if he had such a generator, to install some simple wiring and have electric lighting over the sink, next to his chair, and in the bedroom.

That would mean, he had thought at first, that he could do away with the Coleman lanterns, which would be nice. But then he realized that 1.5 KW was not adequate to power more than one electric hotplate, which meant that the procurement of a generator would not mean that he could dispense with the Coleman stove.

And then he realized that he didn't really want to come out here and watch television, so there was no point in getting a generator to provide power for that purpose.

And then, of course, there were the obvious downsides to having a generator. For one thing, it would make noise. He didn't think that he would really be willing to put up with the sound of a lawn-mower engine running at two-thirds power hour after hour. And it would, of course, require fuel. He would have to bring at least five gallons of unleaded gasoline every time he came to the farm. Carrying gasoline in cans was very dangerous.

It would be much better, he concluded again, not to get a generator. Besides, if he went ahead and got one, there was a very good chance that he wouldn't get to use it very much. Once he had disintegrated the Vice President, all sorts of law enforcement people would begin to look for him. He thought there was very little chance that they would not sooner or later find him.

If indeed, in carrying out the Lord's will at Pennsylvania Station, he didn't end his mortal life.

When he finished breakfast, he pumped the pump and filled the sink in the kitchen with foul-tasting water, added liquid Palmolive dish soap, and washed the plates and flatware and pots and pans he had soiled since his arrival. He put everything in its proper place in the cabinets, and then made up the garbage package.

Until he had finally realized how to solve the problem—like most solutions, once reached, he was surprised at how long it had taken him to figure it out—he had ridden the tractor to the depression carrying the paper bags full of garbage in his arm. It was difficult to drive the tractor with one hand, and sometimes, despite trying to be very careful, he had hit a bump and lost the damn bag anyway, but that was all he could see to do. If he put the garbage in the trailer, by the time he got to the depression, the vibration caused the garbage to come out of the paper sack and spread out all over the trailer. Or even bounce out of the trailer.

The solution was simplicity itself. He made up a garbage package, or packages, by placing one paper sack inside another, and when it was full, sealing it with duct tape. He had then been able to place the sealed bag in the trailer, and then drive, with both hands free, the tractor to the depression.

Ordinarily, when Marion took care of the garbage, he simply drove to the edge of the depression and stood on the edge and threw the garbage packages down the slope.

Today, however, he decided that it would be a good idea if he took another look at the lockers. He had examined them yesterday, of course, but that had been right after he'd set off the devices, and there had been a good deal of smoke and even several small smoldering fires. By now, everything would have cooled down, and if any of the fires were still smoldering, he could be sure they were extinguished.

Throughout the Pine Barrens, were areas that smoldering fires had left blackened and ugly. And one could not completely dismiss the possibility that a smoldering fire could reach the farmhouse, although that was unlikely.

There was still the smell of smoke in the depression, but he could not find any smoke, and it was probably that the converse of "where there's smoke there's fire" was true. No smoke, so to speak, no fire.

He was pleased when he examined the lockers. The devices had functioned perfectly, and with evidence of greater explosive power than he would have thought. The doors of the lockers in which the devices had been detonated had, except for one that hung on a hinge, been blown off. The chain that had been wrapped around the Composition C-4 had functioned as he had hoped it would. The lockers in which the devices had been placed were shredded, as were the adjacent lockers. He found only a couple of dozen chain links, and he found none where more than two links remained attached.

Marion climbed back up the slope of the depression, drove the tractor back to the farmhouse, replaced the tarpaulin over the tractor, and then went into the house. He took a careful look around to make sure that he hadn't forgotten anything, and then left, carefully locking the padlock on the door.

He got in the rental car and started the engine. He looked at his watch. Things couldn't be better. He would get home in plenty of time to do the laundry, go to the grocery store, and then get the rental car back to the airport in time to qualify for the special weekend rate. And then he could get back home in time to watch Masterpiece Theater on the public television station.

That was the television program he really hated to miss.

• • •

Tom O'Mara stopped the car in front of the building that was the headquarters of the Special Operations Division of the Philadelphia Police Department. Over the door there was a legend chiseled in granite: FRANKFORD GRAMMAR SCHOOL A.D. 1892.

Before O'Mara could apply the parking brake and open his door, Supervisory Special Agent H. Charles Larkin said, "This must be the place," and got out of the car.

Matt hurried after him, and managed to beat Larkin to the door and pull it open for him.

"Right this way, Mr. Larkin," he said.

He led him down the corridor to the private door of what had been the principal's office, knocked, and then pushed the door open.

"Mr. Larkin is here, Inspector."

"Fine. Would you ask him to wait just a minute, please, Detective Payne?"

"Yes, sir," Matt said, and turned to Larkin. "The inspector will be with you in just a minute, sir."

"How good of him," Larkin said, expressionless.

Matt knew from checking his watch that Wohl kept Larkin waiting for two minutes, but it seemed like much longer before Wohl pulled his door open.

"Mr. Larkin, I'm Staff Inspector Peter Wohl. Won't you please come in?"

"Thank you."

Wohl gestured for Matt to come in, and then waved Larkin into an armchair.

"Any problems picking you up, sir?"

"None whatever."

"May I offer you a cup of coffee? A soft drink?"

"No, thank you," Larkin said. "But may I use your telephone?"

"Of course," Wohl said, and pushed one of the phones on his desk to Larkin. Larkin consulted a small, leather-bound notebook, and then dialed a number.

Matt could hear the phone ringing.

"Olga? Charley Larkin. How are you, sweetheart?"

Matt saw Wohl looking at him strangely.

"Is that guy you live with around? Sober?"

There was a brief pause.

"How the hell are you, Augie?" Larkin asked.

Staff Inspector Peter Wohl's eyes rolled up toward the ceiling; he shook his head from side to side, smiled faintly, and exhaled audibly.

"I'm in Philadelphia, and I need a favor," Supervisory Special Agent Larkin went on. "I need a good word. For some reason, I got off on the wrong foot with one of your guys, and I'd like to set it right."

"I appreciate it, pal. Hold on a minute."

Larkin handed the telephone to Peter Wohl.

"Chief Wohl would like a word with you, Inspector," he said.

Peter Wohl took the telephone.

"Good morning, Dad," he said.

Larkin, beaming smugly, tapped his fingertips together.

"Yes, I'm afraid Mr. Larkin was talking about me. Obviously, there has been what they call a communications problem, Dad. Nothing that can't be fixed."

Chief Wohl spoke for almost a minute, before Peter Wohl replied, "I'll do what I can, Dad. I don't know his schedule."

He handed the phone back to Larkin.

"Chief Wohl would like to talk to you again, Mr. Larkin."

"I don't know what his plans are for lunch, Augie, but I'm free, and I accept. Okay. Bookbinder's at twelve. Look forward to it."

He reached over and replaced the handset in its cradle.

They looked at each other for a moment, and then Wohl chuckled, and then laughed. Larkin joined in.

"I thought my guy here said 'Wall,'" Larkin said. "I don't know anybody named 'Wall.'"

"Well, while you and my dad have a lobster, that I'll pay for, I'll have a boiled crow," Wohl said. "Will that set things right?"

"I'm sorry I used that phrase," Larkin said. "Nothing has gone wrong yet, but I'm glad I saw your father's picture on the wall. I think you and I could have crossed swords, and that would have been unfortunate. Can I ask a question?"

"Certainly."

"Have you got a hard-on for the feds generally, or is there someone in particular who's been giving you trouble? One of our guys, maybe?"

Wohl, almost visibly, carefully chose his words.

"I think the bottom line, Mr. Larkin, is that I was being overprotective of my turf. They just gave me Dignitary Protection, and I wanted to make sure it was understood who was running it. I really feel like a fool."

"Don't. The Secret Service is a nasty bureaucracy too. I understand how that works."

"When you're aware of your ignorance, you tend to gather your wagons in a circle," Wohl said.

"Well, I'm not the Indians," Larkin said. "And now that we both know that, could you bring yourself to call me Charley?"

"My dad might decide I was being disrespectful," Wohl said.

"Peter, if you keep calling me 'Mr. Larkin,' your dad will think we still have a communications problem."

"Matt," Wohl said. "Go get Captains Sabara and Pekach. I want them to meet Charley here."

"Yes, sir. Lieutenant Malone?"

"Him too," Wohl said.

As Matt started down the corridor to Sabara's office, where he suspected they would all be, he heard Larkin say, "Nice-looking kid."

"I think he'll make a pretty good cop."

*That's very nice. But it's sort of a left-handed compliment. It suggests I will probably be a pretty good cop sometime in the future. So what does that make me now?*

Wohl made the introductions, and they all shook hands.

"There is a new game plan," Wohl said. "There is something I didn't know until a few minutes ago about Mr. Larkin. He and my dad are old pals, and that changes his status from one of them to one of us. And I've already told him that we don't know zilch about what's expected of us. So we're all here to learn. The basic rule is what he asks for, he gets. Mr. Larkin?"

"The first thing you have to understand," Larkin said seriously, "is that the Secret Service never makes a mistake. Our people here in Philadelphia told me that the man in charge of this operation was Inspector Wall. Peter has promised to have his birth certificate altered so that our record will not be tarnished."

He got the chuckles he expected.

"The way this usually works," Larkin went on, "is that our special agent in charge here will come up with the protection plan. I'll get a copy of it, to see if he missed anything, then we present it to you guys and ask for your cooperation. Then, a day or so before the actual visit, either me, or one of my guys, will come to town and check everything again, and check in with your people."

He paused, and looked in turn at everyone in the room—including Matt, which Matt found flattering.

"This time," he went on, "there's what I'm afraid may be a potential problem. Which is why I'm here, and so early."

He picked his briefcase up from the floor, laid it on his lap, opened it, and took out a plastic envelope.

"This is the original," he said, handing it to Wohl. "I had some Xeroxes made."

He passed the Xeroxes around to the others. They showed an envelope addressed to the Vice President of the United States, and the letter that envelope had held.

Dear Mr. Vice President:

You have offended the Lord, and He has decided, using me as His instrument, to disintegrate you using high explosives.

It is never too late to ask God's forgiveness, and I respectfully suggest that you make your peace with God as soon as possible.

Yours in Our Lord,

A Christian.

"Is this for real?" Mike Sabara asked.

Wohl gave him a disdainful look. Matt was glad that Sabara had spoken before he had a chance to open his mouth. He had been on the verge of asking the same question.

"If you're getting a little long in the tooth," Larkin said, "and you've been in this business awhile, you start to think you can intuit whether a threat is real or not. My gut feeling is that it's real; that this guy is dangerous."

"I don't think I quite follow you," Wohl said.

"The Vice President and, of course, the President get all kinds of threatening letters," Larkin said. "There's a surprisingly large number of lunatics out there who get their kicks just writing letters, people in other words who have no intention of doing what they threaten to do. Then there are the mental incompetents. Then there are those with some kind of gripe, something they blame, in this case, on the Vice President—and want fixed."

Larkin paused long enough for that to sink in.

"Everybody, I suppose, has seen *Casablanca*?" He looked

around as they nodded. "There was a great line, Claude Rains said, 'round up the usual suspects,' or something like that. We have a list of suspects, people we think need to be watched, or in some cases taken out of circulation while the man we're protecting is around. This guy is not on our list."

"How could he be on a list?" Matt blurted. "He didn't sign his name."

He glanced at Wohl, and saw Wohl's eyes chill, but then move to Larkin. It was a valid question, and Larkin immediately confirmed this:

"Good question. If they don't have a name, we give them one. For example, No Pension Check. Jew-Hater. Irish-Hater. Sometimes, it gets to be Jew-Hater, Chicago, Number Seventeen. Understand?"

"I think so," Matt said.

"We keep pretty good files. Cross-referenced. As good as we can make them. This guy doesn't appear anywhere."

"What makes you think he's dangerous?" Dave Pekach asked.

"For one thing, he's in Philadelphia, and the Vice President will be in Philadelphia in eight days, a week from Monday. We don't have much time."

"I meant, why do you think he's dangerous, and not just a guy who writes letters to get his kicks?" Pekach persisted.

"Primarily, because he sees himself as an instrument of the Lord. God is on his side; he's doing God's bidding, and that removes all questions of right and wrong from the equation. If God tells you to quote 'disintegrate' somebody, that's not murder."

"Interesting word," Sabara said thoughtfully, " 'disintegrate.' "

Larkin glanced at him. Matt thought he saw approval in his eyes.

"I thought so too," he said.

"So is 'instrument,' " Wohl chimed in. "God using this fellow as his 'instrument.' "

"Yeah," Larkin said. "I sent this off, as a matter of routine, to a psychiatrist for a profile. I'll be interested to hear what he has to say. Incidentally, if you have a good shrink, I'd be interested in what he thinks too."

"Her," Wohl said. "Not a departmental shrink. But she was very helpful when we had a serial rapist, ultimately serial murderer, running around the northwest. When we finally ran him down, it was uncanny to compare what she had to say about him based on almost nothing, and what we learned about him once we had stopped him."

"Interesting," Larkin said.

"Payne's sister. Dr. Amelia Payne. She teaches at the University."

"What's even more interesting, Mr. Larkin . . ." Pekach said.

"Charley, please," Larkin interrupted.

". . . is that Matt, Detective Payne, got this guy. With his next victim already tied up in the back of his van," Pekach concluded.

"Fascinating," Larkin said, looking at Matt.

*He already knew that,* Matt thought. *He's not going to shut Pekach up, but he knew. He really must have some files.*

"Okay, Matt," Wohl ordered. "As a first order of business, run this letter past Dr. Payne, will you, please?"

"Yes, sir."

"Mike, how are we fixed for cars?"

"Not good. Worse than not good."

"Matt's going to be doing a lot of running around," Wohl said. "He's going to need a car."

"Let him use mine," Pekach volunteered. "With or without Sergeant O'Dowd. I can get a ride if I need one."

"With your sergeant," Wohl said. "Matt, take the Xerox—before you go, make half a dozen copies—to Amy. Explain what we need, and why we need it yesterday. On the way, explain this to Sergeant O'Dowd, ask him for suggestions. The minute you can get through to him, call Chief Coughlin and ask him if he can meet us, make sure you tell him Mr. Larkin will be there, at Bookbinder's for lunch. I'll see if I can get Chief Lowenstein to come too."

"It's Sunday. There's no telling where Amy might be."

"Find her," Wohl ordered. "And keep me advised, step by step."

"Yes, sir."

# FOURTEEN

"There are some other things I think we can safely say about this guy," Larkin said after Matt had gone. "For one thing, he's intelligent, and he's well educated. The two don't always go together. You'll notice that he correctly capitalizes all references to the deity. 'His instrument,' for example, has a capital 'H.' "

Sabara grunted.

"And there are no typos on either the letter or the envelope, which were typed on an IBM typewriter. One of those with the ball. So he both knows how to type and has access to an IBM typewriter. Which means probably in an office. Which would mean that he would also have access to a blank sheet of paper, and probably an envelope. He used instead a sheet of typing paper from one of those pads you buy in Woolworth's or McCrory's. There are traces of an animal-based adhesive on the top edge. Actually the bottom, which just means that after he ripped the sheet free, he put it in the typewriter upside down. And he used an envelope from the Post Office. Which probably means that he knows somebody was going to take a good close look at both the letter and the envelope and didn't want us to be able to find him by tracing the paper or envelope."

"Then why write the letter in the first place? Take that risk?" Sabara asked.

"Because he believes that he is a Christian, and is worried about the Vice President's soul," Larkin said. "Which brings us back to someone who thinks he's doing the Lord's work being a very dangerous character, indeed."

"We keep saying 'he,' " Wohl said, but it was a question.

"Two things. Both unscientific," Larkin replied. "Women don't normally do this sort of thing. And there is, in my judgment, a masculine character to the tone of the letter. It doesn't sound as if it's written by a female. But I could be wrong."

"Yeah," Wohl said thoughtfully.

"One more speculation," Larkin said. " 'High explosives.' Technically, there are low-yield explosives and high-yield explosives. Maybe he knows the difference. That could suggest that this guy has some experience with explosives. It could just as easily mean, of course, that he doesn't know the difference, but just heard the term."

"But the whole letter suggests that he isn't thinking of taking a shot at the Vice President," Wohl said.

"Presuming, for the sake of argument, that you're right, that's a mixed blessing. Getting close enough to the Vice President to take a shot at him wouldn't be easy. Using explosives—and I don't think we can dismiss military ordnance, hand grenades, mines, that sort of thing—is something else. And since this guy is doing God's work, I don't think he's worrying about how many other people might have to be 'disintegrated.' "

"I don't suppose there's any chance of having the Vice President put off his visit until we can get our hands on this guy?" Wohl asked.

"No," Larkin said. "Not a chance."

"Has he seen this letter?"

Larkin shook his head, no.

"Well, you tell us, Charley," Wohl said. "How can we help?"

"That's a little delicate . . ."

"You'd rather discuss that in private, is that what you mean?" Larkin nodded.

"Charley, anything that you want to say to me, you can say in front of these people," Wohl said.

Larkin hesitated, and then said, "You are like your dad, Peter. He once told me he never had anyone working for him he couldn't trust."

"There are some I trust less than others," Wohl said. "These I trust, period."

"Okay," Larkin said. "The word that gets back to me is that there is some bad feeling between the Police Department and the feds, the FBI in particular, but the feds generally."

"I can't imagine why anyone would think that," Wohl said, lightly sarcastic.

Larkin snorted.

"There's a story going around that both you, the Department, I mean, and the FBI were going after a big-time car thief. And the first time that either of you knew the other guys were working the job was when your cars ran into each other when you were picking him up."

"Not true," Wohl said.

Larkin looked at him in surprise.

"The real story is that nobody in the Department, except one hard-nosed Irishman, believed that the car thief could possibly be a car thief. We were wrong, and the FBI was right."

"One of your guys, the hard-nosed Irishman?"

Wohl pointed at Jack Malone.

"And I didn't believe him, either," Wohl said. "Walter Davis and I had a long talk to see if we couldn't keep something like that from happening again."

Walter Davis was the SAC, the special agent in charge, of the Philadelphia office of the FBI.

"You get along with Davis all right, Peter?"

"As well as any simple local cop can get along with the FBI," Wohl said.

"Did you almost say 'the feds'?"

"No."

"Out of school," Larkin said. "I hear that part of the problem is a Captain Jack Duffy."

"Out of school, did you hear what Captain Duffy is supposed to have done?"

"What he doesn't do is the problem, is what I hear. Phrased delicately, both Walter Davis and our SAC here . . . Joe Toner, you know him, our supervisory agent in charge?"

Wohl shook his head, no.

". . . tell me that in the best of all possible worlds, Captain Duffy would be a bit more enthusiastically cooperative than he is."

"That's delicately phrased," Wohl said. "But I don't think it's Duffy personally. He takes his guidance from the commissioner."

"Okay. Confession time," Larkin said. "Joe Toner found out somehow that Dignitary Protection had been given to something called Special Operations, which was under an Inspector Wall. So, when I began to suspect that this vice presidential visit was going to present serious problems, I decided I was going to bypass Captain Duffy. I called the Dignitary Protection sergeant . . . you know who I mean, the caretaker sergeant?"

"Henkels," Wohl furnished.

"Sergeant Henkels. And I told him that I wanted to see the supervisor in charge in our office. There, I was going to make sure he found out that Denny Coughlin and I are old pals. The logic being that Henkels and the lieutenant were going to be more impressed with, and more worried about annoying, Chief Coughlin than they would about Duffy. In other words, they would enthusiastically cooperate."

"You think the danger this guy poses is worth really pissing off Duffy and the commissioner?"

"I would rather have both love me, but yes, I do."

"And if getting Henkels and Malone to circumvent normal channels incidentally got them in deep trouble, too bad?"

"My job is to keep the Vice President alive, Peter. If I have to step on some toes . . ."

"You can't simply cut Duffy out of the picture, even if you wanted to," Wohl said.

"Joe Toner's deputy has an appointment with Duffy at eight o'clock Monday morning. We will go through the motions. But what I hoped to get first from Malone, and then from you, was more cooperation than I'm liable to get from Duffy. This is not one of those times when it would be all right for you to say, 'Fuck the feds.' We've got to find this guy before he has a chance to 'disintegrate' the Vice President, and in the process probably a bunch of civilians."

Wohl's face was expressionless, but obviously, Mike Sabara decided, he was giving his response a good deal of thought. Finally, Wohl reached for his coffee cup, picked it up, and then looked directly at Larkin.

"How, specifically, do you think we could help?"

"Some cop in this town has a line on this guy. Either somebody in Intelligence, Sex Crimes, Civil Affairs, something else esoteric, or a detective somewhere, or a beat cop. He's done something suspicious. If we're lucky, done something really out of the ordinary, like buying explosives, maybe. Had some kind of trouble with his neighbors. Done something that would make a good cop suspicious of him, but nothing he would make official."

"If you gave Jack Duffy," Wohl replied, "or, better yet, the commissioner himself what you've just given us, it would be brought up at the very next roll call."

"And laughed at," Larkin said. "But that's what Toner's deputy is going to do tomorrow morning, tell Duffy everything. I told you, we're going to go through the motions. And maybe we'll get lucky. But maybe lucky won't cut it."

"So what do you want from us?" Wohl asked.

"I thought maybe you could tell me what you could do," Larkin said.

The question surprised Wohl; it was evident on his face.

"My dad was not a fan of police vehicles," he said after a moment. "He always said the beat cop, who knew everybody on his beat, could usually stop trouble before it happened. Unfortunately, we don't have many beat cops these days. But that strikes me as the way to go."

"Excuse me?" Larkin said.

"We'll need a good profile, written in simple English, not like a psychiatrist's case record, of this guy. We spread that around the Department, into every district, every unit. 'Does anybody think they know this guy?' And I'll have Dave distribute it, using the Highway Patrol. They're in and out of districts all over the city; they have friends everywhere, in other words. Make it look like a job, not like the brass in the Roundhouse are smoking funny cigarettes."

"Could you do that?" Larkin asked.

"Not without stepping on Duffy's toes, and a lot of other people's," Wohl said. "Do you know Chief Lowenstein?"

"Only that he runs the Detective Division."

"As a fiefdom," Wohl said. "How soon are you going to have the psychological profile you mentioned?"

"Ours, probably tomorrow, the day after. And the FBI's a day or two after that."

"Can that be speeded up?"

"I can have them in your hands, hand carried, within an hour of their delivery to my office in Washington," Larkin said. "Sooner, if you want it read over the phone. But I can't rush our shrink, and certainly not the FBI's."

"Okay. Then we'll have to go with Amy," Wohl said.

"Who?" Larkin asked.

"Dr. Payne. Detective Payne's sister."

"Oh, yeah."

"She'll give us a profile. I'll translate it into English."

The doorman of the large, luxurious apartment building in the 2600 block of the Parkway in which Amelia Alice Payne, M.D., lived paid only casual attention to the blue Ford as it dropped a passenger, a nicely dressed young man, outside his heavy plate-glass doors.

But then, as the young man stepped inside the lobby, the doorman saw, out of the corner of his eye, that the Ford, instead of driving onto the road leading to the parking lot and/or the Parkway had moved into an area close to the door where parking was prohibited to all but the management of the building and those tenants whose generosity to the doorman deserved a little reward.

"Hey!" the doorman called after the nicely dressed young man. "Your friend can't park there."

Matt Payne's childhood and youth had been punctuated frequently by the parental folklore that hay was for horses, and was not a suitable form of address for fellow human beings, the result of which being that he did not like to be addressed as "Hey!"

He turned to the doorman.

"Oh, I think he can," he said.

"Hey, he either moves the car, or I call the cops."

"There's a cop," Matt said helpfully as Jerry O'Dowd, in the full regalia of a sergeant of the Highway Patrol, got out of the car and strode purposefully toward the door.

"What's going on here?" the doorman asked.

"We're finally going to close the floating craps game on the tenth floor," Matt said. "Gambling is illegal, you know."

Sergeant Jerry O'Dowd, who was by nature a very cordial person, at that moment came through the plate-glass door, smiled at the doorman, and said, "Good morning. Nice day, isn't it?"

He then followed Matt to the bank of elevators and into one of them.

The doorman went to the elevator the moment the door closed and watched in some fascination as the indicator needle over the door moved in an arc and finally stopped at ten.

There were four apartments on the tenth floor. The two larger ones were occupied by a dentist and his family, and a lawyer and his family. The two smaller apartments were occupied by single people. One was a male, who, now that the doorman thought of it, did walk a little strangely, but was not the sort of guy who acted like a gambler.

The other was a female, a medical doctor, who he seemed to recall hearing was a teacher at the University of Pennsylvania, even if she didn't look old enough to be a doctor, much less a teacher. The only suspicious thing about her was that ten minutes before the cops showed up a really good-looking blonde had been dropped off by a chauffeur-driven Buick station wagon, asked for the doctor by name, and gone up.

The blonde didn't look like a hooker, but you weren't supposed to be able to tell anymore just by looks. Two young women and two young guys seemed to add up. Mr. Whatsisname in 10D didn't look like he even liked women.

The doorman decided he would just have to wait and see who got off the elevator, later. And then he decided that the young guy was probably pulling his chain. The cop might be a cop, but he was off duty, and the two of them were just going to see their girlfriends.

Just to be sure, he went out and looked at the blue Ford. It looked like a regular car, except that there was at least one extra radio antenna, and when he looked close, he saw a microphone lying on the seat, its cord disappearing into the glove compartment, and when he looked even closer, he could see a speaker mounted under the dashboard.

So it was a cop car. So what it *probably really* was that the sergeant was on duty, and it was Sunday morning, and nothing was going on, so he picked up his buddy and they came to see the girls. And parked wherever the hell they wanted to!

Goddamned cops!

Amy Payne, a slight, just this side of pretty, brown-haired twenty-seven-year-old, peered through the peephole in her door, and then, somewhat reluctantly, opened it just wide enough to look out.

"You are really the last person I expected to see here this morning, Matt," she said.

There was absolutely no suggestion that she intended to open the door.

"I've got to talk to you, Amy," Matt said.

"You've heard of the telephone? People get on the telephone and say, 'Would it be convenient for me to drop by?' "

"This is important," Matt said.

"How did you get past the doorman, come to think of it? Flash your badge at him?"

"Yeah, as a matter of fact. I'm on business, Amy. May we come in?"

She shrugged, and stepped out of the way.

"Amy, Jerry O'Dowd."

"How do you do, Doctor?"

"Why do I suspect you've been talking about me?" Amy said. "I hope you have a sister of your own, Sergeant, so that you will understand that despite the way I talk to him, I really loathe and detest him."

Jerry O'Dowd laughed. "He said you were feisty," O'Dowd said.

Amy realized that she was smiling back at him.

"I'll be with you in a minute," she said. "Go in the living room, Matt, you know where it is. I've got a little surprise for you too."

The surprise was Miss Penelope Detweiler, who was standing by the expanse of glass opening onto the Parkway and the Museum of Art.

"I thought that was your voice!" she said, seemingly torn between surprise and pleasure.

"What are you doing here?"

"That's none of your damned business, Matt!" Amy called from her bedroom. "Who do you think you are, asking a question like that?"

"Oh, I just dropped in to see Amy," Penny said, somewhat lamely.

*Yeah, like hell. Your relationship is professional. Doctor and patient. The only thing personal about it is that you get to come here to Amy's apartment because you are a friend of the family.*

"Penny, this is Sergeant Jerry O'Dowd," Matt said. "Jerry, this is Penny Detweiler, an old buddy of mine and my sister's."

"Hi," Penny said.

"Hello," O'Dowd said. Matt watched his face to see if he made the connection between the pretty blonde and Tony the Zee's junkie girlfriend. There was nothing on his face to suggest that he did.

"We were just having coffee," Penny said. "Real coffee. Amy

even grinds the beans just before she makes it. Would you like some?"

"Please," Matt said.

Penny headed for the kitchen, probably, Matt thought, to get cups and saucers. Matt went and looked out the window. O'Dowd followed him.

"Nice view!" he said enthusiastically.

"Yeah, it is."

"Is that who I think it is?"

"Yeah."

"Pretty girl."

*And you're a good cop. I was trying to read your face and couldn't.*

"Where were you before you went to work for Pekach?" Matt asked.

"Central Detectives, until I made sergeant, and before that in Narcotics. When Pekach was a lieutenant."

"And now Highway? You like riding a motorcycle?"

"You'll notice I'm not riding one. Pekach told me that if Highway was going to be good for his career, it should be good for mine."

"If I have to go to Wheel School and spend time in Highway, I think I'll stay a detective."

"You haven't been a detective long enough, have you, to make that kind of a judgment?"

"No, I haven't."

Amy came into the room, stopping their conversation.

"Okay, Matt," Amy said, "now what's this all about?" She didn't give him time to reply before she noticed that Penny was not in sight. "Where's Penny?"

"She went to get cups and saucers," Matt said. "What did you think?"

Amy ignored the question.

"What is that you're waving around like a field marshal's baton?" she asked.

O'Dowd chuckled. Amy found herself smiling at him again.

"There's nobody nicer anywhere than someone who thinks you're a wit," Matt said.

"Dad said that, not you," Amy said.

Matt peeled one of the Xeroxes from the roll of them he had been carrying in his hand.

"What's this . . ." Amy asked as she took a quick glance, and then she broke off in midsentence. Almost absently, she backed away from Matt and Jerry and sat down on the side arm of her couch.

"My God!" she said, finally. "This is a sick man."

"We'd sort of figured that out," Matt said. "What we need from you is a profile."

"Who's 'we,' you and the sergeant?"

"Peter Wohl, for one. The head of the Vice President's Secret Service detail, for another."

"The Secret Service have their own psychiatrists," Amy said. "I met one of them at Menninger one time. Why me?"

"Wohl said to tell you we need a profile yesterday," Matt said. "We won't get one from the Secret Service until tomorrow. If then."

"Secret Service?" Penny said, coming back into the room with cups and saucers. "That sounds interesting!"

"That's right," Amy said, ignoring Penny, "he is coming to town, isn't he? Next week?"

"Right," O'Dowd said.

"I think I have just been more or less politely told that what's going on here is none of my business," Penny said.

Matt looked at her, saw the hurt in her eyes, and surprised himself by handing her one of the Xeroxes.

"Not to be spread around the Merion Cricket Club, okay, Penny?"

"Thank you," Penny said, and Matt understood that it was not simply ritual courtesy for having been handed a piece of paper. He glanced at O'Dowd and saw in his eyes that he did not approve of what he had done.

*And you're right, Sergeant. I should not have passed that official document to a junkie three days out of the funny farm. And I thank you for not saying so, and humiliating me in front of my sister.*

"You have no idea who this man is?" Amy asked.

"None. That's why we need the profile."

"What are you going to do with it?"

"Circulate it in the Department, 'Do you know someone who fits this description?' "

"Not in public? Not in the newspapers?"

"That didn't come up," Matt said.

"Probably not," O'Dowd said. "That would tend to set off the copycats."

"Yes," Amy said thoughtfully. She looked directly at O'Dowd. "This letter doesn't give me much to go on, you understand?"

"I understand, Doctor," O'Dowd said. "But whatever you could tell us would be helpful."

*He sounds like Jason Washington,* Matt thought. *Stroking the interviewee.*

Jason Washington, late of Homicide, now a sergeant heading up Special Operations Division's Special Investigation Section, considered himself to be the best detective in the Philadelphia Police Department. So did Peter Wohl and Matt Payne.

And then as Matt watched Jerry O'Dowd skillfully draw from his sister a profile of the looney tune who wanted to blow up the Vice President, he had another series of thoughts, which ranged from humbling to humiliating:

*Wohl didn't send Pekach's driver with me so that I could ask him questions. He sent me with Jerry O'Dowd because I could get O'Dowd in to see Amy. My sole role in this was to get him into her presence. She might have, probably would have, told anyone else to call her office and arrange an appointment.*

*Pekach didn't pick this guy to be his driver for auld lang syne, but rather because Jerry O'Dowd is a very bright guy, an experienced detective, and now a sergeant. Both Pekach, when he volunteered O'Dowd to "drive me," and Wohl, when he accepted the offer, knew damned well O'Dowd would take over this little interview sooner or later, probably sooner, and in any event the instant Rookie Detective Payne started to fuck it up.*

Penny handed him a cup of coffee.

"Black, right?"

"Right. Thank you."

"Sergeant?"

"Black is fine with me."

*And that's why O'Dowd was at 30th Street Station when I picked Larkin up. Pekach was not about to tell Wohl that he thought he was making a mistake sending me on an important errand, but he felt obliged to protect his boss by sending O'Dowd there in case I fucked that up.*

Matt had a clear mental image of him patronizing O'Dowd outside the station: *"How are you, Jerry? What's up?"*

*Did your reputation precede you, Detective Payne? Did Captain Pekach say a soft word in Sergeant O'Dowd's ear before he sent him to the station, or did he think that was unnecessary, it would only be a matter of a minute or two before O'Dowd would be able to conclude for himself that Matthew M. Payne was a first-class, supercilious horse's ass?*

"Sergeant, excuse me," Matt Payne said. "I think I'd better call Chief Coughlin, and then check in with Inspector Wohl."

Sergeant O'Dowd looked at Detective Payne with something in his eyes that hadn't been there before.

"Yeah, Matt, please. Go ahead. Tell the inspector that what we're getting from Dr. Payne is very valuable."

Pekach answered Wohl's private number.

"Captain Pekach."

"Payne, sir. I was told to check in."

"The inspector took Mr. Larkin down to Intelligence," Pekach said. "How's things going?"

"Chief Coughlin will meet us for lunch. And Sergeant O'Dowd said to say that what we're getting from my sister is valuable."

"The reservations are for twelve noon. The inspector wants O'Dowd there. Tell him it would be nice if he could get into civilian clothing by then."

"Yes, sir. I have the feeling we're about finished here. There should be time."

In the elevator, Matt said, "Sergeant, Captain Pekach said that you're to go to Bookbinder's, and that if there's time, he'd like you to get out of uniform."

"The inspector probably wants to hear two versions of what we got from your sister," O'Dowd thought out loud, and looked at his watch. "There will be time. I live in Ashton Acres, right by the entrance to Northeast Airport."

The elevator door whooshed open, and they walked to the main door, past the doorman, who made no effort to rush to the door and open it for them.

"See you again," O'Dowd said cheerfully to the doorman, who snorted and pretended to find something on his little desk to be absolutely fascinating.

"I wonder what's wrong with him? Tight shoes?" O'Dowd asked as they were walking to the car.

"Beats me," Matt said. His brilliant repartee earlier with the doorman now seemed nowhere near as witty as it had.

When they were on the Parkway, headed east, O'Dowd said, "Give them a call, tell them where we're going."

Matt picked up the microphone, and then started to open the glove compartment to make sure he was on the right frequency.

"We're on the J-band," O'Dowd said, reading his mind. "And this is the boss's car."

"Highway One-A to Radio," Matt said.

"Highway One-A," the Highway radio dispatcher came back.

"Have you got anything for us?"

"Nothing, Highway One-A."

Matt laid the microphone back on the seat.

"Predictably, I suppose," O'Dowd said, "the only really interesting thing your sister said was when you were on the phone. She said she thinks this guy is asexual. I asked her if she thought that was the cause of his problems, and she said no, she thought it was something else, but that he was asexual, and we should keep that in mind. Do you have any idea what she meant by that?"

"Sergeant, I rarely have any idea what my sister is talking about."

"Have I pissed you off somehow, Payne?"

"Of course not."

"What happened to 'Jerry'?"

"It finally dawned on me that I was out of line at 30th Street Station this morning. A rookie detective should not call a sergeant by his first name."

"I'm not at all shy. If you had been out of line, I would have let you know."

"Thank you."

"So what do you think your sister meant when she said we should keep in mind that this guy is asexual?"

"Beats the shit out of me, Jerry."

O'Dowd laughed. "Better," he said. "Better."

# FIFTEEN

Bookbinder's Restaurant provided a private dining room for the luncheon party, and senior members of the landmark restaurant's hierarchy stopped by twice to shake hands and make sure everything was satisfactory.

*But,* Matt thought, *that's as far as manifestations of respect for the upper echelons of the Police Department are going to go. They might grab the tab if Coughlin or Lowenstein came in here alone. But they are not going to pick up the tab for a party as large as this one. For one thing, it would be too much money, and for another, it would set an unfortunate precedent: Hey, let's get the guys together and go down to Bookbinder's for a free lobster!*

*So what does that mean? That we go Dutch treat, which would make the most sense, or is Peter Wohl going to get stuck with the tab?*

*Fortunately, that is not my problem. So why am I worrying about it?*

He concentrated on his steamed clams, boiled lobster, and on making his two beers last through everything.

*It would be inappropriate for Matthew M. Payne, the junior police officer present, to get sloshed during lunch with his betters.*

Second *junior police officer,* he corrected himself: *I am no longer low man on the Special Operations totem pole. Officer Tom O'Mara is.*

*O'Mara,* Matt thought, somewhat surprised, *does not seem at all uncomfortable in the presence of all the white shirts, and heavy-hitter white shirts, at that. You'd think he would be; for the ordinary cop, chief inspectors are sort of a mix between the cardinal of the Spanish Inquisition and God himself.*

*But, when you think twice, Tom O'Mara is not an ordinary police officer in the sense that Charley McFadden was—and for that matter, detective or not, still is—an ordinary cop. He belongs to the club. His father is a captain. The reputation is hereditary: Until proven otherwise, the son of a good cop is a good cop.*

*Some of that, now that I think about it, also applies to me. In a sense, I am a hereditary member of the club. Because of Denny Coughlin, and/or because both my biological father and my Uncle Dutch got killed on duty.*

*The correct term is "fraternity," an association of brothers, from the Latin word meaning brother, as in* Delta Phi Omicron *at the University of Pennsylvania, where, despite your noble, two years service as Treasurer, you didn't have a fucking clue what the word "fraternity" really meant.*

"You look deep in thought, Matty," Chief Coughlin said, breaking abruptly into his mental meandering. "You all right?"

"I don't think I should have had the second dozen steamed clams," Matt replied. "But aside from that, I'm fine."

"You should have three dozen, Payne," Mr. Larkin said. "I'm paying."

"No, you're not!" Staff Inspector Peter Wohl said.

"We'll have none of that!" Chief Inspector Augustus Wohl said.

"Don't be silly, Charley," Chief Inspector Dennis V. Coughlin said.

"I'll tell you what I'll do, just so we all stay friends," Larkin said, "I'll flip anybody else here with a representation allowance. Loser pays."

"What the hell is a 'representation allowance'?" Chief Wohl asked.

"Your tax dollars at work, Augie," Larkin said. "When high-ranking Secret Service people such as myself are forced to go out with the local Keystone Cops, we're supposed to keep them happy by grabbing the tab. They call it a 'representation allowance.' "

"Screw you, Charley," Coughlin said, laughing. " 'Keystone Cops'!"

"Shut up, Denny. Let him pay," Chief Lowenstein said. "But order another round first."

There was laughter.

"Except for him," Peter Wohl said, pointing at Matt. "I want him sober when he translates that psychological profile into English."

"Sir, I can go out to the Schoolhouse right now, if you'd like."

"What I was thinking, Matt," Wohl said seriously, "was that the most efficient way to handle it would be for you to take it to your apartment and translate it there. Then O'Mara could run it by my dad's house, where we can have a look at it. Then Tom can take it out to the Schoolhouse, retype it, and duplicate it. By then Captain Pekach will have been able to set up distribution by Highway."

"Yes, sir," Matt said. "You don't want me to come by Chief Wohl's house?"

"I don't see any reason for you to come out there," Wohl said.

*Am I being told I don't belong there, or is he giving me time off?*

"Yes, sir," Matt said. "Thank you for lunch, Mr. Larkin."

"Thanks for the ride, Matt," Mr. Larkin said.

The only place there was room in Matt's apartment for a desk was in his bedroom, and even there he had to look long and hard for a desk small enough to fit. He'd finally found an unpainted "student's desk" in Sears Roebuck that fit, but wasn't quite sturdy enough for the standard IBM electric typewriter he had inherited from his father's office. Every time the carriage slammed back and forth for a new line, the desk shifted with a painful squeak.

Tom O'Mara made himself comfortable on Matt's bed, first by sitting on it, and then, when he became bored with that, by lying down on it and watching television with the sound turned off, so as not to disturb Matt's mental labor.

It took him the better part of an hour to translate first Amy's really incredibly bad handwriting, and then to reorganize what she had written, and then finally to incorporate what Wohl and Larkin had brought up in their meeting. Finally, he was satisfied that he had come up with what Wohl and Larkin wanted. He typed one more copy, pulled it from the typewriter, and handed it to O'Mara.

This individual is <u>almost certainly</u>:

Mentally unbalanced, believing that he has a special relationship with God. He may believe that God speaks to him directly.

IMPORTANTLY: He would not make a public announcement of this relationship.

Highly intelligent.

Well educated, most likely a college graduate, but almost certainly has some college education.

Well spoken, possessed of a good vocabulary.

An expert typist, with access to a current model IBM typewriter (one with a "type ball").

This individual is <u>probably</u>:

A male Caucasian.

Twenty-five to forty years old.

Asexual (that is, he's unmarried, and has no wife, or homo- or hetero- sexual partner or sex life).

"A loner" (that is, has very few, or no friends).

Living alone.

Neat and orderly, possibly to an excessive degree, and dresses conservatively.

Of ordinary, or slightly less than ordinary, physical appearance. A chess player, not a football player.

Self-assured, possibly to an excessive degree.

(That is, tends to become annoyed, even angry, with anyone who disagrees with him.)

An Episcopalian, Presbyterian, Methodist, (less likely, a Roman Catholic) but not an active member of any church group.

Works in an office.

A nondrinker.

Either a nonsmoker or a chain cigarette smoker.

This individual is <u>possibly</u>:

An engineer, either civil or electronic, or an accountant, or someone who works with figures.

A veteran, possibly discharged for medical (including psychological) reasons. Possibly a former junior officer.

Someone who has come to the attention of the authorities as the result of a complaint <u>he has made</u> when he has felt he has been wronged. (For example, complaining about neighbor's loud party, or loud radio, damage to his lawn, et cetera, by neighborhood children.)

As O'Mara read it, Matt glanced up at the silent TV mounted on a hospital-room shelf over the door. O'Mara had been watching an old cops-and-robbers movie.

*I wonder how he can tell the good guys from the bad guys? They all look like 1930s-era gangsters.*

"Your sister was able to come up with all this just from that nutty note that screwball wrote?" O'Mara asked, visibly awed.

"My sister is a genius. It runs in the family."

"Shit!" O'Mara said.

*After a pause,* Matt thought, *while he decided I was not serious.*

"Well, I'd better run this out to the brass," O'Mara said, and finally pushed himself upright and got off the bed.

At the head of the stairs, O'Mara stopped. "How do I get out?"

Matt recalled that O'Mara had parked Wohl's car in front of the building. Despite the NO PARKING signs, no white hat was going to ticket what was obviously the unmarked car of a senior white shirt. He had unlocked the plate-glass door to the lobby with his key, and then locked it again after them. It would now be necessary to repeat the process to let O'Mara out.

"I'll let you out," Matt said, and went down the stairs ahead of him.

Matt went into the kitchen and took a bottle of beer from the refrigerator and went into the living room, slumped in his chair and picked up a copy of *Playboy*. He looked at his answering machine. The red, *You Have Messages* light was flashing.

*I really don't want to hear my messages. But on the other hand, Wohl may be wondering what the hell took me so long.*

He reached over and pushed the PLAY button.

There were six calls, five of them from people—

*People, hell, Evelyn is at it again!*

—who had not chosen to leave a message, and one from Jack Matthews, who wanted him to call the first chance he got.

*And I know what you want, Jack Matthews. The FBI wants to know what the hell the Keystone Cops are doing with the Secret Service big shot from Washington. Fuck you!*

As the tape was rewinding, the doorbell, the one from the third floor, at the foot of his stairs, buzzed.

*Now what, O'Mara? Did you forget something?*

He got out of his chair, and pushed the button that operated the solenoid, and then looked down the stairs to see what O'Mara wanted.

Mrs. Evelyn Glover came through the door and smiled up at him.

*Jesus H. Christ!*

"Am I disturbing anything?"

"No," Matt lied. "I was just about to call you. Come on up."

There was an awkward moment at the head of the stairs, when Matt considered if he had some sort of obligation to kiss her and decided against it.

"I guess I shouldn't have done this, should I?" Evelyn asked.

"Don't be silly, I'm glad to see you. Would you like a drink?"

"Yes. Yes, I would."

"Cognac?"

"Yes, please."

She followed him into the kitchen, and stood close, but somewhat awkwardly, as he found the bottle and a snifter and poured her a drink.

"Aren't you having one?"

"I've got a beer in the living room."

"I owe you an apology," Evelyn said.

"How come?"

"I didn't really believe you when you said you had to work," she said. "I thought you were . . . trying to get rid of me."

"Why would I want to do that?"

*Because even as stupid as you are in matters of the heart, you can see where this one is about to get out of control.*

"But then, when I happened to drive by and saw the police car parked in front . . ."

"He just left."

*As if you didn't know. What have you been doing, Evelyn, circling the block?*

"Forgive me?" Evelyn asked coyly.

"There's nothing to forgive."

She had moved close to him, and now there was no question at all that she expected to be kissed.

There was just a momentary flicker of her tongue when he kissed her. She pulled her face away just far enough to be able to look into his eyes and smiled wickedly. He kissed her again, and this time she responded hungrily, her mouth open on his, her body pressing against his.

When she felt him stiffen, she caught his hand, directed it to her breast, and then moved her hand to his groin.

She moved her mouth to his ear, stuck her tongue in, and whispered huskily, pleased, "Well, he's not mad at me, is he?"

"Obviously not," Matt said.

*To hell with it!*

He put his hand under her sweater and moved it up to the fastener on her brassiere.

Marion Claude Wheatley turned the rental car back in to the Hertz people at the airport in plenty of time to qualify for the special rate, but there was, according to the mental defective on duty, 212 miles on the odometer, twelve more than was permitted under the rental agreement. The turn-in booth functionary insisted that Marion would have to pay for the extra miles at twenty-five cents a mile. He was stone deaf to Marion's argument that he'd made the trip fifty times before, and it had never exceeded 130 miles.

It wasn't the three dollars, it was the principle of the matter. Obviously, the odometer in the car was in error, and that was Hertz's fault, not his. Finally, a supervisor was summoned from the airport. He was only minimally brighter than the mental defective at the turn-in booth, but after Marion threatened to turn the entire matter over not only to Hertz management, but also to the Better Business Bureau and the police, he finally backed down, and Marion was able to get in a taxi and go home.

When he got to the house, Marion carefully checked everything, paying particular attention to the powder magazine, to make sure there had been no intruders during his absence.

Then he unpacked the suitcases, and took his soiled linen, bed-clothes, and his overalls to the basement, and ran them through the washer, using the ALL COLD and LOW WATER settings. He watched the machine as it went through the various cycles, using the time to make up a list of things he would need in the future.

First of all, he would need batteries, and he made a note to be sure to check the expiration date to be sure that he would be buying the freshest batteries possible for both the detonation mechanism and for the radio transmitter.

He would need more chain, as well. He was very pleased to learn how well the chain had functioned. He would need six lengths of chain, five for the five devices, and one as a reserve. Each length had to be between twenty and twenty-two inches in length.

He would need two 50-yard rolls of duct tape, and two 25-yard rolls of a good quality electrical tape, tape that would have both high electrical and adhesive qualities. He wouldn't need anywhere near even twenty-five yards of electrical tape, but one tended to misplace small rolls of tape, and he would have a spare if that happened. One tended to lose the larger rolls of duct tape less often, but it wouldn't hurt to be careful.

And he would need five pieces of luggage in which to place the devices. As he had driven back from the Pine Barrens, Marion had decided that what had been "AWOL bags" in the Army would be the thing to get. They were of canvas construction, nine or ten inches wide, probably eighteen inches or two feet long, and closed with a zipper.

It would be necessary to get them with brass, or steel, zippers, not plastic or aluminum. By attaching a wire between a steel or brass zipper and the antennae of the devices, it would be possible to increase the sensitivity of the radio receivers' antennae.

He would also need an attaché case in which to carry the short-wave transmitter. He had seen some for sale in one of the trashy stores along Market Street, east of City Hall. They were supposed to be genuine leather, but Marion doubted that, considering the price they were asking. It didn't matter, really, but there was no sense in buying a genuine leather attaché case when one that looked like leather would accomplish the same purpose.

Marion made two more notes, one to remind himself not to buy the AWOL bags all in one place, which might raise questions, and the other to make sure they all were of different colors and, if possible, of slightly different design.

He was finished making up the list a good five minutes before the washing machine completed the last cycle, and he was tempted to just leave the sheets and everything in the machine, and come back later and hang them up to dry, but then decided that the best way to go, doing anything, was to finish one task completely before going on to another.

He waited patiently until the washing machine finally clunked to a final stop, and then removed everything and hung it on a cord stretched across the basement. Things took longer, it seemed like forever, to dry in the basement, but on the other hand, no one had ever stolen anything from the cord in the basement the way things were stolen from the cord in the backyard.

When he came out of the basement, he changed into a suit and tie, and then walked to the 30th Street Station. He wanted to make sure that his memory wouldn't play tricks on him about the general layout of the station, and what was located where. He had been coming to the 30th Street Station since he had been a child, and therefore should know it like the back of his hand. But the operative word there was "should," and it simply made sense to have another careful look, in case changes had been made or there was some other potential problem.

He spent thirty minutes inside the station, including ten minutes he spent at the fast-food counter off the main waiting room, sitting at a dirty little table from which he could look around.

The Vice President would certainly want to march right down the center of the main waiting room, after he rode up the escalator from the train platform.

Unfortunately, there were no rows of lockers on the platform itself, which would have simplified matters a great deal. If there had been lockers, all he would have had to do was wait until the Vice President walked past where he could have concealed one of the devices, and then detonate it.

He consoled himself by thinking that if there had been lockers there, the Secret Service, who were not fools, would almost certainly make sure they didn't contain anything they shouldn't

Once the Vice President and his entourage reached the main waiting room level of the station, there were three possible routes to where he would enter his official car. There were east, west, and south entrances.

The logical place would be the east exit, but that did not mean he would use it. There were a number of factors that would be considered by those in charge of the Vice President's movements, and there was just no telling, with any degree of certainty, which one would be used.

All three routes would have to be covered. The east and west routes, conveniently, had rows of lockers. If he placed in each of two lockers on both the east and west routes one device, the lethal zone of the devices would be entirely effective. The south route did not have a row of lockers.

Marion thought that it was entirely likely the Lord was sending him a message via the lockers in the Pine Barrens. In other words, why the symbolism of the lockers if they were not in some way connected with the disintegration of the Vice President?

It was unlikely, following that line of thought, that the Vice President would take the south, locker-less route.

But on the other hand, it was also possible that he was wrong. It was also clear that the Lord expected him to be as thorough as humanly possible. That meant, obviously, that he was going to have to cover the south route, even if the Vice President would probably not use it.

There was, of course, a solution. There was always a solution when doing the Lord's work. One simply had to give it some thought. Often some prayerful thought.

There was a large metal refuse container against the wall in the passage between the main waiting room and the doors of the south exit. All he would have to do is put the fifth device in the refuse container. For all he knew—and there was no way to *know* without conducting a test—the metal refuse container would produce every bit as much shrapnel as one of the lockers.

The only problem, which Marion decided could be solved as he left 30th Street Station, was to make sure the metal refuse container would accept one of the AWOL bags through its opening.

Marion bought one of the last copies of the Sunday edition of *The Philadelphia Inquirer* on sale at the newsstand. He sat down on one of the benches in the main waiting room and flipped through it for three or four minutes. Then he left the station by the south route, stopping at the metal refuse container to place the newspaper in it.

He kept the first section. First he opened it and laid it on the opening horizontally, and then tore the paper to mark how wide the opening was. Then he held the paper vertically, and tore it again, this time marking how tall the opening was.

Then he folded the newspaper, tucked it under his arm, and walked out of the station and home.

He had thirty minutes to spare before Masterpiece Theater came on the television.


Magdelana Lanza was waiting for her son Vito on the sidewalk in front of the house on Ritner Street.

"I had to call the plumber," she announced.

"I told you I would go by Sears when I got off work."

"The hot water thing is busted; there was water all over the basement. And the pipes is bad."

"What pipes?"

"What pipes do you think, sonny? The *water* pipes is what pipes."

"What do you mean they're bad?"

"They're all clogged up; they got to go. We have to have new pipes."

*That sonofabitch of a plumber! What he did was figure he could sell an old woman anything he told her she needed. I'll fix his ass!*

"I'll have a look, Mama."

"Don't use the toilet. There's no water; it won't flush."

"Okay, Mama. I'll have a look."

*No water, my ass. What can go wrong with pipes? What I'm going to find when I go in the basement is that this sonofabitch has turned the valve off.*

Vito went in the house and went to his room and took off the good clothes he had worn to take Tony to the Poconos and put on a pair of khaki trousers and an old pair of shoes.

*I got to take a leak. What did you expect? The minute she tells you the toilet won't flush, you have to piss so bad your back teeth are floating.*

He went into the bathroom and looked at the toilet. There was water in the bowl.

*Nothing wrong with this toilet. What the hell was she talking about?*

He voided his bladder, and pulled the chain. Water emptied from the reservoir into the toilet bowl. It flushed. But there was no rush of clean water. The toilet sort of burped, and when he looked down there was hardly any water in the bowl at all, and none was coming in.

Vito dropped to his knees and looked behind the bowl at the valve on the thin copper pipe that fed water to the reservoir, and then put his hand on it.

There was a momentary feeling of triumph.

*The fucking thing's turned off! That sonofabitching plumber! Wait 'til I get my hands on you, pal!*

He turned the valve, opening it fully. No water entered the reservoir. He waited a moment, thinking maybe it would take a second or two to come on, like it took a while for the water to come hot when you turned it on.

*Nothing! Shit!*

*Three hours ago, I was in a bathroom with a carpet on the floor and a toilet you couldn't even hear flushing or filling, and now look where I am!*

*Wait a minute! He wouldn't shut it off here, he'd shut it off in the basement, where nobody would see. I didn't turn that valve on, I turned it off!*

He cranked the valve as far it would go in the opposite direction, and then went down the stairs to the first floor two at a time, and then more carefully down the stairs to the basement, because Mama kept brooms and mops and buckets and stuff like that on the cellar stairs.

His foot slipped on the basement floor, and he only barely kept from falling down. When he finally found the chain hanging from the light switch and got the bare bulb turned on, he saw that the floor was slick wet. Here and there there were little puddles. And it smelled rotten too, not as bad as a backed-up toilet, but bad.

He found the place at the rear of the basement where the water pipes came in through the wall from the water meter out back. And again there was a feeling of triumph.

*There's the fucking valve, and it's off!*

It didn't have a handle, like the valve on the toilet upstairs, just a piece of iron sticking up that you needed a wrench, or a pair of pliers, to turn. He turned and started for the front of the basement, where there was sort of a workbench, and where he knew he could find a wrench.

It was then that he saw the water heater had been disconnected, and moved from the concrete blocks on which it normally rested. Both the water and gas pipes connected to it had been disconnected.

He took a good close look.

*Well, shit, if I was the fucking plumber, I would disconnect the water heater. How the hell would an old lady know whether or not it was really busted? A plumber tells an old lady it's busted, she thinks it's busted.*

And then he saw something else out of the ordinary. There were two pieces of pipe, one with a connection on one end, and the other end sawed off, and a second piece, with both ends showing signs of having just been cut, lying on the floor near the water heater. . . .

*What the fuck did he have to do that for?*

He picked one piece of pipe up, and confirmed that the connection on one end indeed matched the connection on top of the water heater. Then he took the sawed end, and held it up against the pipe that carried the hot water upstairs.

It matched, like he thought it would. Then he saw where there was a break in the cold water pipe, where the other piece had been cut from. Just to be sure, he picked up the other piece of pipe and held it up to see if it fit. It did. And then for no good reason at all, he put the piece of pipe to his eye and looked through it.

*You can hardly see through the sonofabitch! What the fuck?*

He carried it to the bare light bulb fixture and looked through it again.

And saw that it was almost entirely clogged with some kind of shit. Rust. Whatever.

*That's what she meant when she said "the pipes are clogged. They got to go." Jesus Christ! What the fuck is that going to cost?*

Magdelana Lanza was waiting at the head of the cellar stairs when Vito came up.

"I told you not to flush the toilet," she said. "That there's no water. So now what am I supposed to do?"

"Use Mrs. Marino's toilet," he said.

"The plumber wants two thousand dollars' deposit."

"What?"

"He says, you don't get him two thousand dollars by nine tomorrow morning, he'll have to go onto another job, and we'll have to wait. He don't know when he could get back."

*"Two thousand dollars?"*

"He said that'll almost cover materials, labor will be extra, but he won't order the materials until you give him two thousand dollars, and you pay the rest when he's finished."

"Jesus, Mary, and Joseph!"

"Watch your language!"

"And what if I don't have two thousand dollars?"

"Then sell your Cadillac automobile, Mr. Big Shot, you got to have water in the house."

"Who'd you call, Mama, the plumber?"

"Rosselli Brothers, who else?"

"I'll go there in the morning."

"You can get off work? Give me a check, and I'll take it over there."

"I go on four-to-midnight today, Mama. I'll be off in the morning."

"You got two thousand dollars in the bank? After you bought your fancy Cadillac automobile?"

"Don't worry about it, Mama, okay? I told you I would take care of it."

Vito realized that he did not have two thousand dollars in his Philadelphia Savings Fund Society checking account. Maybe a little over a thousand, maybe even twelve hundred, but not two big ones.

*Upstairs, under the second drawer in the dresser, of course, there is some real money. Ten big ones.*

*But shit, I signed a marker for six big ones, which means I got four big ones, not ten. And when I pay the fucking plumber two big ones in the morning, that'll take me down to two.*

*Jesus Christ, where the fuck did it all go? I got off the airplane from Vegas with all the fucking money in the world, and now I'm damned near broke again.*

"You got to take care of it," Magdelana Lanza said. "We got to have a toilet and hot water."

"Mama, I said I'd take care of it. Don't worry about it."

Magdelana Lanza snorted.

"Mama, can you stay with Mrs. Marino tonight? I mean you can't stay here with no water."

"Tonight, I can stay with Mrs. Marino. But I can't stay there forever."

"Okay. One day at a time. I'll see what the plumber says tomorrow, how long it will take him. Now I got to get dressed and go to work. Okay?"

"I'll go ask Mrs. Marino if it would be an imposition."

"You'd do it for her, right? What's the problem?"

"I'll go ask her, would it be an imposition."

She walked out the front door and Vito climbed the stairs to the second floor. He took the second drawer from his dresser, and then took the money he had concealed in the dresser out and sat on his bed and counted it.

It wasn't ten big ones. It was only ninety-four hundred bucks. When there had been twenty-two big ones, six hundred bucks hadn't seemed like much.

Now it means that I don't even have two big ones, just fourteen lousy hundred. Plus, the eleven hundred in PSFS, that's only twenty-five hundred.

Jesus H. Christ!

He changed into his uniform.

*The plumber and his helpers will be all over the house. I better take this money with me; it will be safer than here.*

# SIXTEEN

Officer Jesus Martinez drove into the parking lot of the Airport Police Station in his five-year-old Oldsmobile 98 about two minutes before Corporal Vito Lanza pulled in at the wheel of his not-quite-a-year-old Cadillac Fleetwood.

Martinez would not have seen Lanza arrive had he not noticed that his power antenna hadn't completely retracted. Jesus took great pride in his car, and things like that bothered him. He unlocked the car and got back in and turned the ignition on and ran the antenna up and down by turning the radio on and off.

It retracted completely the last couple of times, which made him think, to his relief, that there was nothing wrong with the antenna, that it was probably just a little dirty. As soon as he got home, he would get some alcohol and wet a rag with it, and wipe the antenna clean, and then lubricate it with some silicone lubricant.

He was in the process of relocking the Olds's door when Corporal Lanza pulled in beside him.

*That's a new Cadillac. Where the fuck does he get the money for a new Cadillac?*

"Whaddaya say, Corporal?"

"Hey! How they hanging, Gomez?"

"It's Martinez, Corporal."

"Sorry."

"Nice wheels."

"Yeah, it's all right. Nothing like a Caddy."

"What's something like that worth?"

"What the fuck is the matter with you? It's not polite to ask people what things cost."

"Sorry, Corporal. Just curious."

"A lot," Lanza said. "Save your pennies, Martinez."

"Yeah."

"Or get lucky, which is how I got that fucker."

"Excuse me?"

"Las Vegas. You want a Caddy like that, you go to Las Vegas and get lucky."

"Yeah, I guess."

"So how do you like the Airport?"

"I haven't been out here long enough to really know. So far it's great. I was in Highway."

*How the fuck did a little Spic like you get into Highway? You don't look big enough to straddle a motorcycle.*

"Yeah, I heard. So why did you leave Highway?"

"They made it plain to me that maybe I would be happier someplace else. Which was all right with me. I wasn't too happy in Highway."

*They didn't want you in Highway as little as you are. Those fuckers all think they're John Wayne. And John Wayne, you're not, Gom—Martinez.*

"Well, walking around an air-conditioned building telling tourists where they can find the pisser sure beats riding a motorcycle in the rain."

"You said it, Corporal."

"The next time they announce a corporal's exam, you ought to have a shot at it."

"Yeah, well, I'm not too good at taking examinations."

"Some people are, and some people aren't. Don't worry about it."

It wasn't until a few minutes after midnight, when he put the key in the Caddy's door, that Vito, with a sinking feeling in his stomach, realized that he had done something really fucking stupid.

He pulled the door open and slid across the seat, and then, cursing, lifted the fold-down armrest out of the way and put his finger on the glove compartment button.

*Shit, it's locked. I don't remember locking the sonofabitch.*

He found the key and unlocked the glove compartment, and exhaled audibly with relief. The Flamingo Hotel & Casino envelope was still there, right where he'd shoved it when he got in the car.

He took it out and glanced into it. There was enough light from the tiny glove compartment bulb to see the comforting thick wad of fifties and hundreds. He closed the envelope and stuck it in his pocket.

*Not that much of it is still mine anymore.*

*I know goddamned well I didn't lock that compartment. Maybe, this is a Caddy, after all, it locks automatically.*

He closed the glove compartment door, slid back across the seat behind the wheel, put the ignition key in, and started the engine.

*Starts right fucking off! There really is nothing like a Caddy.*

He backed out of the parking slot, noticed that the old Olds the Spic kid drove was still there. Well, at least he knew what he was doing in the Airport Unit. The little fucker was too dumb to pass the detective's exam, and too little to be a real Highway Patrolman, so they eased him out. They tossed him Airport Unit as a bone. He wondered if the little Spic was smart enough to know how lucky he was to be in Airport; they could just as easily have sent him to one of the districts, or somewhere else really shitty.

Vito decided he would be nice to the kid. Make sure he knows what a good deal he had fallen into. He might come in useful sometime.

He drove up South Broad Street and then made an illegal left turn onto Spruce.

What the hell it was after midnight, there was no traffic, and he was in his uniform, nobody was going to give him a ticket, even if some cop saw him.

He did decide to put the Caddy in a parking garage. If he didn't, sure as Christ made little apples, some asshole, jealous of the Caddy, would run a key down the side or across the hood. Or steal the fucking hubcaps.

When he parked the car, he remembered this was the garage where the mob blew away a guy, one of their own, who had pissed somebody off. Tony the Zee DeZego. They got him with a shotgun.

Tony met him at the door of her apartment in a negligee. Nice-looking one. Vito had never seen her in it before.

"You didn't have to wait up for me, baby," Vito said.

"I went to bed," she said, kissing him, but moving her body away when he tried to slip his hand under the negligee, "but Uncle Joe called me, and then I couldn't get back to sleep."

"What did he want?"

"He's worried about those markers you signed at Oaks and Pines Lodge."

"Why should he be worried? I'm good for them. And he set it up too, didn't he?"

"Well, that's what happened. He didn't set it up. They just thought he did. But because he sent you there, they told him they were holding him responsible. So he's worried. Six thousand dollars is a lot of money."

"Hey! I'm good for it. I got it in my pocket. You call him up and ask if he wants me to come over there right now with it, or whether he can wait until the morning."

"I'm sure it will be okay," Tony said.

"Call him!" Vito said. "Tell him the only reason I didn't make those markers good sooner was that I had to work."

"Okay, honey," Tony said. "Whatever you say."


Penelope Detweiler, wearing only the most brief of underpants, her naked bosom bouncing not at all unattractively, was chasing Matthew M. Payne around the upstairs sitting room of the Detweiler mansion in Chestnut Hill when the doorbell, actually a rather unpleasant-sounding buzzer, went off.

Matt Payne sat up in his bed suddenly.

*Who the hell is that?*

He looked up at the ceiling, where a clever little clock his sister Amy had given him projected the time by a beam of light. It was almost half past one.

*Christ, don't tell me Evelyn's come back!*

He threw the blankets back angrily and marched naked through the kitchen to the button by the head of the stairs that operated the door lock solenoid and pushed it.

The door opened and Detective Charley McFadden started up the stairs. On his heels was Officer Jesus Martinez, in uniform.

"You took your fucking time answering the doorbell," Detective McFadden said, by way of apology for disturbing Matt's sleep.

"I'll try to do better the next time."

"I thought maybe you had a broad up here," McFadden said as he reached the head of the stairs.

*Not anymore. She finally went home, after reluctantly conclud-
ing that the only way she was going to be able to make it stand up
again was to put it in a splint.*

*That being the case, where did that erotic dream about Precious
Penny come from?*

"If there was, you'd still be down there leaning on the doorbell,"
Matt said. "What do you say, Hay-zus?"

Martinez did not reply.

"You got a beer or something?" McFadden asked. "And why
don't you put a bathrobe on or something?"

"Are we going to have a party?"

"No. This is business. We got to talk."

"You know where the beer is," Matt said, and went in the bedroom for his robe.

*It smells in here.* Essence de Sex.

"You got a Coke or something?" Martinez asked.

"There's ginger ale, Hay-zus," Matt said. "I don't think there's
any Coke."

He went to the refrigerator and found a small bottle of ginger ale
and handed it to Martinez.

"Thank you."

"Hay-zus thinks he's found a dirty cop at the airport,"
McFadden said.

*Then he probably has. But why tell me?*

"Tell Internal Affairs," Matt said.

"I can't go to Internal Affairs. I haven't caught him doing anything, but I got the gut feeling he's dirty," Martinez said.

"I don't understand what you're doing here," Matt said.

"Charley said I should talk to you."

"I don't have the faintest idea what you're talking about," Matt
said. "You want to take it from the beginning?"

"Tell him what you told me, Hay-zus," Charley said, lowering
himself with a grunt into Matt's upholstered chair.

"There's a corporal out there," Jesus said. "A flashy Guinea
named Lanza, Vito Lanza."

Matt did not reply.

"Just bought himself a new Cadillac," Jesus said. "You can't
buy a Caddy on a corporal's pay."

"Maybe his number hit," Matt said, slightly sarcastic.

"He said he won the money in Las Vegas," Jesus said.

"That's possible," Matt said.

"Look at him. He won six thousand when he was out there," McFadden said.

"Yeah, I thought about that. But he's not Lanza."

"What does that mean?" Matt asked.

"You're fucking rich. You don't really give a shit whether you win or lose, and you came home with only six thousand."

"*Only* six thousand? I wish to Christ I had won six thousand," Charley said.

"There's more," Jesus said.

"Like what more?"

"He had almost ten thousand in cash, ninety-four hundred, to be exact, in his car tonight."

"How do you know that?"

"I looked."

"What do you mean, you looked?"

"When Charley and I were in Narcotics, we stopped a guy one night and took a car thief's friend from him," Jesus said. "I kept it."

A car thief's friend, sometimes called a "Slim-Jim," was a flat piece of metal, most commonly stainless steel, suitably shaped so that when inserted into an automobile door, sliding it downward in the window channel, it defeated the door lock.

"In other words, you broke into this guy's car, is that what you're saying?"

"Yeah, and he had ninety-four hundred dollars in an envelope in the glove compartment, an ashtray full of cigarette butts with lipstick on them, and this."

Martinez threw something at Matt who caught it. It was a book of matches. *Oaks and Pines Resort Lodge.*

"What's this?"

"It's a fancy place in the Poconos," Jesus said.

"So?"

"I called a guy I know in Vice and asked him did he ever hear about it, and he told me that there's a room in the back for high rollers; that the word is that the Mob owns it."

"So?"

"This doesn't smell to you, Payne?" Martinez said, seemingly torn between surprise and contempt.

"I take back what I said before. You should not go to Internal Affairs. What you have is a guy that gambles. At this lodge, and in Las Vegas. And right now, he's lucky. The only thing I can see he's done illegally is gamble in the Poconos. That's a misdemeanor, as opposed to a felony. Like being in possession of burglar tools is a felony."

"What did I tell you he'd say, Hay-zus?" Charley McFadden said.

"I got the *feeling*, Charley," Jesus said. "This guy is dirty."

"What's he doing?"

"They're smuggling drugs through the airport, most likely off Eastern Airlines flights from Puerto Rico, and probably from Mexico City flights too."

"You *know* this?"

"Everybody knows it, Matt," Charley said. "The feds, Customs Service, and the Bureau of Drugs and Dangerous Narcotics. . . ."

"Narcotics and Dangerous Drugs," Jesus interrupted to correct him.

"Whatever the fuck they are, they're all over the place."

"They haven't caught this guy, then, have they?" Matt responded.

"*I* want to catch this fucker," Jesus said.

*You're not a detective, Martinez. You're a simple police officer who took the detective's exam and flunked it.*

*You are an arrogant, self-satisfied shit, aren't you, Matthew Payne? Martinez is not only not a rookie, he's spent a lot of time dealing with drug people when he was in Narcotics. He knows what he's talking about.*

"What do you want from me, Hay-zus?"

"I told him he ought to go to Wohl," Charley said. "He says he doesn't want to."

"Why not?" Matt asked, meeting Martinez's eyes.

"I don't work for Wohl anymore, for one thing. And even if I did, how the hell could I go to Wohl and tell him the reason I know this fucker runs around with almost ten thousand in his glove compartment is because I looked?"

" 'Broke into his car' are the words you're looking for," Matt said.

"I told Hay-zus Wohl, or at least Pekach, would listen to him. And he could tell them the car was unlocked."

"That's splitting a hair," Matt thought out loud. "That wouldn't wash with either Wohl or Pekach. And I suppose you know that if you'd found ten thousand dollars' worth of cocaine in his glove compartment, it would be inadmissible evidence."

"Hey, I was a Narc when you were Mr. Joe College Payne," Jesus said. "I know what's admissible and what isn't."

"Hay-zus, you don't have a thing on this guy," Matt said.

"He wants to follow him, and *get* something on him," Charley said.

"You mean, he wants *us* to surveil this guy, right?"

"I told you he'd tell us to go fuck ourselves," Martinez said.

"He can't do it himself, this Dago knows him."

"We're wasting our time. Let's get out of here," Martinez said.

"Hay-zus is usually right, when he smells something," McFadden went on.

"Come on, let's get out of here," Martinez repeated.

"What do you expect to find, Martinez, if we start to follow this guy around?" Matt asked.

"Association with known criminals," Martinez said. "That would give me enough to go to Wohl or Internal Affairs."

*He keeps bringing up Wohl. Why? He doesn't work for Wohl anymore. But I do. That's what this is all about. He figures I could go to Wohl.*

"For the sake of argument, Hay-zus," Matt said. "Let's suppose we follow this guy, and either he spots us before we catch him with some Mob type, or that you're wrong. He'd really be pissed. And we would have some explaining to do."

"In other words, no, right?"

"I didn't say that," Matt said. "I said what if."

"Then I would take my lumps."

"*We* all would take *our* lumps," Matt said.

"This guy is dirty," Martinez said. "We're cops."

Matt exhaled audibly.

"What have you got in mind?"

"You don't look like a cop," Martinez said. "You drive a Porsche. You could get into this place in the Poconos."

"How would we know when he was going to be there? And if we did, what am I supposed to do, tell Wohl I want the day off to take a ride to the Poconos?"

"I don't think he'd be going up there in the daytime," Martinez said. "Except over the weekend. He's got Friday-Saturday off. With a little bit of luck, he'd go up there then."

"And what if he just came across this book of matches some-place? Picked it up in a bar or something? You don't *know* that he's ever even been in this place." Matt picked up the matchbook. "Oaks and Pines Resort Lodge."

"Then I'll think of something else," Martinez said.

"Okay, Hay-zus," Matt said. "Let me know what you want me to do, and when you want me to do it."

"See, Hay-zus," McFadden said. "I told you."

"But don't let your Latin-American temper get out of joint if I can't jump when you call. I may be doing a lot of overtime."

"Overtime, you?" McFadden asked.

*That was an honest question,* Matt decided, *not a challenge.*

"Special Operations has been given Dignitary Protection. The Vice President's coming to Philly. There's a looney tune out there that wants to blow him up."

"No shit?" McFadden asked.

"Yeah, and the Secret Service thinks this guy is for real."

"What's that got to do with you?"

"Malone is in charge. For the time being, I'm working for Malone."

"We'll just have to see what happens," Martinez said. "If you're working, you're working."

When Joe Fierello drove his Mercedes-Benz onto the lot of Fierello Fine Cars at quarter to nine in the morning, he found Vito Lanza waiting for him.

"Don't tell me," Joe said as he got out of his car, "the transmission fell out."

"Not yet," Vito said. "I wanted to take care of my markers."

"Tony tell you I called?" Joe asked, but before Vito could answer, he went on, "Come on in the office. I'm not worth a shit in the morning until I have my coffee."

Fierello's secretary smiled at them as they walked past.

"Darlene, get us some coffee, will you?" Joe said, and as he walked behind his desk, he waved Vito into a chair in front of his desk. "Take a load off. You take anything in your coffee?"

Vito shook his head, no.

"Black both times, darling," Joe called out.

Darlene delivered the coffee and then left, closing the door behind her.

"Nice," Vito said.

"My wife's sister's girl," Joe said. "A *nice* girl."

"That's what I meant," Vito said.

Joe Fierello smiled at Vito. Vito did not like the smile.

"Like Tony," he said.

"Darlene doesn't go off overnight to the Poconos," Joe said. "You understand?"

"Absolutely."

"Don't misunderstand me, Tony's a nice girl. She's over twenty-one and she can do what she likes.

"I'm sorry there was that confusion about the markers," Joe said.

"They offered me the markers," Vito said. "I didn't ask for them."

"You went up there as my guest; they're holding me responsible for the markers. You're a nice fellow, Vito, but I don't like you six big ones worth. How soon can you make them good?"

"Right now, Joe. That's what I came here for."

He reached in his pocket and took out the envelope from the Flamingo.

"Hey, what are you doing?"

"I'm making good my markers," Vito said, now very confused.

"You don't understand," Joe said. "I'm a businessman. You don't make your markers good with me."

"With who, then?"

"You really don't know, do you?"

"You got me pretty confused, to tell you the truth," Vito confessed.

"Let me make a call," Joe said.

He took a small leather notebook from his jacket pocket, found a number, and dialed it.

"This is Joe Fierello," he said when someone answered. "Could I talk to Mr. Cassandro, please?" He covered the microphone with his hand. "Mr. Cassandro is sort of like the local business agent, you know what I mean?"

Vito nodded.

*Business agent, my ass; this Cassandro guy is with the mob.*

"Paulo? Joe Fierello. You know those financial documents you were a little concerned about? Well, don't worry. They're good. Mr. Lanza is right here with me now, and he's anxious to take care of them."

He started nodding, and again covered the microphone with his hand. "He says he's sorry, I don't know what the fuck he means."

He removed his hand from the microphone.

"I'm sure Mr. Lanza would be perfectly willing to come wherever you tell him, Paulo," Fierello said, and there was a reply, and then he went on: "Whatever you say, Paulo. He'll be here."

He hung up the telephone and looked at Vito.

"He's coming right over. He said there was some kind of a

mixup, and he wants to make it right. It'll take him five, ten minutes. You got to be someplace else?"

Vito shook his head. "I really don't understand this," he said.

"Neither do I," Joe Fierello said. "So we'll have our cup of coffee, and in five, ten minutes, we'll both know."

Ten minutes later, a silver Jaguar drove up the driveway into Fierello Fine Cars, and stopped beside Joe Fierello's Mercedes-Benz. Paulo Cassandro, wearing a turtleneck sweater and a tweed sports coat with matching cap, got out of the back seat.

He looked toward the window of Joe Fierello's office.

"I think he wants you to come out there," Joe said.

Somewhat uncomfortable, but not quite sure why he was, Vito nodded at Joe Fierello and walked out of the building and down the stairs.

Joe Fierello opened the drawer of his desk, took out a 35-mm camera in a leather case, went to the window, and started snapping pictures.

"Mr. Lanza, I'm Paulo Cassandro," Paulo said. "I'm sorry about this."

"I don't understand," Vito said.

"We thought you were somebody else," Paulo said. "Lanza is a pretty common name. You, Mario the singer, and a lot of other people, right?"

"I guess so."

"I hate to tell you this," Paulo said, draping a friendly arm around Vito's shoulders, "but one of your cousins, maybe a second cousin, is a deadbeat. He owes everybody and his fucking brother. We thought it was you."

"I can't think of who that would be," Vito said.

"It doesn't matter. With a little bit of luck, you'll never run into him."

"Yeah," Vito said.

"We're sorry we made the mistake. We never should have bothered you or Joe with this. I hope you ain't pissed?"

"No. Of course not. I just want to make my markers good."

"There's no hurry. Take your time. Once we found out you wasn't *Anthony* Lanza, we asked around a little, and *your* credit is as good as gold."

"I always try to pay my debts," Vito said. "I like to think I got a good reputation."

"And now we know that," Paulo said. "So, whenever it's convenient, make the markers good. It don't have to be now. Next month sometime would be fine."

"Let me take care of them now," Vito said. "I already brung the cash."

"You don't have to, but if you got it, and it's convenient, that'd straighten everything out."

Vito handed him the six thousand dollars. Paulo very carefully counted it.

"No offense, me counting it?"

"No. Not at all."

"Watch the fifties, and the hundreds will take care of themselves, right?"

"Right."

Paulo put the money in the pocket of his tweed jacket.

"I want to give you this," he said, and took out a business card. "You want to loan me your back?"

Vito, after a moment, understood that Cassandro wanted to use his back as a desk, and turned around.

"Okay," Paulo said, and Vito turned around again.

Cassandro handed him the card. Vito read it. It said *Paulo Cassandro, President, Classic Livery, Distinguished Motor Cars For All Occasions*.

"You ever get back up to the Lodge, you just give that to the manager," Paulo said. "Turn it over."

Vito turned it over. On it, Cassandro had written, *"Vito Lanza is a friend of mine. And I owe him a big one."*

"You didn't have to do nothing like this," Vito said, embarrassed.

"I don't have to do nothing but pay taxes and die," Paulo said. "Just take that as my apology for making a mistake. Maybe they'll give you a free ice cream or something."

"Well, thank you," Vito said.

"I'm glad we could straighten this out," Paulo said, and wrapped his arm around Vito's shoulder.

Vito felt pretty good until he got to the goddamned plumber's. The sonofabitch was waiting for him, and overnight, he'd gone back on his word. Now he wanted twenty-five hundred before he would fix a fucking thing at the house. That left him with nine hundred. The plumber said it would probably run another thousand, maybe fifteen hundred, for the labor and incidentals.

*There isn't a plumber in the fucking world who ever brought a*

*job in for less than the estimate, and even if this sonofabitch did,
that would leave me, if he wants fifteen hundred, six hundred short.*

*I've got eleven, twelve hundred in the PSFS account, and I can
always borrow against the Caddy.*

*Jesus, I hate to put a loan against the Caddy.*

*Why the fuck didn't I take Cassandro's offer to take my time mak-
ing the markers good? I really didn't have to pay them off that
quick. My credit is good.*

The absence of inhabitants in most of the Pine Barrens does not
obviate the need for police patrols. The physical principle that nature abhors a vacuum has a tangential application to an unoccupied
area. People tend to dump things that they would rather not be connected to in areas where they believe they are unlikely to be found
in the near future.

Enterprising youth, for example, who wish to earn a little pocket
money by stealing someone's automobile, and removing therefrom
parts that have resale value, drive the cars into the Pine Barrens and
strip them there.

And, in the winter, more than one passionate back seat dalliance
in an auto with a leaking exhaust system has ended in tragedy by
carbon monoxide poisoning.

And the Pine Barrens is a good place to shoot someone and dis-
pose of the body. The chances that a shot will be heard are remote,
and a shallow grave even desultorily concealed stands a very good
chance of never being discovered.

There had been an incident of this nature just about a year before, which Deputy Sheriff Daniel J. Springs was thinking about as
he drove, touching sixty, on a routine patrol in his three-year-old
Ford, down one of the dirt roads that crosses the Barrens.

Dan Springs, a heavyset, somewhat jowly man who was fifty
and had been with the Sheriff's Department more than twenty
years, tried to cover all the roads in his area at least once every
three days. Nine times out of ten, he saw nothing but the scrubby
pines and the dirt road, and his mind tended to wander.

One of Springs's fellow deputies, making a routine patrol not far
from here, had come across a nearly new Jaguar sedan abandoned
by the side of the road, the keys still in the ignition, battery hot,
with half a tank full of gas.

That meant somebody had dumped the car there, and driven
away in a second car. They'd put the Pennsylvania plate on the

FBI's NCIC (National Crime Information Center) computer and got a hit.

The cops in Philadelphia were looking for the car. It was owned by a rich guy, a white guy, who had been found carved up in his apartment. The cops were looking for the car, and for the white guy's black boyfriend.

Springs had been called in on the job then, to help with working the crime scene, and to keep civilians from getting in the way. Springs never ceased to be amazed how civilians came out of the woodwork, even in the Pine Barrens, when something happened.

Everybody came in on that job. The State Police, and even the FBI. There was a possibility of a kidnapping, which was a federal offense, even if state lines didn't get crossed, and here it was pretty evident, with a Philadelphia car abandoned in New Jersey, that state lines had been crossed.

Plus, of course, the Philadelphia Homicide detectives working the job. Springs remembered one of them, an enormous black guy dressed like a banker. Springs remembered him because he was the only one of the hotshots who did not go along with the thinking that because the car had been found *here*, that if there *was* a body, it had been dumped/buried anywhere *but* here, and the chances of finding it were zilch.

The black Philadelphia Homicide detective had said he was pretty sure (a) that there was a body and (b) they were going to find it right around where they had found the Jaguar.

And they had. Not a hundred yards from the Jaguar they had found a shallow grave with a black guy in it.

Springs had spoken to the big Homicide detective:

"How come you were so sure we'd find a body, and find it here?"

"I'm Detective Jason Washington," the black guy had said, introducing himself, offering a hand that could conceal a baseball. "How do you do, Deputy Springs? We're grateful for your cooperation."

"Why did you know the body would be here?" Springs had pursued as he shook hands. "Call me Dan."

"I didn't know it would be here," Washington had explained. "But I thought it would be."

"Why?"

"Well, I started with the idea that the doers were not very smart. They would never have stolen the Jaguar, an easy-to-spot vehicle, for example, if they were smart. And I'm reasonably sure they were drunk. And people who get drunk doing something wrong in-variably sober up, and then get worried about what they've done. That would apply whether they shot this fellow back in Philadel-phia, en route here, or here. They would therefore be anxious to get rid of the car, and the body, as quickly as possible. I would not have been surprised if we had found the body in, or beside, the car. And they are both lazy, and by now hung over. I thought it unlikely that they would drag a two-hundred-odd-pound corpse very far."

Just like Sherlock Holmes, Springs had thought. He had *deduced* what probably had happened. Smart guy, as smart as Springs had ever met.

They'd caught the guys, two colored guys, who had shot the one in the Barrens, a couple of days later, in Atlantic City. They had been using the dead white guy's credit cards, which proved Detec-tive Washington's theory that they were not very smart.

They'd copped a plea, and been sentenced to twenty years to life, which meant they would be out in seven, eight years, but Springs now recalled hearing somewhere that they had been indicted for kid-napping, and were to be tried in federal court for that. The white boy's father had political clout, he owned a newspaper, newspapers, and he wanted to make sure that the guys who chopped up his son didn't get out in seven or eight years.

Deputy Springs was thinking of the enormous black Homicide detective who dressed like a banker and talked like a college pro-fessor, wondering if he was still around Philadelphia, when sud-denly the steering wheel was torn out of his hands, and the Ford skidded out of control off the dirt road and into a scraggly pine tree before he could do anything about it.

He hit the four-inch-thick pine tree squarely. He was thrown for-ward onto the steering wheel, and felt the air being knocked out of him. The Ford bent the pine tree, and then rode up the trunk for a couple feet, and then the tree trunk snapped, and the car settled on the stump.

"Jesus, Mary, and Joseph!" Deputy Springs exclaimed. For a moment, he could see the branches of the pine tree, and then, ac-companied by the smell of the water/antifreeze mixture turning to steam, the windshield clouded over.

There was a screeching from the engine compartment as the blades of the fan dug into the radiator.

Springs switched off the ignition, unfastened his seat belt, and pushed his door open. He got out and walked several feet away from the car and stood there for a moment, taking tentative deep breaths to see if he'd broken a rib or something, and bending his knees to see if they were all right.

Then he walked around the front of the car and examined the bumper.

*They're not bumpers, they're goddamned decoration is all they are. Look at the way that "bumper" is bent!*

He walked to the right side of the car and saw what had happened.

He'd blown a tire. The wheel was off the ground, and still spinning, and he could see the steel and nylon, or polyethelene or whatever they were, cords just hanging out of the tire.

*That sonofabitch really blew. It must have been defective from the factory. Christ, it could have blown when I was chasing some speeder on the highway, and I would have been up shit creek.*

He walked back to the driver's side and got behind the wheel and turned the ignition key on. The radio lights went on.

He called in, reporting that he'd had an accident, and approximately where, and that he'd need a wrecker.

They said they'd send someone as quick as they could, and asked if he was hurt. He told them no, he was all right, he had been lucky. He also told them he was going off the air, that he didn't want to have the ignition and the radios on, he might have got a gas line.

They told him to take it easy, they were going to send a State Trooper who was only ten, fifteen miles away, and that the wrecker should be there in thirty, thirty-five minutes.

He turned the ignition off and got out of the car again. He took another look at the shredded tire, and then walked twenty yards away and sat down against another pine tree.

He then offered a little prayer of thanks for not getting hurt or killed, and settled down to wait for the Trooper and the wrecker.

# SEVENTEEN

Detective Matthew M. Payne parked his Bug in the Special Operations parking lot at five minutes to eight Monday morning. At precisely eight, he pushed open a door—on the frosted glass door of which had been etched, before he was born, "Principal's Office."

There was a very natty sergeant, face unfamiliar, sitting inside the door, a stocky man who looked as if he was holding the war against middle-aged fat to a draw.

"May I help you, sir?" the sergeant asked politely.

"Sergeant, I'm Detective Payne, I'm reporting in."

"Oh, yes," the sergeant said, and stood up and offered his hand. "I'm Sergeant Rawlins, Dick Rawlins, the administrative sergeant."

"How do you do?"

"I just had a quick look at your records," Rawlins said. "Haven't had the time for more than a quick look. But I did pick up that you were third on the detective's exam, and that speaks well of you."

"Thank you."

"Have a seat, Payne," Rawlins said. "The captain will see you when he's free."

He gestured toward the door, on which could still be faintly seen faded gilt lettering, *Principal. Private.*

"The captain" was obviously Mike Sabara, whose small office opened off Peter Wohl's office. Captain Dave Pekach's office was down the corridor.

"I wonder what he wants?" Matt thought aloud.

Rawlins's smile faded.

"I'm sure the captain will tell you what he wants, Detective," he said.

*You have just had your knuckles rapped, Detective Payne, and you will not get a gold star for behavior to take home to Mommy.*

*I wonder what Sabara wants with me? He was there when Wohl told me I would be working with Jack Malone. And Malone left a message on the machine that he wanted to see me at eight.*

Five minutes later, the door opened and Mike Sabara stuck his head out. Then, surprised, he saw Matt.

"Hi, Matt. You waiting to see me?"

"Sir, Sergeant Rawlins told me you wanted to see me."

"Come on in," Sabara said, and then added, to Rawlins, "Sergeant, if you see the inspector before I do, would you have him call Chief Coughlin?"

"Yes, sir."

Sabara closed the door to his office behind him.

"Sergeant Rawlins comes to us highly recommended from Criminal Records," he said dryly. "That 'see the captain business' is so either the inspector or I can eyeball newcomers. It didn't apply to you, obviously, and he should have known that. I'm already getting the feeling that he's every bit as bright as that Sergeant Henkels we got stuck with. Does that tell you enough, or should I draw a diagram?"

"I think I get the point, sir."

"Well, our time is not entirely wasted. This gives me the chance to tell you that the inspector was impressed with Sergeant O'Dowd, so for the time being, he'll be working for Jack Malone too, full-time, on the lunatic. And so will Washington, although, of course, with the Black Buddha, the way we say that is 'will be working *with*.' "

"Yes, sir," Matt said, chuckling.

"I think catching this lunatic with the bomb is the first thing that's really interested Jason since Wohl transferred him here. He and Malone are going, maybe have gone, to Intelligence. I don't know what Malone has planned for you, but I think you'd better go down there and see."

"Yes, sir."

"Matt, that was a good job on the lunatic profile."

"That was my sister, not me," Matt said, "but thank you anyway."

"I'm glad you're back. You—or at least your car—lends the place some class."

"I'm driving my Volkswagen, Captain."

"Get out of here," Sabara said.

Matt went back in the outer office as Staff Inspector Wohl came into it from the corridor.

Sergeant Rawlins stood up.

"Good morning, Inspector," he said. "Sir, Captain Sabara said that you are to call Chief Coughlin at your earliest opportunity. And, sir, this is Detective Payne."

"Is it?" Wohl asked, a wicked gleam in his eye.

"Good morning, sir," Matt said.

"Good morning, Detective Payne," Wohl said, and then turned to Rawlins. "Is Captain Sabara in there?"

"Yes, sir. He just interviewed Detective Payne."

"I'm sorry I missed that," Wohl said, and went into his office.

"Did the captain happen to tell you where you will be working, Detective?" Rawlins asked.

"For Lieutenant Malone," Matt said.

"That would be in Plans and Training," Rawlins replied, after consulting an organizational chart. "I'll make a note of that."

"What can I do for you?" Sergeant Maxwell Henkels demanded, making it more of a challenge than a question, as Detective Matthew M. Payne walked through a door on the second floor of the building, above which hung a sign, *Plans and Training Section*.

Henkels was just this side of fat, a flabby man who could have been anywhere from forty to fifty, florid-faced, with what Matt thought of as booze tracks on his nose.

"I'm looking for Lieutenant Malone, Sergeant."

"What for, and who are you?"

*Why, I'm the visiting inspector for the Courtesy in Police Work Program, Sergeant. And you have just won the booby prize.*

"My name is Payne, Sergeant. Detective Payne."

"The lieutenant and Sergeant Washington were waiting for

you," Henkels said. "When you didn't show up, they went to Intelligence. He wants you to meet him there."

"I just transferred in this morning. . . ."

"Yeah, I heard."

". . . and the administrative sergeant said I had to report to Captain Sabara before I came here."

"You should have called me," Sergeant Henkels said. "You're to let me know where you are all the time, understand?"

*Oh, shit!*

Matt nodded.

"Did Lieutenant Malone say anything about a car for me?"

"No."

"I'd better get going."

Sergeant Henkels snorted.

Matt went down the corridor, the oiled wooden boards of which creaked under his footsteps, to another former classroom, this one now the office space provided for the Special Investigations Section of the Special Operations Division. He knew he could both use the phone there and receive a friendly welcome.

This time the uniformed sergeant behind the door was smiling genuinely.

"I told you he'd show up here," Sergeant Jerry O'Dowd said to Officer Foster H. Lewis, Jr., who was even larger than Sergeant Jason Washington, and thus had inevitably been dubbed "Tiny."

"I didn't expect to find you here," Matt said. "You guys know each other?"

"His dad was my first sergeant on my first job out of the Academy," O'Dowd said. "I knew him before he ate the magic growth pills."

"Hey, Matt," Tiny Lewis said, "welcome home."

They shook hands.

"Sergeant Rawlins just introduced me to Inspector Wohl," Matt said.

"Introduced you to Wohl?" Tiny asked.

"That was after my 'welcome to Special Operations' speech from Sabara. And *then* I met Sergeant Henkels."

Lewis and O'Dowd chuckled.

"Which is why I decided to hang out up here," O'Dowd said.

"Was . . . is . . . Malone and/or Washington looking for me?" Matt asked.

"Was," Tiny said.

"They went down to Intelligence," Jerry O'Dowd explained.

"What they wanted to tell you was that I'm now working for Malone, and we're going to work together."

*Well, that's good news. And I really appreciate "work together"; he had every right to say "you'll be working for me."*

"Doing what?"

"Right now, we're waiting for the phone to ring," O'Dowd said, pointing to a desk with a brand-new telephone on it. "That's new. That's the number we're asking people to call in case they think they have a line on our lunatic. If it sounds at all . . . what? credible? possible? . . . we're to go talk to the guy who called it in, and then, if it still looks promising, call Washington and/or Sabara and/or Pekach."

"In that case, I guess I've got time for a cup of coffee."

"You'll have to make it," Tiny said, pointing at the coffee machine. "Unless you want to drink that black whatever from the machine."

"I'll make it," Matt said.

"Rough night, Detective Payne?" O'Dowd asked.

"At half past one," Matt said, more to Tiny Lewis than to O'Dowd, "Detective McFadden and Officer Martinez paid a social call."

"What did Mutt and Jeff have on their minds, so-called?" Tiny asked.

*I cannot tell either of them what Hay-zus has in mind. Is that deceit or discretion?*

"Not much," Matt said. "I think they simply decided that I should not be asleep while they were awake."

"Tough about Hay-zus failing the detective exam," Tiny said.

"Yeah, that surprised me," Matt said.

He went to the coffee machine, picked up the water reservoir and went down the corridor to the door with BOYS lettered on it, and filled it.

Matt Payne, mostly privately, was very much aware of his inadequate capabilities to be a detective. It was a long list of characteristics he didn't have, including experience, but headed by impatience. He had learned, even before Jason Washington had made the point aloud, that a good detective absolutely has to have nearly infinite patience.

The special line telephone did not ring, after either the Highway patrols had come off their seven P.M. to three A.M. tour, or the district patrols had come off their midnight-to-eight tours. Neither did Malone nor Washington call.

His new assignment as one of the inner circle of Special Operations people looking for the lunatic who wanted to disintegrate the Vice President was turning out to be just as thrilling as his assignment as recovered stolen car specialist in East Detectives had been.

His mind began to wander.

His relationship with Evelyn came quickly to mind, with all its potential for disaster, long and near term, and specifically what he was going to do about her tonight, when he got off work, and she would be waiting by her phone for him to call, and if he didn't call, circling Rittenhouse Square until she decided to come up to the apartment and console him in his loneliness and sexual deprivation.

And he thought of Jesus and his dirty corporal at the airport. Going into the guy's car was a monumental act of stupidity. If someone had seen him, the excreta would really have hit the rapidly revolving blades of the electromechanical cooling device.

But maybe that was the way a good cop worked, fighting fire with fire. A dirty cop had to be stopped, even if you bent the law, taking a big chance, in the process.

There would be rewards, of course, if he was right. Maybe that was Jesus' motivation. Failing the detective exam had certainly been humiliating for him.

*If this guy is dirty, is, if nothing else, associating with known criminals, and Hay-zus caught him at it, it would be, to coin a phrase, a feather in his cap. It wouldn't get him a detective's badge, of course, he's going to have to pass the exam to get promoted, but it might get him a better job, maybe in plainclothes someplace, than looking for baggage thieves at the airport.*

*Except that Hay-zus wants* me *to catch this guy associating with known criminals at the—what the hell is it?—*

He fished through his pockets until he came up with the matchbook from the Oaks and Pines Lodge.

*—Oaks and Pines Lodge, Gourmet Cuisine, Championship Golf, Tennis, Heated Pool, Riding, 340 Wooded Acres Only 12.5 miles North of Stroudsburg on Penna. Highway 402. . . .*

*Plus, of course, if Hay-zus is to be believed—and he's probably right—fun and games for high rollers in the back room.*

*What am I supposed to do, just walk into this place and ask where the roulette tables are, and does there happen to be a dirty cop on the premises? I am again functioning from a bottomless pit*

*of ignorance, but I suspect that you have to know someone to get
into the back room. I doubt, even considering Hay-zus' opinion
that I don't look like a cop, that the management is simply going to
let a single guy who wanders into the place into the back room.*

*I may not look like a cop, but I damned well could be an FBI
agent, or an IRS agent, or some other kind of fed. Who handles
gambling for the feds?*

*I could not get in there alone. I would have to be with either a
bunch of guys, out for a good time—that wouldn't work, if there
were a bunch of guys, they would expect at least one of them to be
able to furnish a reference . . .*

*Or a girl. A guy out with a date, who had heard you could play a
little roulette in the back room. A guy driving a Porsche, and with a
nice-looking girl would probably work.*

*What girl? Evelyn? Evelyn would love to take a ride to the
Poconos for dinner, to be followed by several hours of mattress
bouncing in a lodge in the oaks and pines.*

*But (a) Evelyn doesn't look young enough to be my girl and (b) I
don't want to take Evelyn anywhere.*

*Who then? Precious Penny, maybe? Jesus H. Christ, what a lu-
natic idea!*

*But on the other hand, Penny is a bona fide airhead. There's no
way she could be suspected of being an undercover FBI agent.
With Penny, you see what you get, an overprivileged, expensively
dressed inhabitant of Chestnut Hill, the kind of young woman, were
I the operator of an illegal gaming house for high rollers, I would
be anxious to acquire as a client.*

*But what if they spotted her as Penelope Detweiler, aka the ex-
girlfriend of the late Tony the Zee?*

*That would either fuck things up completely, or the opposite.
They would know she was a wild little rich girl who would be looking for something exciting, like gambling, to do.*

*You don't know, Matthew, how well acquainted she is among the
Mob. On the other hand, you don't know which Mob controls Oaks
and Pines Lodge, either. It could be a family out of New York, or
Wilkes-Barre.*

*Very probably, now that I think of it, she probably is not well ac-
quainted with the Mob. Tony the Zee would neither want to share
her with his associates, or to run the risk of one of his associates
telling Mrs. DeZego about Tony's blond girlfriend. Say what you
like about the Mob, they are staunch defenders of the family.*

*Next question: Do you really want to involve Penny in something like this?*

*Involve her in what? All you would be doing would be taking her out to dinner in the Poconos. It would certainly be ill-advised to inform her you were checking out a dirty cop, so she wouldn't know what was going on, beyond being taken out to dinner, by the loyal family friend. And all you would be doing would be checking out the Oaks and Pines. Unless everything fell in place, you might not even inquire about gambling. Just take a look around and give them a face to remember—the guy with the Porsche who was in here a couple of days with the blonde—if you should go and ask about making a few small wagers.*

*And if you were in the Poconos with Penny, the odds are that by, say, midnight, Evelyn would finally become discouraged and stop calling and/or circling Rittenhouse Square.*

*Why not? What is there to lose?*

Martin's Ford and Modern Chevrolet, both of Glassboro, N.J., shared the pleasure of the Sheriff's Department's business. By an amazing coincidence, going back at least fifteen years, when the sheriff announced for competitive bid his need for six suitably equipped for police service automobiles—which he did every year, replacing his eighteen vehicles on a three-year basis—Martin's Ford would submit the lowest bid one year, and Modern Chevrolet the next.

Maintenance of all county light automotive vehicles, including as-needed wrecker service, was similarly awarded, on a competitive bid basis, annually. And by another amazing coincidence, Modern Chevrolet seemed to submit the lowest bid one year, and Martin's Ford the next.

On a purely unofficial basis, both dealerships seemed to feel that it was a manifestation of efficiency in business to "subcontract" repairs to the brand agency. In other words, if, as was the case when Deputy Springs wrecked his Ford patrol car, Modern Chevrolet had that year's county maintenance contract, Modern would "subcontract" the Ford's repairs to Martin's. The next year, if a county-owned Chevrolet needed repair, and Martin's had the contract, Martin's would "subcontract" the repairs to Modern.

And so it came to pass when Modern Chevrolet's wrecker went out in the Pine Barrens to haul Deputy Springs's wrecked Ford off, it never entered the driver's mind to bring the car to Modern

Chevrolet; he hauled it directly into the maintenance bay at Martin's Ford and lowered it onto the grease-stained concrete.

Greg Tomer, Martin's Ford's chief mechanic and service adviser, walked up and shook the hand of Tommy Fallon, the Modern Chevrolet's chief mechanic and wrecker driver. On the first Tuesday of each month, at seven-thirty P.M., they were respectively the senior vice commander and adjutant quartermaster of Casey Daniel Post 2139, Veterans of Foreign Wars.

"What the hell did he hit, Tommy?"

"He blew a tire. Going through the Barrens. Went right off the road. Hit a tree square in the middle. It broke. Had a hell of a time getting the sonofabitch off the tree. Fucked up the pan, I'm sure."

"Springs all right?"

"Yeah. I guess he was wearing his seat belt."

Greg Tomer dropped to his knees and peered under the car.

"Just missed the drive shaft," he said. "But, yeah, he fucked up the pan. I don't think it can be straightened."

"Radiator's gone too. And the fan."

"Maybe the insurance adjuster will says it's totaled. I sure don't want to try to fix it." He got off his knees and leaned in the driver's window. "Sixty-seven thousand on the clock. And no telling whether that's the second time around or the third."

"Well, he was lucky he wasn't hurt, is all I can say."

"Yeah."

"I gotta go, Greg."

"We appreciate your business, Mr. Fallon. Come in again soon."

Tommy Fallon touched Greg Tomer's arm, and then got in the cab on the wrecker, got it into low with a clash of gears, and drove out the back door of the maintenance bay.

"Shit," Greg Tomer said aloud, "I should have asked him to dump it out in back."

He had two options. He could fire up the Martin's Ford wrecker, pick the car up, and haul it out in back himself, or he could change the wheel with the blown tire on it, and push it into a corner of the maintenance bay.

He opened the trunk. There was a spare.

"Harry," he called to the closest of Martin's Ford's three mechanics, "get a jack and change the wheel here, and then we'll push it in the corner."

Harry rolled a hydraulic jack over to the Ford, maneuvered it into place, and raised the car in the bay. As he went to get an air-powered wrench, Tomer jerked the spare from the trunk and rested it against the passenger side door.

Harry removed the wheel with quick expertise, and then stuck his head in the wheel well to see what damage the wreck had caused.

"What the hell is that?" he wondered aloud.

A moment later, after a grunt, he came out of the wheel with something in his hand and handed it to Tomer.

"Look at that?"

"What am I looking at?" Tomer asked. "Where did this come from?"

In his hand was a piece of steel plate, a rough oblong about ten inches long and five inches wide. One edge of the steel was bent at roughly a ninety-degree angle. There were several perforations of the steel, and in one of them was stuck what looked like a link of one-inch chain.

"I took it out of the wheel well, behind the rubber sheet, or whatever they call it," Harry said. "That's what blew his tire. There was nothing wrong with the tire. Look."

He took the piece of steel back from Tomer and laid it on the floor of the garage.

Tomer looked.

"That would certainly blow a tire all right," he said. "Like somebody swinging an ax. I wonder what the hell it is?"

"And it went into the tire far enough so that it got thrown into the wheel well, behind the rubber," Harry said. "I don't know what the hell it is. A piece of junk metal."

"When you get the spare on, Harry, have somebody help you push it into the corner." He pointed. "I'm going to walk across the street to the courthouse and give this to Springs. Souvenir."

"You think he'll want a souvenir?"

"Who can tell."

When Tomer went into the Patrol Division of the Sheriff's Department, they told him that Deputy Springs had slammed his chest into the steering wheel harder than he thought, that they'd x-rayed him at the hospital, nothing was broke, but the sheriff told him to take a couple of days off.

Tomer left the piece of steel, with the sawlike edge and the piece of chain wedged into it, and then walked back across the street to Martin's Ford and went back to work.

● ● ●

There were no telephone calls at all for Sergeant O'Dowd or Detective Payne all morning, until just before lunch, when Lieutenant Malone telephoned to say that he and Detective Washington were going to see Mr. Larkin at the Secret Service office, and that they should wait for their phone to ring; maybe something would happen when the eight-to-four tour came off duty.

Detective Payne and Officer Lewis took luncheon at Roy Rogers' Western Hamburger emporium. When they returned to the office, Sergeant O'Dowd went for his lunch. As soon as he was out the door, Detective Payne called Miss Penelope Detweiler at her residence and asked if she would like to go up to the Poconos for dinner.

Miss Detweiler accepted immediately, and with such obvious delight that it made Detective Payne a bit uneasy. He next called the residence of Mrs. Evelyn Glover and left a message on her answering machine that he had to work, and that if he got off at a reasonable hour, say before nine, he would call.

When he put the telephone back in its cradle, he felt Tiny Lewis's eyes on him, and looked at him.

"The last of the great swordsmen at work, huh?"

"Would you believe me, Officer Lewis, if I gave you my word as a gentleman that carnal activity with either lady is the one thing I don't want?"

"No," Officer Lewis said. "I would not."

It wasn't until Matt went into the parking lot to claim his car that he remembered he was driving the Bug. He glanced at his watch, even though he was fully aware that it was only a minute or two after five.

There would not be time to drive all the way downtown to the apartment to get the Porsche. He had told Penny he would pick her up at five-fifteen, and please not to make him wait, it was going to be at least a two-hour-drive to the Poconos.

He fired up the Bug and drove crosstown to Chestnut Hill. The Bug was not going to be a problem, he could park it, probably, where no one would see it at Oaks and Pines Lodge, and if Penny didn't like it, screw her, let her see up close how the other half lived.

It didn't work out that way.

Surprising him not at all, H. Richard Detweiler answered the door of the Detweiler mansion himself, and informed him first that Penny would be down in a moment.

"Your Porsche is down?" he asked, and then as if that was self-evident went on without giving Matt a chance to reply, "Your dad told me you couldn't bring yourself to sell the Volkswagen."

"An old friend, tried and true," Matt said. "It would have been like selling Amy."

Detweiler smiled a little uncomfortably.

"Tell you what," Mr. Detweiler said. "The Mercedes man was here today. Yesterday. Doing Penny's car. It hadn't been moved, since . . . uh . . . you brought it out here."

The Philadelphia Police Department (specifically then Officer M. M. Payne and then Detective Jason Washington) had returned the victim's automobile, a 1973 Mercedes-Benz 380 SL roadster, to her residence after it had been processed by the forensics experts of the Mobile Crime Lab at the scene of the crime. The scene of the crime had been a Center City parking lot where the victim had been wounded by a shotgun during a homicide in which Mr. Anthony J. DeZego had been fatally shot by unknown person or persons.

*Jesus, that's a great idea! I really didn't want to roll up to the Oaks and Pines in the Bug.*

"It really should be driven," Mr. Detweiler said. "Why don't you take it? It's a long way to Allentown."

*"Allentown"? What the hell does he mean, "Allentown"? And now that I think about it, it's a lousy idea. I don't want Precious Penny reminded of Tony the Zee lying on the concrete with his stomach blown out his back.*

"Is that a good idea?" Matt said. "Bad memories?"

"I thought of that," H. Richard Detweiler said, somewhat impatiently. He touched Matt's shoulder. "Replace bad memories with a good one, right?"

He waited until Matt nodded, then pushed him toward the door.

"Come on in and have a drink, one drink, and I'll have Jensen get the car while we're having it."

Jensen was the Detweilers' chauffeur.

Detweiler led Matt onto the veranda outside the small sitting room where, predictably, Grace Detweiler was also waiting.

"How are you, Matt? You look very nice."

Matt, as he was expected to, kissed her cheek.

Detweiler picked up the telephone.

"Florence," he ordered, "would you please ask Jensen to bring Penny's car around to the front?"

"What's that all about?" Grace Detweiler asked.

"Matt's car is down," Detweiler said. "He's driving his

Volkswagen, which is visibly on its last legs. Or tires. I suggested that he take Penny's car."

"Is that a good idea?" Grace challenged.

"He's a policeman now," Detweiler said. "He doesn't get tickets, he gives them."

"That's not what I meant."

"I know what you meant," Detweiler snapped. "Leave it lie, Grace. They're taking the Mercedes."

"Well, excuse me!"

"Scotch all right, Matt?"

"A weak one, please," Matt said.

Penny and the chauffeur came onto the veranda together.

"Whenever you're ready, Mr. Detweiler," Jensen said.

"Communications problem again," Detweiler said. "Mr. Matt and Penny will be taking the car. I'm not going anywhere."

Penny walked to Matt and leaned up and kissed his cheek. She was wearing a crisp-looking cord suit with a frilly blouse under the jacket.

*Giving the devil his*—the deviless her—*due, she's not a bad-looking female.*

He had a quick, clear mental image of her in his erotic dream and wondered, almost idly, if she really looked that way, au naturel.

*The next line in this little scenario of life in Chestnut Hill will be Detweiler telling me to make sure I get Precious Penny home by twelve, or maybe twelve-thirty.*

"I'll put your bag in the car, Miss Penny," Jensen said.

"Thank you, Jensen," Penny smiled sweetly.

*"Bag"? What bag? And what was that about Allentown?*

"Well, Matt," Penny said. "You said not to keep you waiting. Here I am. Are we going to go or what?"

"One or the other," Matt said. "I don't know what you mean by 'what.' "

"We'll see you later," Penny said, and caught Matt's hand and led him off the veranda.

"Have a good time," Grace Detweiler called after them.

Jensen was waiting by the Mercedes, waiting to close Penny's door. Both doors were open.

Matt got behind the wheel, adjusted the seat, and waited for Penny to get it. The moment she closed the door he could smell her perfume.

*A gas expands to the limits of its containment; there ain't a hell of a lot of space in here. Be nice.*

"You smell good," Matt said.

"Oh, I'm *so* glad you noticed!" Penny said.

*Is that sarcasm?*

Matt looked over at her. Penny was bent over, fixing the carpet, or something, on the floorboard. He got a quick, unintentional look down her blouse. A white brassiere. For some reason, he had always found crisp white feminine undergarments to have a certain erotic quality.

He put the car in gear and started down the driveway.

"You want to tell me what the bag, and Allentown, are all about?"

"I'm glad you waited until we were out of there before you asked that."

"Which means?"

"That in case anybody asks, I was asked by a dear friend of mine, who understands my problems, whose mother is a dear friend of my mother's, GiGi Howser, who lives in *Allentown*, to come to a party. And I called you, and asked you to take me, and you agreed."

"We're going to a place called the Oaks and Pines Lodge," Matt said, without thinking.

"Wherever," Penny said. "I'm helpless in your hands."

"What's with Allentown? And what's with the bag?"

"If the party's fun, and lasts until late, and you have more to drink than you should, we may sleep over."

"Jesus Christ!"

"I thought you'd be pleased," Penny said. "You were the one who told me you automatically shift into the seduce mode."

*What we are going to do is go to the Oaks and Pines and have dinner, and then we are going to come back here and tell the Detweilers we had a lousy time.*

"We're not sleeping over anywhere. I have to be at work at eight o'clock in the morning."

"I don't mind getting up early," Penny said. "I told Mother that might happen. She understands. She'd much rather have you bring me home early in the morning than us get in a wreck because you had too much to drink, the way you usually do."

"And what if she calls your *GiGi* and asks to speak to you?"

"We will have just gone out for pizza or something, and will have to call back. When we get where you're taking me, I'll have to call GiGi and let her know where we are. Don't worry. GiGi is very reliable."

He glanced at her and found that she had shifted on her seat so that she was turned to him. She smiled naughtily at him.

By ten minutes after five, there were very few people left on the tenth floor of the First Pennsylvania Bank & Trust Company, and it would probably be possible to exit the building without being jammed together in an elevator, but Marion Claude Wheatley liked to be sure of things, so he waited until 5:25 before locking his desk and his filing cabinets and walking to the bank of elevators.

Except for a stop at the seventh floor, where it picked up two women—probably secretaries, they seemed a little too bright to be simple clerks—the elevator went directly to the lobby, and it really could not be called crowded with only the three of them on it, and Marion was pleased that he had decided to wait the additional fifteen minutes.

When he left the South Broad Street entrance of the building he turned right, toward City Hall, until he reached Sansom Street, and then walked east on Sansom to South 12th, and then north to Market. That way, he had learned, he could avoid the rush of people headed toward City Hall at this hour of the day.

On Market Street, he turned east, toward the Delaware, and then changed his plans when he saw the Reading Terminal. He had planned to do some of the necessary shopping, take the things home, and then do something about supper. But now it seemed to make more sense to have a little something to eat at one of the concessionaire stands in the Reading Terminal Market before shopping. That would obviate having to worry about supper when he got home. He would, so to speak, be killing two birds with one stone.

Marion believed that the efficient use of one's time was a key to success.

He sat at a counter and had a very nice hot roast beef sandwich with french fried potatoes and a sliced tomato, finishing up with a cup of decaffeinated coffee.

Then he went back out onto Market Street, crossed it again, and after looking in the window of the Super Drugstore on the corner of 11th Street and seeing exactly what he wanted, he went in and bought an AWOL bag. It was on sale, for $3.95, and it had a metal zipper, which was important.

The reason it was on sale, he decided, was because it had a picture of a fish jumping out of the waves on it, with the legend, *Souvenir of Asbury Park, N.J.* Whoever had first ordered the bags had

apparently overestimated the demand for them, and had had to put
the excess up for sale, probably at a loss.

Overestimating demand, Marion thought, was a common fault
with many small businesses. The petroleum business did not have,
simplistically, that problem. They didn't have to produce their raw
material, pump oil from the ground, until they were almost certain
of a market. And even if that market collapsed, it was rarely that oil
had to be put up for immediate sale. It could be stored relatively in-
expensively until a demand, inevitably, arose.

He insisted on getting a paper bag for the AWOL bag—he was
not the sort of person who wished to be seen walking through Center City, Philadelphia, with a reddish-orange bag labeled *Souvenir
of Asbury Park, N.J.*—and then continued walking east on Market
Street.

A very short distance away, just where he had remembered seeing them, which pleased him, there was a tacky little store with a
window full of "leather" attaché cases, on SPECIAL SALE.

*Special Sale, my left foot*, Marion thought. It was a special sale
only because money would change hands. He went in the store,
and spent fifteen minutes choosing an attaché case that (a) looked
reasonably like genuine leather, (b) was deep and wide enough to
hold the shortwave transmitter, (c) had its handles fastened to the
case securely. The last thing he could afford was to have a handle
pull loose, so that he would drop the shortwave transmitter onto the
marble floors of 30th Street Station.

He did not insist on a paper bag for the attaché case. He thought
he would submit that to a little test. He would stop in on the way
home, in one of the cocktail lounges along Chestnut Street that catered to people in the financial industry. He would put the "leather"
attaché case out where people who customarily carried genuine
leather attaché cases could see it, and see if anyone looked at it
strangely.

He had solved the problem of supper, had one AWOL bag and
the attaché case, and there was time, so why not?

# EIGHTEEN

North of Doylestown, on US Route 611, approaching Kintnersville, Matt became aware of a faint siren. When he glanced in the rearview mirror, he saw that it was mounted in a State Police car, and that the gumball machine on the roof was flashing brightly.

"Shit," he said.

Penny turned in her seat and giggled.

There was no place to pull safely to the side of the road where they were, so Matt put a hand over his head in a gesture of surrender, slowed, and drove another mile or so until he found a place to stop.

"Mother will not be at all surprised that we wound up in jail," Penny said cheerfully. "She expects it of you."

Matt got out of the car, making an effort to keep both hands in view, and then went back to the State Police car. A very large State Policeman, about thirty-five, got out, and straightened his Smoky-the-Bear hat.

"Good evening, sir," the State Policeman said, with the perfect courtesy that suggested he was not at all unhappy to be forced to cite a Mercedes driver for being twenty-five or thirty miles over the speed limit.

"Good evening," Matt replied, and took his driver's license from his wallet. "There's my license."

"I'll need the registration too, please, sir."

Matt took out the leather folder holding his badge and photo ID and handed that over.

"That's what I do for a living. How fraternal are you feeling tonight?"

The State Policeman examined the photo on the ID card carefully, then handed it back.

"Being a Philly detective must pay better than they do us. That's quite a set of wheels."

"The wheels belong to the lady."

The State Policeman took a long look at Penny, who, resting her chin on her hands on the back of her seat, was looking back at them, smiling sweetly.

"I don't think I'd have given her a ticket, either," he said. "Very nice."

"Thank you."

"You're welcome," the State Policeman said, and turned back to his car.

Matt got back in the Mercedes.

"We're not going to jail?"

"I told the nice officer that I was rushing you to the hospital to deliver our firstborn," Matt said.

"You would do something like that too, you bastard," Penny said, laughing. "But that's an interesting thought. I wonder what our firstborn would look like?"

The question made Matt uncomfortable.

"I didn't have any lunch," Penny went on. "You're going to have to get me something to eat, or you're going to have to carry me into wherever you're taking me."

"I'm taking you to a restaurant, can't you wait?"

"How far?"

"About an hour from here, I suppose."

"Then no. But I will settle for something simple."

*I don't have dinner reservations for this place*, Matt suddenly thought. *For that matter, I don't even know if it's open to the public for dinner. I better find a phone and call.*

Ten minutes later, just south of Easton, he saw the flashing neon

sign of a restaurant between the highway and Delaware River.
Penny saw it at the same time.

"Clams!" she cried. "I want steamed clams! Steamed clams and
a beer! *Please*, Matthew!"

"Your wish, mademoiselle, is my command."

Inside the restaurant, they found a cheerful bar at which a half
dozen people sat, half of them with platters of steamed clams before them.

Penny hopped onto a bar stool.

"Two dozen clams and an Ortlieb's for me," she ordered, "and
two dozen for him. I don't know if he wants a beer or not. He may
be on duty."

The bartender took it as a joke.

"Two beers, please," Matt said.

Two frosted mugs and two bottles of beer appeared immediately.

"And while I'm waiting for the clams, I'll have a pickled egg,"
Penny said.

"Two," Matt said.

"You're being very agreeable. That must mean you want something from me."

"Not a thing, but your company," Matt said.

"Bullshit," Penny said. "I am not quite as stupid as you think I
am. You didn't invite me to dinner in the sticks because you love
food or drives through the country, and you've made it perfectly
clear that you're not lusting after my body, so what is going on?"

Her eyes were on him, over the rim of her beer mug.

"I want to take a look at the Oaks and Pines Lodge," he said.

"In your line of work, you mean, not idle curiosity?"

Matt nodded.

"You going to tell me why?"

He shook his head, no.

"What I thought was that I would attract less attention if I had a
girl, a pretty girl, with me."

She considered that for a moment.

"Okay," she said. "I'm using you, too. I would have gone to
watch the Budapest Quintet with you—and you know how I hate
fiddle music—if it had gotten me out of the house."

"Pretty bad, is it, at home?"

"Mother's counting the aspirin," Penny said.

"I'm sorry."

"I think you really are," Penny said. "So tell me, is there anything I can do to help you do whatever it is you're not going to tell me you're doing?"

The answer came immediately, but Matt waited until he had taken the time to take a long pull at his beer before he replied.

"I don't even know if this place is open to the public for dinner. Some of them aren't. And I don't have reservations."

"You never were too good at planning ahead, were you?"

"I thought I'd call from here and ask about reservations. . . ."

"But?"

"It would be better, it would look better, if I called and asked for a room."

She smiled at him.

"This is the first time that anyone has proposed taking me to a hotel room, said he did not have sex in mind, and meant it. But okay, Matthew."

"Thank you, Penny," Matt said.

"Why is that, Matt? Because I was on drugs? Because of Tony DeZego? Or is it that you simply don't find me appealing?"

"I find you appealing," Matt blurted. "I just think it would be a lousy idea."

Before she had a chance to reply, he got off his bar stool and went to the pay phone he had seen in the entrance.

When he returned, having learned that he was in luck, the Oaks and Pines Lodge, having had a last-minute cancellation, would be able to accommodate Mr. and Mrs. Payne in the Birch Suite, the clams had been served, and Penny was playing airhead with the bartender, who was clearly taken with her.

Charley Larkin, jacket off, tie pulled down, was sitting behind the very nice mahogany desk and SAC Joseph J. Toner was sitting on the couch with Wohl.

*Mr. H. Charles Larkin,* Wohl thought, *has taken over the office of the supervisory agent in charge of the Secret Service's Philadelphia office.*

*Is it a question of priorities or rank? Certainly, keeping the Vice President from being disintegrated has a higher Secret Service priority than catching somebody who prints his own money or other negotiable instruments, and it would follow that the guy in charge of that job would be the one giving the orders. But it might be rank too. Larkin has been in the Secret Service a long time. He probably outranks Toner too. What difference does it make?*

One of the telephones on Toner's desk rang. Larkin looked to see which one it was, and then picked it up.

"Larkin," he said, and then a moment later, "Ask them to come in, please."

Lieutenant Jack Malone, in plainclothes, and Sergeant Jason Washington, in a superbly tailored, faintly plaided gray suit, came into the office.

"Charley, you know Jack," Wohl said. "The slight, delicate gentleman in the raggedy clothes is Sergeant Jason Washington. Jason, Charley Larkin. Watch out for him, he and my father and Chief Coughlin are old pals."

Larkin walked around the desk to shake Washington's hand.

"You know the line, 'your reputation precedes you'?" he asked. "I'm glad you're working with us on this, Sergeant. Do you know Joe Toner?"

"Only by reputation, sir," Washington said. He turned to Toner, who, obviously as an afterthought, stood up and put out his hand.

"How are you, Sergeant?"

"Pretty frustrated, right now, as a matter of fact, Mr. Toner," Washington said.

"I'm Joe Toner, Lieutenant," Toner said, and gave his hand to Malone.

"You mean you didn't come here to report we have our mad bomber in a padded cell, and we can all go home?" Wohl asked.

"Boss, we laid an egg," Washington replied. "We've been through everything in every file cabinet in Philadelphia, and we didn't turn up a looney tune who comes within a mile of that profile."

"And we just checked the Schoolhouse. There has been no, zero, zilch, response from anybody to the profiles we passed around the districts."

"Who's holding the phone down?" Wohl asked.

"Lieutenant Wisser," Malone replied. "Until two. Then a Lieutenant Seaham?"

"Sealyham?" Wohl asked.

"I think so. Captain Sabara arranged for it. He'll do midnight to eight, and then O'Dowd will come back on," Malone said. "We stopped by the Schoolhouse, and talked to them. *Sealyham* on the phone. If they get anything that looks interesting, they're going to call either Washington or me."

Wohl nodded his approval.

"You've had a busy day," he said.

"Spinning our wheels," Jason said.

"I don't offer this with much hope," Charley Larkin said, "but this is the profile the FBI came up with. Did you stumble on anyone who comes anywhere near this?"

He handed copies to both Washington and Malone.

"There's coffee," Larkin said. "Excuse me, I should have offered you some."

Both Malone and Washington declined, silently, shaking their heads, but Washington, not taking his eyes from the sheet of paper, lowered himself onto the couch between Wohl and Toner. The couch was now crowded.

"This is just about what Matt's sister came up with," Washington said.

" 'Matt's sister'?" Toner asked.

"Dr. Payne, sir," Washington said. "A psychiatrist at the University of Pennsylvania. She's been helpful before. Her brother is a detective, Matt Payne."

"Oh," Toner said.

"The FBI says that this guy is probably a 'sexual deviate,' " Malone quoted, "Dr. Payne says he's 'asexual.' What's the difference?"

"Not much," Washington replied. " 'Celibacy is the most unusual of all the perversions,' Oscar Wilde."

Larkin and Wohl chuckled. Toner and Malone looked confused.

"And anyway," Washington went on, "Jack and I went through the files in Sex Crimes too. Same result, zero."

"Who's Oscar Wilde?" Malone asked.

"An English gentleman of exquisite grace," Washington said. "Deceased."

"Oh."

"Sergeant Washington," Larkin said. "Would you mind if I called you 'Jason'?"

"No, sir."

"Jason, I'd like to hear your wild hairs," Larkin said. "I think we all would."

"Yeah," Wohl agreed.

"This chap is going to be hard to find," Washington said. "He's the classic face in the crowd. Law-abiding. Respectable. Few, if any, outward signs of his mental problems."

"We know that," Wohl said, a touch of impatience in his voice.

"Possibly a rude question: How wide have we thrown the net?" Washington asked.

"Meaning?" Toner asked.

"Wilmington, New Jersey, even Baltimore. For that matter, Doylestown, Allentown? Is there a record that matches the profile right over the city border in Cheltenham?"

"Our people, Sergeant," Toner said, somewhat coldly, "have taken care of that. Plus seeking cooperation from other federal agencies, making that profile available to them."

"It was a question worth asking, Jason," Wohl said, flashing Toner an icy look.

"Please ask whatever pops into your mind," Larkin said.

"What about the Army? For that matter, the Navy, the Marines? Coal companies, whatever? Have there been any reports of stolen explosives?"

"Not according to Alcohol, Tobacco and Firearms," Larkin said. "Or the State Board of Mines, in Harrisburg."

Washington shrugged.

"I don't even have any more wild hairs," he said.

"In that case, there is obviously only one thing to do," Larkin said, and waited until the others were all looking at him. "Consult with John Barleycorn. It would not be the first time in recorded history that a good idea was born in a saloon."

*Supervisory Special Agent Toner*, Wohl thought, *looks shocked at the suggestion. But Larkin means that, and Christ, he may be right.*

"I'll drink to that," Wohl said, and pushed himself up off the couch.


"We don't have any luggage," Matt said as he drove up the curving road to the Oaks and Pines Lodge Resort. "That's going to look funny."

"Yes, we do," Penny replied. "And neither the bellhop nor the desk clerk will suspect that there's nothing in there but my clothes, including, incidentally, a rather risqué negligee."

Matt remembered Jensen saying he would put her bag in the car. He looked in the back seat. There was a fairly large suitcase, made out of what looked like a Persian rug.

"You really came prepared, didn't you?" he asked.

"Life is full of little surprises," Penny said. "What's wrong with being prepared?"

A bellman came out to the Mercedes in front of the lodge.

"Good evening, sir," he said. "Checking in?"

"Yes."

"I'll take the luggage, sir, and I'll take care of the car. If you'll just leave the keys?"

Penny took his arm as they walked across the lobby to the desk.

"My name is Payne," Matt said to the man behind the desk. "I have a reservation."

"Yes, sir, I spoke to you on the phone."

Matt handed him his American Express card.

"I have to be in Philadelphia at eight," he said. "Which means I—*we*—will have to leave here in the middle of the night. Is that going to pose any problems?"

"None at all, sir. Let me run your card through the machine. And then just leave, whenever you wish. We'll mail the bill to your home."

He pushed a registration card across the marble to him, and handed him a pen. At the very last moment, Matt remembered to write "M/M," for "Mr. & Mrs.," in front of his name.

"Thank you," the desk man said, and then raised his voice. "Take Mr. and Mrs. Payne to the Birch Suite, please."

They followed the bellman to the elevator, and then to a suite on the third floor. The Birch Suite consisted of a large, comfortably furnished sitting room, a bedroom with a large double bed, and a bath, with both a sunken bathtub and a separate tile shower.

Matt tipped the bellman and he left.

"The furniture's oak," Matt said. "They should call it 'the oak suite.' "

"Don't be critical," Penny called from the bedroom.

"I'm not being critical. It's very nice."

"The food's good too."

"How do you know that?"

"I've been here before, obviously."

*With Tony the Zee? Is this where that Guinea gangster brought you? Why not? It's supposed to have a Mob connection.*

"With my parents," Penny said. "Not what you were thinking."

"How do you know what I was thinking?"

"I usually know what you're thinking," Penny said. "Come look at this."

*If you're referring to the double bed, I've seen it.*

He walked to the bedroom door. Penny pointed at a bottle of champagne in a cooler, placed conveniently close to the bed.

"For what they're charging for this, a hundred and a half a night, they can afford to throw in a bottle of champagne," Matt said.

"How ever do you afford all this high living on a policeman's pay, Matthew?"

"Don't start being a bitch, Penny."

"Sorry," she said, sounding as if she meant it. "I'm curious. Have you got some kind of an expense account?"

"Not for this, no," Matt replied. "What were your parents doing here?"

"Daddy likes to gamble here."

*Why does that surprise me? It shouldn't. He apparently is no stranger in Las Vegas. But why the hell is he gambling? With all his money, what's the point? He really can't care if he wins or loses.*

"You didn't say anything, before, when I told you we were coming here."

"I didn't want to spoil your little surprise. You said we were coming here, you will recall, before you made it clear that whatever you had in mind, it was not rolling around between the sheets with me."

"I want to get a look inside the gambling place."

"That shouldn't be a problem."

"You still hungry?"

"Always," she said.

"Come on then, we'll go have a drink at the bar and then have dinner."

"And save that for later?" she asked, pointing at the champagne.

"We could have it now, if you would like."

"I'd really rather have a beer," she said. "If you romanced me like this more often, Matt, you'd learn that I'm really a cheap date."

"Economical," he responded without thinking, "not cheap."

"Why, thank you, Matthew."

She walked past him out of the bedroom and to the corridor door.

They sat at the bar where Penny drank two bottles of Heineken's beer, which for some reason surprised him, and he had two drinks of Scotch.

The entertainment was a pianist, a middle-aged woman trying to look younger, who wasn't half bad. Much better, he thought, than the trio who replaced her when they went to a table for dinner.

And Penny was right. The food was first class. Penny said she remembered the chateaubriand for two was really good, and he indulged her, and it was much better than he expected it to be, a perfectly roasted filet, surrounded by what looked like one each of every known variety of vegetable. They had a bottle of California Cabernet Sauvignon with that, and somehow it was suddenly all gone.

"If you'd like, we could have another," Penny said as he mocked shaking the last couple of drops into his glass. "And have cheese afterward, and listen to the music. I don't think the gambling gets going until later."

The cheese was good, something the waiter recommended, something he'd never had before, sort of a combination of Camembert and Roquefort. They ate one serving, spreading it on crackers and then taking a swallow of the wine before chewing, and then had another.

Penny said she would like a liqueur to finish the meal, and he passed, saying he'd already had too much drink, and instead drank a cup of very black, very strong coffee.

When he'd finished that, Penny inclined her head toward the rear of the room.

"It's over there, if you want to give it a try," she said.

Matt looked and saw a closed double door, draped with red curtain and guarded by a large man in a dinner jacket.

As they walked to it, Penny leaned up and whispered in his ear: "You did remember to bring money?"

"Absolutely," he said, although he wasn't really sure.

The man in the dinner jacket blocked their way.

"May I help you?" he asked.

"We want to go in there," Penny said.

"That's a private party, I'm afraid, madam."

"Oh, come on. I've been in there before."

"Are you a club member?"

"I'm not, but if there's a club, my father probably is."

"And your name, madam?"

"My maiden name was Detweiler," Penny said.

*That rang a bell*, Matt thought, *if widening eyes and raised eyebrows are any criteria.*

"First name?"

"Richard. H. Richard."

"Just a moment, please, madam," the man in the dinner jacket said. He pulled open a cabinet door in the wall Matt hadn't noticed—it was covered with wallpaper—and spoke softly into a telephone. After a moment, he hung up and pushed the door closed.

"Sorry for the delay, Miss Detweiler," he said as he pulled the door open. "Good luck!"

"*Mrs. Payne,*" Penny corrected him, smiling sweetly at Matt.

There were very few people in the room, although croupiers stood waiting for customers behind every table.

*Do you call the guys who run the craps games and the blackjack "croupiers" too?* Matt wondered. *Or does that term apply only to roulette? If not, what* do *you call the guy who runs the craps table? The crapier?*

"Roulette all right with you, Penny?"

"It's fine with me," she replied. "But I'm surprised, I thought you would be a craps shooter."

Matt took out his wallet. He had one hundred-dollar bill and four fifties and some smaller bills.

*The hundred must be left over from the Flamingo in Las Vegas. I never take hundreds from the bank. You can never get anyone to change one.*

He put the hundred-dollar bill on the green baize beside the roulette wheel.

"Nickles," he said.

The croupier slid a small stack of chips to him.

He placed two of them on the board, both on One to Twelve. The croupier spun the wheel, twenty-three came up, and he picked up Matt's chips.

Matt made the same bet again.

"There's a marvelous story," Penny said. "A fellow brought a girl here, or to a place like this, and gave her chips, and she said, 'I don't know what to bet,' so he said, 'Bet your age,' so she put fifty dollars on twenty-three. Twenty-nine came up. The girl said, 'Oh, *shit!*' "

The croupier laughed softly. Matt didn't understand. Penny saw this: "The moral of the story, Matthew darling, is 'Truth pays off.' "

He laughed.

Thirty-three came up, and the croupier picked up Matt's chips again.

"You're not too good at this, are you, darling?"

"Just getting warmed up," Matt said. He put five chips on 00.

Sixteen came up.

"Have you ever considered getting an honest job?" Penny asked.

*Not only isn't this much fun, but I've seen about all of this place that there is to see. It's about as wicked as a bingo game in the basement of McFadden's parish church.*

*Hay-zus is off base on this one. There's nobody in this room who looks like a mobster; my fellow gamblers look like they all belong to the Kiwanis. And/or the Bible Study Group.*

*I will buy Penny a drink, and try to show her the wisdom of driving back to Philadelphia now, rather than in the morning. We can get back by one, maybe a little sooner.*

When the croupier had removed his five chips from 00, Matt pushed what was left of his stack onto 00.

"I don't think this is my night," Matt said to the croupier.

"You never can tell," the croupier said.

00 came up.

"And we have a winner," the croupier said.

"There must be some sort of mistake," Penny said. "Clearly, God doesn't want him to win."

"God must have changed His mind," the croupier said. "Would you like some quarters, sir? That's going to be a lot of nickles."

"I think I'd rather cash out. I'm too shocked to play anymore."

A pit boss appeared, saw what happened, and nodded his approval. The croupier wrote something on a slip of paper, handed it to the pit boss, who signed it and handed it back. The croupier handed Matt the slip of paper. On it was written $2035.

"Thank you," Matt said. "Where's the cashier?"

The croupier inclined his head, and Matt followed his eyes and saw a barred window near the entrance door. At the last moment, he remembered that winning gentlemen gamblers tip the croupier. He took a fifty-dollar bill from his wallet and handed it to the croupier.

"Is this what's known as quitting when you're ahead?" Penny asked.

"You got it."

He took the chit to the cashier, exchanged it for a nice thick wad of hundred-dollar bills, put them in his inside jacket pocket, and then led Penny out of the casino and toward the bar.

"Are we going to the bar?" Penny asked.

"I thought we'd have a drink to celebrate."

"We have a bottle of champagne in the room," Penny said.

*We have to go to the room anyway to get her bag. And there will be no one in the room, as there would be at the bar, to eavesdrop on our conversation, and wonder why a healthy-appearing young man was trying to talk a good-looking healthy blonde out of spending the night in a hotel.*

"I forgot," Matt said as he nudged her toward the elevator.

While they had been downstairs, the bed had been turned down.

There was a piece of chocolate precisely in the center of each of the pillows.

"Open the champagne," Penny said as she went into the bathroom. "See if it's still cold."

It was still cold. Whoever had turned down the bed had also refilled the cooler with ice. As he wrestled with the cork, he could hear the toilet flush and then water running.

The cork popped and he poured champagne into the glasses. He sipped his.

*Nice.* He looked at the label. California champagne, a brand he'd never heard of.

Methode Champagnois, *whatever the hell that means. What did you expect, Moet et Chandon?*

He heard, or at least sensed, the bathroom door opening, and turned with Penny's glass extended.

She had—*Jesus, how did she do that so quickly?*—taken off her clothes and changed into a negligee—or peignoir, whatever a pale blue, lacy, nearly transparent garment of seduction was called— and brushed her hair so that it hung straight down to her shoulders.

The light in the bathroom was still on, which served to illuminate the thin material of her negligee from the rear. She was, for all visual purposes, quite naked.

"Jesus, Penny!"

"I figured, what the hell? Matt knows all my secrets. What have I got to lose?"

She came into the bedroom, took the champagne glass from him, and walked to the draped window.

"I guess it didn't work, huh?" she said after a moment.

*What the fuck am I supposed to do now?*

*I can't see through her nightgown anymore. Jesus, that made my heart jump!*

He saw her raise and drain her champagne glass, and then she turned.

"Go and wait in the other room," she said, her voice flat and bitter. "I'll get dressed, and we can go."

She walked toward him.

"Go on, Matt. Get out of here."

Tears were running down her cheeks.

He put his hand to her face.

"Don't," she said. "Don't pity me, you sonofabitch!"

"It would be stupid, Penny."

"*Life* is stupid, you jackass. It's a bitch, and then you die."

He chuckled.

She raised her eyes to his.

And then her hand came up and touched his cheek.

"What are you thinking, Matt?"

"You don't want to know what I'm thinking."

*I am thinking that I could cheerfully spend the rest of my life like this, with my arm around you, my fingers on your backbone, your face on my chest, your absolutely magnificent breasts pressing on me, the smell of your hair in my nostrils. Feeling the way I do. Jesus, what made it so good? The champagne?*

"Yes, I do."

"Great set of boobs on this broad."

"Fuck you!"

"We've already done that."

"And no comment about that? You usually have an opinion about everything."

Matt kissed the top of her head.

She raised her head.

"Is that in lieu of a comment?"

He kissed her. It was exquisitely tender. She shifted her body against his, so that her mouth was in his neck.

"The reason I'm curious," Penny said softly, carefully, "is because I really don't know what it's supposed to be like."

"I don't understand."

"There was Kellogg Winters," Penny said softly. "And then Anthony. And now you."

"Kellogg Winters? He's an ass."

*Is she telling me I'm the third?*

"Yes, he is. But I was seventeen, and I wanted to, so I let him. In the back seat of a car at Rose Tree Hunt Club. It was his birthday."

"Kellogg *Winters*?" he chuckled.

"And I thought, if this is what everybody's so excited about, that's really much ado about nothing."

Without thinking, horrified as he heard his own words, he asked, "And Tony the Zee? What was that like?"

He felt her body tense, and then relax.

"Different. Better."

"And Matthew Payne?"

"It was not like anything else. Is it always like that for you?"

*Oh, shit!*

*Tell her the truth. If you make a four-star ass of yourself, so what?*

"It has never been, before, like it was with you."

For a moment she didn't reply or move. Then she raised her head and looked down into his eyes.

"Really? God, please don't try to be charming, Matt!"

"I'm not being charming, I'm trying to figure it out."

She looked into his eyes for a long moment, and then lowered her head into his neck again.

"I'm going to take an enormous chance and believe you," she said. Her arm slowly tightened around him. He held her as tightly as he could.

A long moment later, Matt asked throatily, "How would you feel about seeing if we can do the same thing again?"

"Really?" She giggled in his ear. "Could you?" Her hand slid down over his chest and stomach. "Oh, how nice!"

She rolled over on her back, and pulled him onto her.

"Look in my eyes!" she ordered. He did. He felt her guiding him into her body.

"Oh, God, Matt!" she called softly.

# NINETEEN

Penny started to go through the door of the Birch Suite into the corridor, but then stopped and looked around.

"If I had my druthers," she said, "we would just stay here for a while longer. Like forever."

"We've already had that discussion. What we're going to do is take one more look around Las Vegas East, and then we go back to Philadelphia."

"You still haven't told me what we're—what *you're*—looking for."

"I really don't know. I think this is a bum lead, but I want to be sure before I go back and say so."

"That doesn't make much sense," she said as she walked past him and out into the corridor.

Matt went to the desk, settled the bill, and then handed a bellman Penny's bag and five dollars and told him to bring the Mercedes to the door.

"I'll be out in a few minutes," he said. "I'm going to give you a chance to get a little of your money back."

From the uncomfortable smile on the desk clerk's face, Matt understood that making reference to the casino was not considered good form.

He glanced at his watch as they approached the casino door. It was quarter to two.

*If it was nearly deserted at half past nine, I'll give you five to one that it will be me and the croupier again.*

He was wrong. The room was not crowded, but there were gamblers at all but one of the tables.

He reached into his jacket and took out some of the hundred-dollar bills. He looked and counted. There were six.

"Here," he said, handing them to Penny.

She took the money, looked at it, and then at him, then shrugged.

"Is that the going rate?" she asked, "Or is that five hundred, plus a hundred tip?"

"Oh, Jesus Christ!"

"Sorry," she said, again sounding as if she meant it. She touched his arm, just above the elbow, and gently squeezed it. "Our new relationship is going to take some getting used to."

*That, madam, qualifies as the understatement of the millennium.*

She turned from him and walked directly to the blackjack table. He followed her and got there in time to watch her hand the money to the dealer.

"Quarters," she said.

*This is not the first time she's done this.*

He looked around the room, and then at the others at the blackjack table.

*There are some people in here now who look like gamblers, as opposed to the Bible Study Group who was in here earlier. But where is it written that a gambler has to wear a two-tone coat and a pastel shirt open to his navel, like that clown at the end of the table? Or, for that matter, where is it written that a Mafioso cannot buy his clothes at Brooks Brothers and look like he went to Princeton?*

He watched Penny gamble. She grew intense, to the point of pursing her lips. He had watched her apply lipstick in the room, after she had put on her underwear, before she had put her dress back on. It had been a curious mixture of innocence and eroticism. She had seen him watching her in the mirror and pursed her lips in a kiss.

She quickly lost most of her chips, and then as quickly began to increase the size of the two stacks before her, subconsciously making the stacks even as the game progressed.

*She's good at this. Better than I am. I always lose my shirt playing blackjack.*

She bumped her rear end against him, and when he looked down, she nodded her head toward her chips.

"Not only economical," she said. "But maybe even profitable."

"The evening is young," he said.

He saw that the clown in the pastel shirt at the end of the table was looking at him curiously.

*You could be a mobster, my friend. The question is, have you made me as a cop?*

"Nature calls, Penny," he said. "I'll be right back."

She nodded absently.

He glanced around the room, found the rest rooms sign, and walked to it. The men's room was empty. He relieved himself, and then looked at himself in the mirror.

*You don't look like a cop. Hay-zus was right about that. On the other hand, you have achieved a certain fame, or infamy, for taking down Mr. Warren K. Fletcher, aka the Northwest serial rapist, and also by getting yourself shot, getting your picture in the newspapers and everything. Is that why El Mafioso has made you?*

*You don't know he's made you. He may just be wondering where a nice, clean-cut young man like you gets the money to play games in here. Or he may be wondering how he can get a good-looking blonde like the one you're playing with.*

*And why are you so sure that guy is wrong? He probably has a used car lot in Wilkes-Barre or someplace.*

Matt turned from the men's room mirror and went back into the casino. He looked around the room again, but didn't see anyone who attracted his interest. The only guy who was at all interesting was the Mafioso Used Car Salesman at Penny's table.

Penny turned and smiled when she sensed he was again standing behind her.

"Whatever you were doing, do it again," she said. "Look!"

She now had four stacks of chips in front of her, each ten, eleven, maybe twelve chips high.

"You want to quit when you're ahead?"

"Can I have fifteen more minutes?"

"Sure."

A waitress appeared, in a regular uniform, not the short skirt and mesh stockings of Las Vegas, and asked if she could get them something to drink.

"Not for me, thank you," Penny said.

"Could I get some black coffee?" Matt asked.

When the waitress delivered the coffee, Matt felt the eyes of the Used Car Salesman Mafioso on him again, and this time met his glance. The man smiled at him.

*Now what the hell does that mean? That he's made me? And is laughing at me? Or that he thinks maybe we went to elementary school together, but isn't sure?*

Matt, just perceptibly, nodded his head.

His eyes dropped to the chips in front of his new friend. He was playing quarters too, but he wasn't having the luck Penny was. He was down to six chips, and he lost those in the next two hands.

He turned from the table and walked toward the cashier's window. A woman, a peroxide blonde with spectacular breastworks, trailed after him.

*How come you didn't notice that before? You always react to bosoms such as those as if they were electromagnets. Matthew, my boy, you are sated, that is why. Or maybe because you have changed your criteria for magnificent breasts. After tonight, you will always define magnificent breasts as rather small, pink-tipped, and astonishingly firm.*

"Time's up," Matt said to Penny. "Daddy has to go into the office early tomorrow."

"Okay," Penny said, without argument. She slid two quarter chips across the table to the dealer, and then scooped up the rest. There were so many she could barely hold them.

"He would have cashed those in for you."

"I wanted to carry them," Penny said. "To savor my triumph."

The Mafioso Used Car Salesman was leaning over the cashier's marble counter.

*He's signing a—what do you call it?—an IOU? He needs more chips. He's been losing.*

*That bulge under his arm is a gun. In a shoulder holster. He is a Mafioso. Only Mafiosos and cops carry guns.*

*Christ, he's a cop! That's what's wrong with him!*

The Mafioso/Cop slid the IOU, or whatever it was properly called, under the cashier's grill, and she slid a plastic tray full of quarter chips back out to him.

There were eight stacks of chips, each of ten chips, each chip worth twenty-five dollars. Matt did the math quickly in his head.

*That tray is worth two thousand dollars! Cops can't afford that kind of gambling money. Bingo!*

Vito Lanza turned from the cashier's window. The guy who looked familiar was standing behind him in line.

*With the blonde who also looks familiar. And she's been doing a lot better than I have. Well, hell, maybe with her going, my luck will change,* Vito thought.

"Don't I know you from somewhere, pal?" Vito asked the young guy.

"I don't think so."

"You look kind of familiar, you know?"

"I was thinking the same thing."

"You come here a lot?"

"Second time."

"Well . . . Vegas! You ever go to Vegas?"

"Yeah, sure."

"And you was there last week, right?" Vito asked triumphantly.

"Right."

"At the Flamingo, right?"

"Right again."

"And you flew back to Philadelphia on American, right? The both of you. In first class?"

"Right," Matt said. "So that's where it was. I knew I'd seen you somewhere."

"Well, how about that!" Vito said.

"How about that," Matt parroted.

"Small world, right?" Vito said. He handed the tray of chips to Tony, and put out his hand. "Vito Lanza. This is Tony."

"Matt Payne, this is Penny."

"Pleased to meet you," Tony said.

"Hi!" Penny said.

"How's your luck, Vito?" Matt asked.

"Aw, you know how it goes. Win a little, lose a little. The night's young."

"That's what I keep telling him," Penny said, and walked between Vito and Tony to the cashier's window and dumped her chips on the cashier's counter.

"Well, see you around," Vito said.

"See you around."

In the Mercedes, Penny leaned over and stuffed bills into Matt's jacket pocket.

"You didn't have to do that," he said.

"Yes, I did. If you're going to buy me off, it's going to take a lot more than a lousy six hundred dollars. Besides, I've got twenty-two hundred more."

"My God, that much?"

"That much," she said. "Tonight, in more ways than one, has been my lucky night."

"I think we had better proceed very, very slowly," Matt said.

"I thought you would say something like that once you'd had your wicked way with me," Penny said. "That was him, wasn't it? Who you were looking for all the time?"

He looked at her in surprise, then nodded.

"You going to tell me about it?"

"No."

"Well, I'm glad I was able to be helpful," she said. She caught his hand, and moved it to her mouth, and kissed it.

The large, illuminated clock mounted on the Strawbridge & Clothier Department Store in Jenkintown showed quarter to five when Matt looked up at it from Penny's Mercedes.

That meant he would be at her place at five, or a few minutes after. He looked over at her, expecting to find her still curled up asleep.

She was not asleep. She was awake and had apparently been reading his mind again.

"I think we could make this little deception of ours more credible if I arrived home at, say, seven," she said. "We having left GiGi's at, say, five. What time do you have to be at work?"

"Eight."

"We could find an all-night diner, I suppose," Penny said. "Or we could go to your apartment. I've never been to your apartment."

"I've got to change clothes," Matt said. "And reclaim my car."

"Or we could go to your apartment," Penny repeated.

*Where we are likely to find Evelyn circling the block, looking for her missing lover. That does not rank as one of the good ideas of all time.*

"Is that an indecent proposal?"

"More like female curiosity," Penny said. "Would your delicate male ego be crushed if I told you that I have had enough romance for the next day or two?"

He chuckled.

She reached out her hand and rubbed her fingers across his cheek.

"Make that '*physical* romance'," she said. "You can hold my hand, if you want."

She moved her hand to his on the steering wheel and caught it and moved it to her chest.

*That is a tender, as opposed to erotic, gesture.*

"You need a shave," she said. "Are you going to take me to your apartment, Matthew?"

"I suppose that's best, even for someone whose delicate male ego has just been crushed flat."

"Women have the right to change their minds," she said cheerfully. "Didn't anyone ever tell you that?"

She suddenly let go of his hand and sat up.

"I know. Look for an all-night grocery store. We'll get eggs and bacon, or maybe Taylor Ham, and coffee and orange juice, and I'll make us breakfast."

"You're hungry again?"

"I can't imagine why."

"It would be easier to find a diner."

"I want to make us breakfast!"


"It's tiny," Penny said. "Where did you ever find this place?"

The red light on the answering machine, surprising Matt not at all, was blinking.

"My father owns it," he said. "The kitchen is that place back there with all the white things."

He motioned her ahead of him, and then ducked and pulled the answering machine's plug out of its socket.

"Does it have a toilet?"

"Off the bedroom," he said, catching up with her and pointing.

He unpacked the groceries, setting them on the kitchen counter. Then he went to the refrigerator and threw away all the food he had purchased with the noble intention of making his own meals, and which was now spoiled.

She came back into the kitchen.

"Would it help your crushed ego to learn that I am very sore?"

"Jesus," he said. "I'm sorry."

She walked quickly to him and kissed him lightly on the lips.

"I'm not," she said. "Cheap at twice the price."

He put his hands on her shoulders, and then slid them down to her waist and pulled her against him. He ran the balls of his fingers along her spine and wondered why he found that so erotic.

After a moment, she pushed him away.

"Tarzan sit," Penny said. "Jane make food."

He went into the living room and put his pistol on the mantelpiece, and then sat down in his armchair. He looked at the dead answering machine.

And then he reached for the telephone, lifted it up, and consulted a typewritten list of telephone numbers.

Officer Jesus Martinez answered, sleepily, on the third ring.

"Martinez."

"This guy you're interested in: dark-skinned, maybe thirty, thirty-five, five-nine or . . ."

"Payne?" Jesus asked incredulously.

". . . five-nine or ten. Maybe one-seventy. Wears his shirts unbuttoned to the navel?"

"What the hell?"

"You said his name is Lanzo, Lanza, something like that?"

"Lanza, Vito Lanza. What about him?"

"At two o'clock this morning, he was signing a two-thousand-dollar IOU in the back room at the Oaks and Pines Lodge," Matt said.

There was a long silence.

*"Marker,"* Martinez said, finally. "Not an IOU, a marker."

"I stand corrected."

"What were you doing up there?"

"Is this your guy, Hay-zus?"

"Yeah. I'm sure. How did *you* know who he was?"

"He was carrying. I made him as a cop. And he made me . . ."

"Shit!"

"Not as a cop. I was in Las Vegas when he was. He recognized me from Vegas and spoke to me."

"You're sure he didn't make you as a cop?"

"As you're so fond of telling me, Hay-zus, I don't look like a cop."

There was another pause.

"Payne, keep this under your hat, will you?"

"Who would I tell? What would I tell? 'Inspector, I just happened to be in an illegal gambling joint, and you know what, I wasn't the only cop in there'?"

"Just keep it under your hat, Payne, okay?"

"Okay. Are you forgetting something, Hay-zus?"

"What?"

"Try, 'Thank you very much, Detective Payne.' "

"Thanks, Payne," Jesus said. "I'll get back to you."

He hung up.

Matt said, "You're welcome, Hay-zus," and put the phone back in its cradle. He pushed himself out of the chair and went into the kitchen.

Penny was at the stove, and there was the peculiar smell of frying Taylor Ham.

"One egg or two? Over light or sunny side up?"

"Two. Up. Have I got time for a shower?"

"A quick one."

When he came back into the kitchen, Penny was in the process of wiping up the last of her egg yolk with a piece of toast.

"Boy, for a fat girl, you sure don't eat much."

"Your eggs are probably cold, which serves you right. What is that I smell?"

"Some kind of after-shave that comes from the Virgin Islands or somewhere. I get a ritual bottle of it from Amy on suitable occasions."

"Nice," she said. "Who's 'Hay-zus'?"

"Martinez. A cop."

"You don't like him much, do you? I could tell from the tone of your voice."

"No, I don't suppose I do like him. He's a good cop, though."

"Are you a good cop?"

"You haven't been reading the newspapers. I'm a goddamned Dick Tracy."

"You almost got killed, didn't you?"

"Yes, I guess I did."

"You know I don't understand you being a cop at all, don't you?"

"There's a good deal about you I don't understand, either."

"Was that a simple statement of fact, or are we back to Tony? And other things?"

"Are we going to fight now? Are things back to normal?"

"I don't know if we're going to fight or not, but I don't think things are ever going to be the same between us." She paused. "Do you?"

"No. How could they be?"

"If you can keep your lust under control, you can kiss me, Matthew."

He leaned across the table and kissed her lightly on the lips.

"I like kissing you better than fighting with you," Penny said. "Let's try that for a while and see what happens."

Peter Wohl, lying in his bed, had just decided that his delicate condition, the session with Larkin, Washington, Malone, and John Barleycorn having lasted until after ten, indicated a couple of soft boiled eggs on toast, rather than a restaurant breakfast, when his door buzzer sounded.

*Who the hell is that, at quarter to seven?*

He got out of bed, put on a bathrobe, and walked barefoot to the door.

"Hello, Hay-zus," he said. "How are you? Come on in."

*What the hell do you want? That you couldn't have said on the telephone?*

"I brought this back," Martinez said, thrusting the loose-leaf notebook with BUREAU OF NARCOTICS AND DANGEROUS DRUGS Investigator's Manual FOR INTERNAL USE ONLY stamped on its cover at Wohl.

*At seven o'clock in the goddamned morning?*

"Thank you," Wohl said.

"And I wanted to talk to you," Martinez said a little uncomfortably. "I thought it would be better if I came. Instead of calling, I mean."

"Absolutely. Do you know how to make coffee?"

"Yes, sir."

"You make the coffee, then, while I catch a quick shower," Wohl said, and pointed toward his kitchen.

"Yes, sir."

"What's on your mind, Hay-zus?" Wohl asked, walking into the kitchen buttoning the cuff of his shirt.

"Inspector, the last time I was here . . . sir, you asked me if I had a gut feeling about anybody, anybody dirty, I mean, and I told you I didn't."

*And now you're going to tell me, right?*

"I remember."

"I did, but I didn't want to say anything."

"I understand. What's your gut feeling, Hay-zus?"

"There's a corporal out there, name of Vito Lanza."

"And you think he's dirty? Why?"

"He just came back from Las Vegas with a lot of money. Enough to buy a new Cadillac."

"Your pal Matt Payne was just in Vegas and did about the same thing."

"Payne's different. Payne's got money. He can afford that kind of money to gamble."

"Is that all you've got to go on, Hay-zus?"

"The day before yesterday, this Lanza had a lot of money, in cash, ninety-four hundred dollars, in his glove compartment."

*Maybe he is onto something. That's a lot of money. Christ knows, I never had ninety-four hundred dollars in cash. But then I never gambled in Las Vegas, either. And how the hell does he know that?*

"How do you know that?"

Martinez's face flushed.

*The reason he knows that is that he went into this guy's car. My God!*

"Forget I asked that question. That way you won't have to lie to me," Wohl said. "Anything else?"

"There was also a matchbook from a place in the Poconos, called the Oaks and Pines Lodge," Martinez said. "I called a guy I know in Vice and asked him about it, and he said they gamble in the back room of that place."

"Fortunately, that's no concern of ours, our jurisdiction ending as it does at the city line."

*Why did you do that? This guy is trying, and sarcasm is not in order.*

"At two o'clock this morning, Lanza signed a marker for two thousand dollars at this place."

"How do you know that? What did you do, for Christ's sake, follow him?"

"No, sir. But I got it from a good source."

"You're supposed to be undercover, Martinez. That means you don't talk to people about what you're doing. Who's your source?"

"I don't want to get him in trouble, Inspector."

"Cut the crap, Martinez. Who's your source?"

"Well, I knew I never could get in this place. And even if I did, Lanza would recognize me. I had to find out."

"Once again, Martinez, cut the crap. Let's have it."

"Payne went up there, Inspector."

"You asked Payne to follow this guy?" Wohl asked incredulously.

"I asked him if he would, if I found out Lanza was going up there."

"And you heard he was going up there?"

"No. Payne went up there on his own. Last night. And he called me about five this morning and told me he saw Lanza sign a marker for two thousand dollars."

"How did he know who Lanza was?"

"He was carrying, and Payne made him as a cop, and then Lanza recognized Payne. . . ."

"Lanza made Payne?"

"Not as a cop. He recognized him from Las Vegas, or something like that. But Payne said he was sure Lanza did not make him as a cop."

*I don't need this. A bona fide lunatic is trying to disintegrate the Vice President of the United States, and we have no idea who he is or where he is, and I don't need to be distracted by a possibly dirty cop at the airport, or another proof that Matt Payne has a danger-ous tendency to charge off doing something stupid.*

"What we have here is a lucky gambler. The only law we know he's broken is to gamble in the Poconos. We wouldn't have a police department if every cop who gambles got fired."

"This guy is dirty, Inspector. I know it," Martinez said.

*On the other hand we have here a guy who gambles big time in Las Vegas, had almost ten thousand dollars in cash in his glove compartment yesterday, and yet was signing a marker for two thousand in a joint in the Poconos. Which means, unless he used the ten thousand to pay off his mortgage or something, that he lost it, and signed a marker for more. The money bothers me. Cops do not have that kind of money. Honest cops don't.*

*And Martinez is not Matt Payne. He had two years undercover in Narcotics, and was damned good at it. He's had the time to de-velop the intuition. And he's not going off half-cocked, either, strictly on intuition. The last time he was here, he wouldn't give me this guy's name.*

Wohl got up from the table and went into his bedroom. He took a small notebook from his bedside table, looked up a number, and dialed it.

"Chief Marchessi, this is Peter Wohl. Sorry to disturb you at home, sir. I think our man has come up with something. Have you got time in your schedule this morning to talk to us, sir?"

There was a pause.

"Thank you, Chief. We'll be there."

He hung up and went back in the kitchen.

"At half past eight, Hay-zus, we're going to see Chief Inspector Marchessi at Internal Affairs. You know where it is?"

"Yes, sir. At Third and Race."

"Be there."

"Yes, sir."

When Martinez had gone, Wohl went to the phone on the coffee table in his living room and dialed another number, this one from memory.

There was no answer on Detective Payne's line, and his answering machine did not kick in, although Wohl let it ring a long time.

Finally, he hung up and looked at his watch.

*Christ, I won't get any breakfast at all!*

At ten minutes past seven, Matt Payne very nearly drove Miss Penelope Detweiler's Mercedes into the wrought-iron gate of the Detweiler estate in Chestnut Hill.

He stopped so suddenly that Penny was thrown against the dashboard.

"When the hell did you start closing the goddamned gate?"

"No, I don't think I'm hurt, but thank you for asking, darling."

"Sorry. Are you all right?"

"I'm going to be sore all over," Penny said innocently. "If it's not one thing, it's another. Whatever am I going to do about you, Matthew darling?"

"What's with the gate?"

"There's some kind of a machine on it. It closes automatically at ten, something like that, and then opens automatically when it gets light in the morning."

"Not this morning."

He got out of the car and went to a telephone box and lifted a telephone receiver. It rang automatically.

"May I help you?" a voice said.

"Princess Penelope seeks entrance to the castle," Matt said.

"Yes, sir," the voice, which Matt now recognized as that of Jensen, the chauffeur, said. He did not seem amused.

The right half of the double gates creaked majestically open.

"I'll tell you something else that gate does," Matt said as he drove through it. "It permits your parents to know when your boy-friends bring you home."

"Don't be silly," she said.

H. Richard Detweiler, in a quilted silk dressing gown, came out of the front door as Matt drove up, holding a cup of coffee.

"He doesn't do that too well, does he?" Penny said.

"Do what?"

"Manage to look like he just happened to be there?"

Matt drove right past Detweiler, waving cheerfully at him, and around to the garage. His Volkswagen was parked to one side.

"You lie to your father," Matt said. "I'm getting out of here."

"You're underestimating him. I'll bet there's no keys in your Bug."

There were not.

It was necessary to walk back to the house, where Penny gave an entirely credible, but wholly false, report of GiGi's party, and why they had decided to stay over and come back first thing in the morning.

Matt was at first amused. Then it occurred to him that if Penny could lie that easily to her father, she could lie as easily to someone else, say M. Payne, Esq., and it no longer seemed amusing.

And then he realized that H. Richard Detweiler didn't believe a word Penny had told him.

*He has no idea where we really were, but he knows damned well we were* not *at GiGi's. So why isn't he mad? Aren't fathers supposed to be furious when young men screw their daughters?*

*As a general rule of thumb, yes. But not when the young gentleman is an old, dear, and more importantly,* responsible *friend of the family, and the young lady in question has previously been involved in things that make a night between the sheets seem quite innocent, indeed.*

"I really have to go."

"I'll have Jensen bring your car around," Detweiler said.

"Just get me the keys, please, I can get it myself."

"Thank you for a lovely evening, Matt," Penny said. "Ask me again, soon."

When she was sure her father's back was turned, she winked lewdly at him.

At two minutes before eight, Matt Payne pushed open the door to the Special Investigations Section. Two sergeants were waiting for him.

"Payne," Sergeant Maxwell Henkels said, "I told you once before. This is the second time, I'm not going to tell you again. I want to know where you are located all the time."

*Somebody, obviously, has been looking for me.*

"I wasn't aware that applied when I'm off duty," Matt said.

"Yeah, well, now you do. You understand me, I'm not going to tell you again?"

"I understand, Sergeant."

"Payne," Sergeant Jerry O'Dowd said uncomfortably, a strange smile on his face. "You have thirty-one minutes to meet Inspector Wohl at Chief Marchessi's office in Internal Affairs."

"What?"

"What are you, deaf or what?" Sergeant Maxwell Henkels demanded.

"I'll handle this, Sergeant," O'Dowd said. "And to make things easier for everybody concerned, I'll keep track of Detective Payne's whereabouts. Will that be all right with you?"

"The inspector asked me where he was, and I felt like an asshole when I didn't know."

"Well, that won't happen again. Payne will keep me advised of his location, on and off duty, won't you, Payne?"

"Right."

Henkels left the office.

"You'd better get moving, Payne," O'Dowd said. "With the early morning traffic, you're going to have to push it."

"Do you know what this is all about?"

"No. But right now, you're not one of his favorite people. He made that pretty clear."

Matt tried to figure that out, but came up with nothing.

"I guess nothing happened overnight? About the lunatic?"

"Not a thing."

"Well, Sergeant," Matt said. "You know where I'll be."

Jerry O'Dowd nodded.

# TWENTY

At twenty-nine minutes after eight, Matt entered the outer office of Chief Inspector Mario Marchessi, of the Internal Investigations Bureau, which was housed in a building about as old as the Schoolhouse, literally under the Benjamin Franklin Bridge, which connects Philadelphia with Camden, N.J.

Staff Inspector Peter Wohl and Officer Jesus Martinez were already there.

"Good morning, sir," Matt said.

Wohl did not reply. He gestured for Martinez and Payne to follow him out into the corridor.

"I want to make this clear before we go in to see Chief Marchessi," Wohl said. "This is to see what, if anything, can be salvaged as a result of you two going off like you thought you were the heroes in a cops-and-robbers movie on TV. Do you understand what I'm saying?"

"No, sir," Matt said. Martinez shook his head no.

"Jesus!" Wohl said disgustedly. "Martinez, you were sent to the airport to keep your eyes and ears open, and to report what you thought you heard or saw to me . . ."

*What does he mean, "Martinez, you were sent to the airport"?*

". . . but when I asked you to tell me your gut feelings, you decided, to hell with him, I'll play it close to my chest; I'm Super Cop. I'll catch this dirty cop by myself."

Matt looked at Martinez, who looked crushed.

"And you!" Wohl turned to Matt. "Whatever gave you the idea that you could, without orders, surveil anyone, much less a police corporal of a district you have absolutely no connection with at all, anywhere, much less to somewhere in another county, for Christ's sake, where you knew illegal gambling was going on?"

"Inspector, I didn't . . ."

"Shut up, Matt!"

". . . follow anyone anywhere."

"I told you to shut up," Wohl said. "I meant it."

He went back into Chief Marchessi's outer office.

Matt looked at Jesus Martinez.

"What did he mean when he said you were sent to the airport?"

Martinez raised his eyes to his, but didn't reply.

"Well?" Matt asked impatiently.

Wohl put his head back out into the corridor.

"Okay, let's go," he said.

They followed Wohl into Chief Marchessi's office. He pointed to where he wanted them to stand, facing Marchessi's desk, then closed the door to the outer office, then sat down on a battered couch.

"Okay, Peter, what's going on?" Chief Marchessi asked.

"My primary mistake, Chief, was in assuming that Detectives Martinez and Payne . . ."

*Detectives Martinez and Payne?*

". . . had a good deal more common sense than is the case."

"I don't follow you, Peter," Marchessi said.

"At two o'clock this morning, Detective Payne, having followed him there, observed an Airport Unit corporal signing a marker for two thousand dollars in a gambling joint in the Poconos."

"What gambling joint?" Marchessi asked.

"What was the name of this place, Payne?" Wohl asked.

"The Oaks and Pines Lodge," Matt replied. "Sir, I didn't follow . . ."

"Speak when you're spoken to," Wohl said.

"Let him talk," Marchessi said. "What were you saying?"

Wohl didn't let him.

"The reason he followed this fellow to the Oaks and Pines," Wohl went on, "was because Detective Martinez asked him to."

Marchessi put up his hand, palm out, to silence Wohl.

"Did you follow this Corporal . . . have we got a name?"

"Lanza, sir. Vito Lanza," Martinez said.

"Did you follow this Corporal Lanza to this place in the Poconos?" Marchessi asked.

"No, sir."

"Inspector Wohl thinks you did."

"The inspector is mistaken, sir. May I explain?"

"I wish somebody would."

"Officer Martinez believes . . ." Matt began.

"*Detective* Martinez," Marchessi interrupted. "Let's get that, at least, straight."

*Jesus! That means Hay-zus was working the Airport undercover,* and *as a detective.*

"Detective Martinez became suspicious of Corporal Lanza, sir," Matt started again.

"Whoa!" Marchessi said. "Why were you suspicious of Corporal Lanza, Martinez?"

"His life-style, sir," Martinez said. "He had too much money. And a new Cadillac. And he gambles."

Marchessi looked at Wohl.

"That's all?" he asked.

"He had almost ten thousand dollars in cash in the glove compartment of his Cadillac, Chief," Martinez said.

"How do you know that?"

"I saw it."

"He showed it to you?"

"No, sir."

"Does this Corporal . . . Lanza . . . know you know he had all this cash?"

"We hope not," Wohl said sarcastically. "We think Detective Martinez's breaking and entering of Corporal Lanza's personal automobile went undetected."

Marchessi snapped his head to look at Martinez. He was on the verge of saying something, but, visibly, changed his mind.

"And with all this somewhat less than incriminating evidence in hand," Marchessi said, "you enlisted the aid of Detective Payne to surveil Corporal Lanza, and he followed him to this lodge in the Poconos?"

"Not exactly, sir," Jesus said.

"Tell me, *exactly*."

"I asked Detective Payne if he would be willing to follow Lanza there if I found out he was going."

"Why?"

"You mean why did I ask Payne?"

Marchessi nodded.

"Because my friend in Vice said it was a high-class place and I figured Payne could get in. I couldn't follow him myself."

"And did you tell Detective Payne what you're doing at the Airport Unit?"

"No, sir. Just that I thought I found a dirty cop."

"And you learned that Lanza was going to this place, and told Payne, and Payne followed him up there. Is that correct?"

"No, sir," Matt said.

"I'm asking Martinez," Marchessi said.

"I didn't tell him Lanza was going there," Martinez said. "He went up there on his own."

*Was that a simple statement of fact, Hay-zus, or are you trying to stick it in me?*

"Why did you do that, Payne?"

"Hay-zus is a good cop, sir . . ."

"Who the hell is '*Hay-zus*'?" Marchessi interrupted.

"That's the Spanish pronunciation of 'Jesus', sir."

"Whether '*Hay-zus*' is a good cop seems to be open to discussion," Marchessi said. "Go on."

"I thought if he said he had a dirty cop, he probably had one."

"Just as an aside, Detective Payne, there is a departmental policy that states that police officers having reason to suspect brother officers of dishonesty will——*will*, not *may*——bring this to the attention of Internal Affairs."

"Yes, sir. Martinez asked me if I would be willing to go to this place to see if Lanza was associating with known criminals . . ."

"And if he was, I was going to tell you his name, Inspector," Martinez said to Wohl.

". . . and I agreed," Matt went on. "Then it occurred to me it would make sense if I knew where I was going. To take a look at the place before I followed Lanza there, in other words. So I went up there."

"No one, correct me if I'm wrong, told you to do so. Just your buddy Martinez asked you, right?"

"Yes, sir."

"Is there anyone else involved in this? Another buddy?"

Martinez and Matt looked at each other.

"Okay, who?" Marchessi asked, correctly interpreting the exchanged glances.

"He didn't do anything, sir," Martinez said.

"*Who*, dammit?"

"I talked about Lanza to Detective McFadden, sir."

"He's the officer you worked with in Narcotics?" Marchessi asked.

"Yes, sir."

*If he knows that*, Matt thought, *he knows that it was Hay-zus and Charley who brought down the guy who killed Uncle Dutch. That ought to be worth something.*

"Anybody else?"

"No, sir."

"Just the three of you, huh? Your own private detective squad within the Department, huh?"

Marchessi looked between them until it was clear that neither dared reply to that, and then went on.

"You have any trouble getting in this place, Payne?"

"No, sir."

"It's open to the public?"

"I believe it's operated as a club, sir. I was with someone who belonged."

"That could be interpreted to mean that you are associating with known criminals."

"Not in this case, sir," Matt said quickly.

*But that's bullshit. Penny is a known narcotics addict, as well as someone known to associate with known criminals. Jesus!*

"And this Corporal Lanza was there?"

"Yes, sir."

"Associating with known criminals?"

"I don't know, sir."

"The truth of the matter, Payne," Wohl said, "is that, with the possible exception of somebody like Vincenzo Savarese, you wouldn't recognize a known criminal if you fell over one. Isn't that so?"

"Yes, sir."

"Tell me about the two-thousand-dollar marker," Marchessi said.

"Sir, as I was cashing out, I saw Lanza sign a marker for two thousand dollars' worth of chips. He was in the line ahead of me."

"I thought you said you didn't follow him up there."

"I didn't. He was there."

"You knew him by sight? That would suggest he knows you by sight."

"Yes, sir. But not the way that sounds, sir."

"Clarify it for me."

"I didn't know who he was. But I made him as a cop. He was carrying."

"People, other than policemen, sometimes go about armed."

"I had a gut feeling he was a cop, sir, and then he spoke to me."

"What did he say?"

"I had apparently run into him in Las Vegas, sir. And on the airplane from Las Vegas home. He recognized me. Not as a cop."

"You made him, is that what you're saying, as a cop, but he didn't make you as a cop?"

"I'm sure I could have told if he had, sir."

"I admire your confidence in your own judgment, Payne," Marchessi said. "And then what did you do?"

"I came back to Philadelphia and called Off . . . *Detective* Martinez and told him (a) that Lanza had been in the Oaks and Pines and (b) had signed a marker for two thousand dollars."

"And then I went to see you, sir," Martinez said to Wohl.

"Tell me, Martinez," Marchessi said. "Have you any *evidence* to connect Corporal Lanza with the smuggling of narcotics, or, for that matter, of anything else, or any other criminal activity, at the airport?"

"No evidence, sir. But it has to be him."

" 'Has' to be him?" Marchessi replied, softly sarcastic.

He looked at Wohl, who shrugged his shoulders.

"You two wait outside. In the corridor," Marchessi said.

Matt and Martinez turned around and left his office.

"You want some coffee, Peter?" Marchessi asked.

"What I would like is a stiff drink."

"At this hour of the morning?"

"Figure of speech," Wohl said.

"Both of them talked about 'gut feelings,' or implied it," Marchessi said. "My gut feeling is that they've found who we're looking for."

"But have they blown it?" Wohl asked. "Dammit, I asked him to give me a name."

"Give him the benefit of the doubt. He didn't want to point a finger until he was sure."

"And while he was making sure, there was a good chance this guy would smell that he was being watched. And breaking into his car was absolute stupidity."

Marchessi chuckled.

"There was a story going around that one of my staff inspectors, carried away with enthusiasm, tapped the line of a Superior Court judge without getting the necessary warrant."

"Ouch!" Peter said.

"I didn't believe it, of course," Marchessi said. "I don't know what I would have done if somebody had discovered the tap."

"What, to change the subject, Chief, do we do about this?"

"Well, I think we've already been shifted into high gear, whether or not we like it," Marchessi said.

He pushed one of the buttons on his telephone, then picked up the receiver.

"Ollie, can you come in here a minute?" he said, and hung up.

Less than a minute later, Captain Richard Olsen, a large, blond-haired man of forty, wearing a blue blazer and a striped necktie, opened Marchessi's door without knocking.

"Sir?"

"Come in and close the door, Ollie. You remember Peter, of course?"

"What brings you slumming, Inspector?"

Captain Olsen, whose exact title Wohl could not remember, provided administrative services to the fourteen staff inspectors assigned to the Internal Investigations Bureau. The staff inspectors, from whose ranks Wohl had been transferred to command of Special Operations, handled sensitive investigations, most often involving governmental corruption. Wohl liked and respected him.

"How are you, Ollie?"

"Ollie," Marchessi asked, "if I wanted around-the-clock, moving surveillance of an off-duty Airport Unit corporal, starting right now, what kind of problems would that cause?"

Olsen thought that over for a minute.

"What squad is he assigned to?"

"Three squad, four to midnight," Wohl furnished.

"I can handle the next twenty-four hours, forty-eight, with no trouble. After that, I'll need some bodies. What are we looking for?"

"For openers, association with known criminals. Ultimately, to catch him smuggling drugs out of the airport."

"Watching him on the job would be difficult."

"I'm wondering if I can strike a deal with the feds. I know god-damned well they have people undercover out there. If I told them I'll give them a name, if they let us have the arrest . . ."

"And if they won't go along?" Wohl asked.

"That would bring us back to Hay-zus, wouldn't it, Peter?" Marchessi said thoughtfully.

"Yeah," Wohl said.

"You call it, Peter, you know him better than I do."

"We'd be betting that Lanza has accepted the story that Martinez is out there because he failed the detective's examination," Wohl thought aloud. "And I would have to impress on Martinez that all, absolutely all, that he's to do is watch him on the job. . . . Screw the feds. I don't like the idea of having the feds catch one of our cops dirty. Let's go with Martinez."

"I have no idea," Olsen said, "who or what either of you are talking about."

"I think we should bring Martinez back in here," Marchessi said. "I don't think we need Payne. Except to tell him to keep his nose out of this."

"I'll handle Payne," Wohl said. "I don't think you need me, either, do you, Chief?"

"No. And you're on the mad bomber too, aren't you? How're you doing?"

"We don't have a clue who he is," Wohl said, getting off the couch. "Thank you very much, Chief. You've been very understanding."

"I have some experience, Peter, with bright young men who sometimes get carried away. Every once in a while, they even catch the bad guys. You might keep that in mind."

"Just between you, me, and the Swede here, I'm not nearly as angry with those two as I hope they think I am," Wohl said.

"You could have fooled me," Marchessi said. "Send in Martinez, will you, Peter?"

"I guess I'll be seeing you, Peter?" Olsen said, extending his hand.

"More than you'll want to, Ollie," Wohl said.

At 9:24, Mr. Pietro Cassandro pulled up before Ristorante Alfredo's entrance at the wheel of a Lincoln that had been delivered to Classic Livery only the day before. On the way from his home, Mr. Vincenzo Savarese had been concerned that there was something wrong with the car. It smelled of something burning.

Mr. Cassandro had assured Mr. S. that there was no cause for concern, that he had personally checked the car out himself, that it was absolutely okay, and that what Mr. S. was smelling was the preservatives and paint and stuff that comes with a new car, and burns off after a few miles. Like stickers and oil, for example, on the muffler.

Mr. S. had seemed only partially satisfied with Pietro's explanation, and Pietro had decided that maybe he'd made a mistake in picking up Mr. S. in the car before he'd put some miles on it. He would never do so again. The next time Mr. S. was sent a new car, it would have, say, two hundred miles on it, and wouldn't smell of burning anything.

Mr. Gian-Carlo Rosselli got out of the passenger seat and walked quickly to the door. Ristorante Alfredo didn't open until half-past eleven, and Pietro hoped that Ricco Baltazari had enough brains to have somebody waiting to open the door when Rosselli knocked on it. Mr. S. did not like to be kept waiting in a car when he wanted to go someplace, especially when the people knew he was coming.

Mr. Cassandro's concerns were put to rest when the door was opened by Ricco Baltazari himself before Rosselli reached it. Rosselli turned and looked up and down the street, and then nodded to Pietro, who got quickly out from behind the wheel and opened the door for Mr. S.

Mr. S. didn't say "thank you" the way he usually did, or even nod his head, but just walked quickly across the sidewalk and into the restaurant. Pietro was almost sure that was because he had business on his mind, and not because he was pissed that the car smelled, but he wasn't positive.

He wondered, as he got back behind the wheel, if he raced the engine, would that speed up the burn-the-crap-off process, so that the car wouldn't smell when Mr. S. came out.

He decided against doing so. What was likely to happen was that, sitting still, the smoke would just get more in the car than it would if he just let things take their natural way.

But then he decided that he could take a couple of laps around the block and burn it off that way. Mr. S. probably wasn't going to come out in the next couple of minutes, and if Rosselli looked out and saw the car wasn't there, he would think the cop on the beat had made him move the car.

Sometimes, the cops would leave you alone, let you sit at the curb, if there was somebody behind the wheel, but other times, they would be a pain in the ass and tell you to move on.

Pietro put the Lincoln in gear and drove off. At the first red light, he raced the engine. A cop gave him a strange look. Fuck him!

"Good morning, Mr. S.," Ricco Baltazari said as he carefully shook Mr. S.'s hand. "I got some nice fresh coffee, and I sent out for a little pastry."

"Just the coffee, thank you, Ricco," Mr. S. said, and then changed his mind. "What kind of pastry?"

"I sent out to the French place. I got croissants, and eclairs, and . . ."

"Maybe an eclair. Thank you very much," Mr. S. said.

"Would you like to go to the office? Or maybe a table?"

"This will do nicely," Mr. S. said and sat down at a table along the wall.

Gian-Carlo Rosselli looked as if he didn't know what he should do, and Mr. S. saw this.

"Sit down, Gian-Carlo, and have a pastry and some coffee. I want you to hear this."

"I'll get the stuff," Ricco said.

When he came back, Mr. S. asked after his family.

"Everybody's doing just fine, Mr. S."

Mr. Savarese nodded, then leaned forward and added cream and sugar to the cup of coffee Ricco had poured for him.

"There's a little business problem, Ricco," Mr. S. said.

"With the restaurant?" Ricco asked, concern evident in his voice. He glanced nervously at Gian-Carlo.

Mr. S. looked at him for a moment, expressionless, before replying and when he did it was not directly.

"I had a telephone call yesterday from a business associate in Baltimore," he said. "A man who has always been willing to help me, when I asked for a favor. Now he wants a favor from me."

"How can I help, Mr. S.?"

"His problem, he tells me, is that the feds, the Customs people, and the Narcotics and Dangerous Drugs people have been making a nuisance of themselves at Friendship. You know Friendship? The airport in Baltimore?"

"I know it, Mr. S."

"He says that he don't think it will last, that what they're doing is fishing, not looking for something specific, but he has decided that it would be best if he didn't try to bring anything through

Friendship for the next week or ten days. As a precaution, you understand."

"Certainly."

"And he asked me, would I do him the favor of handling his merchandise through Philadelphia. The point of origin is San Juan, Puerto Rico."

"We don't have anybody at the airport. . . ."

"There are two reasons I told this man that I would be happy to help him," Mr. S. said. "The first being that I owe him, and when he asks . . . And the second being that I did not want it to get around, and it would if I told him, that at this moment, I don't have anybody at the airport."

"I understand."

"So what I want to know from you, Ricco, how are things going with your friend who works at the airport?"

"I had a telephone call at eight this morning, Mr. S. Our friend was up there last night and he had bad luck, and he signed four thousand dollars' worth of markers."

"You ever think, Ricco, that somebody's bad luck is almost always somebody else's good luck?"

"That's very true, Mr. S."

"So you have these markers?"

"No, sir. They're going to have a truck coming to Philadelphia today, this afternoon, and they'll bring the markers with them then."

"I think I would like to have them sooner than that. Do you think you could call them up and ask them, as a favor to you, if they could maybe put somebody in a car and get them down here right away?"

"Or we could send a car up there, Mr. S.," Gian-Carlo suggested.

"Let them, as a favor to Ricco, bring the markers here to the restaurant. Then, when they come, Ricco can call me, at the house, and say that he has the papers you were looking for, and you'll come pick them up, and take them, and also those photographs Joe Fierello took at the car lot, over to Paulo, and then Paulo can go have a talk with this cop."

"Right, Mr. S."

"Where would you say this cop would be, Ricco, in, say, three hours?"

"I don't know, Mr. S., to tell you the truth."

"You know where he is now? I thought I asked you to have that girl keep an eye on him."

"He's at her apartment now, Mr. S. But what you asked is where he'll be at about noon. He may be there. He may go by his house, Tony told me he had to have new pipes put in, or he may just stay at Tony's apartment until it's time for him to go to work. I just have no way of telling."

"I understand. All right. The first thing you do is you get on the phone and ask them to please send the markers right away to here. Then, can you do this, you call this girl, and you tell her if she can to keep the cop in her apartment as long as she can, and if she can't, she's to call you the minute he leaves, and tell you where he's going. And I think it would be best if you made the calls from a pay phone someplace."

"I'll have to leave the keys to the restaurant with Gian-Carlo, otherwise you'd be locked in."

"There's nobody else here?"

"The fewer people around the better, I always say."

"And you're right. But I'll tell you what. We'll leave, and then you go find a pay phone and make the call, and when you find out something, you call the house and all you have to say is 'yes' or 'no.' You understand?"

"That would work nicely."

"And besides, if I stayed here, I'd eat all this pastry, it's very good, but it's not good for me, too much of it."

"I understand, Mr. S."

Gian-Carlo got up and walked to the door and pushed the curtain aside and looked for Pietro.

"He's not out there, Mr. S."

"He probably had to drive around the block," Mr. S. said. "He'll be there in a minute."

For the next three minutes, Gian-Carlo, at fifteen-second intervals, pushed the curtain aside and looked out to see if Pietro and the Lincoln had returned.

Finally he had.

"He's out there, Mr. S.," Gian-Carlo said.

Mr. Savarese stood up.

"Thank you for the pastry, even if it wasn't good for me," he said, and shook Ricco's hand.

Then he walked out of the restaurant and quickly across the sidewalk and got into the Lincoln. As soon as Gian-Carlo had got in beside him in the front seat, Pietro drove off.

"I'll tell you, Pietro, if anything, it smells worse than before."

"As soon as I get a chance, Mr. S., I'll take it to the garage and swap it."

"Why don't you do that?" Mr. S. replied.

"Anthony, something has come up," Mr. Ricco Baltazari, proprietor of Ristorante Alfredo, said to Mr. Anthony Clark (formerly Cagliari), resident manager of the Oaks and Pines Lodge, over the telephone. Mr. Clark was in his office overlooking the third tee of the Oaks and Pines Championship Golf Course. Mr. Baltazari was in a pay telephone booth in the lower lobby of the First Philadelphia Bank & Trust Building on South Broad Street.

"What's that?"

"The financial documents you're going to send me . . ."

"They're on their way, Ricco, relax. The van just left, not more than a couple minutes ago."

"That's not good enough. It'll take him for fucking ever to get to Philly."

"What do you want me to do, get in my car and bring them my fucking self?" Mr. Clark said, a slight tone of petulance creeping into his voice.

"It's not what I want, Anthony. It's what you know who, our mutual friend, wants," Mr. Baltazari said. "He wants those financial documents right fucking now."

There was a moment's silence.

"The only thing I could do, Ricco," Mr. Clark said, "is put somebody in my car and send him after the van, see if he could catch it, you understand?"

"Do it, Anthony. Our mutual friend is very anxious to get his hands on those financial documents just as soon as he can."

"If I had known he wanted those documents in a hurry, I would have brought them myself, you understand that?"

"If I had known he wanted them, I would have come up and got the fuckers myself," Mr. Baltazari replied. "I just left him. He said I should tell you he wants them, as a special favor, right now."

"I'll do what I can, Ricco. You want I should call our friend and tell him what I'm doing, in case my guy can't catch the van? Or will you do that?"

"He don't give a shit what you're doing. All he wants is the fucking markers. How you do that is your business."

"I tell my guy to take them right to our mutual friend?"

"You tell your guy to bring them to me, at the restaurant. When I got them, I'm to call our friend."

"Ricco, I would be very unhappy if I was to learn that you weren't telling me the whole truth about this."

"Anthony, get your guy on the way, for Christ's sake!"

"Yeah," Mr. Clark said, and hung up.

Mr. Clark took a pad of Oaks and Pines notepaper from his desk, and a pen from his desk set.

On one sheet of paper, he wrote, "Give Tommy the envelope I gave you, A.C." and on the other he wrote Ristorante Alfredo, Ricco Baltazari, and the address and telephone number.

Then Mr. Clark went down to the money room off the casino. There he found Mr. Thomas Dolbare sitting all alone on one of the stools in front of the money counting table, on which now sat a small stack of plastic bank envelopes. Mr. Dolbare, a very large and muscular twenty-eight-year-old, was charged with the security of last night's take until the messenger arrived from Wilkes-Barre to take it for deposit into six different, innocently named bank accounts in Hazelton and Wilkes-Barre.

"Tommy," Mr. Clark said, "what I want you to do is take my car and chase down the van. He just left. He always goes down Route 611. Stop him, give him this, and he'll give you an envelope. You then take the envelope to Mr. Baltazari. I wrote down the address and phone number."

Mr. Clark gave Mr. Dolbare both notes.

"Right."

"As soon as you have it, go to a pay phone and call me. Or if you can't catch the van, call me and tell me that too."

"I'll catch it," Mr. Dolbare said confidently. He was pleased that he was being given greater responsibility than sitting around in a fucking windowless room watching money bags.

"Don't take a gun," Mr. Clark said. "You won't need it in Philadelphia."

"Right," Mr. Dolbare said, and took off his jacket and the .357 Magnum Colt Trooper in its shoulder holster, and then put his jacket back on.

"Don't drive like a fucking idiot and get arrested, or bang up my car," Mr. Clark said.

"Right," Mr. Dolbare said.

The van that Mr. Dolbare intercepted on Highway 611 between Delaware Water Gap and Mount Bethel was a year-old Ford, which had the Oaks and Pines Lodge logotype painted on both its doors and the sides. It made a daily, except Sunday, run to Philadelphia

where it picked up seafood and beef and veal from M. Alcatore &
Sons Quality Wholesale and Retail Meats in South Philadelphia.

M. Alcatore & Sons was a wholly owned subsidiary of Food
Services, Inc., which was a wholly owned subsidiary of South
Street Enterprises, Inc., in which, it was believed by various law
enforcement agencies, Mr. Vincenzo Savarese held a substantial
interest.

It was also believed by various law enforcement agencies that
through some very creative accounting the interlocked corpora-
tions were both depriving the federal, state, and city governments
of all sorts of taxes, and at the same time laundering through them
profits from a rather long list of illegal enterprises.

So far, no law enforcement agency, city, state, or federal, had
come up with anything any of the respective governmental attor-
neys believed would be worth taking to court.

Tommy Dolbare gave the van driver Mr. Clark's note, and the
van driver gave him a sealed blank envelope.

Tommy got back in Mr. Clark's Cadillac Sedan de Ville, and
continued down Highway 611 to Easton, where he had to take a
piss, and stopped at a gas station. He decided, on his way back to
the car, that Mr. Clark would probably like to hear that he had intercepted the van, so he went into a telephone booth and called Oaks
and Pines Lodge.

Then he got back in the Sedan de Ville and continued down US
Highway 611 toward Philadelphia. It is one of the oldest highways
in the nation, and from Easton south for twenty miles or so parallels the Delaware Canal.

Shortly after Mr. Dolbare passed the turn off to Durham, a tiny
village of historical significance because it was at Durham that
Benjamin Franklin established the first stop of his new postal service, and from the canal at Durham that George Washington took
the Durham Boats on which he floated across the Delaware to attack the British in Princeton, Mr. Dolbare took his eyes from the
road a moment to locate the cigarette lighter.

When he looked out the windshield again, there was a dog on the
road. Mr. Dolbare, although he did not have one himself, liked
dogs, and did not wish to run over one. He applied his brakes as
hard as he could, and simultaneously attempted to steer around the
dog.

The Cadillac went out of control and skidded into the post-and-
cable fence that separates Highway 611 from the Delaware Canal.

The fence functioned as designed. The Cadillac did not go into the Delaware Canal. The cables held it from doing so. Only the front wheels left the road. Mr. Dolbare was able to back onto the road, but when he did so, one of the cables, which had become entangled with the grill of the car, did not become unentangled, and held. This caused the grill of the Cadillac, and the sheet metal that held the grill and the radiator in place, to pull loose from the Cadillac.

There was a scream of tortured metal as the fan blades struck something where the radiator had been, and then antifreeze erupted from the displaced radiator hose against the engine block.

"Oh, shit!" Mr. Dolbare said.

He got out of the car. He looked in both directions down the highway. He could see nothing but the narrow road in either direction. He did not recall what lay in the direction of Philadelphia, but he estimated that it was not more than a couple of miles back toward Easton where he had seen a gas station and a bar, which would have a telephone.

He slammed the door of Mr. Clark's Cadillac as hard as he could, and started walking back up Highway 611 toward Easton, his heart heavy with the knowledge that he had really fucked up, and that he was now in deep shit.

Mr. Dolbare had just passed a sign announcing that the Riegelsville Kiwanis met every Tuesday at the Riegelsville Inn and had just learned that the Riegelsville American Legion welcomed him to Riegelsville when he saw a familiar vehicle coming down Highway 611.

He stepped into the road and flagged it down.

"What the fuck are you doing walking down the highway?" the driver inquired of him.

"We have to find a phone," Mr. Dolbare said. "You see one back there?"

"What the hell happened?"

"Some asshole forced me off the road; I had an accident."

"You wrecked Clark's car?" the Oaks and Pines van driver replied, adding unnecessarily, "Boy, is your ass in deep shit."

"No shit? Get me to a fucking phone."

Fifteen minutes later, Mr. Anthony Clark telephoned to Mr. Ricco Baltazari, at the Ristorante Alfredo, to inform him that there had been an accident, some asshole had forced his guy off the road in the sticks, but that the van had caught up with him, and those financial documents they had been talking about were at this very minute on their way to him.

Mr. Baltazari told Mr. Clark, unnecessarily, that he would pass the progress report along to their mutual friend, who wasn't going to like it one fucking bit.

"He's going to want to know, Anthony, if you didn't have somebody reliable to do this favor for him, why you didn't do it yourself."

"Accidents happen, Ricco, for Christ's sake!"

"Yeah," Mr. Baltazari said, and hung up.

He looked at his watch. It was quarter to twelve. He thought that although it wasn't his fault, Mr. S. was going to be pissed to hear that the goddamned markers were still somewhere the other side of Doylestown.

Somewhat reluctantly, he dialed Mr. S.'s number.

# TWENTY-ONE

Chief Marchessi had ordered surveillance of Corporal Vito Lanza "starting right now." Captain Swede Olsen had done his best to comply with his orders, but Internal Affairs does not have a room full of investigators just sitting around with nothing else to do until summoned to duty, so it was twenty minutes after eleven before a nondescript four-year-old Pontiac turned down the 400 block of Ritner Street in South Philadelphia.

"There it is," Officer Howard Hansen said, pointing to Corporal Lanza's residence. "With the plumber's truck in front."

"Where the hell am I going to park?" Sergeant Bill Sanders responded. "Jesus, South Philly is unbelievable."

Officer Hansen and Sergeant Sanders were in civilian clothing. Hansen, who had been handling complaints from the public about police misbehavior, was wearing a suit and tie, and Sanders, who had been investigating a no-harm-done discharge of firearms involving two police officers and a married lady who had promised absolute fidelity to both of them, was wearing a cotton jacket and a plaid, tieless shirt.

"Go around the block, maybe something'll open up," Hansen said.

"I don't see a new Cadillac, either."

"If you had a new Cadillac, would you want to park it around here?"

"We don't even know if he's here," Sanders said as he drove slowly and carefully down Ritner Street, where cars were parked, half on the sidewalk, along both sides.

Suddenly he stopped.

"Go in the bar," he ordered, pointing. "See if you can get a seat where you can see his house. I'll find someplace to park."

Hansen got quickly out of the car and walked in the bar. He saw that if he sat at the end of the bar by the entrance, he could see over the curtain on the plate-glass window, and would have a view of most of the block, including the doorway to Lanza's house.

He ordered a beer and a piece of pickled sausage.

Sergeant Sanders walked in ten minutes later.

"Well, I'll be damned," he said. "Long time no see!"

They shook hands.

"Let me buy you a beer," Hansen said.

"I accept. Schaefers," he said to the bartender, and then to Hansen: "I got to make a call."

The bartender pointed to a phone, and then drew his beer.

Sanders consulted the inside of a matchbook, then dropped a coin in the slot and dialed a number.

On the fourth ring, a somewhat snappy female voice picked up.

"Hello?"

"Is Vito there, Mrs. Lanza?"

"Who's this?"

"Jerry, Mrs. Lanza. Can I talk to Vito?"

"If you can find him, you can talk to him. I don't know where he is. Nobody is here but me and the plumbers."

"I'll try him later, Mrs. Lanza, thank you."

"You see him, you tell him he's got to come home and talk to these plumbers."

"I'll do that, Mrs. Lanza," Sanders said, and hung up.

He walked back to the bar.

"His mother doesn't know where he is. She's all alone with the plumbers."

Hansen nodded, and took a small sip of his beer.

"Is there anything on the TV?" he called to the bartender.

"What do you want?"

"Anything but the soap opera. I have enough trouble with my own love life; I don't have to watch somebody else's trouble."

The bartender started flipping through the channels.

At five minutes to twelve, Marion Claude Wheatley left his office in the First Pennsylvania Bank & Trust Company, rode down in the elevator, and walked north on South Broad Street to the City Hall, and then east on Market Street toward the Delaware River.

He returned to the Super Drugstore on the corner of 11th Street where he had previously purchased the *Souvenir of Asbury Park, N.J.* AWOL bag, and bought two more of them, another *Souvenir of Asbury Park, N.J.* and one with the same fish jumping out of the waves, but marked *Souvenir of Panama City Beach, Fla.* He thought it would be interesting to know just how many different places were stamped on AWOL bags the Super Drugstore had in the back room.

And then he thought that Super Drugstore was really a misnomer. There was a place where one presumably could have a prescription filled, way in the back of the place, and there were rows of patent medicines, but he would have guessed that at least eighty percent of the available space in the Super Drugstore was given over to nonpharmaceutical items.

It was more of a Woolworth's Five and Dime, he thought, than a Super Drugstore. They really should not be allowed to call it a drugstore; it was deceptive, if not downright dishonest.

He had almost reached the entrance when he saw a display of flashlight batteries, under a flamboyant *S A L E !* sign. He knew all that meant, of course, was that the items were available for sale, not on sale at a reduced price. But he headed for the display anyway, and saw that he was wrong.

The Eveready Battery Corporation, as opposed to the Super Drugstore itself, was having a promotional sale. He could tell that, because there were point-of-purchase promotional materials from Eveready, reading "As Advertised On TV!"

The philosophy behind the promotion, rather clever, he thought, was *"Are you* sure *your batteries are fresh? Be Sure With Eveready!"*

This was tied in, Marion noticed, with a pricing policy that reduced the individual price of batteries in a sliding scale tied to how many total batteries one bought.

This triggered another thought. Certainly, there would be nothing suspicious if he acted as if he were someone taken in by

Eveready's advertising and bought all the batteries he was going to need.

And then he had a sudden, entirely pleasing insight. There was more to his having come across this display than mere happenstance. The Lord had arranged for him to pass by this display. He had, of course, planned to *Be Sure* his batteries were fresh. But he had planned to buy four batteries here, and four batteries there, not all twenty-four at once.

The Lord had made it possible for him to buy everything he needed to *Be Sure With Eveready* at one place, and in such a manner that no one would wonder what he was doing with all those batteries.

He paid for the batteries, and then put them in the *Souvenir of Asbury Park, N.J.* AWOL bag, and then folded that and put it in the *Souvenir of Panama City Beach, Fla.* AWOL bag, and then asked the girl at the cashier's counter for a bag to put everything in.

He didn't want to walk back to the office, much less into the office, carrying a bag with *Souvenir of Panama City Beach, Fla.* painted on it.

When he got back to the office, he got out the telephone book, and a map of Philadelphia, and carefully marked on the map the location of all hardware stores that could reasonably be expected to sell chain, which were located within a reasonable walking distance of the house.

He would, he decided, hurry home after work, leave the lunchtime purchases just inside the door, and see how much chain he could acquire before he really got hungry, and the headaches would come back, and he would have to eat.

At twenty-five minutes past one o'clock, Mrs. Antoinette Marie Wolinski Schermer telephoned to Mr. Ricco Baltazari at the Ristorante Alfredo and informed him that Corporal Vito Lanza had just left her apartment.

"Jesus Christ! I told you to keep him there!"

"Don't snap at me, Ricco, I did everything I could. He said he had to go by his house and see the plumbers."

"I didn't mean to snap at you, baby," Mr. Baltazari said, sounding very contrite. "But this was important. This was business. You sure he went to his house?"

"I'm not sure, that's what he said."

"Okay, I'll get back to you."

Mr. Baltazari was thoughtfully drumming his fingers on his

desk, trying to phrase how he could most safely report this latest development to Mr. S. when there was a knock at the door.

"What?"

"Mr. Baltazari, it's Tommy Dolbare."

Mr. Baltazari jumped up and went to the door and jerked it open.

"I got this envelope for you," Tommy said.

Mr. Baltazari snatched the extended envelope from Mr. Dolbare's hand and looked into it.

"Where the fuck have you been, asshole?" he inquired.

"I had a wreck. I got forced off the road," Tommy said, hoping that he sounded sincere and credible.

"Get the fuck out of here," Mr. Baltazari said, and closed the door in Mr. Dolbare's face.

Mr. Baltazari then telephoned Mr. S.'s home. Mr. Gian-Carlo Rosselli answered the telephone.

"I got those financial documents Mr. S. was interested in," Mr. Baltazari reported. "They just this minute got here. Our friend's guy got in a wreck on the way down. Or so he said."

"Fuck!" Mr. Rosselli said.

"I just talked to the broad. She says our other friend just left there to go home, to talk to the plumbers."

"She was supposed to keep him there," Mr. Rosselli said.

"She said she couldn't."

"I'll get back to you, Ricco," Mr. Rosselli said, and hung up.

"That was Ricco," Mr. Rosselli said to Mr. Savarese, who was reading *The Wall Street Journal*. He waited until Mr. S. lowered the newspaper. "He's got the markers. That bimbo of his called him and said that the cop left her place; he had to go to his house and talk to the plumbers. What do you want me to do?"

Mr. Savarese, after a moment, asked, "Did he say why it took so long to get the markers?"

"He said something about Anthony Cagliari's guy . . ."

*"Clark,"* Mr. Savarese interrupted. "If Anthony wants to call himself Clark, we should respect that."

". . . Anthony's guy getting in a wreck on the way down from the Poconos."

"This was important. I told Ricco to tell Anthony it was important. Either Ricco didn't do that, or he didn't make it clear to Anthony. Otherwise Anthony would have brought those markers himself."

"You're right."

"Maybe you had better say something to Ricco," Mr. Savarese said. "When things are important, they're important."

"I'll do that, Mr. S. Right now, if you want."

"What I want you to do right now is go get the markers from Ricco. Take the photographs and give them to Paulo. You know where this cop lives?"

"Yes."

"I don't know what this business with the plumbers is," Mr. Savarese said. "If possible, without attracting attention, you and Paulo try to have a talk with the cop. But I don't want a fuss in the neighborhood, you understand?"

"I understand, Mr. S."

"You tell Paulo I said that. You tell him I said it would have been better if you could have talked to the cop in the girl's apartment. But sometimes things happen. Anthony's driver had a wreck; the cop's toilet is stopped up. It's not the end of the world. If you can't talk to him at his house, it might even be *better* if Paulo and you talked to him at this woman's apartment. Use your best judgment, Gian-Carlo. Just make sure that we get what we're after."

"I'll do my best, Mr. S."

Mr. Savarese nodded and raised *The Wall Street Journal* from his lap and resumed reading it.

"Ricco," Mr. Rosselli said to Mr. Baltazari when he answered the telephone. "What I want you to be doing is standing on the sidewalk in ten minutes with those things in your hand, so I don't have to waste my time coming in there and getting them, you understand?"

"Right," Mr. Baltazari said. "I'll be waiting for you."

"There's a new Cadillac parking," Sergeant Bill Sanders said to Officer Howard Hansen. "Is that our guy?"

Hansen consulted a notebook, stuck into which was a photograph of Corporal Vito Lanza.

"Yeah, that's him."

"If I was dirty, and lived in this neighborhood," Sergeant Sanders said, "I think I would take what that Cadillac cost and move out of this neighborhood."

"But then you wouldn't be able to impress the neighbors with your new Caddy," Hansen said. "Why be dirty if you can't impress your neighbors?"

"Did you hear what this guy is supposed to have done? I mean, anything besides he may be taking stuff out of the airport?"

"Olsen said that Peter Wohl was in the chief's office first thing this morning. He had the kid—he just made detective, by the way—that got himself shot by the Islamic Liberation Army, Payne, and some little Puerto Rican with him. I worked with Wohl on the job where he put Judge Findermann away. He does not go off half-cocked."

"The little Puerto Rican was a cop?"

"I think he was the guy, one of the guys, who got the junkie who shot Captain Dutch Moffitt."

Sanders nodded.

"You think to bring the camera from the car?"

Hansen nodded, and patted his breast pocket.

"Just in case we lose this guy when he leaves, I think you'd better take his picture."

Hansen nodded again.

"There's not *a* plumber," Mr. Paulo Cassandro said, looking out the back window of his Jaguar as it moved slowly down the 400 block of Ritner Street, "there's a whole fucking army of them."

"These houses is old; the pipes wear out," Mr. Rosselli replied absently.

On the way here, Mr. Cassandro had given some thought to how he was going to handle the situation if the place was full of plumbers, or Lanza's mother, or whatever. He had what, after some reflection, seemed to be a pretty good idea.

Starting with the bill of sale for the Cadillac, all the paperwork involved in dealing with the cop had been Xeroxed. It was the businesslike thing to do, in case something should get lost, or fucked up, or whatever. Including the bill for the comped room at the Oaks and Pines, and the markers, both the ones he'd paid, and the ones he'd just signed.

The thing they had to do now was make the cop nervous. He thought he had figured out just how to do that.

*I will just go in the cop's house, and hand him the markers from last night. And tell him I want to talk to him, and why don't you let me buy you a drink when you get off work, say in the bar in the Warwick. He probably won't come, he wants to bang the broad, but he will wonder all fucking day what getting handed the markers is all about, and what I want to talk about. And if he don't show up at the Warwick by say one o'clock, I know where to find the fucker. Rosselli and I will go to the broad's apartment.*

"Let me out of the car, Jimmy," Mr. Cassandro said to his driver, "and then drive around the block until I come out."

"You don't want me to come with you?" Mr. Rosselli asked.

"I want you to drive around the block with Jimmy until I come out."

"You will never believe who I just got a picture of getting out of a Jaguar and walking toward Lanza's house," Officer Howard Hansen said softly as he returned to the bar where Sergeant Bill Sanders was watching a quiz program on the television.

"Who?"

"Paulo Cassandro."

"You sure?" Sergeant Sanders asked.

Hansen nodded.

"And, unless I'm mistaken, the guy driving the Jaguar was Jimmy Gnesci, 'Jimmy the Knees,' and—what the hell is his name?—*Gian-Carlo* Rosselli was in the back seat with Cassandro."

"You get his picture, *their pictures* too?"

Hansen nodded.

"This is getting interesting," Sanders said.

"I told you, I've been on the job with Wohl. He don't go off half-cocked."

The fucking plumbers had just told Vito Lanza that it would be at least three days until there was cold water to flush the toilets, and probably a day more until there was hot water and he could take a bath and shave, when he heard somebody call, "Yo, Vito! You in here?" upstairs at the front door.

He went up the stairs and there was Paulo Cassandro standing there, just inside the open door. He was smiling.

"What the hell have you got going here, Vito? You really need all these plumbers?"

"Well, hello. How are you?"

Paulo Cassandro was the last person Vito expected to see inside his house, and for a moment there was concern that Paulo was there about the markers he had signed at the Oaks and Pines.

He shook Cassandro's hand.

"You wouldn't believe what they're charging me," Vito said.

"I would believe. There's only two kinds of plumbers, good expensive plumbers and bad expensive plumbers. I've been through this."

"So what can I do for you, Mr. Cassandro?"

"You can call me 'Paulo' for one thing," Cassandro said. "I just happened to be in the neighborhood, I was down by Veteran's Stadium, and I had these, and I thought, what the hell, I'll see if Vito's home and give them to him."

He handed Vito the markers, four thousand dollars' worth of markers, that he had signed early that morning at Oaks and Pines.

"To tell you the truth, Paulo, until I can get to the bank, I can't cover these."

*I don't have anywhere near enough money in the bank to cover those markers. My fucking luck has been really bad!*

"Did I ask for money? I know you're good for them. Take care of them at your convenience. But I had them, and I figured, what the hell, why carry them around and maybe lose them. You know what I mean?"

"Absolutely."

"And we know where you live, right?"

"Yeah."

"So I'll see you around, Vito," Paulo said, and started to leave, and then, as if it was a thought that had suddenly occurred to him, turned back to Vito. "What time do you get off?"

"Eleven," Vito said.

*What the hell does he want to know that for?*

"That's what I thought," Paulo said. "Hey, Vito. We're all going to be at the bar at the Warwick a little after midnight. Why don't you come by, and we'll have a shooter or two?"

"Jees, that's nice, but when I get off work, I'm kind of beat. And I went up to the Poconos last night. I think I'm just going to tuck it in tonight. Let me have a raincheck."

"Absolutely. I understand. But if you change your mind, the Warwick Bar. On the house. We like to take care of our good customers."

Paulo punched Vito in a friendly manner on the arm, smiled warmly at him, and walked out of his house.

He stood on the curb for almost five minutes until his Jaguar came around the block and pulled to the curb.

The relationship between the Federal Bureau of Alcohol, Tobacco and Firearms and local law enforcement agencies has rarely been a glowing example of intergovernmental cooperation.

This is not a new development, but goes back to the earliest days of the Republic when Secretary of the Treasury Alexander Hamilton convinced the Congress to pass a tax on distilled spirits. Some of the very first federal revenue officers were tarred and feathered when they tried to collect the tax, more than once as local sheriffs and constables stood by looking in the opposite direction.

In July, 1794, five hundred armed men attacked the home of General John Neville, the regional tax collector for Pennsylvania, and burned it to the ground. Since local law enforcement officers seemed more than reluctant to arrest the arsonists, President George Washington was forced to mobilize the militia in Virginia, Maryland, New Jersey, and Pennsylvania to put the Whiskey Rebellion down.

During Prohibition, the New Jersey Pine Barrens served both as a convenient place to conceal illegally imported intoxicants from the federal government, prior to shipment to Philadelphia and New York, and as a place to manufacture distilled spirits far from prying eyes. And again, local law enforcement officers did not enforce the liquor laws with what the federal government considered appropriate enthusiasm. Part of this was probably because most cops and deputy sheriffs both liked a little nip themselves and thought Prohibition was insane, and part was because, it has been alleged, the makers of illegally distilled intoxicants were prone to make generous gifts, either in cash or in kind, to the law enforcement community as a token of their respect and admiration.

Even with the repeal of Prohibition the problem did not go away. High quality, locally distilled corn whiskey, or grain neutral spirits, it was learned, could be liberally mixed with fully taxed bourbon, blended whiskey, gin, and vodka and most people in Atlantic City bars and saloons could not tell the difference. Except the bartenders and tavern keepers, who could get a gallon or more of untaxed spirits for the price of a quart of the same with a federal tax stamp affixed to the neck of the bottle.

And the illegal distillers still had enough of a profit to be able to comfortably maintain their now traditional generosity toward the local law enforcement community.

While the local law enforcement community did not actively assist the moonshine makers in their illegal enterprise, neither did they drop their other law enforcement obligations to rush to the assistance of what had become the Bureau of Alcohol, Tobacco and Firearms in their relentless pursuit of illegal stills.

It boiled down to a definition of crime. If they learned that someone was smuggling firearms to Latin America, the locals would be as cooperative as could be desired. And since the illegal movement of cigarettes from North Carolina, where they were made and hardly taxed at all, to Atlantic City, where they were heavily taxed by both the state and city, cut into New Jersey's tax revenues, the locals were again as cooperative as could be expected in helping to stamp out this sort of crime.

And if they happened to walk into a still in the Pine Barrens, the operator, if he could be found, would of course be hauled before the bar of justice. It was simply that other aspects of law enforcement normally precluded a vigorous prosecution of illegal distilling.

Additionally, there was—there is—a certain resentment in the local law enforcement community toward neatly dressed young men who had joined ATF right out of college, at a starting salary that almost invariably greatly exceeded that of, for example, a deputy sheriff who had been on the job ten years.

Whatever else may be said about them, ATF agents are not stupid. They know that they need the support of the local law enforcement community more than it needs theirs. They are taught to be grateful for that support, and made aware that it would be very foolish indeed to make impolitic allegations, much less investigations.

When Special Agent C. V. Glynes, of the Atlantic City office of the Bureau of Alcohol, Tobacco and Firearms, making a routine call, just to keep in touch, walked into the Sheriff's Department in the basement of the county courthouse, he knew very well that if he was going to leave with any information he had not previously had, it would be volunteered by either the sheriff himself, or one of his deputies, and not the result of any investigative genius he might demonstrate.

He waved a friendly greeting at the sheriff, behind his glass-walled office, and then bought a Coca-Cola from the machine against the wall.

He studied the bulletin board, which was more devoted to lawn mowers, mixed collie and Labrador puppies, washing machines and other household products for sale, than to criminal matters until the sheriff, having decided he had made the fed wait long enough, waved him into his office.

"Good morning, Sheriff," Special Agent Glynes said.

"How are you, Glynes? I like your suit."

"There was a going-out-of-business sale, Machman's, on the

Boardwalk? Fifty percent off. I got two of them for a hundred and twenty bucks each."

The sheriff leaned forward and felt the material.

"That's the real stuff. None of that plastic shit."

"Yeah. And I got some shirts too, one hundred percent cotton Arrow. Fifty percent off."

"Anything special on your mind?"

Glynes shook his head, no.

"Just passing through. I thought I'd stop in and ask about Dan Springs. How is he?"

"He must have really hit his steering wheel. If he hadn't been wearing his seat belt, he'd probably have killed himself. He's got three cracked ribs. He said it doesn't hurt except when he breathes."

Glynes chuckled. "What happened?"

"He was out in the Barrens," the sheriff said, "and he run over something. Blew his right front tire, run off the road, and slammed into a tree."

"Jesus!"

The sheriff raised his voice and called, "Jerry!"

A uniformed deputy put his head in the office.

"Jerry, you know Mr. Glynes?"

The deputy shook his head, no.

"Revenoooooer," the sheriff said. "Don't let him catch you with any homemade beer."

"How do you do, Mr. Glynes? Jerry Resmann."

*"Chuck,"* Special Agent Glynes said, smiling and shaking Resmann's hand firmly. "Pleased to meet you."

"Jerry, is that piece of scrap metal still on Springs's desk?" the sheriff asked.

Deputy Resmann went to the door and looked into the outer office.

"Yeah, it's there."

"Why don't you go get it, and give our visiting Revenooooer a look?"

"Right."

Resmann went into the outer office and returned and handed the twisted piece of metal to Glynes.

"Can you believe that thing?" the sheriff asked. "They found it in the wheel well, up behind that plastic sheeting, when they hauled Dan's car in. No wonder he blew his tire."

*Jesus Christ! What the hell is this? That's one-eighth, maybe three-sixteenth-inch steel. And it's been in an explosion. One hell of an explosion, otherwise that link of chain wouldn't be stuck in it.*

"You have any idea what this is, Sheriff?"

"It's what blew Dan's tire," the sheriff said. "A piece of junk metal. Probably fell off a truck when some asshole was dumping garbage out in the Barrens, and then Dan drove over it."

"You know, it looks as if it's been in an explosion," Glynes said.

"Why do you say that?" Resmann asked.

"Look at this link of chain stuck in it. The only way that could happen is if it struck it with great velocity."

The sheriff took the piece of metal from Glynes.

"There's burned areas too," the sheriff said. "I read one time that in a hurricane, the wind gets blowing so hard, so fast, that it'll stick pieces of straw three inches deep into a telephone pole."

Glynes took the piece of steel back and lifted it to his nose, and then, carefully, touched the edge of the burned area with his fingertip, and then looked at his fingertip. There was a black smudge. When he touched his finger to it, it smeared.

"The explosion happened recently," he said, handing the steel to the sheriff. "You can smell it, and the burned area is still moist."

The sheriff sniffed. "I'll be damned. I wonder what it is?"

"I'd like to know. I'd like to run it by our laboratory. You think I could have this for a while?"

"Would we get it back?"

"Sure."

"I know Dan would want that for a souvenir."

"I can have it back here before he comes back to work."

"What do you think it is?"

"You tell me. Have there been any industrial explosions, anything like that around here?"

The sheriff considered that for a moment, and then shook his head, no.

"Take it along with you, Chuck, if you want. But I really want it back."

"I understand."

Special Agent Glynes was halfway to Atlantic City when he pulled to the side of the road.

*I don't need the goddamned laboratory to tell me that piece of metal has been involved in the detonation of high explosives. What I want to know is where it came from.*

*It could be nothing. But on the other hand, if somebody is blow-*

*ing things up around here with high explosives, I damned sure
want to know who and why.*

He made a U-turn, stopped at the first bar he encountered,
bought a get-well bottle of Seagram's 7-Crown for Deputy
Springs, and asked for the telephone book.

He found a listing for *Springs, Daniel J.*, which was both unusual and pleased him. Most law enforcement officers, including
Special Agent Glynes, did not like to have their telephone numbers
in the book. It was an invitation to every wife/mother/girlfriend
and male relative/acquaintance of those whom one had met, *professionally,* so to speak, to call up, usually at two A.M., the
sonofabitch who put Poor Harry in jail.

He carefully wrote down Springs's number and address, but he
did not telephone to inquire whether it would be convenient for
him to call. It was likely that either Dan Springs or his wife would,
politely, tell him that it would be inconvenient, and he was now determined to see him. If he showed up at the front door with a smile
and a bottle of whiskey, it was unlikely that he would be turned
away.

Glynes had been on the job nearly fifteen years. When he saw
advertisements in the newspapers of colleges offering credit for
practical experience, he often thought of applying. He had enough
practical experience to be awarded a Ph.D., summa cum laude,
in Practical Psychology.

He found Springs's house without difficulty. There was no car in
the carport, which was disappointing. He thought about that a moment, then decided the thing to do was leave the whiskey bottle,
with a calling card, *"Dan, Hope you're feeling better. Chuck."* That
just might put Springs in a charitable frame of mind when he came
back in the morning.

But he heard the sound of the television when he walked up to
the door, and pushed the doorbell. Chimes sounded inside, and a
few moments later a plump, comfortable-looking gray-haired
woman wearing an apron opened the door.

"Mrs. Springs, I'm Chuck Glynes. I work sometimes with Dan,
and I just heard what happened."

"Oh," she seemed uncomfortable.

*Why is she uncomfortable? Ah ha. Dear Old Dan isn't as inca-
pacitated as he would have the sheriff believe.*

"I'm not with the Sheriff's Department, Mrs. Springs. I work for
the federal government in Atlantic City. I brought something in
case Dan needed something stronger than an aspirin."

"Dan went to the store for a minute," Mrs. Springs said. "My arthritis's been acting up, and I didn't think I should be driving."

"Well, maybe I can offer some of this to you."

"Come in," she said, making up her mind. "He shouldn't be long."

Deputy Springs walked into his kitchen twenty minutes later.

*He's not carrying any packages. And his nose is glowing. If I were a suspicious man, I might suspect he was down at the VFW, treating his pain with a couple of shooters, not at the Acme Supermarket.*

"How are you, Mr. Glynes?"

"The question, Dan, is how are you? And when did you start calling me 'Mr. Glynes'? My name is Chuck."

"Cracked some ribs," Dan said. "But it only hurts when I breathe."

Glynes laughed appreciatively.

"Doris get you something to drink, Chuck?"

"Yes, she did, thank you very much," Glynes said.

"I think I might have one myself," Springs said.

"Well, then, let's open this," Glynes said, and pushed the paper sack with the Seagram's 7-Crown across the table toward him.

"I don't know what happened," Dan Springs said, ten minutes later, as he freshened up Chuck Glynes's drink. "I'm riding down the road one second, and the next second I'm off the road, straddling a tree."

"I know what happened," Glynes said.

"You do?" Springs asked, surprised.

"Let me go out to the car a minute and I'll get it," Glynes said.

Springs walked out to the car with him. Glynes handed him the explosive-torn chunk of metal.

"You ran over that," Glynes said. "It opened your tire like an ax."

"Jesus, I wonder where that came from?"

"Well, they found it in your wheel well, up behind that rubber sheet. But I'd like to know, professionally, where it came from."

"Excuse me?"

"That piece of steel has been in an explosion, Dan. Look at that link of chain stuck in it."

"I'll be damned!"

"I'd really like to see where you had the wreck."

"Out in the Pine Barrens."

"Could you find the spot again?"

"Sure," Springs said. "But not tonight. By the time we got there, it would be dark."

"Would you feel up to going out there tomorrow?"

"I'm on sick leave."

"Well, hell, the sheriff wouldn't have to know."

"Yeah," Springs said, after a moment's thought. "I could take you out there tomorrow, I guess."

"I'd appreciate it, Dan. We like to know who's blowing what up."

"Yeah, and so would I."

Mrs. Springs insisted that Chuck stay for supper. He said he would stay only if she let him buy them dinner.

At dinner, when he said he would have to head back to Atlantic City, Mrs. Springs said there was no reason at all for him to drive all that way just to have to come back in the morning, they had a spare bedroom just going to waste. He said he wouldn't want to put her out, and she said he shouldn't be silly.

# TWENTY-TWO

"I have just had one of my profound thoughts," Officer Howard Hansen said to Sergeant Bill Sanders as they watched Corporal Vito Lanza drive his Cadillac into the area reserved for police officers on duty at the airport.

"And you're going to tell me, right?"

"I'm not saying Lanza is a nuclear physicist, but he's not really a cretin, either. . . ."

"What's a cretin?"

"A high-level moron."

"Really?"

"Take my word for it, a cretin is a high-level moron. You want to hear this or not?"

"I wouldn't miss it for the world."

"So for the sake of argument, let's say Lanza is smart enough to know that people, especially other cops, are going to ask questions about that Cadillac of his. 'Where did he get the money?'"

"So?"

"He doesn't seem to give a damn, does he?"

"Howard, what are you talking about?"

"If I were dirty and had bought a Cadillac with dirty money, I wouldn't drive it to work."

"Maybe you're smarter than Lanza."

"And maybe he inherited the money and isn't dirty, and if somebody asks him, he can say 'I got it from my mother's estate,' or something."

"And what about those Guinea gangsters we saw at his house? What were they doing, selling Girl Scout cookies?"

"If I was dirty, I think I'd be smart enough to tell the Mob to stay away from my house. And the Mob, I think, is smart enough to figure that out themselves."

Sergeant Sanders grunted, but did not reply.

After a moment, Hansen said, "Well, what do you think?"

"I think I'm going to call Swede Olsen and tell him that after Lanza bought Girl Scout cookies from Paulo Cassandro, Jimmy the Knees, and Gian-Carlo Rosselli, he went to work, and does he want us to keep sitting on him or what."

He opened the door of the Pontiac and went looking for a telephone.

Officer Paul O'Mara stuck his head in Peter Wohl's office.

"Inspector," he said, "there's a Captain Olsen on 312. You want to talk to him?"

"Paul, for your general fund of useful knowledge," Wohl replied as he reached for his telephone, "unless the commissioner is in my office, or the building's on fire, I always want to talk to Captain Olsen."

He punched the button for 312.

"How are you, Swede? What's up?"

"Inspector, I put Bill Sanders and Howard Hansen on Lanza. You know them?"

"Hansen, I do. Good cop. Smart. What about them?"

"Sanders is a sergeant. Good man. He just called from the airport. Lanza just went to work. They picked him up at his house. Before he went to work, Paulo Cassandro paid him a visit at his house."

"Vincenzo Savarese's Paulo Cassandro?" Wohl asked, and then, before Olsen could reply, went on, "We're sure about that?"

"Sanders said he went in, was inside maybe five minutes, and while he was, Gian-Carlo Rosselli and Jimmy the Knees Gnesci rode around the block in Rosselli's Jaguar."

"I suppose it's too much to hope, Swede, that we have photographs?"

"We have undeveloped film," Olsen said. "But Hansen's pretty good with a camera."

"I know. How soon can we have prints?"

"As soon as I can get it to the lab in the Roundhouse. Our lab is temporarily out of business, which is really why I called. I'm out of people, Inspector, I was hoping maybe you could help me out."

"When are you *not* going to be out of people?"

"I had the feeling this was special, and that we should have good people on it. I'll be out of *good* people until about eight o'clock tonight . . ."

"This is special," Wohl interrupted without meaning to.

". . . when I have two good people coming in. What I need between now and then is some way to get Hansen's film to the Roundhouse lab. And if possible to relieve them."

"They don't like overtime?"

"I like to change people. I don't want Lanza to remember seeing them on Ritner Street."

"Yes, of course," Wohl said, feeling more than a little stupid. "Swede, let me get right back to you. Where are you? Give me the number."

He wrote the number down, put the telephone in its cradle, and then sat there for a moment, thinking.

*I need one, better two, good men from now until eight. Who's available? Jason Washington won't do. Every cop in the Department knows him. Tony Harris? Jerry O'Dowd?*

He pushed himself out of his chair and walked quickly out of his office, stopping at O'Mara's desk.

"Call the duty lieutenant and find out what kind of an unmarked car we have that doesn't look like an unmarked car," he ordered, and then walked out without further explanation.

He walked quickly down the corridor to the door of the Special Investigations Section and pushed it open. Detective Tony Harris was there, and so were Sergeant Jerry O'Dowd, Officer Tiny Lewis, and Detective Matthew M. Payne. Only Lewis was in uniform.

"Tony," Wohl began without preliminaries, "do you know a cop named Vito Lanza, now a corporal at the airport?"

"Yeah, I know him. He's sort of an asshole."

"Damn! Jerry?"

"No," O'Dowd said, after a moment to think it over. "I don't think so."

"What's going on around here?" Wohl asked.

"We're waiting for the phone to ring," Matt Payne said.

"I'm beginning to suspect the mad bomber is not going to call," Tony Harris said.

"Spare me the sarcasm, please," Wohl snapped.

"Sorry," Harris said, sounding more or less contrite.

"I need somebody to surveil Lanza from right now until about eight," Wohl said. "O'Dowd, I think you're elected."

"Yes, sir."

"You know a Sergeant Sanders? Officer Hansen?"

"Both."

"Okay. They're sitting on Lanza, who went on duty at three at the airport. I presume they're parked someplace where they can watch Lanza's car."

"Yes, sir."

"I've got O'Mara looking for an unmarked car for you."

"I've got my car here, Inspector, if that would help."

"No. You might have to follow this guy, and you'd need a radio."

"Let him take mine," Harris said.

*You have tried, Detective Harris, and succeeded in making amends, for letting your loose mouth express your dissatisfaction for being here, instead of in Homicide.*

"Good idea. Thank you, Tony," Wohl said. "How are you with a camera, O'Dowd?"

"I can work one."

"Take Larsen's camera from him," Wohl ordered. "Payne, you follow him down there. On the way, unless there's some around here, get some film. I'm sure it's 35mm. Sergeant O'Dowd will have the rolls of film Hansen has shot. Take them to the Roundhouse, have them developed and printed. Four copies, five by seven. Right then. If they give you any trouble, call me. Take a look at the pictures. See if you recognize anybody from your trip to the Poconos. If you do, call me. In fact, call me in any case. Then take three copies of the prints to Captain Olsen, in Internal Affairs. Bring the fourth set out here, and leave them on my desk."

"Yes, sir."

"Could I help, sir?" Officer Lewis asked.

"Looking for a little overtime, Tiny? Or are you bored waiting for the phone to ring?"

The moment the words were out of his mouth, Wohl regretted them, and wondered why he had snapped at Lewis.

"More the bored than the overtime, sir," Tiny Lewis said. There was a hurt tone in his voice.

"When do you knock off here?"

"Five, sir."

"When your replacement comes, change into civilian clothing, and then go see if you can make yourself useful to Sergeant O'Dowd. You don't know Corporal Lanza, do you?"

"No, sir."

"Tony, you sit on the phone. I'll have the duty lieutenant send somebody to help you. Or maybe O'Mara?"

"O'Mara would be fine," Harris said.

Wohl had another thought.

"Let me throw some names at you two," he said, nodding at O'Dowd and Lewis. "Do you know Paulo Cassandro, Gian-Carlo Rosselli, or Jimmy the Knees Gnesci?"

Tiny Lewis shook his head, no, and looked embarrassed.

"Cassandro, sure," O'Dowd said. "The other two, no."

"Five sets of prints, Matt," Wohl ordered. "The first three to Captain Olsen, then take a set to the airport and give them to Sergeant O'Dowd, and then bring the last set here. Got it?"

"Yes, sir."

"We have," Wohl explained, "photographs of these three going into Corporal Lanza's house. If he leaves the airport before you're relieved, follow him. See if he sees these guys again."

"And if he does?"

"Try to get a picture of them together. But not if there is any chance he'll see you. Pictures would be nice, but we already have some. Understand?"

"Yes, sir."

"Get going, this is important. You think you can find Sergeant Sanders?"

"It would be helpful to know where he is."

"Near where Lanza would park his car. If you can't find him, call me."

"Yes, sir."

For some reason, the words to "Sweet Lorraine" had been running through Marion Claude Wheatley's mind all afternoon, to the point of interfering with his concentration.

Something like that rarely happened. He often thought that if there was one personal characteristic responsible for his success, it was his ability to concentrate on the intellectual task before him.

This was true, he had reflected, not only at First Philadelphia Bank & Trust, but had also been true earlier on, at the University of Pennsylvania, and even in Officer Candidate School in the Army. When he put his mind to something, he was able to shut everything else out, from the noises and incredibly terrible music in his barracks, to the normal distractions, visual and audible, one encountered in an office environment.

He had been working on a projection of how increasing production costs in the anthracite fields, coupled with decreased demand (which would negatively affect prices to an unknown degree) would, in turn, affect return on capital investment (and thus stock prices) in a range of time frames. (One year, two years, five years, and ten years.)

It was the sort of thing he was not only very good at, but really enjoyed doing, because of the variable factors involved. Normally, working on something like this, nothing short of an earthquake or a nuclear attack could distract him.

But "Sweet Lorraine" kept coming into his mind. For that matter, into his voice. He several times caught himself humming the melody.

He had no particular feelings regarding the melody. He neither actively disliked it, nor regarded it as a classic popular musical work.

That left, of course, the possibility that the Lord was sending him a message. He considered that possibility several times, and could make no sense of it.

He thought he had it once; it might be the name of someone close to the Vice President, but that wasn't it. He called the Free Public Library and a research librarian told him the Vice President's wife's name was Sally. And she couldn't help him when he asked if she happened to know if there was someone on the Vice President's staff named Lorraine, maybe his secretary.

She had the secretary's name, Patricia, and she said, as far as she could tell, everyone else on the Vice President's staff was a male.

That left only one possibility, presuming that it was not simply an aberration, that the Lord was alerting him to something that would happen later, something that, when he saw it, would answer the mystery.

Once he had come to that analysis, he had been able to return to *A Projection of Anthracite Production Economic Considerations* without having his concentration disrupted. He made good progress, and was very nearly finished when the sounds of people getting ready to go home broke into his concentration again.

Marion was so close to being finished with the *One-Year Time Frame* that he considered staying and finishing it, but finally decided against that. He knew himself well enough to know that if he finished the *One-Year* he would be tempted to just keep going.

The priority, of course, was to get the things on the list not yet acquired. The list was just about complete. All he needed now was the chain and two more AWOL bags. He would get the chain today, and the remaining two AWOL bags tomorrow. It would not be wise to return to the Super Drugstore at all, and certainly not so soon.

First the chain and then the AWOL bags. Perhaps, when he went shopping for the chain, he would see another store that had AWOL bags on sale. Perhaps even bags that met the metal zipper and other criteria, but which at least would not have *Souvenir of Someplace* painted on them, and with a little bit of luck would be of a different design.

Marion waited, of course, until the office herd had thundered out and ridden the cattle cars down to the lobby before putting the *A Projection of Anthracite Production Economic Considerations* material back into its folders and then into his desk file.

When he came out onto Broad Street, he had an interesting thought. Instead of looking for a hardware store in the streets down toward the river, he would get on a bus and ride up North Broad Street.

He vaguely remembered seeing a decent-looking hardware store in a row of shops on the west side of North Broad Street, five or six blocks north of the North Philadelphia Station of the Pennsylvania Railroad.

He started to walk up South Broad Street toward City Hall. As he approached it, he decided he would let the Lord decide, by His timing of the traffic lights that controlled the counterclockwise movement of vehicular traffic around City Hall, whether He wanted him to go to North Broad Street by walking through the City Hall passageways, or if He preferred that Marion turn right at Market Street and walk the long way around, on the sidewalk past John Wannamakers, et cetera.

The Lord apparently wanted him to get to North Broad Street quickly, for just as he approached Market Street, the vehicular light turned to red, the pedestrian light turned to green, and without

breaking stride he was able to cross the street and enter the arch-
way of City Hall.

The same thing happened as he emerged from the north arch-
way. The vehicular light turned to red and the pedestrian to green
just as he reached the street, and he was again able to keep walking
without stopping at all.

And then as he reached the bus stop at the next corner, a bus was
just swallowing the last of the line of people who had been waiting
for it. Marion climbed aboard without having to break pace.

He thought for a moment that the Lord had wanted him to board
this particular bus, but then decided that wasn't true. There was
only one empty seat, and that was on the right side of the bus. If the
Lord had wanted him to get on this bus, He would have saved him
a seat on the left side, from which he could look for the hardware
store he remembered seeing somewhere past the North Philadelphia Station.

*Perhaps,* Marion thought, *by the time we get to the North Philadelphia Station, someone now sitting on the left side will have gotten off
the bus and I can move over.*

Sometime later, Marion wasn't sure how much later, because he
had been thinking that he had forgotten to factor into *A Projection
of Anthracite Production Economic Considerations* the cost of new
federal government mine safety regulations, he became aware that
the bus was not moving.

He looked out the window. They were stopped at Ridge Avenue.
The bus was now filled with mutterings. His fellow passengers
were growing angry that the bus wasn't moving. Marion raised
himself in his seat and tried to look out the windshield. There was
a long line of cars in front of the bus, but he could see nothing that
explained why they weren't moving.

Marion glanced out the side window again, and saw that they
were stopped in front of the hotel that belonged to that rather amusing, viewed in one light, and rather pathetic, viewed in another, re-
ligious sect founded by a Philadelphia black man who called
himself Father Divine.

Father Divine had convinced an amazing number of colored
people, and even some white people, that he had been anointed by
the Lord to bring them out of their misery, spiritual and temporal,
primarily by turning over all of their assets to him.

His wife, Marion recalled, had been a white woman, and she had
lived rather well as the mate of Father Divine. They were supposed

to own property and businesses all over Philadelphia. And New York too. And Washington, D.C.

He wondered if Mrs. Father Divine was still living well, now that Father Divine had been called to Heaven.

*I wonder what Father Divine said to Saint Peter?*

*There really had been a lot of money. The hotel, before they bought it, with cash, closed the bar, and renamed it, after Mrs. Divine, of course, the* Divine Lorraine *Hotel, had been a rather decent hotel.*

*The Divine* Lorraine *Hotel!*

The bus began to move.

Marion broke out in a sweat.

When the bus stopped in front of the old Reading Railroad Terminal at Lehigh Avenue, not far at all from the Pennsylvania Railroad's North Philadelphia Station, the four people sitting in the two seats to the left of Marion all got up at once and exited the bus.

Marion quickly moved across the aisle. The sweating had stopped, but it left him feeling clammy and uncomfortable.

*There is no question that the Lord wants me to do something in connection with the Divine Lorraine Hotel. But what?*

Three blocks past the North Philadelphia Station, Marion saw the hardware store he thought he remembered. And it was even larger, and thus more likely to carry what he needed to complete the list, than he had remembered.

He got off the bus at the next stop, crossed North Broad Street, and walked back toward the hardware store.

He passed a Super Discount Store, the windows of which were emblazoned with huge signs reading SALE!

And in one of the windows, under a SALE! sign with an arrow pointing downward there was a stack of AWOL bags. These were not only of better quality than the three he had bought on Market Street, but of different design. Their straps went completely around the bag. They had metal zippers, and they did not have *Souvenir of Asbury Park, N.J.,* and a fish leaping out of the surf gaudily painted on their sides.

Marion went into the Super Discount Store and bought two of the AWOL bags, one in a rather nice shade of dark blue, the other in sort of a rusty brown. He put the blue one inside the brown one, and thought that he would have plenty of space left over for the chain.

The clerk in the hardware store told Marion that they stocked a wide variety of chains, and if Marion would tell him what he wanted the chain for, six lengths each twenty-two inches long, they could make sure he was getting the right thing.

Marion was fairly certain that the man was more garrulous than suspicious, but he could not, of course, tell him what he really wanted the chain for. He had considered this sort of question coming up, of course, and was ready for him. He told the clerk that he had to lock six steel casement windows, and that he would also need six padlocks.

The clerk told him that not only did the store stock a wide array of padlocks, but that he thought it would be possible to furnish six locks all of which would operate with the same key.

Marion told him that would be unnecessary but nice.

The clerk was similarly garrulous when Marion informed him that he would need both duct and electrical tape. Marion was astonished at the wide selection available, and made his choice by selecting the most expensive tapes he was shown. That would, he believed, make the clerk happy.

Marion was not annoyed with the clerk. Quite to the contrary. In this day and age it was a pleasant surprise to find a clerk who seemed genuinely interested in pleasing the customer.

He paid for the tape and the chain, and put it all in the AWOL bag, shook the clerk's hand, thanked him for his courtesy, and went back out onto Broad Street.

That completed acquisition of the items on the list.

But now there was a new problem. The Divine Lorraine Hotel.

*Was that simply coincidence? Thinking of "Sweet Lorraine" to the point of distraction all day? Or is the Lord telling me something?*

Marion stood on the curb for a minute or two, considering that problem.

A taxicab, thinking he was seeking a ride, pulled to the curb.

Marion was on the verge of waving it away, when he suddenly had a thought, almost as if the Lord had put it there.

*There were half a dozen ways to get from where I stand to the house. Only one of them leads back past the Divine Lorraine Hotel. If the Lord has nothing in mind vis-à-vis the Divine Lorraine Hotel, the chances are five, or more, out of six that the taxi driver will elect not to pass in front of the Divine Lorraine Hotel. On the other hand, if the taxi driver elects to drive past the Divine Lorraine Hotel, the odds*

*that the Lord wishes me to do something involving the hotel would
certainly be on the order of six to one.*

Marion got in the taxicab and gave him his address.

The driver headed right down North Broad Street. When they
reached Ridge Avenue, the traffic light was red. Marion looked out
the window at the Divine Lorraine Hotel.

When the traffic light turned green, and the taxi driver put his
foot to the accelerator, the car stalled.

Marion broke out in another sweat.

He looked at the Divine Lorraine Hotel again. A very large colored lady with some kind of white napkin or something wrapped
around her head and neck smiled at him.

Marion smiled back.

A taxi pulled up in front of the hotel, and a man got out and carried suitcases toward the door.

*It is a hotel still, I forgot that. A hotel that caters, apparently, to
those who believe in Father Divine, whom they believe is either
God, or close to Him. It would follow, therefore, that a Christian of
that persuasion would stay at the Divine Lorraine Hotel.*

*Any Christian! That's what it is, of course. How could I have
been so stupid? The Lord wants me to go there. But why? It is not
mine to question the Lord, but it would help me to carry out His
will if I knew what He wanted of me.*

The answer came: *I have probably made an error somewhere,
and the Secret Service is looking for me. Or will be looking for me
at the house after I carry out the Lord's will and disintegrate the
Vice President.*

*No one would think of looking for Marion Claude Wheatley in
the Divine Lorraine Hotel.*

*Thank you, Lord! Forgive me for taking so long to understand
what it was You wanted of me.*

The taxi driver got the motor running again.

Marion leaned back against the cushions. He felt euphoric.

*I am in the Lord's hands. I walk through the valley of death, but
I feel no evil, for Thou art with me.*

Matt's Volkswagen started with difficulty, and he made the immediate decision to swap cars at his apartment as his first order of
business. The one thing he did not need was to have the Bug die on
him when he was running errands for Peter Wohl.

The Bug performed flawlessly on the way from the Schoolhouse
to the basement garage of his apartment and he wondered if swap-

ping cars was now such a good idea. Silver Porsche 911s attracted attention; battered Bugs did not.

He walked out of the basement garage, waving at the rent-a-cop on duty, went to the convenience store around the corner and bought five rolls of 36-exposure ASA 200 Kodak black and white film, and went back to the garage.

*The Porsche was conspicuous, but on the other hand, people didn't think of cops when they saw one. And the Bug might just have been teasing me when it ran so well on the way down here.*

He drove out to the airport, and found Sergeant Jerry O'Dowd with less trouble than he thought he would have. O'Dowd gave him a roll of film, then told him to wait a second, and removed the film from the camera and gave him that too.

"I haven't taken any pictures," O'Dowd said. "But I forgot to ask Hansen if he had."

"I'll be back as soon as I can."

O'Dowd handed him several bills.

"How about stopping at a Colonel Sanders and getting my supper? You better get something for Lewis too."

"Sergeant, you don't make enough money to feed Tiny," Matt said.

He drove to the Roundhouse and for once found a parking spot without trouble. And there was no trouble getting the film souped and printed right away, either.

"Inspector Wohl called," the civilian in charge behind the counter said. "It'll take me forty-five minutes, if you have something else to do."

There was no fried chicken place anywhere near the Roundhouse that Matt could think of. And Jerry O'Dowd had specified fried chicken. But on the other hand, Jerry was a gentleman of taste, and as such would certainly prefer Chinese to fried chicken, no matter how many spices and flavors it was coated with.

He walked to Chinatown, bought a Family Dinner For Four, and went back to the photo laboratory.

The prints were already coming off the large, polished stainless-steel drier. Matt looked at all of them. He recognized no one but Corporal Vito Lanza, and decided that he would not have recognized Lanza in uniform if he didn't know who he was looking at. Corporal Lanza did not look like the guy on the airplane home from Vegas or in the back rooms of the Oaks and Pines Lodge.

He called Peter Wohl from the photo lab, first at the School-house and then at his apartment.

Wohl only grunted when he told him he recognized no one but Lanza, but then said, "Remind Sergeant O'Dowd of what I said about making sure Lanza, or anyone else, doesn't see him taking pictures."

"Yes, sir."

"I'll wait here for you, Matt," Wohl said, and hung up.

Matt delivered three sets of photographs to Captain Olsen in Internal Affairs, and then drove back to the airport. Tiny Lewis had joined O'Dowd while he had been gone, and had had the foresight to bring supper—barbecued ribs—for the both of them with him.

Tiny was not at all reluctant to add a little Chinese to his supper menu, however, and accepted half of the food Matt had brought with him.

*It will not be wasted,* Matt decided, as he headed for Peter Wohl's apartment in Chestnut Hill. *Wohl likes Chinese. What I should have done was get some of Tiny's ribs.*

Peter Wohl, a crisp white shirt and shaving cream behind his ears indicating he was dressed to go out, was not only not at all interested in the Chinese, but didn't even invite Matt in, much less in for a beer. He just took the envelope of photographs from Matt, muttered "thank you," and started to close the door.

"Is there anything else you need me for, sir?"

Wohl looked at him.

"I think you have made quite enough of a contribution to the Department in the last twenty-four hours for one detective, Payne. Why don't you go home? And stay there?"

He closed the door.

Matt, as well as he knew Wohl, was not sure whether Wohl was pulling his chain, or whether Wohl was still sore about his having gone to the Oaks and Pines Lodge.

Matt got back in the Porsche and drove back to Center City. He was almost at Rittenhouse Square before he thought of Evelyn.

*She probably ran the answering machine out of tape,* he thought as he drove into the underground garage. *What the* hell *am I going to do about her?*

The red light on the answering machine was blinking, and when he played the tape, there had been thirteen callers who had elected not to leave their names, plus two calls from, of all people, Amelia Payne, M.D., who sounded, he thought, as if she had just sat on a nail, and demanded that he call her the moment he got in.

"Screw you, Sister Mine," Matt said aloud. "I am not in the mood for you."

He carefully arranged the Chinese goldfish buckets on his coffee table, got a cold beer from the refrigerator, and sat down to his supper.

The Chinese was cold.

He carried everything to the kitchen and warmed it in the microwave, carried it back to the coffee table, and sat down again.

The doorbell sounded.

*Evelyn, Jesus Christ! Well, if she's at the door, she knows I'm here. I might as well face the music.*

He went to the head of the stairs and pushed the button that activated the solenoid.

His visitor came through the door.

She looked up at him and called: "You miserable sonofabitch, how could you?"

It was not Evelyn, it was Amelia Payne, M.D.

"That would depend on which of my many mortal sins you have in mind. Come on in, Amy. Soup's on, and it's always a joy to see you."

"I have been angry with you before," Amy said as she reached the top stair. "And disgusted, but this really is despicable."

He was concerned.

*Amy is really angry, and that means she thinks I have done something really despicable. But I haven't.*

"Are you going to tell me what you're talking about?"

The telephone rang. Without thinking, he picked it up.

"Hello?"

"Hello, Matt," Evelyn said.

"I can't talk to you right now. Let me call you back."

"But you won't, will you?" Evelyn said, her voice loaded with hurt, and then she hung up.

"Jesus!" Matt said. He looked at Amy. "How about an egg roll?"

"What I'm talking about, Matt," Amy said, back in control of her temper, "is you going to bed with Penny."

*Jesus Christ! How did she hear about that? The answer to that, obviously, is that Penny told her. Patients tell their psychiatrists everything.*

"What in the world were you thinking?" Amy demanded.

*She has shifted into her Counselor of Mankind tone of voice.*

"I don't know," he said, his mouth running away with him. "What do you think about when you hop in bed with some guy?"

Amy slapped him. His vision blurred, his ears rang, and his eyes watered.

He looked at her for a moment as his eyes came back into focus.

"I should not have done that," Amy announced. But it was as if she was talking to herself.

"You're goddamned right you shouldn't have," he replied angrily. "You slap a cop, you're likely to get slapped right back."

"Is that what it was, Matt?" Amy asked. "Just Detective Payne hopping into bed with the nearest available female?"

"It happened, Amy," Matt said.

"Like hell 'it happened.' You didn't take her to dinner in the Poconos to look at the trees. Matt, she's a sick girl. And you know she is."

"You can believe this or not, but taking . . . but taking Penny to bed was the last thing I had in mind when we went up there."

"Why did you go up there, then?"

He met her eyes.

"I was working. I needed a girl to look legitimate."

*She is not going to believe that, and that's all I'm going to tell her.*

"Oddly enough, I believe you," Amy said, after a moment. "That doesn't make things any better, but I have the odd notion you're telling the truth."

"I am."

"She's in love with you," Amy said. "Or thinks she is, which is the same thing. The one thing she doesn't need right now is that kind of stress."

"She was behaving perfectly normal up there. I did not seduce the village idiot girl. Amy, she *wanted* to."

"And your monumental ego got in the way, right? It never occurred to you that she wanted the approval of the Rock of Gibraltar, complete to badge and gun, wanted it so desperately that she was willing to pay for it by going to bed with you?"

He did not reply.

"So what are you going to do about it?" Amy asked.

"How does suicide strike you? I could jump out the window."

"God *damn* you! Don't be flip!"

"What am I going to do about what?"

"You haven't been listening to me. How are you going to deal with this notion of hers that she's in love with you?"

"I don't know," Matt said.

"Obviously, you're not in love with her."

*Now that you bring it up, I really don't know how I feel about that.*

He had a sudden, painfully clear mental image of Penny naked in his arms. Of how good that felt.

"May I speak?" Matt asked.

"I'm waiting."

"I'm not going to hurt Penny. Period. I don't really think that . . . what happened . . . hurt her."

"And what are you going to do when she realizes that you don't love her?"

"I never told her I did."

"When she learns about the rest of your harem?" Amy asked, and pointed to the telephone. "Like the one who just called?"

Matt shrugged.

"I can only repeat that I will not hurt her," Matt said.

"You've already set the stage to do exactly that. She sees you as a life preserver, someone she can lean on. I don't know how she's going to react when she finds out, inevitably, that's not true. Certainly, you're not willing to assume emotional responsibility for her. And even if you were, I don't think you could handle it."

He didn't reply.

"Penny cannot be just one more notch on your gun, Matt."

"I never thought of her that way," Matt interrupted.

Amy ignored his response.

"You can't, when she becomes an inconvenience, tell Penny, the way you told that woman on the telephone just now, 'I can't talk to you right now. I'll call you right back.' She cannot take that kind of rejection, for that matter, any rejection right now. It would put her right back in The Lindens."

"Okay, you made your point."

"You're going to have to disabuse her of the notion that she's in love with you very gently."

"I told you, you made your point."

Amy glowered at him, but after a moment her face softened.

"Okay, Matt. I *have* made my point. And you're not really a sonofabitch. You're incredibly stupid and insensitive, of course, and you do most of your thinking with your penis. A typical male, I would say."

He looked at her and smiled.

"How about an egg roll?"

"You bastard!" Amy said, but she sat beside him on the couch and helped herself to an egg roll.

When she left, half an hour later, and he steeled himself to call Evelyn back, there was no answer.

He knew that if he stayed in the apartment he would get drunk, so he called Charley McFadden, and Charley's mother said he was out with his girlfriend.

He walked up Rittenhouse Square to the Rittenhouse Club, and stood at the bar and ordered a Scotch. There were some people there whom he knew vaguely, and who smiled at him. He moved down the bar and tried to join their conversation.

Before he finished his first drink, he realized that he was wholly disinterested in what they were talking about.

*I look like them. I act like them. I am a product of the same socio-economic background. But I am no longer like them. I'm a cop.*

*So where does that leave me with Penny?*

He motioned to the bartender, so that he could sign the chit, and then he went back to his apartment.

# TWENTY-THREE

Matt woke instantly at the first ring of the telephone, and was instantly wide awake, and aware that he was in his armchair in the living room. He glanced at the clock on the mantelpiece. It was quarter past eleven.

The telephone rang a second time. On the third ring, the answering machine would kick in.

*Evelyn, of course. Who else? And Jesus, I don't want to talk to her!*

He picked up the telephone a half second after the answering machine began to play his message.

He spoke over it. "I'm here. Hang on until the machine does its thing."

"Did I wake you up?" Sergeant Jerry O'Dowd asked.

"Yeah, but it's all right. What's up?"

"I thought if you didn't have anything better to do, you might want to put in some unpaid overtime."

*No, as a matter of fact, I would* not *want to put in some overtime, paid or otherwise. But he wouldn't ask if it wasn't important.*

"Sure. What's up?"

"Not to be repeated, okay?"

"Sure."

"I was not impressed with the two guys Olsen sent to relieve us at the airport. I know one of them, and he couldn't be trusted to follow an elephant down Broad Street."

"You want me to go out there? Lanza knows me."

"I thought about that. And decided it was worth the risk. But I wouldn't drive the Porsche."

*Wohl doesn't know about this. If he did, he would tell me to stay at least five miles away from the airport.*

As if he had read Matt's mind, O'Dowd said, "If there is any static, from Wohl especially, I'll take the heat. With a little bit of luck, no one will ever know about this but you and me. I'll be proven wrong about the guy I know."

"You'll have to explain that."

"If I'm wrong, and I hope I will be, the guys on Lanza will be able to follow him. If they can follow him, wherever he's going, fine, we'll hang it up. But if they lose him, which wouldn't be surprising, at midnight in that area, I want to be on him. Then I'll get on the radio and tell the other guys where he is."

"You want me to go with you?"

"No. I want both of us to follow him. That would have three people following him. I don't think all three of us would lose him. But if they did, and I did, and you didn't . . ."

"Okay. Where do I meet you?"

"There's an all-night diner on South Broad right across from the stadium. You know it?"

"Uh-huh."

"Twenty minutes?"

"I'll be there."

"Thanks, Matt. I've got one of those feelings about tonight."

"Twenty minutes," Matt repeated. "You still have Tony Harris's car?"

"Yeah," O'Dowd said, and hung up.

At ten minutes after eleven, Corporal Vito Lanza came out of the Airport Unit, went to the parking lot, unlocked his Cadillac, and entered the sparse stream of traffic leaving the airport in the direction of Philadelphia.

So did a four-year-old Pontiac, with two men in it; a new Ford sedan with one man in it; and a twelve-year-old Volkswagen driven by Detective M. M. Payne, who brought up the tail of the line.

Corporal Lanza took Penrose Avenue, sometimes known as Bridge Avenue, which carried him across the Schuylkill River to the stop light at the intersection of Pattison Avenue. Until this point, he had been driving in the left lane, and so had the Pontiac and the Ford. At the last moment, Corporal Lanza jerked the Cadillac into the right lane, and as the light turned red, he turned right onto Pattison Avenue.

The line of traffic closed up, and left the Pontiac and the Ford with no choice but to wait for the light to turn green again, with the hope that Corporal Lanza intended to get on South Broad Street, and that they could intercept him by following Penrose as it turns into Moyamensing Avenue, which angles to the right, and intersects South Broad Street at Oregon Avenue just north of Marconi Plaza.

Detective Payne, in the twelve-year-old Volkswagen, had not been able to get in line behind the Pontiac and the Ford in the left lane, and consequently was already in the right lane when Corporal Lanza abruptly moved into it.

He saw that the Pontiac and the Ford were trapped in the left lane, and thought, as the drivers of the Pontiac and the Ford did, that they could probably catch up with Lanza at South Broad and Oregon. But in the meantime, there was only one possible course of action for him to take, and he took it.

He drove the Bug onto the sidewalk, down the sidewalk to Pattison Avenue, and then down Pattison past the U.S. Naval Hospital and Franklin Delano Roosevelt Park to South Broad Street.

As he approached South Broad, as he saw Lanza's Cadillac turn left onto South Broad Street, the traffic light turned orange and then red. Matt ran it, which caused the horns of several automobiles to sound angrily. But he did not lose Lanza, even though Lanza was driving like hell.

*Policemen tend to do that,* Matt thought wryly, remembering his encounter with the State Trooper on the way to the Oaks and Pines Lodge, *secure in the knowledge they are unlikely to get a ticket from a brother officer.*

The traffic lights at first Oregon Avenue and then Snyder Avenue were green, permitting the Lanza Cadillac and the Payne Volkswagen to sail through without stopping. They were stopped at Passyunk Avenue and South Broad Street, however, which gave

Detective Payne the opportunity to search in vain in his rearview mirror for either a Ford or a Pontiac.

Corporal Lanza turned left at the intersection of South Broad and Spruce Streets, and then wove his way around to the Penn-Services Parking garage, which he entered.

Detective Payne was familiar with the Penn-Services Parking garage, which was around the corner from the Bellvue-Stratford Hotel and not far from his apartment and the Union League Club. It was in the Penn-Services Parking garage that Mr. Anthony "Tony the Zee" DeZego had met his untimely end at the hand of assassin or assassins unknown. Where Matt found Miss Penelope Detweiler lying in a pool of her own blood.

Matt drove around the block until he saw Corporal Lanza come out of the building. Lanza did not look at the Volkswagen as it passed him.

Matt parked the Volkswagen illegally in an alley and ran down the alley and saw Lanza crossing a street. He followed him as discreetly as he could, very much afraid that Lanza would sense his presence and turn around.

But he didn't. He walked purposefully down a street and entered an apartment building. Matt looked around for a pay telephone but couldn't see one.

He backtracked to the next block and found a tavern. He went inside, went to the phone booth, and searched his pockets futilely for coins. The bartender was visibly reluctant to make change for someone who didn't even buy a lousy beer, but finally came through.

Matt called Police Radio and asked the dispatcher to pass to William Five (Harris's radio call sign) his location.

Sergeant Jerry O'Dowd, in Tony Harris's Ford, pulled up in front of the tavern less than ten minutes later. Before he was completely out of the car, the Pontiac pulled up behind him, and two men Matt had never seen before got out of it.

"Lanza's in an apartment around the corner," Matt said to O'Dowd.

"Good man," O'Dowd said.

"Until you called me on the radio, O'Dowd, I didn't know you were in on this," one of the two men from the Pontiac said. He pointed at Matt. "Or him. He works for you?"

"Excuse me," O'Dowd said politely. "Sergeant Framm, Detective Pillare, this is Detective Payne."

Both men shook Matt's hand.

"It's a good thing we were, wouldn't you say, Framm?" O'Dowd asked. "You lost Lanza before you got to the Naval Hospital."

There was no doubt in Matt's mind that Sergeant Framm was the man O'Dowd would not trust to follow an elephant down Broad Street.

"I got caught in traffic . . ." Framm began.

"Nobody, Olsen or Wohl, has to know about this," O'Dowd interrupted. "Payne did not lose Lanza. Everything is fine."

"Yeah, well . . . Hell, all's well that ends well, right?"

"Show us the apartment, Matt," O'Dowd said, "and then you can get some sleep."

When Matt got back to the apartment, the red light on the answering machine was flashing.

"I knew you wouldn't call me back," Evelyn's recorded voice said. "What have I done wrong, Matt?"

Mssrs. Paulo Cassandro, Joseph Fierello, Francesco Guttermo, Ricco Baltazari, and Gian-Carlo Rosselli were sitting at a table at the end of the bar off the lobby of the Hotel Warwick.

Mr. Rosselli took an appreciative sip of his Ambassador 24 Scotch, set the glass delicately down on the marble tabletop, and consulted his Rolex Oyster wristwatch.

"It's almost one," he announced, and then inquired, "How long does it take to drive from the airport?"

"At this time of night," Frankie the Gut replied, "twenty minutes, thirty tops."

"You're saying you don't think he's coming here?" Mr. Cassandro asked.

"Do you see him?" Mr. Rosselli asked. He turned to Mr. Fierello. "Why don't you call your 'niece' and see if he's there?"

"I don't have the number."

"I got it," Mr. Baltazari said, and took a gold Parker ballpoint pen from his pocket, wrote a number inside a Hotel Warwick matchbook, and handed it to Mr. Fierello.

"That's right," Mr. Rosselli said, "I forgot. You know Joe's niece, don't you, Ricco?"

Mr. Fierello and Mr. Cassandro laughed, but it was evident that Mr. Baltazari did not consider the remark amusing.

Mr. Fierello got up from the table and went to one of the pay telephones in the lobby. He was back at the table in less than two minutes.

"He's there."

Mr. Rosselli nodded. He sat thoughtfully for a moment and then nodded again. He stood up.

"Just in case, Ricco, I think you'd better give me the key to the apartment."

"You don't want me to go?"

"Paulo and I can handle it," Mr. Rosselli said. "And I wouldn't want that your jealousy should get in the way."

Mr. Cassandro and Mr. Guttermo laughed.

"Shit!" Mr. Baltazari said.

He removed a key from a ring and handed it to Mr. Rosselli.

"Take care of the bill, will you, Frankie?" Mr. Rosselli asked.

"My pleasure," Mr. Guttermo said.

Mr. Rosselli and Mr. Cassandro left the bar by the door leading directly to the street. They turned south.

"What do you want to do about the car, Carlo?" Mr. Cassandro asked.

"Leave it in the garage," Mr. Rosselli said, his tone suggesting the answer should have been evident. "Jesus, Paulo, you leave a car like a Jaguar on the street, you come back, it'll either be gone or there'll be nothing left but the windshield."

"Yeah," Mr. Cassandro agreed, his tone suggesting that he regretted raising the question.

They walked to the apartment building in which Mrs. Antoinette Marie Wolinski Schermer maintained her residence. There was a four-year-old Pontiac parked halfway down the block on the other side of the street, but neither gentleman paid it more than cursory attention.

The interior lobby door was locked. Mr. Cassandro took a small, silver pocketknife, which was engraved with his initials, from his pocket, opened it, and slipped the blade into the lock. He then pushed open the door and held it for Mr. Rosselli to pass inside.

They took the elevator to the fifth floor, and walked down the corridor.

"Here it is," Mr. Cassandro said, stopping before the door to Apartment 5-F.

"Ring the bell," Mr. Rosselli ordered.

Sixty seconds later, Mrs. Antoinette Marie Wolinski Schermer, wearing a bathrobe, opened the door.

"Hi, ya, Tony," Mr. Rosselli said. "Sorry to disturb you. But we have to talk to Vito. Is he here?"

Mrs. Schermer looked distinctly uncomfortable. She stepped back from the door, and waited for them to come into the apartment, then closed the door after them.

"Yo, Vito! It's Gian-Carlo Rosselli. You there?"

"He's in the bedroom," Tony Schermer said. "Give him a minute."

"Take your time, Vito," Mr. Rosselli called cheerfully. "Put your pants on."

Mr. Cassandro chuckled.

"Can I offer you something?" Tony asked.

"You got a little Scotch and water, I wouldn't say no. Paulo?"

"Yeah, me too."

Tony went into the kitchen.

Corporal Lanza came out of the bedroom, which opened onto the living room, barefoot, wearing a T-shirt and his uniform trousers.

"Hey," he greeted his callers somewhat uncomfortably. "What's up?"

"Well, when you didn't show up at the Warwick, we figured, what the hell, we'll go see him. I hope we didn't interrupt anything?"

"Nah. The reason I didn't come over there—I wanted to—was I didn't have any decent clothes to change into at the airport, and I can't be seen drinking in uniform. They'd have my ass."

"I understand," Mr. Rosselli said. "Anyway, a cop would make the customers nervous."

"Yeah."

Tony came into the room carrying two glasses.

"Can I fix you one, honey?" Tony asked.

"Why not?" Vito replied.

There were several minutes of somewhat awkward silence while Tony went into the kitchen and made Vito a drink.

"Honey, there's no reason for you to lose your beauty sleep," Mr. Rosselli said. "We're just going to sit around and have a couple of shooters. Why don't you go to bed? When we need another, Vito'll make it. Right, Vito?"

"Right," Vito said.

"Okay, then," Tony said. "If you're sure you don't mind, Vito."

"Go to bed," Vito said.

When she had closed the door behind her, Mr. Rosselli said, "I like her. She's a nice girl, Vito."

"Yeah, Tony's all right," Vito agreed.

"Vito, I'm going to tell you something, and I hope you'll believe me," Mr. Rosselli said.

"Why shouldn't I believe you?"

"You should. When I asked you to come by the Warwick for a couple of shooters, a couple of laughs, that was all I had in mind. You believe me?"

"Absolutely. And I wanted to come, and if I had the clothes, I would have. Next time."

"Right. Next time," Mr. Rosselli said. "But between the time I seen you and the plumbers . . . what's all that going to cost you, by the way?"

"A fucking bundle is what it's going to cost me. Those bastards know they've got you by the short hair."

"Yeah, I figured. Well, what the hell are you going to do? You can bitch all you want, but in the end, you end up paying, right?"

"Right."

"Like I was saying, Vito, between the time I was at your house and tonight, something has come up. We got a little problem that maybe you can help us with."

"What kind of a problem?"

"You ever hear of the guy that broke the bank at Monte Carlo?" He waited until Vito nodded, and then went on: "We had a guy between nine o'clock and nine-fifteen tonight, that goddamned near broke the bank at Oaks and Pines."

"No shit?"

"Sonofabitch was drunk, which probably had a lot to do with it, a sober guy wouldn't have bet the way he did."

"Like how?"

"He was playing roulette. He bet a hundred, split between Zero and Double Zero. He hit. That gave him eighteen hundred. He let that ride. He hit again . . ."

"Jesus!"

"That gave him, what? Thirty thousand, thirty-two thousand, something like that."

Vito thought: *Jesus Christ, that's the kind of luck I need!*

He said, "I'll be goddamned!"

"Yeah," Mr. Rosselli agreed. "At that point, right, a good gambler, a good *sober* gambler, would know it was time to quit, right?"

"You said it!"

"This guy let it ride," Mr. Rosselli said, awe in his voice.

"Don't tell me he hit again?"

"Okay, I won't tell you. With the kind of luck you've been having, it would be painful for you."

"He hit?" Vito asked incredulously.

"You understand how this works, Vito? Let me tell you how it works: A small place, like Oaks and Pines, it's not the Flamingo in Las Vegas, we have to have table limits."

"Sure," Vito said understandingly.

"On roulette, it's a thousand, unless the pit boss okays it, and then it's twenty-five hundred. Except . . ."

"Except what?"

"You can let your bet ride if you win," Mr. Rosselli explained. "You're a gambler, you understand odds. The chances of anybody hitting the same number twice in a row are enormous. And hitting it three times in a row? Forget it."

"Right," Vito said.

"The house understands the odds. And it would be bad business to tell the players when they're on a roll, that they can't bet no more, you understand?"

"I understand. Sure."

"By now, the pit boss is watching the action. They do that. That's what they're paid for, to make judgments, and to keep the games honest . . . you would be surprised, even being a cop, how many crooks try to hustle someplace like Oaks and Pines . . ."

"I wouldn't be surprised," Vito said solemnly.

"So the pit boss is watching when this guy hits three times in a row. And he knows he's not a crook. He's a rich guy, coal mines or something, from up around Hazleton. But when this guy says 'let it ride' . . . and he's got thirty-two thousand, thirty-three, something like that, the pit boss knows he can't make that kind of a decision, so he suspends play and calls Mr. Clark. You know Mr. Clark?"

Vito shook his head, no.

"Mr. Clark is the general manager of Oaks and Pines. Very fine guy. So the pit boss calls Mr. Clark, and Mr. Clark sees what's going on, and he makes his call. First of all, he knows that the odds against this guy making it four times in a row are like . . . like what? Like Paulo here getting elected pope. And this guy is a good customer, who'll be pissed if they tell him he can't make the bet. So he says, 'Okay.' Guess what?

"You won't believe it. Double Zero. It pays sixteen times the thirty-two, thirty-three big ones this guy has riding."

"Jesus!" Vito said, exhaling audibly.

"Can you believe this?" Mr. Cassandro asked rhetorically.

"So that's eighteen times thirty-three, which comes to what?"

"Five hundred big ones," Vito offered, making a rough mental calculation.

"Closer to six," Mr. Rosselli said.

*One of these days,* Vito thought, *I'm going to get on a roll like that.*

"So, as I understand it, this is what happened next," Mr. Rosselli went on. "Mr. Clark has just decided he cannot let this guy let six hundred big ones ride. Maybe the fucking wheel is broken. Maybe this is one of those things that happens. But Oaks and Pines can't cover a bet like that, and even if it means pissing this guy off, Mr. Clark is going to give him the money he's won . . . you understand, Vito, we have to do that. We run an absolutely honest casino operation. Mr. Clark has just decided to tell this guy he's sorry, that's all the casino can handle . . ."

"I understand."

"When the guy starts pulling all the chips toward him, Mr. Clark figures the problem has solved itself, so he don't say nothing. The biggest problem he figures he has is how to tell this guy that he don't have six hundred big ones in cash in the house, and he's going to have to wait until tomorrow . . . you understand how that works, don't you?"

"I'm not sure what you mean," Vito confessed.

"I'm surprised, you being a cop," Mr. Rosselli said. "But let me tell you. If there is a raid, by the local cops, the state cops, or the feds, and the feds are the ones that cause the trouble, they're always after gamblers when they should be out looking for terrorists . . . If there's a raid, they confiscate the equipment and whatever money they find. So naturally, you don't keep any more money around than you think you're going to need."

"Yeah," Vito said thoughtfully.

"I don't mind telling you how this works, because you're a good guy and we trust you. What we do up there is keep maybe fifty big ones in the cashier's cage. If somebody has a run of luck, and there's a big dent in the fifty, which sometimes happens, then we have more money someplace a couple of miles away. We send somebody for it. You understand?"

"Yeah, sure."

"In the other place, there's a lot of money. Two hundred big ones, at least. But not enough to pay off this character who's won six hundred big ones. You understand?"

"So what do you do?" Vito asked, genuinely curious.

"You know what the interest is on one hundred big ones a day?"

"What?"

"I asked if you ever thought how much the interest on a hundred thousand dollars is by the day?"

"No," Vito said, now sounding a little confused.

"A lot of money," Mr. Rosselli said seriously. "And on a million, it's ten times that a lot of money."

"Right."

"So keeping two hundred thousand around in a safe, without getting no interest, is one thing, it's the cost of doing business. But a million dollars is something else. You can't afford to keep a million dollars sitting around in a safe someplace not earning no interest, just because maybe someday you're going to need it. Right?"

"Right," Vito replied.

"My glass's got a hole in it or something," Mr. Rosselli said. "You suppose I could have another one of these, Vito?"

"Absolutely. Excuse me, I should have seen it was empty."

"Get Paulo one too, if you don't mind. He looks dry."

Vito took the glasses and went into the kitchen and made fresh drinks.

He wondered for a moment what Gian-Carlo Rosselli wanted from him, wondered if despite what he had said at the house about not having to worry about making the markers good, he was here to tell him that had changed and he wanted the money, but that was quickly supplanted by the excitement of thinking about this guy at Oaks and Pines who had hit four times in a row.

*Jesus Christ, winning six hundred big ones in four, five minutes! If I had that kind of luck, I could get my own place somewhere, maybe in Bucks County. And have enough left over to invest, so there would be a check every month, and I wouldn't have to raise a finger.*

He carried the drinks back into Tony's living room. Gian-Carlo Rosselli had moved to the couch, and now had his feet up on the cocktail table. Vito, after a moment's hesitation, sat down beside him.

"I was telling you about this guy who hit his number four times in a row," Mr. Rosselli said.

"Yeah. I sure could use a little of that kind of luck."

"Yeah, you could," Mr. Rosselli said significantly. "Luck's been running against you, hasn't it? How much are you down? You mind my asking?"

"No. I don't mind. I'm down about twelve big ones."

"What the hell, it happens, but twelve thousand is a lot of money, isn't it? And what are your markers?"

"I think it's four thousand," Vito said, hoping that it looked as if it was unimportant to him, and that he had to think a moment before he could come up with the figure.

"Yeah, right. Four thousand," Mr. Rosselli said. "Pity it's not a hell of a lot more. We could call them, and pay off the million two we owe the guy at the Oaks and Pines."

"Million two?" Vito asked. "I thought you said he won six hundred big ones."

Mr. Rosselli looked as if he were surprised for a moment, and then said, "No. It's a million two."

"You said the general manager cut him off," Vito said.

"Mr. Clark. What I said, I guess I stopped before I was finished, was that Mr. Clark *was* going to cut him off, but when he started collecting his chips, he figured he didn't have to. And then the guy changed his mind . . ."

"He bet six hundred big ones?"

"No. Just the bet. Just the thirty-two thousand whatever it was. He took the nearly six hundred thousand off the table, and then said, 'One more time, just to see what happens' and bet the thirty-two thousand."

"Don't tell me he won?"

"He won. Which meant another nearly six hundred thousand we owed him. Altogether, it comes to a million two."

"And then the manager shut him off?"

"Then the guy said he was going to quit when he was ahead."

"And walked out with a million two?"

"No. He's a good customer. He knows how it works, and he sure didn't want to take a check. You pass a check for that kind of money through a bank, and the IRS is all over you."

"Yeah," Vito said. "So what did Mr. Clark do?"

"He took the croupier out in the woods and shot him in the ear," Mr. Rosselli said, smiling broadly.

Mr. Cassandro laughed appreciatively.

"Kidding, of course," Mr. Rosselli went on. "No, what Mr. Clark did was make a couple of phone calls to get the money."

"I thought you said there was only a couple of hundred big ones in the other place," Vito asked.

"There was," Mr. Rosselli replied, and then asked, "Vito, what do you know about offshore banks?"

"Not a hell of a lot," Vito confessed.

"The thing they got going for them is their banking laws," Mr.

Rosselli explained. "They don't have to tell the fucking IRS anything. How about that?"

"I heard something about that," Vito said. "Fuck the IRS."

"You said it. So what happens is that if you have to have, say, a couple of million dollars where you can get your hands on it right away, instead of a safe, where it don't earn no interest, you put it in an offshore bank, where it does. Understand?"

"Yeah," Vito said appreciatively.

"So Mr. Clark makes the telephone calls, and says he needs a million two right away to pay a winner, and it's set up. It's really no big deal, it happens all the time, not a million two, but five, six hundred big ones. Once a month, sometimes once a week. It goes the other way too, of course. Some high roller drops a bundle, and we put money *in* the offshore banks."

"Yeah, sure," Vito replied.

"But this time, we run into a little trouble," Mr. Rosselli said.

"No million two in the bank?" Vito asked with a smile.

"That's not the problem. The problem is moving the money. A million two is twelve thousand hundred-dollar bills. That's a *lot* of green paper. You can't get that much money in an envelope, and drop it in a mailbox."

Vito tried to form a mental image of twelve thousand one-hundred-dollar bills. He couldn't remember whether there were fifty or one hundred bills in one of those packages of money with the paper band around them. But either way, it was a hell of a lot of paper stacks of one-hundred-dollar bills.

"So what we have is people who carry the money for us," Mr. Rosselli said. "I guess, you're a cop, you know all about this?"

"No," Vito said honestly. "I figured it had to be something like that, but this is the first time I really heard how it works."

"It's a problem, finding the right people for that job," Mr. Rosselli said. "First of all, you don't hand a million dollars to just anybody. And then, with IRS and Customs watching—they're not stupid, they know how this is done—you can't use the same guy all the time, you understand?"

"I can see how that would work," Vito said.

"Anyway, the way it usually works, we take the money out of the bank, offshore, and give it to one of our guys, and he goes to Puerto Rico, and gets on the plane to Philly, and somebody meets him and takes the bag."

"Yeah," Vito said.

"The problem we have is that we think that IRS is watching the only guy we have available," Mr. Rosselli said.

"Oh," Vito said.

"So the way those IRS bastards work it is they make an anonymous telephone call, anonymous my ass, to either Customs or the Bureau of Narcotics and Dangerous Drugs, and tell them somebody, they give a description of our guy, is smuggling drugs. So when he's picking up his bag at the carousel, they search his bag. The Narcotics guys don't have to have the same, what do you call it, probable cause, that other cops do. You know what I mean."

"Probable cause," Vito said. "You need it to get a search warrant."

"Well, they don't need that. They can just search your bags, 'looking for drugs.' They don't find no drugs, of course, but they do find all that money."

"And then what happens? You lose the money?"

"No. Nothing like that. It's just a big pain in the ass, is all. They take it, of course. And then you have to go to court and swear you won it gambling in Barbados or someplace. And you have to pay a fine for not declaring you have more than ten thousand in cash on you, and then you have to pay income tax on the money. Gambling income is income, as I guess you know."

"Yeah, right. The bastards."

"But there's no big deal, like if they caught somebody smuggling drugs or something illegal. The worst that can happen is that they keep the money as long as they can, and you have to pay the fine."

Mr. Rosselli took a sip of his drink.

"Vito, you got anything against making a quick ten big ones?" Mr. Rosselli asked.

Vito looked at him, but did not reply.

"The four you owe us on the markers, and six in cash. It'd pay for your plumbing problem."

"I don't understand," Vito said softly, after a moment.

"Now, we don't know for a fact that this is going to happen," Mr. Rosselli said. "But let's just say that the IRS does know our guy who will have the million two in his suitcase. And let's just say they do make their anonymous fucking telephone call to Customs or the Narcotics cops, giving them his description and flight number. Now, we don't *know* that's going to happen, but we're businessmen, and we have to plan for things like that."

"Yeah," Vito said softly.

"So what would happen? They would wait for him at the baggage carousel and search his bags, right?"

"Right. I've seen them do that. Sometimes they call it a random search."

"Right."

"So they search his bags and find the money, and we have to go through the bullshit of paying the fine and the income tax on a million two. And also have to get another million two out of the bank to pay the guy in the Poconos. Right?"

"Yeah, I understand."

"So, I figured we could help each other. We don't want to take the chance of having to go through the bullshit that *might* happen. Including paying the IRS tax on a million two of gambling earnings. And you need money for your fucking plumbing, and to make good the four big ones you owe us."

"What do you want me to do?"

"Just make sure when our guy's airplane lands at Philadelphia, one of his bags don't make it to the carousel. There will be nothing in his other bag but underwear, *if,* and I keep saying, *if* they search it."

Mr. Rosselli paused.

"Look, Vito, we know you're a cop and an honest cop. We wouldn't ask you to do nothing *really* against the law, something that would get you in trouble with the Department. But you got a problem, we got a problem, and I thought maybe we could help each other out. If you think this is something you wouldn't want to do, just say so, and that'll be it. No hard feelings."

Vito Lanza looked first at Mr. Rosselli and then at his hands, and then back at Mr. Rosselli.

"How would I know which bag?" he asked, finally.

"Jesus, Carlo," Mr. Cassandro said to Mr. Rosselli as they left the apartment building. "I got to hand it to you. You played him like a fucking violin!"

"That did go pretty well, didn't it?" Mr. Rosselli replied. "And he wants in. That's a lot better than having to show him the photographs and the Xeroxes and all that shit."

"Yeah," Mr. Cassandro agreed.

"It's always better," Mr. Rosselli observed philosophically, "to talk people into doing something. If it's their idea, they don't change their minds."

Neither Mr. Rosselli nor Mr. Cassandro noticed that the four-year-old Pontiac was still parked halfway down the block on the other side of the street.

# TWENTY-FOUR

Special Agent C. V. Glynes woke at seven A.M., which, considering how far they had lowered the level in the bottle of Seagram's 7-Crown before they went to bed, was surprising.

He went down the corridor to the bathroom and made as much noise as possible voiding his bladder, flushing twice, and dropping the toilet seat back into the horizontal position as loudly as he could manage.

He heard the creak of bed springs and other sounds of activity in the Springs's bedroom, and went back to his room to finish dressing and to wait for the Springs's announcement that breakfast was ready.

Logic told him that he was not likely to find anything at all, much less anything of interest to the Bureau of Alcohol, Tobacco and Firearms when he got Deputy Dan Springs out into the Pine Barrens. And that meant that this whole business would have been a waste of time, and moreover would cause some minor difficulty with H. Howard Samm, Jr., the special agent in charge of the Atlantic City office of the Bureau of Alcohol, Tobacco and Firearms.

"Sam Junior," as he was known by his not-too-admiring staff, liked to have what he called "his team" present each morning for an eight-thirty conference, aka "the pep talk," and Glynes knew he wasn't going to make that.

On the other hand, finding a chunk of three-eighth-inch steel with a link of chain imbedded in it by the force of high explosives was not an everyday occurrence, and Glynes had a hunch he was onto something. Sometimes his hunches worked, and sometimes they didn't—more often than not they didn't—but they had over the years worked often enough so that he knew that he shouldn't ignore them.

Sam Junior's pontifical pronouncements vis-à-vis scientific crime detection to the contrary, Glynes believed what really did the bad guys in was almost always sweat, experience, luck, and following hunches, in just about that order.

In other words, Glynes felt, he just might find something of professional interest to ATF out in the Pine Barrens. He was either right or wrong, but in either case, the sooner he got out in the Pine Barrens the better.

Overnight, Marion Claude Wheatley had given a good deal of thought to the Lord having directed him to the Divine Lorraine Hotel.

There had to be a reason, of course. The Lord was not whimsical. One possibility was that the Lord knew that once the Vice President had been disintegrated the Secret Service and the FBI would learn that Marion had been responsible, and come looking for him. If he was not in his office, or at the house, but rather in the Divine Lorraine Hotel, obviously they would not be able to find him.

If that scenario were true, the Lord would certainly furnish him additional information and assistance once the disintegration had been accomplished.

But after more reflection, Marion came to believe that the Lord was concerned that the Secret Service was already, somehow—they were not stupid, quite the contrary—aware of Marion's existence and intentions. And that they would somehow keep him from carrying out the disintegration.

Before or after the disintegration, the last place, obviously, except perhaps the cells in the Police Administration Building, that the authorities would think to look for Marion Claude Wheatley would be in the Divine Lorraine Hotel.

At eight A.M. Marion got out the telephone book, and laid it on his desk. He took a paper clip from the desk drawer, and straightened one end. He held the clip in his left hand, then closed his eyes and opened the telephone book with his right hand. He stabbed it with the paper clip and then opened his eyes. The paper clip indicated EDMONDS, RICHARD 8201 HENRY AVENUE, 438-1299.

Marion thought about that for a moment, and then, being careful not to disturb the position of the paper clip, took a notebook and a ballpoint from the desk and began to write:

> Richard H. Edmonds
> Henry R. Edmonds
> Edmund R. Henry
> Henry E. Richards

Then he looked elsewhere in the telephone book until he found the number, and then telephoned to the Divine Lorraine Hotel.

"Divine Lorraine Hotel. Praise Jesus!"

*That,* Marion decided, *is a colored lady.*

He had a mental image of a large colored lady wearing one of those white whatever-they-were-called on her head.

"I'm calling with regard to finding accommodations for the next few days."

"Excuse me, sir, but do you know about the Divine Lorraine Hotel?"

"Yes, of course, I do," Marion said.

*What an odd question,* Marion thought. And then he understood: *As I heard in her voice that she's colored, she heard in mine that I am white.*

"This is a Christian hotel, you understand," the woman pursued. "No drinking, no smoking, nothing that violates the Ten Commandments and the teachings of Father Divine."

"I understand," Marion said, and then added, "I am about the Lord's work."

"Well, we can put you up. No credit cards."

"I'm prepared to pay cash."

"When was you thinking of coming?"

"This morning, if that would be convenient."

"We can put you up," the woman said. "What did you say your name was?"

"Henry E. Richards," Marion said.

"We'll be expecting you, Brother Richard. Praise Jesus!"

"That's 'Richards,'" Marion said. "With an 'S.' Praise the Lord."

At half past eight, Captain Michael Sabara picked up the private line in his office in the Schoolhouse.

"Captain Sabara."

"Peter Wohl, Mike."

"Good morning, sir."

"Something's come up, Mike. When I get off, call Swede Olsen in Internal Affairs. I just got off from talking to him. He'll bring you up-to-date on what's going on. I don't think anything's going to happen this morning, but if it does, just use your own good judgment."

"Yes, sir. I guess you're not coming in?"

"No."

"Is there anyplace I can reach you?"

Wohl hesitated.

"For your ears only, Mike," he said, finally. "I'm in the Roundhouse. I made inspector. My dad and my mother are here. We're waiting for the mayor."

"Jesus, Peter, that's good news. Congratulations!"

"Thank you, Mike. I'll call in when I'm through. But if anyone asks, I'm at the dentist's."

"Yes, sir, *Inspector!*"

"Thanks," Wohl said, and hung up.

At five minutes to nine, Special Agent Glynes placed a collect call, he would speak with anyone, to the Atlantic City office of the Bureau of Alcohol, Tobacco and Firearms from a pay telephone in a Shell gasoline station in Hammonton, N.J.

"Odd that you should call, Glynes," Special Agent Tommy Thomas, an old pal, said, "Mr. Samm has been wondering where you are. He at first presumed that you had fallen ill, and had simply forgotten to telephone, but when *he* telephoned your residence, there was no answer, so he knew that couldn't be it."

"Is he there, Tommy?"

"Yes, indeed."

"Put him on."

Special Agent Thomas turned his back to Special Agent in Charge Samm and whispered into the phone: "Careful, Chuck. He's got a hair up his ass."

Then he spun his chair around again to face Special Agent in

Charge Samm, who was standing by the coffee machine across the room, and raised his voice.

"It's Glynes, sir."

"Good," Mr. Samm said, coming quickly across the room and snatching the telephone from Thomas. "Glynes?"

"Yes, sir."

"How is it that you were neither at the eight-thirty meeting or called in?"

"Sir, I was in the Pine Barrens. There was no phone."

"What are you doing in the Pine Barrens?"

"I've got something out here I think is very interesting."

"And what is that?"

"I've got six, maybe more, pay lockers, you know, the kind they have in airports and railroad stations, that, in what I would say the last week, maybe the last couple of days, have been blown up with high explosives."

There was a very long pause, so long that Glynes suspected the line had gone out.

"Sir?" he asked.

"Chuck, I have been trying to phrase this adequately," Mr. Samm said. "I confess that I have suspected you never even read the teletype. And that teletype isn't even twenty-four hours old, and you're onto something."

*What the hell,* Special Agent C. V. Glynes wondered, *is that little asshole talking about?*

"You're confident, Chuck, that it is high explosives?"

"Yes, sir. Nothing but high-intensity explosives could do this kind of damage."

"Good man, Chuck," Mr. Samm said. "Thomas, pick up on 303. Get this all down accurately."

Tommy Thomas's voice came on the line. "Ready, sir."

"Thomas," Mr. Samm said, "with reference to that Request for All Information teletype of yesterday, Glynes has come up with something."

"Yes, sir," Thomas said, his tone of voice suggesting to Glynes that Thomas hadn't read the teletype either.

"Okay, Chuck," Mr. Samm went on. "Give Thomas your location. I'm going to get on another phone and get in touch with the Secret Service and the FBI."

"Yes, sir."

"And, Glynes, make sure you keep the scene clean. Keep the locals out."

"Yes, sir."

"I'll be there as soon as I can."

"Yes, sir."

"Good work, Glynes. Good work."

At two minutes past nine o'clock, Marion Claude Wheatley telephoned Mr. D. Logan Hammersmith, Jr., vice president and senior trust officer of the First Pennsylvania Bank & Trust Company and told him he had come down with some sort of virus and would not be able to come into work today, and probably not for the next few days.

Mr. Hammersmith expressed concern, told Marion he should err on the side of caution and see his physician, viruses were tricky, and that if there was anything at all that he could do, he should not hesitate to give him a call.

"Thank you," Marion said. "I'm sure I'll be all right in a day or two."

"No sense taking a chance, Marion. Go see your doctor," Mr. Hammersmith said, added "Good-bye," and hung up.

Marion called for a taxi, and while he was waiting for it to come, he took all his luggage from where he had stacked it by the front door and carried it out of the house and down the stairs and stacked it on the second step up from the sidewalk.

When the taxi came, he helped the driver load everything into the trunk and, when it would hold no more, into the back seat. Finally, he returned to the steps and picked up the two attaché cases, one of which held the detonators and the other the shortwave transmitter (batteries disconnected, of course, there was no such thing as being too careful around detonators) and took them with him into the rear seat.

"The airport," he ordered. "Eastern Airlines. No hurry. I have plenty of time."

At the airport, he secured the services of a skycap, and told him he needed to put his luggage in a locker. The skycap rolled his cart to a row of lockers. Marion needed two to store what he was going to temporarily leave at the airport. He kept out the attaché case with the detonators, and two suitcases, one of which held what he thought would be enough clothing for a week, and the other half of the devices.

He paid off the skycap, tipping him two dollars, and then carried the two suitcases and the attaché case to a coffee shop where he had a cup of black coffee and two jelly-filled doughnuts. While he ate, he flipped through a copy of the *Washington Post* that a previous customer had left on the banquette cushion.

He then got up and carried his luggage down to the taxi station, waited in line for a cab, and when it was finally his turn, he told the driver to take him to the Divine Lorraine Hotel.

The driver turned and looked at him in disbelief.

"The Divine Lorraine Hotel?"

Marion smiled.

"I'm going to North Broad and Ridge," he explained. "Some drivers don't know where that is. *Everybody* knows where the Divine Lorraine Hotel is."

"You had me going there for a minute," the driver said. "You didn't look like one of Father Divine's people."

*I'll have to remember that,* Marion thought. *Someone such as myself, who does not fit in with the Divine Lorraine Hotel, would naturally attract curiosity and attention by taking a taxi there.*

*But no harm done, and a lesson learned.*

When they reached Ridge Avenue, Marion told the driver to turn right. A block down Ridge, he told the driver to let him out at the corner.

He walked down Ridge Avenue until the taxi was out of sight, then crossed the street and walked back to North Broad Street and into the Divine Lorraine Hotel.

There was a colored lady wearing sort of a robe and a white cloth, or whatever, behind the desk.

"My name is Richards, Henry E. Richards," Marion said. "I have a reservation."

"Yes, sir, we've been expecting you," the colored lady said. She was not, to judge from her voice, the same one he had spoken with on the telephone.

She gave him a registration card to sign, and he filled it out, and she said she could either give him a single room with a single bed, or a single room with a double bed, or a small suite with a double bed in the bedroom and a sitting room.

"Does the small suite have a desk?" Marion asked.

"Yes, and so does the single with a double bed," the woman said.

"Then the single with the double bed, please," Marion said. "I need a desk."

She told him how much, and he asked if there was a weekly rate, and she told him there was, so he paid for a week in advance, and asked for a receipt.

He counted the money in his wallet while she was making out the receipt. He had only one hundred and four dollars.

*I probably will not need more,* Marion decided, *but it is always good to be prepared. When I go out later, I will find a branch of Girard Trust Bank and cash a check.*

Another colored lady in a robe and a white whatchamacallit around her head appeared and tried to take his suitcases.

He was made uncomfortable by the notion of a woman carrying his bags.

"I'll take those," Marion said.

"You take one, and I'll take the other," she said with a smile.

She led him to the elevator, which she operated herself, and took him to a very nice room on the sixth floor that overlooked North Broad Street.

He gave her a dollar.

"For the Lord's work, you understand," she said.

"Of course."

"I hope you enjoy your stay with us."

"Thank you."

"Praise Jesus!"

"Praise the Lord!"

The room, Marion found on inspection, was immaculate. Everything seemed a bit old, and well worn, but the state of cleanliness left nothing to be desired.

*Cleanliness,* Marion thought, *is next to godliness.*

He went to the suitcases, hung up the clothing they contained, and then picked up the Bible that was neatly centered on the desk. He sat down in an upholstered chair.

He closed his eyes, and then opened the Bible, and then put his finger on a page.

*If the Lord wants to send me a message, what better way? And then, in an hour or so, I will go back out to the airport and get the rest of my things. This time I will have the driver drop me two blocks farther up North Broad Street.*

He opened his eyes to see what passage of Holy Scripture the Lord might have selected for him.

He saw that he was in the second chapter of Haggai, the seventeenth verse.

Marion was not very familiar with Haggai.

"17. I smote you with blasting and with mildew and with hail in all the labours of your hands; yet ye turned not to me, saith the Lord."

Marion read it again and again and again, trying to understand what it meant.

At quarter to ten the private number on the desk of Staff Inspector Peter Wohl rang. Officer Paul O'Mara answered it in the prescribed manner.

"Inspector Wohl's office, Officer O'Mara speaking, sir."

"This is H. Charles Larkin, Secret Service. May I speak with the inspector, please?"

"I'm sorry, sir. The inspector is not available."

"This is important. Where can I reach him?"

"Just a moment, sir."

O'Mara went quickly to Captain Sabara's office.

"Captain, that Secret Service guy is on the inspector's private line. He says it's important."

"Does he have a name?"

"Mr. Larkin, sir."

Sabara went into Wohl's office and picked up the telephone.

"Good morning, Mr. Larkin. Mike Sabara. Can I help you?"

"I really wanted to talk to Peter, Mike."

"He won't be here until after lunch, and I don't really know how to reach him."

"That's not a polite way of saying he doesn't want to talk to me, is it?"

"No," Sabara said. "I . . . Not for dissemination, he's been promoted to Inspector. He's in the Commissioner's office."

"Well good for him," Larkin said, then added, "Something has come up. *May* have come up. An ATF guy from Atlantic City has found evidence of a recent series of high-explosive detonations under odd circumstances."

"Really?"

"I just this minute got the call. It may or not be our guy. But on the other hand, it's all anybody's turned up. I'm going to the scene . . . it's in the Pine Barrens in Jersey . . . and I'd sort of hoped Peter would either go with me, or send somebody else."

"I can't leave," Sabara said.

"What about Malone?"

"He's at the Roundhouse, and I don't expect him back for at least an hour."

"What about Payne? He at least knows what we're up against."

"When and where do you want him?"

"Here. Ten minutes ago."

"He'll be twenty minutes late. He's on his way."

"Thank you, Mike. I appreciate the cooperation," Larkin said, and hung up.

En route from the Schoolhouse to the Federal Courts Building in Captain Mike Sabara's unmarked car, Detective Payne realized that he had no idea where in the Federal Courts Building he was to meet Supervisory Special Agent H. Charles Larkin. For that matter, he didn't know where in the building the Secret Service maintained its offices, and he suspected that he would not be allowed to drive a car into the building's basement garage without the proper stickers on its windshield.

*Fuck it,* he decided. *I'll park right in front of the place, and worry about fixing the ticket later.*

His concerns were not justified. When he pulled to the curb, Larkin was standing there waiting for him. He pulled open the passenger side door and got in.

"Good morning, Detective Payne," he said cheerfully. "And how are you this bright and sunny morning?"

Matt opened his mouth to reply, but before a word came out, Larkin went on: "Has this thing got a whistle?"

*He means "siren,"* Detective Payne mentally translated.

He looked down at the row of switches mounted below the dash. He saw Larkin's finger flip one up and the siren began to howl.

"A Jersey State Trooper is waiting for us on the Jersey side of the Ben Franklin Bridge," Larkin said.

Matt looked into his rearview mirror and pulled into the stream of traffic.

No one got out of his way, despite the wailing siren, and, Matt presumed, flashing lights concealed behind the grill.

Larkin read his mind:

"If you think this is bad, try doing it in New York City. They get out of the way of a whistle only when it's mounted on a thirty-ton fire truck."

There was a New Jersey State Trooper car waiting in a toll booth lane on the Jersey side of the bridge, the lights on its bubble gum machine flashing. As Matt pulled up behind it, a State Trooper, his brimmed cap so low on his nose that Matt wondered how he could see, came up.

"Secret Service?"

"Larkin," Larkin said, holding out a leather identification folder. "I appreciate the cooperation."

"We're on our way," the Trooper said and trotted to his car.

There were more vehicles than Matt could count around what looked like a depression off a dirt road in the Pine Barrens, so many that a deputy sheriff had been detailed to direct traffic. He waved them to a stop.

"I'm Larkin, Secret Service," Larkin said, leaning across Matt to speak to him.

"Yes, sir, we've been waiting for you," the sheriff said. "Pull it over there. Everybody's in the garbage dump."

Matt parked the car and then followed Larkin to the depression, which he saw was in fact a garbage dump.

A tall, slender man with rimless glasses detached himself from a group of men, half in one kind or another of police uniform, a few in civilian clothes, and several in overalls with FEDERAL AGENT printed in large letters across their backs.

"Mr. Larkin?" the man asked, and when Larkin nodded, he went on, "I'm Howard Samm, I have the Atlantic City office of ATF."

"I'm very glad to meet you," Larkin said. "I can't tell you how much I appreciate your help with this."

"I like to think we have a pretty good team," Samm said. "And Agent Glynes was really on the ball with this, wasn't he? We didn't get that Request for All Information teletype until yesterday."

"He certainly was," Larkin said. "Mr. Samm, this is Detective Payne of the Philadelphia Police Department. He's working with us."

Samm shook Matt's hand.

*Well, that's very nice of you, Mr. Larkin, but it's bullshit. Unless driving you around and running errands is "working with you."*

"Well, what have we got?" Larkin asked.

"Somebody has been blowing things—specifically metal lockers, the kind you find in airports, bus stations—up with high explosives. My senior technician—the large fellow, in the coveralls?—says he's almost sure it's Composition C-4."

"When will we know for sure?"

"We just finished making sure the rest of the lockers weren't booby-trapped. The next step is taking a locker to the lab."

He pointed. Matt looked. Two of the men in coveralls were dragging a cable from a wrecker with MODERN CHEVROLET painted on its doors down to the remnants of a row of rental lockers. A Dodge van with no identifying marks on it waited for it, its rear doors open.

"We have any idea who's been doing this?" Larkin asked.

"That's going to be a problem, I'm afraid," Samms said.

"Not even a wild hair?" Larkin asked. "Who owns this property? Has anybody talked to him?"

"We don't know who owns the property. One of the deputies found a cabin a quarter of a mile over there. But there's no signs of life in it."

"A deserted cabin?"

"Well, of course, we haven't been able to go inside. So I really don't know."

"You haven't gone inside?"

"We don't have a search warrant."

"We'll go inside," Larkin said. "I'll take the responsibility."

Samm, visibly, did not like that.

"Christ," Larkin said. "Don't you think we have reasonable cause, even if there wasn't a threat to the Vice President?"

"You're right, of course," Samm said. He raised his voice. "Meador!"

The large man in the coveralls with FEDERAL AGENT on the back looked at him. Samm waved him over.

"This is Mr. Larkin of the Secret Service," he said. "He wants to have a look inside that house. Will you check it for booby traps, please?"

"No search warrant?" Meador asked.

"Just open the place for me, please," Larkin said. "I'll worry about a search warrant."

"Okay," Meador said.

Meador, with Larkin, Samm, and Matt following him, went to the van and took a toolbox from it, and led the way to the house. They stood to one side as he carefully probed a window for trip wires, and then smashed a pane with a screwdriver.

When he had the window open, he crawled through it. He was inside a minute or two, and then crawled back out.

"The door's clean," he said. "What do I do with the padlock?"

"You got any bolt cutters in that box?" Larkin asked.

Meador was putting bolt cutters in place on the padlock when two men in business suits walked up. Matt was surprised to see Jack Matthews, who was also surprised to see him. The other man, somewhat older, was a redhead, pale-faced, and on the edge between muscular and plump.

"Mr. Larkin," he said, "I'm Frank Young, Criminal A-SAC [Assistant Special Agent in Charge] for the FBI in Philadelphia."

"I think we've met, Frank, haven't we?" Larkin said.

"Yes, sir, now that I see you, I think we have met. Maybe Quantico?"

"How about Denver?" Larkin asked.

"Right. I was in the Denver field office. This is Special Agent Jack Matthews."

"We've met," Larkin said. "And I think you know Matthews too, don't you, Matt?"

"Yes, indeed," Matt said. "How nice to see you, Special Agent Matthews."

"Why do I think he's needling him?" Larkin said. "Payne is a Philadelphia detective. Do you know each other?"

"I know who he is," Young said, and shook Matt's hand. "What are we doing here?"

"Well, Frank, if you're the Criminal A-SAC, this will be right down your alley," Larkin said. "Detective Payne and I were walking through the woods and came across this building. Into which, I believe, person or persons unknown have recently broken in. We were just about to have a look."

Meador of ATF looked at Larkin and smiled.

"I wouldn't be at all surprised," he said as he lowered his bolt cutters, "if the burglar used a bolt cutter to cut through that padlock."

"That's very astute of you," Larkin said.

"What are we looking for?" Young asked.

"Signs of occupancy. If we get lucky, a name. So we can ask if he's noticed anything strange, like loud explosions, around here."

"There are tractor tracks that look fresh," Jack Matthews said, pointing.

"Take a look at the dipstick in the tractor engine," Young ordered. "I'll take a look inside."

"Yes, sir."

"Don't open any doors or cabinets until Meador here checks them," Larkin said. "And it would probably be a good idea to watch for trip wires."

"You think this is your bomber?" Young asked.

"I don't know that it's not," Larkin said.

Matthews came into the cabin after a minute or two to report that the tractor battery was charged, and from the condition of the dipstick, he thought the engine had been run in the last week or ten days.

Matt wondered how he could tell that, but was damned if he would reveal his ignorance by asking.

Jack Matthews moved quickly and efficiently around the cabin, and seemed to know exactly what he was looking for. Matt felt ignorant.

There were no trip wires or booby traps, but there was evidence of recent occupancy.

"There is something about this place that bothers me," Larkin said thoughtfully. "It's too damned neat and clean for a cabin in the boondocks."

"Yeah," Young agreed thoughtfully.

"I think we have to find out who owns this, who comes here."

"County courthouse?" Young said.

"Unless one of the deputies knows offhand," Larkin said.

"Are you going back to Philadelphia?" Young asked.

"I don't see what else I can do here," Larkin said.

"Why don't I send Jack to the county courthouse with my car?" Young asked. "And catch a ride back with you?"

"Great," Larkin said. He turned to Meador of ATF. "Meador, look into your crystal ball and tell me what he used for detonators."

"The explosive looks like C-4," Meador said. "Somebody with access to C-4 would probably have access to military detonators. I'll know for sure when I'm finished in the laboratory."

"Depressing thought," Larkin said.

"Sir?"

"Somebody with access to C-4 and military detonators who blew up those lockers the way he did knows how to use that stuff, wouldn't you say?"

"Yeah," Meador said.

"Well, at least it gives us a lead or two," Larkin said. "Which is a lead or two more than we had when I woke up this morning."

He put his hand out to H. Howard Samm.

"Your team really did a fine job, Samm. I think my boss would like to write a letter of commendation."

"Why," Samm said. "That would be very nice, but unnecessary."

"Nonsense. A commendation is in order," Larkin said, and then touched Matt's shoulder. "Let's go home, Matthew."

● ● ●

A moment after they turned off the dirt road onto the highway, Larkin said, "You noticed, Frank, how Mr. Samm was so anxious to make sure that his guy who found that place got the credit?"

"I noticed. His name wasn't mentioned."

"His names is Glynes," Larkin said. "C. V. Glynes."

"And he gets the commendation?"

"They both do. And Meador too. But on his, Samm gets his name misspelled," Larkin said.

Young laughed, and Larkin joined in.

"I don't know why we're laughing," Young said. "Now we *know* we have a lunatic on our hands who knows what he's doing with high explosives, and presumably has more in his kitchen closet."

# TWENTY-FIVE

Inspector Peter F. Wohl, of the Philadelphia Police Department, who had, ten minutes before, been Staff Inspector Wohl, came out of Commissioner Czernich's office in the company of Chief Inspector (retired) and Mrs. Augustus Wohl.

*They are happy about this*, Peter Wohl thought, *but they are in the minority. Czernich, despite the warm smile and the hearty handshake, didn't like it at all. And a lot of other people aren't going to like it either, when they hear about it.*

Part of this, he felt, was because before he had become a staff inspector, he had been the youngest captain in the Department. And there was the matter of the anomaly in the rank structure of the Philadelphia Police Department: Captains are immediately subordinate to staff inspectors, who are immediately subordinate to Inspectors. The insignia of the ranks parallels that of the Army and Marine Corps. Captains wear two gold bars, "railroad tracks"; staff inspectors wear gold oak leaves, corresponding to military majors; and inspectors wear, like military lieutenant colonels, silver oak leaves.

There were only sixteen staff inspectors in the Department, all of them (with the sole exception of Wohl, Peter F.) assigned to the Staff Inspection Office of the Internal Affairs Division. There they handled "sensitive" investigations, which translated to mean they were a group of really first-rate investigators who went after criminals who were also high governmental officials, elected, appointed, or civil service.

Being a staff inspector is considered both prestigious and a good, interesting job. Many staff inspectors consider it the apex of their police careers.

Consequently, the promotion path from captain to inspector for most officers usually skips staff inspector. A lieutenant is promoted to captain, and spends the next five or six or even ten years commanding a District, or in a special unit, and/or working somewhere in administration until finally he ranks high enough on an inspector's examination—given every two years—to be promoted off it.

Peter Wohl, who everyone was willing to admit was one of the better staff inspectors, had been transferred out of Internal Affairs to command of the newly formed Special Operations Division. Officially, this was a decision of Police Commissioner Taddeus Czernich. Anyone who had been on the job more than six months suspected, correctly, that Wohl's transfer had been made at the "suggestion" of Mayor Jerry Carlucci, whose suggestions carried about as much weight with Czernich as a Papal pronouncement, ex cathedra.

Anyone who had been on the job six months also was aware that Wohl had friends in high places. Chief Inspector Augustus Wohl, retired, it was generally conceded, had been Mayor Carlucci's rabbi as the mayor had climbed through the ranks of the Department. And Peter Wohl was close to Chief Inspectors Lowenstein and Coughlin. It was far easier, and much more satisfying for personal egos, to conclude that Wohl's rapid rise in rank was due to his closeness to the mayor than to give the mayor the benefit of the doubt, and to believe Carlucci had given Wohl Special Operations, and had the expired Inspector's List reopened, because he really believed Wohl was the best man in the Department for the job, and that he deserved the promotion.

When the Wohls came out of the Commissioner's office door into one of the curving corridors of the Roundhouse, and started walking toward the elevators, Captain Richard Olsen of Internal Affairs walked up to them.

"Looking for me, Swede?" Wohl asked.

"Yes, sir."

"I guess you know my dad? What about my mother?"

"Chief," Olsen said. "Good to see you again. How do you do, Mrs. Wohl?"

"I'm doing very well, thank you, after what just happened in there," Olga Wohl said.

"And just what happened in there?"

"Say hello to the newest inspector," Chief Wohl said.

"No kidding?" Olsen said. "Jesus, Peter, congratulations. Well deserved."

He took Wohl's hand and shook it with enthusiasm.

*Swede seems genuinely pleased. But my fans are still outnumbered by maybe ten to one.*

"Thanks, Swede. It will not be necessary for you to kiss my ring."

"Peter!" Olga Wohl said. "Really!"

"What's up Swede? You *were* looking for me?"

"First of all, don't jump on Mike Sabara for telling me where I could find you. I practically had to get down on my knees and beg."

"That's not good enough," Wohl said. "As my first official act as an inspector, I'll have him shot at sunrise. Did your guys come up with something last night?"

"Yeah. Could you give me a minute?"

"Peter, I understand," Chief Wohl said. "We'll get out of your way."

He hugged his son briefly, but affectionately, and then, after she'd kissed their son, propelled Olga Wohl toward the elevator.

"You want to go get a cup of coffee or something?" Olsen asked.

"I didn't have any breakfast," Wohl said. "So I need some, which I think, under the circumstances, I'll even pay for."

"I know just the place," Olsen said. "If that was an invitation."

Olsen led him, on foot, to The Mall, a bar and restaurant on 9th Street. It was popular not only with the Internal Affairs people, but also with Homicide detectives. Wohl had spent a lot of time and money in The Mall as both a staff inspector and when he'd been in Homicide. It was just what he wanted now, for it offered a nice menu and comfortable chairs at a table where their conversation would not be overheard.

He ordered Taylor ham and eggs, hash browns and coffee.

"Same for me, please," Olsen said, and waited for the waitress to leave.

"I sent for Sergeant Framm and Detective Pillare first thing this morning . . ." Olsen began.

"They're the two you had on Lanza?" Wohl interrupted.

Olsen nodded.

". . . Framm opened the conversation by saying, 'It couldn't be helped, Captain, he dodged through traffic.' "

"Oh, shit, they lost him?"

"They did," Olsen said. "And your Sergeant O'Dowd did . . ."

"O'Dowd was there too?"

Olsen nodded again. "And he lost him too, but your man Payne stayed with him."

"Detective Payne was there too?"

*Goddammit, Lanza knows Matt, and he shouldn't have been anywhere near him. I am going to have to sit on him, and hard.*

"And he followed him to an apartment house in Center City, and then arranged for a somewhat chagrined Sergeant Framm, Detective Pillare, and Sergeant O'Dowd to join him."

*If O'Dowd was there, and what the hell was he doing there, he knew Payne was there, and should not have been there. Unless, of course, O'Dowd told Matt to be there. Jesus Christ!*

"You lose people. It happens to everybody. It's certainly happened to me," Wohl said.

"Shortly after Lanza got to the apartment building, Mr. Gian-Carlo Rosselli *and* Mr. Paulo Cassandro entered the premises, stayed approximately twenty minutes, and then left, obviously pleased with themselves, and went to the bar at the Hotel Warwick where they stayed until closing."

"Who did Lanza see in the apartment building?"

"A lady," Olsen said, and handed Wohl a photograph. "Brilliant detective work by myself this morning identified her as Antoinette Marie Wolinski Schermer, believed by Organized Crime to be the girlfriend of Mr. Ricco Baltazari, proprietor of Ristorante Alfredo."

"What's she doing with Lanza? He spend the night there?"

"Yeah, and it's not the first time."

The waitress delivered the coffee.

"I'm going to need another one of these," Wohl said to her.

She nodded and left. Wohl took a sip, then another, then looked at Olsen.

"It would seem he has nice friends, our Corporal Lanza," Wohl said.

"Yeah, doesn't he?" Olsen replied. "So I took this to Chief Marchessi . . ."

"Right," Wohl said.

"Peter, I didn't mention to him that Framm and Pillare lost Lanza. He's . . . Framm is, this is not the first time he's lost somebody . . . and he's already on the chief's shit list."

*If Olsen is covering for Framm, he has his reasons, and it's not because Framm's a nice guy.*

"He wasn't lost, that's all that counts," Wohl said.

"Thank you," Olsen said. "The chief asked what you thought of all this, and I told him you were unavailable . . . At this point in time, Mike Sabara was still stonewalling me."

"Good for him," Wohl said.

"So the chief said that what we should do is bring the airline security people in on this. You remember Dickie Lowell?"

"Sure."

*Before my time*, Wohl thought. *But I remember him. H. Dickenson Lowell had been one of the first, if not the first, black staff inspectors. And then he made inspector. Well, dammit, I am not the first staff inspector to have the gall to try to get myself promoted.*

"Well, they had him running the Headquarters Division in the Detective Bureau and he didn't like it, all the paperwork, so he took retirement. He's chief of security for Eastern at the airport. More important, he and Marchessi are old pals."

"He was a good cop, as I recall," Wohl said.

"Marchessi called him, and explained the situation. Lowell is going to have his people keep an eye on Lanza, and he told Marchessi he has some friends, other airlines security, that he can go to. He will not go to the feds, which is important to Marchessi . . ."

"And me," Wohl interjected.

". . . but he will call Marchessi or me if Lanza does something suspicious. And we'll keep sitting on Lanza when he's not on the job."

"Good," Wohl said. "Very good."

"And then the chief told me to find you and bring you in on this and see if it's all right with you, or if you had anything, a suggestion, or what."

Wohl didn't reply for a moment, then he said, "There's only two loose ends that I can think of. This woman, Schermer, you said?"

Olsen nodded.

"I'd like to know if she was the woman Payne saw with Lanza in the Poconos. And then there's Martinez. I don't want him to go off half-cocked and screw anything up."

"The chief said maybe I should mention Martinez to you."

The waitress appeared with their ham and eggs.

Wohl looked at his plate, and then stood up.

"I think I know how to kill two birds with one stone," he said, and walked to a pay telephone.

Five minutes later he was back.

"That didn't work," he said.

"What didn't work?"

"I called the Schoolhouse. I was going to tell Payne to find Martinez, and bring him here. Payne could have told us whether that was the woman Lanza had with him in the Poconos, and we both could have impressed on both of them that neither of them are to get anywhere near Lanza until we finish this."

"What happened?"

"Payne is in New Jersey with the Secret Service, they may have a lead on the guy who wants to blow up the Vice President, and when I called Martinez, his mother told me he's got the flu, and called in sick."

"You've got Payne working on the screwball?" Olsen asked, surprised.

"Mike sent him," Wohl said. "When I have him shot in the morning, I'll have them pick up the body and shoot him again."

He looked at Olsen.

"And my eggs are probably cold. I think this is going to be one of those days."

At five minutes past one, Marion Claude Wheatley left his room in the Divine Lorraine Hotel, rode the elevator to the lobby, left his key at the desk, and walked out onto North Broad Street.

He turned north, walked three blocks, and then crossed the street. There he waited for a bus, rode it downtown into Center City, got off, and walked to Suburban Station. He went downstairs, picked up a Pennsylvania Railroad Timetable from a rack, and went back out to the street.

He flagged a cab and had himself driven to the airport, giving American Airlines as his destination. Inside the airport, he went to a fast-food restaurant and had a hot dog with sauerkraut and mustard and a medium root beer.

When he was finished, he went to the locker where he had left his things earlier, picked them up, and went to the taxi stand.

He gave the driver an address on Ridge Avenue, and when he got there, carried his luggage into a small office building until he was sure the cab had driven away.

Then he went back to the Divine Lorraine Hotel, sorted everything out on the bed, repacked everything, and put it in the closet. The closet had a key, which he thought was fortuitous, and he removed it and put it in his pocket.

Then he sat down at the desk and looked at the Bible again, and reread the passage the Lord had directed him to. He could by now practically recite Haggai 2:17 by heart, but he was no closer to understanding what "17. I smote you with blasting and with mildew and with hail in all the labours of your hands; yet ye turned not to me, saith the Lord" meant than he had been when the Lord had first directed his attention to it.

Marion decided the only thing to do was pray.

He knelt by the bed, and with the Bible before him, he prayed for understanding.

When Inspector Wohl walked into his office, a few minutes after two, it was immediately apparent to Captain Mike Sabara that he had a hair up his ass about something, and Sabara wondered if he had done the wrong thing in sending Matt Payne off with the man from the Secret Service.

"Do you have any word from Payne, Mike?" Wohl asked.

"No, sir."

"When he gets back, let me know," Wohl said, and went into his office and closed the door.

Twenty minutes later, Officer O'Mara put his head in Wohl's door and said that Mr. Larkin was here, and could the inspector see him?

"Ask him to come in," Wohl said, "and if Payne is out there, don't let him get away."

"Yes, sir," Officer O'Mara replied crisply, and then promptly misinterpreted his instructions. Detective Payne, at Officer O'Mara's bidding, followed Supervisory Special Agent Larkin into Inspector Wohl's office.

"Well, Peter," Larkin asked as they shook hands, "how did the promotion ceremony go?"

*Does everybody in Philadelphia know I've been promoted? And what the hell is Matt doing in here?*

"I did all right until the Commissioner kissed me."

He stopped.

*I'll show Payne the photograph and then throw him out.*

"Yes, sir?"

"Excuse me, Charley. This won't take a minute," Wohl said, and handed Matt the photograph. "You ever see this woman before?"

Matt looked at it.

"That's the girl Lanza had in the Poconos."

"Okay. Call Captain Olsen in Internal Affairs and tell him that," Wohl ordered.

"Right now?"

"Right now," Wohl said sharply.

"Peter," Larkin said. "Excuse me, but is that as important as our lunatic?"

*No, of course it isn't. I am just having one of my goddamned bad days. What the hell is the matter with me?*

"No, of course not," Wohl said. "Sorry. Payne, that will wait."

"Yes, sir."

"I'm reasonably sure, Peter, that we know where our man has been," Larkin said. "But we don't have an idea who he is, or where."

"What happened in New Jersey?"

"A deputy sheriff came across a piece of steel that showed evidence of having been involved in a high-explosive detonation," Larkin said. "Actually, he ran over it. Anyway, an ATF guy out of Atlantic City ran it down, and they called us. What we found, in a garbage dump in the middle of the Pine Barrens, were half a dozen railroad station, airline terminal, bus station rental lockers that had been, recently, blown up. The ATF expert said he was almost sure it was Composition C-4, and that it was set up with GI detonators. This guy knows his way around explosives."

"That's not good news, is it?"

"It may not be all bad. It may give us a line on him. We're already back-checking with the military. And if he knows what he's doing, that would lessen the chance of his explosives going off accidentally."

"But you don't know who he is?"

"That's the bad news. Where we stand is that the FBI is searching records in the county courthouse over there to find out who owns the property. There's a house, more of a cabin, on the property. Someone has been there in the past week or ten days, which coincides with when the ATF explosives guy says the explosions took place. And, for a cabin, the place was out-of-the-ordinary neat and clean. Which ties in with the psychological profile. Both of them. Ours and Dr. Payne's. I have a gut feeling he could be our guy."

"But no name?"

"Not yet. And I could be wrong. Maybe the people who own the property have nothing to do with what happened there. But that's all we have to go on, unless we get a name from the Defense Department, some explosives guy with mental problems."

"How can we help?" Wohl asked.

"*If* we come up with a name, we're going to have to move fast. It would help if we had a search warrant that had the important parts left blank."

"Denny Coughlin," Wohl said. "I'll call him. He's good at that. He knows every judge in the city."

"You're not?"

"There's a Superior Court judge named Findermann in the slam," Wohl said. "Since I put him there, I have not been too popular with the bench."

"The only people worse than doctors and Congressmen when it comes to protecting their own are judges," Larkin said, and then went on: "If we get a name and an address, *and* a search warrant, we'll need some explosives people, maybe even a booby-trap expert."

"I thought of that," Wohl said. "We call it 'Ordnance Disposal.' It's in the Special Patrol Bureau. When I called over there, they told me, 'You tell us where, and we'll be there in ten minutes.'"

"Good. I appreciate your cooperation, Peter."

"You keep saying that."

"I keep saying it because I mean it. We couldn't handle this by ourselves."

"I have the simple solution to this problem," Wohl said. "Tell the Vice President to stay the hell home."

"No way," Larkin chuckled. "What I think I should do now is go back to the office and see if I can lean on the Defense Department to come up with some names. Can Matt take me?"

"Sure. On your way back, go see Hay-zus Martinez. Tell him . . ." He stopped, and then went on. "Hell, when all else fails, tell the truth. Tell Hay-zus that other people are watching Lanza. If he goes back to work, he is to stay away from Lanza. If he sees him doing something, he is to telephone either Captain Olsen or me. He's not to do anything about it."

"If he goes back to work?" Matt asked.

"His mother said he has the flu. Make sure he understands the message, Matt."

"Yes, sir."

"If he goes off half-cocked, he's liable to blow the whole thing," Wohl went on.

"I'll tell him, sir."

"And then come back here, of course, so Captain Sabara can have his car back."

"Yes, sir."

The red light was blinking on the answering machine when Matt came into his apartment at twenty minutes after five.

*I don't want to listen to any goddamned messages. I'm just going to have to bite the goddamned bullet.*

He reached down and pushed the ERASE button before he could change his mind. Nothing happened.

*You have to play the goddamned messages before you can erase them! Damn!*

He pushed the PLAY button and walked into the kitchen and took a beer from the refrigerator. He could hear that there had again been a number of callers who had elected not to leave their names.

Nature called, and he went to the bathroom off his bedroom. He had just begun to void his bladder when there was a familiar voice, somewhat metallically distorted.

*Penny! Jesus, I can't understand a word she's saying! I wonder what the hell she wanted?*

By the time he had zipped up his fly and returned to the answering machine, all the recorded messages, including the hangups, had played.

*Do I want to push REWIND so that I can hear what Precious Penny wants? No, I do not want to hear what Precious Penny wants.*

He pushed the ERASE button, and this time it worked.

*Banishing forever into the infinite mystery of rearranged microscopic metallic particles whatever Penny wanted to tell me. Why did I do that?*

He went into the kitchen, picked up the beer bottle, returned to the telephone, and dialed Evelyn's number.

It was a brief, but enormously painful conversation, punctuated by long, painful silences.

He told Evelyn the truth. He could not see her tonight because he was on orders to keep himself available. That was the truth, the whole truth, and nothing but the truth. Peter Wohl had even told him to take an unmarked car home with him in case he would need a car with radios and a siren.

Evelyn, her voice made it quite plain, did not believe a word he was saying. Nor did Evelyn believe him when he said he really didn't know about tomorrow, but that he thought the same thing would be true then. That was also the unvarnished truth. Until they found the lunatic who wanted to disintegrate the Vice President, everyone would be either working or keeping themselves available around the clock for a summons.

But he couldn't tell Evelyn that, of course. Not just on general principles, but because Wohl had made it an order. They didn't want the lunatic knowing they were looking for him, which he would if it got into the newspapers or on television.

He told her he would call her when he was free, and Evelyn didn't believe that, either. In this latter incidence, he had not told her the truth, the whole truth, and nothing but the truth. Even as he spoke, he had wondered if maybe Evelyn would take a hint, that her feminine pride would be offended, and if he didn't call, she would give up.

He strongly suspected that Evelyn was crying when she hung up.

"Shit!" he said aloud after he slammed the handset into its cradle.

Then he went into the kitchen and put a cork in the beer bottle and put it back into the refrigerator. He took down a bottle of Scotch and after carefully pouring a dollop into a shot glass, he tossed it down. And then had another.

All it did was make him feel hungry.

*And I don't want to be shit-faced if Wohl summons me to single-handedly place into custody our lunatic. Or more likely, orders me to play taxi driver to Mr. Larkin again.*

*What I will do is grab a shower, change clothes, call in and say I'm going to supper, and then go either to the Rittenhouse Club or the Ribs Place and have my supper, not washing anything down with wine or anything else.*

He was vaguely aware, as he showered, of a noise that could very possibly be the sound of his doorbell, but he wasn't sure, and he wasn't concerned. It could not be Evelyn. There was no way she could have made it into Center City from Upper Darby that quickly. And if Wohl or anybody else at Special Operations wanted him, they would have phoned. It could be Charley McFadden, or Jack Matthews, but in that happenstance, fuck 'em, let 'em wait.

When he turned the shower off, there was no longer a question whether the doorbell was being run. Whoever was pushing it was playing "Shave and a Haircut, Two Bits" on it.

Still dripping, Matt wrapped a towel around his waist and headed for the solenoid button. The doorbell musician played another verse of "Shave and a Haircut" before he got to the button.

"Keep your goddamned pants on!" he called as he looked down the stairwell.

The door opened. Penny came in.

"Tired of me so soon, are you?"

"Jesus! Penny, this is a very bad time."

She stopped halfway up the stairs. She saw that he was dressed in a towel.

"Am I interrupting anything?" she asked, and Matt did not like either her tone of voice or the kicked puppy look in her eyes.

"Come on in," he said. "There's always room for one more in an orgy."

"Is someone with you, Matt?" Penny asked, quite seriously.

"Hell, no. Come on in. You caught me in the shower."

Her face changed. The smile came back on her face and into her voice.

"I knew you were here, the guard told me," she said.

*Jesus, she looks good!*

"Make yourself at home," Matt said. "Let me get some clothes on."

She was by then at the head of the stairs.

"You called," she said. "And said that if I came into Center City, we could go to the movies."

"Did I?"

"And Daddy, over Mommy's objections, said he thought it would be all right, if I came home right after the movie, if I drove myself."

He looked at her. Their eyes met.

"Are you sore, Matt?" Penny asked softly.

"No, of course not," he said.

And then somehow, his arms went around her, and her face was on his chest, and he could feel her breath and smell her hair.

"I was sort of hoping you'd do that," she said, and then pushed him away. "For God's sake!" she said furiously. "Don't you dry yourself when you get out of your shower? I'm soaked!"

"Sorry," he said.

"Big date tonight?" Penny asked.

"I'm on call," he said.

"Which means?"

"Just what it sounds like. I have to make myself available. They'll probably call me before long."

"Oh."

"I was just about to go out and get something to eat. Ribs, I thought. Sound interesting?"

"How hungry are you?"

"What?"

"You said they were probably going to call you before long."

"I don't know what the hell you're talking about."

"Think about it, Matthew," Penny said, and then, a naughty look in her eyes, she put her hand to the towel around his waist and snatched it away.

"Jesus!" he said.

"You ever hear of first things first?" she said.

A very large man of about thirty-five who had been sitting with what the General Services Administration called a Chair, Metal, Executive, w/arms FSN 453 232234900 tilted as far back as it would go, and with his feet on what the GSA called a Desk, Metal, Office, w/six drawers, FSN 453 232291330, moved with surprisingly speed and grace when one of the three telephones on the desk rang, snatching the handset from the cradle before the second ring.

"Six Seven Three Nineteen Nineteen," he said.

"Mr. Larkin, please," the caller said.

"May I ask who's calling?" the large man said, then covered the microphone with his large hand. "For you, sir," he called.

Across the room, H. Charles Larkin, who had been lying, in fact half dozing, on what the GSA called a Couch, Office, Upholstered, w/three cushions, FSN 453 232291009, pushed himself to an erect position. He looked at the clock on the wall. It was 6:52.

"My name is Young, I'm the Criminal A-SAC, FBI, for Philadelphia."

"Young, FBI," the large man said, and took his hand off the microphone. "One moment, please, Mr. Young."

Larkin walked to the desk, grunting, his hand on the small of his back.

*I'm getting old*, he thought. *Too old for that goddamned couch.*

He took the phone from the large man.

"Hello, Frank."

"Charley, we have a name," Young said. "Matthews just called. That property is owned by Richard W. and Marianne Wheatley, husband and wife."

"Spell it, please," Larkin said, snatching a ballpoint pen extended in the hand of the large man.

"What about an address?" Larkin asked when he had written the name down.

"No. Just the address of the property."

"Damn!"

"And we've checked the Philadelphia area, plus Camden and Wilmington phone books. No Richard W. Wheatley."

"Maybe the Philadelphia cops can help," Larkin said. "Let me get back to you, Frank. Where are you?"

"I'm in the office about to go home. Let me give you that number. I've told our night guy what's going on."

Larkin wrote down Young's home phone number, and repeated, "Let me get back to you, Frank. And thank you."

He hung up, and turned to the large man.

"Get on the phone to Washington. Have them send somebody over to the Pentagon. Tell them that Richard W. and Marianne might be parents' names. Tell them to get me anything with Wheatley."

"You don't think the FBI will be on that?"

"I think they will, but I don't know they will," Larkin said sharply. "Just do it."

He took out his notebook, found Peter Wohl's home telephone number, and dialed it.

Detective Matthew M. Payne thought that one of the great erotic sights in the world had to be a blonde wearing a man's white shirt, and nothing else, especially when, whenever she leaned forward to help herself to the contents of one of the goldfish boxes from the Chinese Take-out, it fell away from her body and he could see an absolutely perfect breastworks.

"Here," Penny said, putting an egg roll in his mouth. "This is the last one. You can have one bite."

"Your generosity overwhelms me," Matt said.

"I try to please."

"Are you going to tell my sister that you came here and seduced me?"

"Meaning what?"

"You told her what happened in the Poconos."

"She's my shrink," Penny said. "She said I seemed very happy, and wanted to know why, so I told her. I didn't think she'd tell you!"

"She is convinced that I'm taking advantage of you."

"I can't imagine where she got that idea."

"She was pretty goddamned mad," Matt said.

"I'm pretty goddamned mad that she told you I told her."

"She's afraid that . . . that this won't be good for you."

"That's my problem, not hers. How did we get on this subject?"

"Penny, the last thing I want to do is hurt you."

"Relax. I'm making no demands on you. But that does raise the question I've had in the back of my mind."

"Which is?"

"Have you got someone?"

"No," he said.

"I didn't think so," Penny said. "Otherwise you would have taken her to the Poconos."

She looked at him, and she was close enough to kiss, and he did so, tenderly.

The phone rang.

"Damn!" Penny said.

*Please God, don't let that be Evelyn!*

"Payne," Matt said to the telephone.

"We have a name," Peter Wohl said, without any preliminaries. "Just a name. Do you know where Tiny Lewis lives?"

"Yes, sir."

"Go pick him up, he'll be waiting, and then come to Chief Lowenstein's office in the Roundhouse."

"Yes, sir."

Wohl hung up.

Matt put the telephone down.

"I've been called."

"So I gathered."

He swung his legs out of the bed and went searching for underwear in his chest of drawers.

Penny watched him get dressed.

"You want to take me to the movies again, sometime?"

"Why not?" he asked.

"Would it be all right with you if I hung around here until the movie would be over?"

"Of course. There's an *Inquirer* in the living room. Go look up what we saw, so we can keep our stories straight."

She got out of bed with what he considered to be a very attractive display of thighs and buttocks and went into the living room.

When he had tied his tie and slipped into a jacket he went after her.

"They're showing *Casablanca* for the thousandth time. How about us having seen that?"

" 'Round up the usual suspects,' " he quoted. "Sure. Why not?"

He went to the mantelpiece and picked up his revolver and slipped it into a holster.

"I suppose that's what cops' wives go through everyday, isn't it?"

"What?"

"Watching their man pick up his gun and go out, God only knows where."

"You are not a cop's wife, and you are very unlikely to become a cop's wife."

"You said it," she said.

He went and bent and kissed her, intending that it be almost casual, but she returned it with a strange fervor that was somehow frightening.

"I'll call you," he said.

"Enjoy the movie," Penny said.

He went down the stairs.

Penny looked at the mantel clock and did the mental calcuations. She had an hour and a half to kill, before she went home after an early supper and the movies.

She gave in to feminine curiosity and went around the apartment opening closets and cabinets, and when she had finished, she sat down in Matt's chair and read the *Inquirer*.

The doorbell sounded.

"Damn!" she said aloud. "What do I do about that?"

She went to the solenoid button and pushed it and looked down the stairwell.

A woman came in, and looked up at her in surprise.

"Who are you?" Evelyn asked.

"To judge by the look on your face, I'm the other woman," Penny said. "Come on up, and we'll talk about the lying sonofabitch."

# TWENTY-SIX

The commissioner's conference room in the Police Administration Building was jammed with people. Every seat at the long table was filled, chairs had been dragged in from other offices, and people were standing up and leaning against the wall. There were far too many people to fit in Lowenstein's office, which was why they were in the commissioner's conference room.

"You run this, Peter," Chief Inspector Matt Lowenstein declared from his chair at the head of the commissioner's conference table. "Denny Coughlin and I are here only to see how we can help you, Charley, and Frank."

Chief Inspector Dennis V. Coughlin, Supervisory Special Agent H. Charles Larkin of the Secret Service, and Assistant Special Agent in Charge (Criminal Affairs) Frank F. Young of the FBI were seated around him.

*And if I fuck up, right, you're off the hook? "Wohl was running the show."*

Peter Wohl immediately regretted the thought: *While that might apply to some, most, maybe, of the other chief inspectors, it was not fair to apply it to either Lowenstein or Coughlin.*

*Worse, almost certainly Lowenstein had taken the seat at the head of the table to establish his own authority, and then delegating it to me. Lowenstein is one of the good guys. And I know that.*

"Yes, sir. Thank you," Wohl said. He looked around the table. With the exception of Captain Jack Duffy, the special assistant to the commissioner for inter-agency liaison, only Captain Dave Pekach and Lieutenant Harry Wisser of Highway Patrol were in uniform.

"Indulge me for a minute, please," Wohl began. "I really don't know who knows what, so let me recap it. An ATF agent from Atlantic City, in response to a 'furnish any information' teletype from the Secret Service, came up with evidence of high-explosive destruction of a bunch of rental lockers. We're still waiting for the lab report, but the ATF explosives expert says he's pretty sure the explosive used was Composition C-4, and the detonators were also military. He also said that whoever rigged the charges knows what he's doing.

"Mr. Larkin went down there. There is a house, a cabin, on the property. Mr. Larkin feels that the unusual neatness, cleanliness, of the cabin fits in with the psychological profile the psychiatrists have given us of this guy.

"The FBI has come up with the names of the people who own the property. Richard W. and Marianne Wheatley. No address. I don't know how many Wheatleys there are in Philadelphia . . ."

"Ninety-six, Inspector," Detective Payne interrupted. Wohl looked at him coldly. He saw that he had a telephone book open on the table before him.

"None of them," Matt went on, "either Richard W. or Marianne. Not even an R. W."

"I was about to say a hell of a lot of them," Wohl said, adding with not quite gentle sarcasm, "Thank you, Payne. If I may continue?"

"Sorry," Matt said.

"And of course we don't know if these people live in Philadelphia, or Camden, or Atlantic City."

"Peter," Frank Young said. "Our office in Atlantic City has already asked the local authorities for their help."

"I'll handle Camden," Denny Coughlin announced. "I'm owed a couple of favors over there."

"What about Wilmington, Chester, the suburbs?" Wohl asked him.

"I'll handle that," Coughlin said.

"Then that leaves us, if we are to believe Detective Payne, ninety-six people to check out in Philadelphia. It may be a wild goose chase, but we can't take the chance that it's not."

"How do you want to handle it, Peter?"

"Ring doorbells," Wohl said. "I'd rather have detectives ringing them."

"Done," Lowenstein said.

"What I think they should do, Chief," Wohl said, "is ring the doorbell, ask whoever answers it if their name is Wheatley, and then ask if they own property in the Pine Barrens. If they say they do, they'll either ask why the cops want to know, and the detective will reply—or volunteer, if they don't ask—that the Jersey cops, better yet, the sheriff has called. There has been a fire in the house. The people have to be notified, and since Richard W. and Marianne Wheatley are not in the book, they are checking out all Wheatleys."

"What if it's the guy?" Captain Duffy asked.

"I don't really think," Wohl said, aware that he was furious at the stupidity of the question, and trying to restrain his temper, "that the guy is going to say, 'Right, I'm Wheatley, I own the garbage dump, and I've been using it to practice blowing up the Vice President' do you, Jack?"

"If I may, Peter?" Larkin asked.

"Certainly."

"We have to presume this fellow is mentally unstable. And we know he's at least competent, and possibly expert, around explosives. *If* we find him, we have to be very careful how we take him."

"Yes, sir," Captain Duffy said. "I can see that."

"Let me lay this out as I see it," Wohl said. "The reason I want detectives to ring the bell, Chief Lowenstein, is that most people who answer the doorbell are going to say 'No, I don't own a farm in Jersey' and any detective should be able to detect any hesitation. For the sake of argument, they find this guy. There will have to be a reaction to a detective showing up at his door. The detective does his best to calm him down. There was a fire, he's simply delivering a message. The detective goes away. Then we figure how to take him."

"We'd like to be in on that, Peter," Frank F. Young of the FBI said.

"How do you want to handle it, Peter?" Chief Lowenstein said.

"Depends on where and what the detective who's suspicious has to say, of course," Wohl replied. "But I think Stakeout, backed up by Highway."

"We've got warrants," Chief Coughlin said. "We just take the door, is that what you're saying?"

"It'd take us up to an hour to set it up," Wohl said. "Ordnance Disposal would be involved. And the district, of course another field Detective Division. By then, I hope, he would relax. And taking the doors would be, I think, the way to do it."

Coughlin grunted his agreement.

"And in the meantime, sit on him?" Lowenstein said.

"Different detectives," Wohl said, "in case he leaves."

"And what if nobody's home?" Mike Sabara asked.

"Then we sit on that address," Wohl said. "An unmarked Special Operations car, until we run out of them, and then, if nothing else, a district RPC." He looked at Lowenstein and Coughlin, and then around the table. "I'm open to suggestion."

"I suggest," Lowenstein said, breaking the silence, "that Detective Payne slide that phone book down the table to me, and somebody get me a pen, and we'll find out where these ninety-six Wheatleys all live."

The telephone book, still open, was passed down the table to Chief Lowenstein. Sergeant Tom Mahon, Chief Coughlin's driver, leaned over him and handed Chief Lowenstein two ballpoint pens.

As if they had rehearsed what they were doing, Chief Lowenstein read aloud a listing from the telephone directory, the whole thing, name, address, and telephone number, then said, "North Central" or "West" or another name of one of the seven Detective Divisions.

Most of the time, Coughlin would either grunt his acceptance of the location, or repeat it in agreement, but every once in a while they would have a short discussion as to the precise district boundaries. Finally, they would be in agreement, and Lowenstein would very carefully print the name of the Detective Division having jurisdiction over that address in the margin.

Everyone in the room watched in silence as they went through the ninety-six names.

*They could have taken that to Radio,* Peter Wohl thought. *Any radio dispatcher could have done the same thing.*

But then he changed his mind. *These two old cops know every street and alley in Philadelphia better than any radio dispatcher. They're doing this because it's the quickest way to get it done, and done correctly. But I don't really think they are unaware that everybody at this table has been impressed with their encyclopedic knowledge.*

When he had written the last entry, Lowenstein pushed the telephone book to Coughlin, who examined it carefully.

"Take this, Matty," Coughlin said, finally, holding up the telephone book. "Type it up, broken down into districts. Tom, you go with him. As soon as he's finished a page, Xerox it. Twenty-five copies, and bring it in here."

"Yes, sir," Sergeant Mahon said.

The two left the commissioner's conference room.

"Peter, are you open to suggestion?" Lowenstein asked.

"Yes, sir. Certainly."

"There's three of us, you, Coughlin, and me. I think that list, when he's finished sorting it out, we can break down into thirds. I'll take one, you take one, and Denny can take the third. We'll have the detective teams, I think we should send two to each doorbell, report to whichever of us it is. That make sense to you?"

"Yes, sir. It does."

"Sort of supervisory teams, right?" Frank F. Young of the FBI said. "Do you think it would be a good idea if I went with one of them, with you, Chief Lowenstein, and I'll get two other special agents to go with Chief Coughlin and Inspector Wohl."

"Better yet," Lowenstein said, "why don't you and Charley go with Peter? He's the man in overall charge."

"Whatever you say, of course," Young said, visibly disappointed.

Wohl thought he saw Coughlin, not entirely successfully, try to hide a smile.

When the neatly typed and Xeroxed lists were passed around, it was evident that the Wheatleys were scattered all over Philadelphia. Lowenstein, after first tactfully making it a suggestion to Wohl, assigned himself to supervise the operation in the Central and North Central detective districts. He also "suggested" that Chief Coughlin supervise the operation in the South and West Detective Divisions, which left Wohl to supervise the detectives who would be working in the East, Northeast, and Northwest Detective Divisions.

At that point, although the CONFERENCE IN PROGRESS—DO NOT ENTER sign was on display outside the conference room, the door suddenly opened and the Honorable Jerry Carlucci, mayor of Philadelphia, marched into the room.

"What's all this going to cost in overtime?" he asked, by way of greeting. "I suppose it's too much to expect that anybody would think of telling me, or for that matter the commissioner, what the hell is going on?"

"I was going to call you, Jerry . . ." Lowenstein began.

"Mr. Mayor to you, Chief, thank you very much."

". . . right about now. Peter just decided how this is going to work."

"So you tell me, Peter."

Wohl described the operation to the mayor.

He listened carefully, asked a few specific questions, grunted approval several times, and then when Wohl was finished, he stood leaning against the wall thinking it all over.

"What do the warrants say?" he asked finally.

"As little as legally possible," Lowenstein said. "Denny got them."

"They're city warrants?" Carlucci asked.

"Right," Coughlin said.

"Not federal?" the mayor asked, looking right at Frank F. Young of the FBI.

"Reasonable belief that party or parties unknown by name have in their possession certain explosives and explosive devices in violation of Section whateveritis of the state penal code," Coughlin said.

"That, of course," Young said, "unlawful possession of explosive devices is a violation of federal law."

"Have you got any warrants, Charley?" the mayor asked H. Charles Larkin.

"Mr. Mayor, we haven't tied, this is presuming we can find the guy with the explosives, we haven't tied him to the threatening letter sent to the Vice President. So far as we're concerned, getting this lunatic off the streets, separated from his explosives, solves our problem."

"So, if you want to look at it this way, Charley, you're here just as an observer?"

"That's right, Mr. Mayor."

"Would that describe the FBI's role in this, Mr. Young?" the mayor asked.

"Pretty well," Young said uncomfortably. "The FBI, of course, stands ready to provide whatever assistance we can offer."

"We appreciate that," the mayor said. "And I'm sure Inspector Wohl will call on you if he thinks he needs something."

He looked at Young to make sure that he had made his point. Then he turned to Peter Wohl.

"Before you take any doors, let me know," the mayor said. "I think I would like to be in on it."

"Yes, sir."

With that, the mayor walked out of the conference room.

*I wonder,* Peter Wohl thought, *if the mayor just happened to hear about this meeting via somebody on the night shift here, or whether Lowenstein or Coughlin called him up, and told him what was going on, sure that he would be anxious to keep the arrest, if there was one, from being taken over by the FBI or the Secret Service. Now that I think about it, Charley Larkin didn't seem very surprised when the mayor honored us with his presence.*

The food in the dining room of the Lorraine Hotel was simple, but quite tasty, and, Marion thought, very reasonably priced. There was no coffee or tea. Apparently, Marion reasoned, Father Divine had interpreted Holy Scriptures to mean that coffee was somehow sinful. He wondered how Father Divine had felt about what had been reported by Saint Timothy vis-à-vis Jesus Christ's attitude toward fermented grapes. There was no wine list, either, in the Divine Lorraine Dining Room.

It was not going to be a problem, Marion thought. He habitually took a little walk after dinner to settle his stomach. He would take one now, and was certain to come across someplace where he could get a cup of coffee.

On his way through the lobby to North Broad Street, he saw that the bulletin board in the lobby announced, *"Sacred Harp Singing, Main Ball Room, 7:30. All Welcome!"*

He wondered what in the world that meant.

When he returned from his walk, which included two cups of coffee and a very nice piece of lemon meringue pie at a Bigger Burger, the lobby was full of pleasant voices, singing, a cappella, "We Will Gather at the River."

He followed the sound of the voices, passing and noticing for the first time an oil portrait of a white middle-aged woman, wearing the whateveritwas these people wore on their heads. He wondered if that was Mrs. Father Divine, and then if she was called "Mother Divine."

He found the source of voices. It was in the main ballroom. A neatly dressed black man put out his hand, said, "Welcome, brother. Make yourself at home. Praise the Lord."

"Praise the Lord," Marion replied, and went into the ballroom and took a mimeographed program, which included the words to the hymns and spirituals on the program, from a folding chair.

He was a little uncomfortable at first but the music was lovely, and the sincerity and enthusiasm of the singers rather touching, and after a few minutes, he was quite caught up in the whole thing.

He had always liked "Rock of Ages," and other what he thought of as traditional hymns, and he had never before had the opportunity to not only hear Negro spirituals, but to join in with the singers.

Afterward, when he went to his room, he wondered if perhaps somehow the last two hours, which certainly could be interpreted as worship, would now give him an insight into Haggai 2:17.

He read it again, standing up at the desk where he had left the Bible open to it: "17. I smote you with blasting and with mildew and with hail in all the labours of your hands; yet ye turned not to me, saith the Lord."

He thought perhaps he had an insight. Viewed from one perspective, it was possible, even likely, that it was what the Lord might be saying to the Vice President, rather than directed to him.

That made a certain sense vis-à-vis "blasting," but while one might be smitten with "blasting" and "hail," being smitten with mildew made no sense. Mildew was what grew in the grouting around the tiles of a bathroom.

He undressed and took a shower, and then took the Bible to bed with him. But even after praying for insight, Haggai 2:17 made no sense to him at all.

Marion Claude Wheatley dropped off to sleep, propped up against the headboard, with the Holy Bible open on his lap.

Mr. Vincenzo Savarese, Mr. Paulo Cassandro, Mr. Gian-Carlo Rosselli, and Mr. Ricco Baltazari were seated at a table in the rear of Ristorante Alfredo. A screen had been erected around the table, to keep the customers from staring. No place had been set for Mr. Baltazari, the proprietor, who thought it might be considered disrespectful to break bread with Mr. Savarese uninvited.

"I like your Chicken Breast Alfredo," Mr. Savarese said to Mr. Baltazari, "how is it made?"

"It's really very simple, Mr. S.," Mr. Baltazari said. "Some oregano, some thyme, some chervil, a little sweet paprika for color, you grind them up, then add maybe a half cup olive oil; you marinate maybe an hour, then you broil, and then, at the last minute, a slice of cheese on top, and that's it."

"Not only is it nice, I see by the price on the menu that it probably makes a nice profit."

"Absolutely, chicken is always good that way. I'm pleased that you're pleased."

"Ricco, I have to make a decision," Mr. Savarese said. "I want your advice."

"I'm honored that you would ask me, Mr. S.," Mr. Baltazari said.

"You understand that I am under an obligation to some friends in Baltimore," Mr. Savarese said. "An obligation that I would like to meet."

"I understand," Mr. Baltazari said.

"They telephoned me just before I came here," Mr. Savarese said. "They are very anxious to make the shipment we talked about. Their man is waiting word that it's all right to come to Philadelphia."

Mr. Baltazari nodded his understanding.

"Gian-Carlo and Paulo tell me that they think everything is arranged with our new friend at the airport," Mr. Savarese said. "And on one hand, I trust their judgment. But on the other hand, I am a cautious man. I am always concerned when things seem to be going too easily. You understand?"

"Yes, Mr. Savarese, I understand."

"There are two things that concern me here," Mr. Savarese said. "One may be as important as the other. We think we have this policeman's cooperation. *Think*. It would be very embarrassing for me if he changed his mind at the last minute. And costly. If the shipment was lost, I would, as a man of honor, have to make good the loss. You understand?"

"I understand, Mr. S."

"The second thing that concerns me is the possibility that if he is not what Paulo tells me he believes he is, that, in other words, if he went either to the Narcotics Division or to the Federal Narcotics people . . . You understand?"

"Mr. S.," Mr. Rosselli said very carefully, "that word never even came up. Narcotics."

"Mr. S.," Mr. Cassandro added, "he thinks the shipment is money."

"So you have told me," Mr. Savarese said. "My question is,

would he be tempted by that much money? We certainly could not complain to the authorities that we had lost a large sum of money, could we?"

"He's not that smart, Mr. S.," Mr. Rosselli said.

"Yes. He is not smart. That worries me. He is a fool, a fool without money. Fools without money do foolish, desperate things."

"I see what you mean, Mr. S.," Mr. Rosselli said.

"We could test him," Mr. Savarese said. "That is one option. I could tell my associates in Baltimore that in the interests of safety, we should have nothing of interest to the authorities in the bag, just to be sure."

"That's an idea," Mr. Baltazari said.

"But that would make me look as if I don't have things under control here, wouldn't it?"

"I can see what you mean," Mr. Baltazari said seriously.

"Or, we can take the chance. I will tell Gian-Carlo to telephone Baltimore and tell them everything is in order. So my question to you, Ricco, is what should I do?"

Mr. Baltazari thought it over for a very long moment before he replied.

"Mr. S.," he said carefully. "You asked me, and I will tell you what I honestly think. I think we have to trust Gian-Carlo's and Paulo's judgment. If they say the cop is going to be all right, so far as I'm concerned, that's it."

Mr. Baltazari felt a flush of excitement.

*I handled that perfect,* he thought. *If I had said,* "I go for the test," *that would have meant that I thought Gian-Carlo and Paulo were wrong, that they were going to get Mr. S. in trouble. That would have really pissed them off. This way, they set it up, it fucks up somehow, it's their fault, and I'm out of it.*

Mr. Savarese nodded, then put another piece of Chicken Breast Alfredo into his mouth and chewed it slowly.

"I thank you for your honest opinion," he said, finally. "So this is what we're going to do. I'm going to have Gian-Carlo call the people in Baltimore and tell them to go ahead."

"There's not going to be a problem with the cop, Mr. S.," Mr. Rosselli said. "He needs to get out from under them markers, and he needs the cash so bad, he's pissing his pants."

"Give Ricco the information," Mr. Savarese said.

Mr. Rosselli handed Mr. Baltazari a sheet of notepaper. On it was written, "Eastern 4302. 9:45."

"That's from San Juan," Mr. Savarese explained. "Tomorrow

night, it arrives. The shipment will be in a blue American Tourister plastic suitcase. On both sides of the suitcase will be two strips of adhesive tape with shine on it."

Mr. Baltazari then asked the question foremost in his mind. He held up the piece of paper with "Eastern 4302" on it. "Mr. S., what am I supposed to do with this?"

"I value your judgment, Ricco," Mr. Savarese said. "I want you to give that to the cop. Tell him about the tape with the shine on the blue American Tourister suitcase. Look at his eyes. Make up your mind, is he reliable or not? If it smells like bad fish, then we do the test. It'll be a little embarrassing for me to have to call Baltimore, but there'll be plenty of time if you see the cop when he gets off duty, and better a little embarrassment than taking a loss like that, or worse. You agree?"

"Right, Mr. S.," Mr. Baltazari said.

His stomach suddenly hurt.

"You go see him after midnight, at that woman's apartment, and then you call Gian-Carlo. If you make the judgment that everything will be all right, then that's it. If he sees something wrong, Gian-Carlo, then you call me at the house, understand?"

"Right, Mr. S.," Mr. Rosselli said.

"I feel better," Mr. Savarese said. "Now that we've talked this over. I think I might even have a little cognac. You got a nice cognac, Ricco?"

"Absolutely, Mr. S.," Mr. Baltazari said, and got up from the table.

In the kitchen, he put a teaspoon of baking soda in half a glass of water, dissolved it, and drank it down.

Then he went and got a fresh bottle of Rémy Martin VSOP, which he knew Mr. Savarese preferred, and carried it back to the table.

At about the same time that his reliability was being discussed in Ristorante Alfredo, Corporal Vito Lanza told Officer Jerzy Masnik, his trainee, that he was going to take a break, get some coffee and a doughnut, get the hell out of the office for a few minutes, he was getting a headache.

He made his way to the Eastern Airlines area of the airport, and used his passkey to open a door marked CLOSED TO THE PUBLIC—DO NOT ENTER.

It opened on a flight of stairs, which took him down to the level of the ramp. He walked to the office from which the Eastern baggage handling operation was directed, and asked the man in charge if it would be all right if he borrowed one of the baggage train tractors for a couple of minutes.

"Help yourself," the Eastern supervisor told him.

Vito drove slowly among the airplanes parked at the lines of airways, watching as baggage handlers loaded luggage into, and off-loaded it from, the bellies of the airplanes. Twice, he stopped the tractor and got off, for a closer examination. Once he actually went inside the fuselage of a Lockheed 10-11.

No one questioned his presence. Cops are expected to be in strange places.

The way to get a particular piece of luggage off a particular airplane, Vito decided, was to stand by the conveyor belt and watch for it as it was off-loaded from the airplane, seeing on which of the carts of the baggage train it had been placed.

Once he knew that, he would drive his tractor to the door where luggage was taken from the baggage carts and loaded on the conveyor belt that would transport it, beneath the terminal, to the baggage carousel.

Taking it from the airplane or the baggage carts at the airplane would look suspicious. But with the baggage handlers busy throwing bags on the conveyor belt under the terminal, no one would notice if he removed a bag from the other side of the cart.

And if they did notice him, and someone actually asked him what he was doing, he would say that it was his mother's, or his sister's, and he was just saving her a trip to the baggage carousel.

Nobody questioned what a cop did. And he was only going to do this once. If he did it all the time, somebody might say something about it.

Vito told himself that there were laws and laws. Everybody broke some kind of law, except maybe the pope. And screwing the IRS was something everybody did. And that's all he was going to be doing, was keeping the IRS from making a pain in the ass of itself. It wasn't like he was smuggling drugs or jewels. He wouldn't be able to do that.

What he was doing, Vito convinced himself, was helping a friend, repaying a favor.

*It wasn't anything worse than some chief inspector fixing a speeding ticket for his next-door neighbor.*

*The reason Gian-Carlo Rosselli, or really the people who own the Oaks and Pines, are willing to come up with ten big ones, the four I owe them on the markers, and six besides, is like them buying*

*insurance. It's the cost of them doing business. It's not like they're
bribing me or anything. They want all that money to arrive safely
so they can pay that coal-mine guy—that lucky sonofabitch, he
probably doesn't even need it—what he won.*

*It was just lucky. They knew me, and I needed the money. That
fucking plumber is going to want his money, and with my luck
lately, I just don't have it. So this way, everybody is happy. The
plumbers, the people who own Oaks and Pines, and especially that
fucker with the coal mines who hit his number four times in a row.*

*And my run of bad luck can't keep on for fucking ever!*

Vito drove around the aircraft parking area a few minutes more,
trying to figure the best way to get the suitcase, once he had taken
it from the baggage cart, out to his car. That turned out to be simplicity itself.

There was a gate leading from the work area under the terminal
to the outside. There was a rent-a-cop working it. No rent-a-cop
was going to stop a real cop and ask him what he was doing.

*I'll just drive one of these goddamned tractors out the gate, go to
the parking lot, put the suitcase in the trunk of the Caddy, and drive
back in and give them their tractor back.*

He decided to try it. It worked like a jewel. He went out of the
gate, drove to the parking lot, went in the trunk of the Caddy, got
back on the tractor, and drove back through the gate. The rent-a-
cop didn't look at him twice.

*Why should he? I'm a police corporal. If I'm riding around on
an Eastern Airlines tractor, so what? What business was that of a
rent-a-cop?*

Vito drove the tractor back to the Eastern office and told the guy
he'd returned it.

"Anytime," the Eastern guy said. "Support your local sheriff,
right?"

Starting at fifteen minutes to midnight, within minutes of each
other, automobiles carrying Chief Inspectors Matt Lowenstein and
Denny Coughlin, Supervisory Special Agent H. Charles Larkin of
the Secret Service, and A-SAC (Criminal) Frank F. Young of the
FBI arrived at the headquarters of the Special Operations Division.

The building, and especially the corridor outside Peter Wohl's—
what had been the principal's—office, and the office itself were
crowded with senior police officers. All the participants in the
earlier meeting in the commissioner's office, except Mayor
Carlucci, were present. In addition, the commanding officers of

Central, North Central, and Northwest Detective Divisions; the commanding officers of Ordnance Disposal and Stakeout; and Captain Jack Duffy, the special assistant to the commissioner for inter-agency liaison, had either been summoned or had naturally migrated to the Schoolhouse as the center of the operation.

Three inspectors, who had been neither summoned nor invited, were also in Peter Wohl's office when Chief Lowenstein marched in. They were the commanding officers of the South and North Detective Divisions and the Tactical Division. Their subordinates had made known to them the orders they had received from Chiefs Lowenstein and Coughlin, and they wanted to know what was going on.

Lowenstein ordered everyone out of Wohl's office but Coughlin, Wohl, and the three inspectors and the federal agents.

"Peter and I decided to hold this here, rather than in the Roundhouse," Lowenstein began, "for a couple of reasons. First of all, it's on my way home . . ."

He paused for the expected chuckle.

*"Peter and I decided"? Wohl thought. Inspector Peter Wohl is not only outranked by you, but, until very recently, by everybody else in this room. Despite his reputation within the Department as a real hard-ass, Lowenstein sometimes can be very gracious and kind.*

". . . and for another, all these white shirts showing up at the Roundhouse at midnight might give the gentlemen of the press the idea that something's going on. Charley Larkin thinks, and I agree, that the less the press is involved until we catch this guy, the better."

"The less the press is involved, the better, period," Inspector Wally Jenks said.

There were chuckles and grunts of approval.

"There's a real nasty copycat aspect to something like this," Charley Larkin said. "A lunatic who has been sitting around harmlessly studying his navel sees another lunatic is getting a lot of attention in the papers and on TV, and promptly decides the thing for him to do to get some attention is also blow something up. If I had my druthers, not a word of this would appear in the papers."

"Sometimes, Charley," Frank F. Young of the FBI said, "it's a good idea to let the taxpayers know where their money is going."

"Let me bring everybody up-to-date on where we stand," Lowenstein said, cutting off what could have been an argument about dealing with the press.

He went on: "We had ninety-six Wheatleys on the list. Eighty-nine of them have been contacted, and are off the list, which means we are down to seven. These are Wheatleys who were not at home when we rang doorbells. Or didn't answer the doorbell.

"We have detectives in unmarked cars sitting on the seven, backed up by Highway RPCs. If anyone leaves those seven houses, we will talk to them.

"Of the seven, two look more promising than the others. One is listed under the name of Wheatley, Stephen J., in the 5600 block of Frazier Avenue, and the other is Wheatley, M. C., in the 120 block of Farragut. Both these houses are in middle class neighborhoods, which fits in both with somebody owning property in the sticks in Jersey and with the psychological profile we have of this guy. He's well educated, and it would figure he's making a decent living.

"Inspector Wohl believes, and Chief Coughlin and I agree, that taking either of these doors tonight would probably be counterproductive."

"Can I ask why?" Inspector Jenks asked.

"Worst case scenario, Inspector," Wohl said. "He's in there. He's got explosives. He sets them off, and takes half the neighborhood with him."

"Next worse case scenario, Wally," Chief Coughlin said. "He's not in there. He's the editor of the *Catholic Messenger*. On his way to complain to the cardinal archbishop that while he and wife were having a retreat at Sacred Heart Monastery, the cops took his front and back doors and scared hell out of his cat, he stops by the Philadelphia *Ledger* to tell Arthur Nelson what Carlucci's Commandos have done to him."

That produced more outright laughter than chuckles.

"And Jerry Carlucci, Wally," Lowenstein added, "said he wants to be there if we take anybody's door."

"I agree with Inspector Wohl too," H. Charles Larkin said. "I don't think, if our man is in one of these houses, that he's liable to do anything tonight. Unless, of course, we panic him. Then all bets are off."

"So what Peter has come up with is this," Lowenstein went on. "At half past seven tomorrow morning, it gets light at six-fifty, we are going to send detectives to the houses adjacent to the houses in question and see what the neighbors know about Wheatley, Stephen J., and Wheatley, M. C. If it looks at all that there's a chance he's our guy, we evacuate the houses in the area, and then we take the door. Stakeout will take the door, backed up by Highway and Ordnance Disposal."

"And what if he's not our man?" Inspector Jenks asked.

"Then we take a look at the other five houses where nobody was home. There will be people still on them, of course."

*And if we shoot blanks there too,* Wohl thought, *we're back to square one.*

"So what happens now?" Inspector Jenks asked.

"I don't know about you, Wally," Coughlin said, "but I'm going to go home and go to bed."

"You each, you and Chief Lowenstein, are going to take one of these houses?" Jenks asked.

"That's up to Inspector Wohl," Lowenstein said. "Peter?"

"I'm going to be between the two houses," Wohl said. "Which door we take first, if we take any at all, will depend on what the detectives come up with when they talk to the neighbors. We'll do them one at a time."

"And the mayor's going to be there?"

"Yes, sir. That's what he said."

"And we'll be with Peter and the mayor," Lowenstein said. "Denny's going to pick him up at his house in Chestnut Hill at seven."

Lowenstein put a match to a large black cigar, then turned to Wohl.

"Is that about it, Peter?"

"Yes, sir. All that remains to be done is to pass the word."

"Then I'm going home," Lowenstein said, and walked out of the room.

The meeting was over.

# TWENTY-SEVEN

As Mr. Ricco Baltazari walked down the corridor to the door of Mrs. Antoinette Marie Wolinski Schermer's apartment, at quarter to one in the morning, he was aware that several things were bothering him.

There was the obvious, of course, that he was between the rock (Mr. Savarese) and the hard place (Mssrs. Gian-Carlo Rosselli and Paulo Cassandro) about this goddamned cop. If the cop either didn't look like he could handle what was required of him or, worse, that he was maybe setting them up, he would have to tell Mr. S. that he thought so, or risk winding up pushing up grass in the Tinnicum Swamps out by the airport, if something went wrong.

But if he did that, it was the same thing as saying that Gian-Carlo and Paulo were a couple of assholes who were going to get Mr. S. in trouble. They would be insulted, and they both had long memories.

And that wasn't all. There was the business between the goddamned cop and Tony. He was having trouble remembering that all she was, was a dumb Polack who he liked to screw and nothing

402

more. That had been possible as long as he hadn't actually seen what was going on.

But now he was going to be in her apartment, actually *their* apartment, where they'd had some really great times in the sack, and where she was now fucking the goddamned cop.

*Well, shit, there's nothing I can do about it.*

He pushed her doorbell and in a moment Tony answered it, wearing a fancy nightgown he'd bought her, and which he now clearly remembered taking off her.

"Whaddaya say, Tony?"

"Hello, Ricco."

"Your boyfriend here? I'd like a word with him."

"Come on in, Ricco," Tony said, and then raised her voice. "Vito, honey, it's Mr. Baltazari. He wants to talk to you."

"It's who?"

"I'm a friend of Mr. Rosselli, Vito," Ricco said.

The goddamned cop came into the living room in his underwear.

*My living room, I'm paying the freight. And my girl, I'm paying the freight there too. And here's this sonofabitch* in his underwear.

"Vito," Ricco said, putting out his hand, "Mr. Rosselli got tied up. He had to go to the Poconos, as a matter of fact, and he asked me to drop by and pass a little information to you."

"What did you say your name was?"

"Baltazari, Ricco Baltazari. I run the Ristorante Alfredo."

"Oh," the goddamned cop said. He did not offer to shake hands. "You know Tony?"

"We seen each other around, right, Tony?"

"You could put it that way, I guess," Tony said.

"So what's the message?"

"Tony, could you give us a minute alone? Get yourself a beer or something?"

"Whatever you say, Mr. Baltazari," Tony said and went into the bedroom. She turned as she closed the door and gave him a look.

"That shipment you and Mr. Rosselli was talking about?" Ricco began.

"What about it?"

"It's coming in tomorrow night. I mean tonight, it's already today, ain't it? On Eastern Flight 4302 from San Juan. At nine forty-five."

Vito Lanza nodded.

"It's going to be in a blue American Tourister suitcase, one of the plastic ones, and there will be two red reflective strips on each side of the suitcase," Ricco went on.

Vito nodded again.

"That going to pose any problems for you, Vito?"

"What kind of problems?"

"You're not going to write that down, or anything?"

"I can remember Eastern 4302 at nine forty-five."

"From San Juan."

"Eastern 4302 is always from San Juan," Vito said. "Every day but Sunday."

*He's a wiseass. He's an asshole who gambles with money he doesn't have, a fucking cop too dumb to know he's being set up, or that the only reason he's fucking Tony is because I told her to fuck him, and he's a wiseass.*

"I'm going to ask you again, Vito. Is that going to pose any problems?"

"What kind of problems?"

"Money does funny things to people. Nothing personal, you understand. But you understand why I have to ask."

"I understand."

"I'm sure you're not that kind of a guy. Mr. Rosselli speaks very well of you, but there are some people, when they get around that kind of money, they do foolish things. Foolish things that could get them killed."

"I'm not that kind of guy," Vito said evenly.

"I'm sure you're not," Ricco said.

"But I do have a couple of questions."

"What kind of questions?"

"Two questions. What do I do with the suitcase once I get it out of the airport?"

*Jesus Christ, I don't know. Didn't they tell him, for Christ's sake?*

"Didn't Mr. Rosselli tell you what to do with it?"

"If he had told me, I wouldn't be asking," Vito said calmly.

"Then I guess we'll have to ask him, won't we?" Ricco replied. "What was the other question?"

"When and where do I get my money?"

*You're a greedy sonofabitch too, aren't you? Well, I guess if I was into Oaks and Pines for four grand worth of markers, four grand that I didn't have, I'd be a little greedy myself.*

"You don't worry about that, Vito. You carry out your end of the deal, Mr. Rosselli will carry out his."

"Yeah."

Ricco walked to the telephone and dialed Gian-Carlo Rosselli's number.

"Yeah?"

"Ricco. I'm with our friend."

"How's things going?"

"He wants to know what he should do with the basket of fruit."

"Shit, I didn't think about that," Rosselli said. There was a long pause. "Ask him if he could take it home, and we'll arrange to pick it up there."

Ricco covered the microphone with his hand.

"Mr. Rosselli says you should take it home, and he'll arrange to have it picked up. You got any problem with that?"

"No," Vito said, after thinking it over for a moment. "That'd be all right."

"He says that's fine," Ricco said.

"Okay. And everything else is fine too, right?"

"Everything else is fine too."

Mr. Rosselli hung up on Mr. Baltazari.

"Okay," Ricco said. "Everything's fine. I'll get out of your hair."

Vito Lanza nodded.

Ricco turned and walked to the door and opened it. Then he turned.

"I got to make the point," he said. "You know what happens to people who do foolish things, right?"

"Yeah, I know," Vito said. "And I already told you I'm not foolish."

"Good," Ricco said and went through the door.

When, a few minutes before one A.M., Matt Payne drove into the underground garage at his apartment at the wheel of the unmarked Special Operations Division car he had been given for the business tomorrow morning, he was surprised to find that the space where he normally parked the Bug was empty.

*As if I need another reminder that my ass is dragging, I have no idea where the Bug is. It's almost certainly at the Schoolhouse—where else would it be?—but I'll be damned if I remember leaving it there.*

He parked the Ford, and rode the elevator to the third floor, and then walked up the stairs to his apartment.

The red light on the answering machine, which he had come to hate with an amazing passion toward an inanimate object, was blinking.

*I don't want to hear what messages are waiting for me. They will be, for one thing, probably not messages at all, but the buzz, hummm, click indication that my callers had not elected to leave a message, in other words, that Evelyn was back dialing my number. Or it might actually be a message from Evelyn, which would be even worse.*

*On the other hand, it might be a bulletin from the Schoolhouse; Wohl might have thought of some other way in which I can be useful before I meet O'Dowd at half past six, which is 5.5 hours from now.*

He was still debating whether to push the PLAY button when the phone rang.

*It has to be either Wohl or O'Dowd. And if it's not, if it's Evelyn, I'll just hang up.*

"Payne."

"Christ, where the hell have you been?" Charley McFadden's voice demanded.

"What the hell do you want?"

"Have you been at the sauce?"

"No, as a matter of fact, I haven't. But it seems like a splendid idea. You running a survey, or what?"

"Matt, you better get your ass out here, right now," Charley said.

"Out where, and why?"

"I'm on the job. Northwest Detectives. Just get your ass out here, right now," McFadden said, and hung up.

*What the hell is that all about?*

*But Charley's not pulling my chain. I can tell from his voice when he's doing that. Whatever this is, it is not a manifestation of Irish and/or police humor.*

He had, in what he thought of as a Pavlovian reflex, laid his revolver on the mantelpiece. He reclaimed it and went down the stairs and took the elevator to the basement.

The Porsche was where he remembered parking it, and he took the keys to it from his pocket and was about to put them in the door when he reconsidered.

*Whatever Charley McFadden wants, it's personal, and I don't want to be about personal business when I run into one of Wohl's station wagons full of nuns. But on the other hand, it was made goddamned clear to me that Wohl wants to know where I am, second by second, and there's no radio in the Porsche. The minute I drive the Porsche out of here, Wohl will call, and when he gets the answering machine, will get on the radio. And I won't answer.*

He got in the unmarked car and drove out of the garage. There wasn't much traffic, and he was lucky with the lights. The only one he caught was at North Broad Street and Ridge Avenue, which gave him a chance to look at the Divine Lorraine Hotel, and wonder what the hell went on in there.

*Wouldn't the bishop of the Episcopal Diocese of Philadelphia have a heart attack if there was suddenly a booming voice from heaven saying, "You're wrong, Bishop; my boy Father Divine has it right"?*

He remembered he hadn't reported in. He switched to the J frequency and told Police Radio that William Fourteen was en route to Northwest Detectives.

He then wondered, as he continued up North Broad Street, whether what Charley was so upset about was the missing Bug.

*I know goddamned well I left it at the apartment. Stolen? Out of the basement, past the rent-a-cop, who knows who it belongs to? And who the hell would steal the Bug when the Porsche was sitting right next to it? Who would steal the Bug if nothing was sitting right next to it?*

That impeccable logical analysis of the situation collapsed immediately upon Detective Payne's entering the parking lot of Northwest Detectives, which shares quarters with the 35th District at Broad and Champlost Streets.

There was the Bug.

*Jesus, what the hell is this all about?*

He went in the building and took the stairs to the second floor two at a time.

"I'm Detective Payne of Special Operations," Matt said, smiling at the desk man just inside the squad room. "Charley . . ."

"I know who you are," the desk man said with something less than overwhelming charm. He raised his voice: "McFadden!"

Charley appeared around the corner of a wall inside.

"What's with my car?" Matt asked.

McFadden, who looked very uncomfortable, didn't reply. He came to Matt, and motioned for him to follow him down the stairs.

They went into the district holding cells.

"You got him?" Matt asked. "Brilliant work, Detective McFadden!"

"You better take a look at this," Charley said, pointing at one of the cells.

A very faint bulb illuminated the cell interior just enough for Matt to be able to make out a figure lying on the sheet steel bunk.

As his eyes adjusted to the gloom, Matt saw that the figure was in a skirt, and thus a female, and there was just enough time for the thought, *Christ, a* woman *stole my Bug?* when he recognized the woman.

"Jesus Christ!" he said.

Charley McFadden tugged on his sleeve and pulled him out of the detention cell area.

"Okay, what happened?" Matt asked, hoping that he was managing to sound matter-of-fact and professional.

"I was out, serving a warrant, and when I brought the critter in here, two Narcotics undercover guys, I know both of them, brought her in."

"On what charges?"

McFadden did not reply directly.

"They were watching a house on Bouvier, near Susquehanna," he said, avoiding Matt's eyes. "Thinking maybe they'd get lucky and be able to grab the delivery boy."

"What delivery boy? What are you talking about?"

"You know where I mean? Bouvier, near Susquehanna?"

Matt searched his memory and came up with nothing specific, just a vague picture of Susquehanna Avenue as it moved through the slums of North Philadelphia near Temple University.

"No," Matt confessed. "Not exactly."

"You don't go in there alone, you understand?" Charley said.

Matt understood. He was not talking about it being the sort of place it was unwise for Miss Penelope Detweiler of Chestnut Hill to visit alone, he was talking about a place where an armed police officer did not go alone, for fear of his life.

He nodded.

"So they see this white girl in a Volkswagen come down Bouvier, and that attracts their attention. So she circles the block, they think looking for the house they're sitting on. And weaving. They think she's either drunk or stoned. These are not nice guys, Matt, do-gooders. But the thought of what was liable to happen to a white girl, stoned or drunk, going in that house was too much."

"Oh, God!"

"So one of them got out of the car and ran down the block, and the next time she came around, he flagged her down. She almost ran over him. But he stopped her, and saw she was drunk. . . ."

*"Drunk?"* Matt asked.

*Please, God!* Drunk*, not drugged.*

"Drunk," Charley said. "So he put cuffs on her and got in her car. She told them she's your girlfriend. So they tried to call you, and when they couldn't find you, brought her here. They know we're pals."

"They know who she is?"

"No. Just that she's your girl. She didn't have an ID. For that matter, not even a purse. Just a couple of hundred-dollar bills in her underwear."

"What's she charged with?"

"Right now, nothing. I called in some favors."

"Jesus, Charley!"

"Yeah, well, you'd do the same for me," McFadden said.

*Absolutely. The very next time that your girlfriend, Miss Mary-Margaret McCarthy, R.N., who is probably the only virgin over thirteen that I know, gets herself hauled in by an undercover Narcotics officer, I'll pull in whatever favors I can to get her off.*

*Christ, I feel like crying.*

"I don't suppose you have any handcuffs, do you?"

*Jesus Christ, handcuffs? What for?*

Matt shook his head, no.

McFadden reached behind him, where he wore his handcuffs draped over his belt. He handed them to Matt.

"You got a key?"

Matt nodded.

*The cuffs are so it will appear to the uniforms in the lobby that I'm taking her out of here under arrest.*

"She's . . . uh. She was pretty drunk, Matt. And mad about being in here."

"You're saying, I'm going to need the cuffs?"

McFadden nodded.

"She's passed out. But if she wakes up in the car, I think you'd be better off if she was cuffed."

"God!"

"Dailey!" McFadden called.

The turnkey, a tired-looking uniform who looked to be about fifty, came up to them.

"Pete Dailey, Matt Payne," McFadden made the introductions. The two men shook hands, but neither said a word.

"Open it up, please, Pete," McFadden said.

The turnkey unlocked the cell, slid the barred door open, and then walked away.

Penny Detweiler did not stir.

Charley went into the cell. Matt followed him. Charley looked at

Matt, then put out his hand for the handcuffs. When Matt gave them to him, he pulled Penny's wrists behind her, and put the cuffs on her wrists.

The smell in the cell was foul. Matt wondered if he was going to further embarrass himself by being sick. And then he realized that the smell was coming from Penny.

She had lost control of her bowels, and probably her bladder as well.

*The proper word for that,* Detective Payne thought, *is "incontinent."*

And then he was swept by nausea, and barely made it to the lidless toilet in the corner of the cell in time.

After a moment, as he became aware that he was soaked in a clammy sweat, he heard Charley ask, "You okay, buddy?"

"Yeah," Matt said, and forced himself to his feet.

He went to the bunk, and the two men pulled Penny erect. She was limp, and surprisingly heavy.

*Jesus, she stinks!*

They half carried, half dragged her from the detention cell area to the desk.

Officer Peter Dailey appeared with a newspaper.

"What are you driving?" he asked.

"A blue unmarked Ford," Matt said.

Officer Dailey preceded them out of the building and to the car, where he opened the rear door and spread the newspaper over the seat.

"I'll take her shoulders," Charley McFadden said. "You take her feet."

McFadden backed into the rear seat, dragging Penny after him, and then exited the car by the other door.

He came around the back as Matt was closing the opposite door.

"You going to be able to handle her?" Charley asked.

"Yeah," Matt said.

*What the hell am I going to do with her? I can't take her home in this condition. And I can't take her to the apartment. What would I do with her when I have to go to work?*

"I can get off to go with you."

"Charley, what you can do is call my sister. She's not in the book. The number is 928-5923. Call her and tell her I'm on my way."

"Nine Two Eight, Five Nine Two Three," Charley repeated, setting the number in his memory. "Do I tell her why?"

"Tell her I need some help," Matt said. "Tell her to come down into the lobby and wait for me."

"I can go with you, buddy."

"I can handle it," Matt said. "Thank you, Charley."

"Forget it," McFadden said, and touched Matt's arm gently. "I'm sorry, Matt."

Matt walked around the front of the Ford and got behind the wheel.

He had not gone more than four blocks south on North Broad Street before there was the sound of retching and the smell of vomitus was added to the smell of feces and urine.

He rolled down his window so that he would not be sick again.

Amelia Payne, M.D., fully dressed, came out of the plate-glass doors leading to the lobby of 2601 Parkway as Matt pulled up.

He got out of the car.

"Where is she, in the back?"

*Did Charley tell her what happened? Or did she figure that out herself?*

"Yes. She's in pretty bad shape."

"What did she take, do you know? She may have overdosed. You should have taken her to University Hospital."

"I think she's just drunk," Matt said. "I don't know. Can you tell?"

"Just drunk? How fortunate for you," Amy said.

She pulled open the rear door and climbed in. Matt saw the bright light of a flashlight, and when he looked, saw that Amy had pushed Penny's eyes open and was shining the light into her eyes. Then she slapped her, twice, three times.

"What have you taken?" Matt heard Amy ask, several times, but could not hear a reply, if there was one.

Amy backed out of the car.

"Let's get her upstairs," she said. "Can you manage? Should I get the doorman?"

"Just make sure the doors are open," Matt said.

He reached in the car and pulled Penny out, bent and threw her over his shoulder in the fireman's carry, and carried her into the lobby and into the elevator.

Amy followed him in and pushed the button. The door closed and the elevator began to rise. Amy turned to face him.

"You sonofabitch, I told you this was liable to happen!" she said bitterly.

"I don't know what happened. She came to the apartment, we had Chinese, and then I went to work."

"I'll tell you what happened. One of your harem showed up at your apartment. Penny called me about nine-thirty."

He didn't reply.

"God *damn* you, Matt," Amy said as the elevator door opened at her floor. She walked off the elevator and down the corridor and by the time Matt got there had the door open.

"Take her in the bathroom," Amy ordered, and led the way.

She turned on the bathtub faucets, then turned to Matt.

"We're going to have to get those things off her wrists and undress her," Amy said. "How we're going to do that in here, I don't know. Can you lower her to the floor?"

"I can try," Matt said.

He dropped to his knees, and then Amy turned from the tub and helped him lower Penny to the tiles of the bathroom floor. He unlocked the handcuffs.

"Help me undress her," Amy said, and then when she saw the look on his face: "Don't look shocked, dammit, you've seen her naked before. And it's your fault she's like this."

Amy, somewhere in the process, disappeared for a moment and returned with a roll of paper towels, with which she cleaned up most of the mess around Penny's groin. Then Matt lowered Penny into the tub, and Amy finished the cleaning process.

Penny made noises, not quite groans, but much like them, but was not fully conscious. Once, she slipped down in the tub and Amy ordered Matt to slide her back up.

Finally, rather coldly, Matt thought, Amy turned on the shower, and as the water drained, she used it to rinse Penny off, as a hose might be used to clear a sidewalk.

"Get her out of there," she said, finally. "Be careful. She's slippery."

Matt got Penny out of the tub and held her up by locking his hands under her arms and breasts. Amy made a halfhearted effort to dry her with a towel, then bent and picked up her feet, and they carried her into Amy's spare bedroom and put her between the sheets.

"For what the hell it's worth," Matt said. "I'm sorry."

"So am I," Amy said. "And for what the hell it's worth, it just occurred to me that if you were not a cop, this would probably be more of a disaster than it is."

"What happens now?"

"You get out of here. I call the Detweilers, who probably need a padded cell themselves by now, and tell them Penny is here with me. What happens in the morning, God knows."

"From what I understand, the Narcs got her before she could buy any drugs," Matt said.

"You sound as if you actually care," Amy said.

"Fuck you, Amy! God damn you! Of course I care."

"Get out of here, Matt," Amy said.

When he got back to the underground garage at his apartment, Matt took the newspaper from the back seat. They had protected the upholstery from Penny's incontinence, but when she had vomited, that had gone onto the floor carpet, where there were no newspapers.

He went up to his apartment and returned with Lysol and everything else in the under the sink cabinet he thought might be helpful in cleaning the carpet and getting rid of the smell.

It still smelled like vomitus, so he went back to the apartment and got the bottle of Lime after-shave Amy had given him for Christmas and sprinkled all that was left over the interior of the car.

It was three when he climbed the stairs for the last time.

*The fucking smell has followed me up here!*

He then realized that his suit was soiled, probably ruined.

*Can you get that shit, accurate word, shit, out of suiting material?*

He took his clothing off, down to his skin, put on a bathrobe, and then carried the suit, the shirt, the necktie, and the underwear down to the basement and jammed it into one of the commercial garbage cans.

Then he went back to his apartment and showered and shaved and waited for it to grow light by watching television. He fell asleep in his armchair at four-thirty. At five-thirty, the alarm went off.

At ten minutes to six, as Peter Wohl was measuring coffee grounds into the basket of his machine, his out-of-tune "Be It Ever So Humble" door chimes sounded.

He went quickly through the door, wondering who the hell it could be. Usually, a telephone call preceded an early morning call.

*Unless, of course, it's my father, who, I suspect, really hopes to catch me with some lovely in here.*

It was Captain Richard Olsen, of Internal Affairs.

"Good morning, Swede," Wohl said. "What gets you out of bed at this hour?"

"I need to talk to you, and I didn't want it to be over the phone."

*Olsen wouldn't do this unless he thought it was necessary.*

"Come on in. I'm just making coffee."

"It's been a long time since I've been here. I remember the couch. What was her name?"

"What was whose name?"

"That interior decorator. You really had the hots for her."

"I forget," Wohl said.

"The hell you do," Olsen chuckled.

"You had breakfast?"

"No. But that doesn't mean you have to feed me."

"There's bacon and eggs. That all right?"

"Fine. Can I help?"

"You can make bacon and eggs while I get dressed," Wohl said. "And I'll finish the coffee."

"Lanza is dirty," Olsen said. "Or it goddamned well looks that way."

"I hope it won't require action between seven and nine this morning," Wohl said.

"No."

"Good, then I can get dressed," Wohl said, and went into his bedroom.

When he came out, he said, "What I really am curious about is why you couldn't have told me that on the phone?"

"We have a wiretap of questionable legality," Olsen said.

"How questionable?"

"Absolutely illegal," Olsen said.

"Oh, shit," Wohl said. "And it was found? Are you in trouble, Swede?"

"The tap is gone, and we were not caught."

"Who's we? You knew about this?"

"No, of course not. Can I start at the beginning?"

"The bacon's burning," Wohl said.

Olsen quickly took the pan off the burner and quickly forked bacon strips out of it.

"Well done, not destroyed," he said.

"Thank God for small blessings," Wohl said. "*I'll* make the eggs. Can you handle the toaster?"

"I don't know. I used to think I could fry bacon without a problem."

"Give it a try. Tell me about the tap."

"You remember I told you about Sergeant Framm and Detective Pillare losing Lanza at the airport, and your man Payne saving their ass?"

"Yeah."

"Yeah, well, Framm was humiliated by that. So he thought he'd make up for it by being Super Cop. He tapped the Schermer woman's line."

"How did you find out?"

"You really want to know?"

"Yeah, I think I better know."

"He told me," Olsen said.

"Oh, Jesus! Now I'm sorry I asked."

"He means well, Peter. I think he just watches too many cop shows on the TV. *They* don't have to get a warrant for a tap."

"We do. I hope you told him that."

"What do you think?"

"Not that we could use it, but what did he hear?"

"They tailed Lanza from the airport when he went off tour at midnight. He went to the Schermer woman's apartment. At quarter to one, he was visited by Mr. Ricco Baltazari. . . ."

"The Ristorante Alfredo Ricco Baltazari?"

"One and the same. He stayed about ten minutes. While he was there, a male, almost certainly Baltazari, called somebody, no name, but Organized Crime told me the number is the unlisted number of Mr. Gian-Carlo Rosselli."

"You didn't tell Organized Crime why you wanted to know, I hope?"

"No. Just asked if they had a name to go with the number."

Olsen took a notebook from his pocket, and opened it.

"Ricco told the no-name guy he was with quote, our friend, end quote, and that the friend, quote, wants to know what he should do with the basket of fruit, unquote."

"Swede, did you listen to the tape?"

"What tape?"

"Is that how you're going to play it?"

Olsen shrugged helplessly.

"Was there a reply?" Wohl asked.

"No name replied, quote, Ask him if he could take it home, and we'll arrange to pick it up there, unquote. Then Ricco replied, quote, He says that's fine, unquote."

Wohl grunted.

"That's all?"

"Two more lines: Unnamed, quote, Okay. And everything else is fine too, right? unquote, to which Ricco replies, quote, Everything else is fine too, unquote."

"Being the clever detective that I am, I don't think the basket of fruit is oranges and grapefruit and things of that nature," Wohl said. "Drugs?"

"What else?" Olsen said. "Rosselli is a heavy hitter."

"Lanza is going to somehow get his hands on this 'fruit basket' at the airport, get it away from the airport, and take it home. Where Rosselli will arrange to have it picked up, right?"

"That's how I see it, Peter."

"God, I'd like to bag Rosselli and Baltazari picking it up," Wohl said.

"Maybe we can," Olsen said.

"Don't hold your breath," Wohl said. "They'll send some punk. They don't take risks."

"Maybe we'll get lucky," Olsen said.

"I have the feeling this will happen tonight," Olsen said.

"Then get Sergeant Whatsisname off the job."

"Framm. He's gone. I have a suggestion, or maybe I'm asking for a favor . . ."

"Either way, what?"

"Sergeant O'Dowd. Can I have him?"

"Sure," Wohl replied after a just perceptible hesitation. "Can I make a suggestion?"

"Of course."

"Have somebody, preferably two men, on both Lanza's house and the girlfriend's apartment, from right now until whatever happens with the fruit basket happens."

"That may take two or three days, longer."

"So what? I don't want this to go wrong. Maybe we *can* catch Rosselli or Baltazari too."

"I don't suppose there's anybody else you could let me have?"

"Not until we catch this fruitcake who wants to disintegrate the Vice President."

"How's that going?"

"At eight o'clock, we may or may not take a couple of doors behind which he may or may not be hiding. Not well, in other words."

"I'll handle the Lanza thing myself if it comes down to that. If I haven't forgotten how to surveil somebody."

"I'll send Tony Harris down to you. I'll have him call you. You tell him when and where. I really would like to put one of these Mafiosos in the slam with our dirty cop."

"Thank you," Olsen said.

"I didn't hear anything you said about an illegal tap, Swede. The bacon was burning or something."

"Thank you, Peter."

# TWENTY-EIGHT

At 7:25 A.M., as they sat in a nearly new Ford sedan in the 1100 block of Farragut Street, a very large, expensively tailored police officer turned to a somewhat smaller, but equally expensively tailored police officer and smiled.

"You are really quite dapper this morning, Matthew, my boy," Sergeant Jason Washington said approvingly. "I like that suit. Tripler?"

"Brooks Brothers. Just following orders. Sergeant: You told me to dress like a lawyer."

"And so you have. But despite looking like one of the more successful legal counsel to the Mafioso, somehow I suspect that all is not perfect in your world. Is there anything I can do?"

"Things are not, as a matter of fact, getting better and better, every day, in every way," Matt said.

"My question, Matthew, my boy, was, 'Is there anything I can do?' "

"I wish there were," Matt said.

"Try me," Washington said. "What is the precise nature of your problem? An *affaire de coeur*, perhaps?"

"A couple of undercover guys from Narcotics arrested Penny Detweiler last night, as she was cruising in the vicinity of Susquehanna and Bouvier."

The joking tone was gone from Washington's voice when he replied, replaced with genuine concern.

"Damn! I'm sorry to hear that. I'd hoped that—what was that place they sent her? In Nevada?—would help her."

"The Lindens. Apparently the fix didn't take."

"What have they charged her with?"

"Nothing. They picked her up for drunk driving before she was able to make her connection. She gave them my name. They couldn't find me, but they knew that Charley McFadden and I are close, so they took her to Northwest Detectives, and he got them to turn her loose to me."

"Aside from trying to make a buy, there is no other reason I can think of that she would be in that area," Washington said.

"No, there's not. She was trying to make a buy. And according to McFadden, if the undercover guys hadn't taken her in, she'd probably have had her throat cut."

"If she was lucky," Washington said. "I'm sorry, Matt. That slipped out. But McFadden is right. Where is she now?"

"I took her to my sister. My sister the shrink."

"*I* admire your sister," Washington said. "That was the thing to do."

"William Seven," the radio went off. "William One."

Matt grabbed the microphone.

"Seven," he said.

"It's that time," Wohl's voice metallically announced.

Matt looked at Washington, who nodded.

"On our way," Matt said into the microphone.

They got out of the Ford. Washington opened the trunk and took out a briefcase, and then a second, and handed one to Matt.

They walked up Farragut Street, hoping they looked like two successful real estate salesmen beginning their day early, crossed the intersection, and walked halfway down the block.

There they climbed the stairs of a house, crossed the porch, and rang the doorbell.

They could hear footsteps inside but it was a long minute before the door was finally opened to them by a woman of maybe thirty-

five, obviously caught three quarters of the way through getting
dressed for work.

"Yes, what is it?" she asked, somewhat shy of graciously, looking with curiosity between them.

Washington held out his identification.

"Madam, I'm Sergeant Washington of the Police Department
and this is Detective Payne. We would very much like a moment of
your time. May we please come in?"

The woman turned and raised her voice.

"Bernie, it's the cops!"

"The cops?" an incredulous voice replied.

A moment later Bernie, a very thin, stylishly dressed, or half-
dressed, man appeared.

"Sir, I'm Sergeant Washington of the Police Department and this
is Detective Payne. We would very much like a moment of your
time. May we please come in?"

"Yeah, sure. Come on in. Is something the matter?"

"Thank you very much," Jason Washington said. "You're Mr.
and Mrs. Crowne, is that right?"

"I'm Bernie Crowne," Bernie said.

The woman colored slightly.

*You are not, I deduce brilliantly,* Matt thought, Mrs. *Crowne.*

"Say, my wife's not behind this is she? My ex-wife?" Bernie
Crowne asked.

"No, sir. This inquiry has to do with your neighbor, Mr.
Wheatley."

"Marion?" Bernie asked. "What about him?"

"We've been trying to get in touch with Mr. Wheatley for several days now, Mr. Crowne, and we can't seem to catch him at
home."

"What did he do? Rob a bank?"

"Oh, no. Nothing like that. Actually, we're not even sure we
have the right Mr. Wheatley. There has been a fire in New Jersey, at
a summer place, in what they call the Pine Barrens. The New Jersey State Police are trying to locate the owner. And they don't have
a first name."

"Bullshit," Mr. Crowne said. "They don't send sergeants and detectives out to do that. My brother is a lieutenant in the 9th District,
Sergeant. So you tell me what this is all about, or I'll call him, and
he'll find out."

"Call him," Washington said flatly. "If he has any questions about what I'm doing here, tell him to call Chief Inspector Lowenstein."

Bernie looked at Washington for a moment.

"Okay. So go on. Marion's got a house in Jersey that burned down?"

"Do you have any idea where we could find Mr. Wheatley?"

"He works somewhere downtown. In a bank, I think."

"And Mrs. Wheatley?"

"There is no Mrs. Wheatley," the woman said.

Bernie held his hand at the level of his neck and made a waving motion with it, and then let his wrist fall limp.

"You don't *know* that, Bernie," the woman said.

"If it walks like a duck, quacks like a duck, right, Sergeant?"

"Most of the time," Washington agreed.

"Say," the woman said suddenly, triumphantly, pointing at Matt. "I thought you looked familiar. I know who you are! You're the detective who shot the Liberation Army, *Islamic* Liberation Army guy in the alley, aren't you?"

"Actually," Matt said, "the ILA guy shot me."

"Yeah," Bernie said. "But *then* you shot *him*, and killed the bastard. My brother, the lieutenant, thinks you're all right. You know Lieutenant Harry Crowne?"

"I'm afraid not," Matt said.

"Harry and I are old pals," Jason Washington said. "But can we talk about Mr. Wheatley now?"

"Well, I'll tell you this," the woman said. "The one thing Marion isn't is some Islamic nut. He's Mr. Goody Two Shoes. I don't know if he's what Bernie thinks he is, but he's not some revolutionary. He wouldn't hurt a fly."

"Well, I'm glad to hear that," Washington said. "Is there anything else you can tell us about him?"

"I hardly ever see him to talk to," Bernie said. "He mostly keeps to himself."

"You wouldn't happen to know," Jason asked, "if he was in the Army?"

"Yeah, that I know. He was. We were both in 'Nam at the same time. He told me, it could be bullshit, excuse the language, Doris, he told me he was a lieutenant in EOD. That means Explosive Ordnance Disposal."

"Yes, I know," Washington said. "Give me the radio, Matt."

Matt opened his briefcase and handed Washington the radio.

"William One, William Seven."

"One."

"Mr. Wheatley is a bachelor who has told his neighbor he served as a lieutenant in EOD in Vietnam," Washington said.

"Bingo!" Wohl said. "Stay where you are, Jason."

Marion Claude Wheatley was wakened at half past seven by the sound of screeching brakes and tearing metal. He got out of bed, went to the window, and looked down at the intersection of Ridge Avenue and North Broad Street.

Even though he looked carefully up and down both streets as far as he could, he could see no sign of an auto accident.

He turned from the window, took off his pajamas and carefully hung them on a hanger in the closet, then took a shower and shaved and got dressed.

He went down to the restaurant and had two poached eggs on toast, pineapple juice, and a glass of milk for breakfast. He ate slowly, for he had at least half an hour to kill; he hadn't planned to get up until eight, and had carefully set his travel alarm clock to do that. The wreck, or whatever it was, had upset his schedule.

But there really wasn't much that one can do to stretch out two poached eggs on toast, so when he checked his watch when he went back to his room, he saw that he was still running twenty minutes ahead of schedule.

And, of course, into the schedule, he had built in extra time to take care of unforeseen contingencies. With that it mind, he was probably forty-five minutes ahead of what the real time schedule would turn out to be.

He decided he would do everything that had to be done but actually leave the room, and then wait until the real time schedule had time to catch up with the projected schedule.

That didn't burn up much time, either. AWOL bag #1 (one of those with *Souvenir of Asbury Park, N.J.* on it) was already prepared, and it took just a moment to open it and make sure that the explosive device and the receiver were in place, and that the soiled linen in which it was wrapped was not likely to come free.

He sighed. All he could do now was keep looking at his watch until it was time to go.

And then he saw the Bible on the bed. He picked it up and carried it to the desk, and sat down.

"Dear God," he prayed aloud. "I pray that you will give me insight as I prepare to go about your business."

He read, "17. I smote you with blasting and with mildew and

with hail in all the labours of your hands; yet ye turned not to me, saith the Lord," and then he read it aloud.

Haggai 2:17 made no more sense to him now than it ever had.

He wondered if he had made some kind of mistake, if the Lord really intended for him to read Haggai 2:17, but decided that couldn't be. If the Lord didn't want him to read it, the Lord would not have attracted his attention to it.

It was obviously his failing, not the Lord's.

 Supervisory Special Agent H. Charles Larkin of the Secret Service walked across the intersection of Kingsessing Avenue and Farragut and looked down the 1200 block.

He was honestly impressed with the efficiency with which Peter Wohl's men were evacuating the residents of the houses surrounding the residence of M. C. Wheatley. There was no panic, no excitement.

*Obviously,* Larkin decided, *because the people being evacuated were being handled by cops who were both smiling and confident, and seemed to know exactly what they were doing. If the man in the blue suit, the figure of authority, looks as if he is about to become hysterical, that's contagious.*

And since Wohl was really a nice guy, Charley Larkin decided it wouldn't hurt a thing to offer his genuine approval out loud, in the hearing of the Honorable Jerry Carlucci, mayor of the City of Brotherly Love, who had shown up five minutes after he had heard that Wohl intended to take M. C. Wheatley's door.

Larkin turned around, crossed Farragut Street again, and returned to where Carlucci and Wohl were standing by Wohl's car, just out of sight of the residence of M. C. Wheatley.

"I think they're about done," Larkin said. "I'm impressed with the way they're doing that, Peter," he said.

The mayor looked first at Larkin and then at Wohl.

"So am I," Wohl said. "Jack Malone set it up. He put them through a couple of dry runs in the dark at the Schoolhouse."

*I suppose that proves,* Larkin thought, *that while you can't cheat an honest man, you can't get him to take somebody else's credit, either.*

"Peter does a hell of a job with Special Operations, Charley," His Honor said. "I think we can now all say that it was an idea that worked. It. And Peter going in to command it."

" 'The Mayor said,' " Wohl replied, " 'just before the 1200 block of Farragut Street disappeared in a mushroom cloud.' "

"You think he's got it wired, Peter?" Mayor Carlucci asked.

"I believe he's crazy," Wohl said. "Crazy people scare me."

"William One, William Eleven," the radio in Wohl's car went on. William Eleven was Lieutenant Jack Malone.

Officer Paul O'Mara, sitting behind the wheel, handed Wohl the microphone.

"William One," Wohl said.

"All done here."

"Seven?" Wohl said.

"Seven," Jason Washington's voice came back.

"Have you seen any signs of life in there?"

"Nothing. I don't think anybody's in there."

"Your call, Jason. How do you want to take the door?"

"You did say, 'my call'?"

"Right."

"I'll get back to you," Washington said.

"Jason?"

There was no answer.

"Jason?"

"Jason. William Seven, William One."

There was no reply.

"That will teach you, Peter," Mayor Carlucci said, "Never tell Jason 'your call.' "

"William Eleven, William One."

"Eleven."

"Can you see Seven?"

"Payne just jumped onto the porch roof."

"Say again?"

"Payne came out onto the roof over the porch of the house next door, jumped over to the next one, and just smashed the window and went inside."

A bell began to clang.

"What did he say about Payne?" the Mayor asked.

"I hope I didn't hear that right," Wohl said.

He tossed the microphone to Officer O'Mara and quickly got in the front seat beside him, gesturing for him to get moving.

They were halfway down Farragut Street toward the residence of M. C. Wheatley when the radio went off:

"William One, Seven."

Wohl grabbed the microphone and barked, "One," as O'Mara pulled up, with a screech of brakes, in front of the house.

"Boss," Washington's voice came over the radio, "you want to send somebody in here to turn off the burglar alarm?"

There were more screeching brakes. A van skidded to a stop, and discharged half a dozen police officers, two of them buried beneath the layers of miracle plastic that, it was hoped, absorbed the effects of explosions, and all of them wearing yellow jackets with POLICE in large letters on their backs.

As the two Ordnance Disposal experts ran awkwardly up the stairs, the mayoral Cadillac limousine pulled in beside Peter Wohl's car, and Sergeant Jason Washington walked casually out onto the porch.

"Jason, what the hell happened?" Wohl called.

"When Payne let me in, the burglar alarm went off," Washington said innocently.

"That's not what I mean, and you know it," Wohl shouted. "God *damn* the both of you!"

"Where's that mushroom cloud you were talking about, Peter?" the mayor asked, at Wohl's elbow.

"God *damn* them!" Wohl said.

"I don't think he really means that, Charley, do you?" the mayor asked.

"Mr. Mayor," Wohl said. "I think you'd better stay right here."

"Hey, Peter," the mayor said as he started quickly up the stairs of the residence of Mr. M. C. Wheatley. "The way that works is that *I'm* the mayor. I tell *you* what to do."

At 8:25, as the schedule called for, Marion Claude Wheatley picked up AWOL bag #1, left his room in the Divine Lorraine Hotel, caught a bus at Ridge Avenue and North Broad street, and rode it to the North Philadelphia Station of the Pennsylvania Railroad.

There he purchased a coach ticket to Wilmington, Delaware, went up the stairs to the track, and waited for the train, a local that, according to the schedule, would arrive at North Philadelphia at 9:03, depart North Philadelphia at 9:05, and arrive at 30th Street Station at 9:12. Marion didn't care when it would depart 30th Street Station for Chester, and then Wilmington. He wasn't going to Chester or Wilmington.

At 9:12, right on schedule, the train arrived at 30th Street Station. The conductor hadn't even asked for his ticket.

Marion rode the escalator to the main waiting room, walked across it, deposited two quarters in one of the lockers in the passageway to the south exit, deposited AWOL bag #1 in Locker 7870, and put the key into his watch pocket.

Then he went back to the main waiting room, bought a newspaper, and went to the snack bar, where he had two cups of black coffee and two pieces of coffee cake.

There was no coffee cake in the dining room of the Divine Lorraine Hotel, Marion reasoned, because there was no coffee in the dining room of the Divine Lorraine Hotel. He wondered if that was it, or whether Father Divine had found something in Holy Scripture that he thought proscribed pastry as well as alcohol, tobacco, and coffee.

When he had finished his coffee, Marion left the coffee shop and left 30th Street Station by the west exit. He walked to Market Street, and since it was such a nice morning, and since the really important aspect of trip #1, placing AWOL bag #1 in a locker, had been accomplished, he decided he would walk down Market Street, rather than take a bus, as the schedule called for.

The exercise, he thought, would do him good.


"Well, goddammit, then get it from Kansas City!" Supervisory Special Agent H. Charles Larkin said, nearly shouted, furiously. "I want a description, and preferably a photograph, of this sonofabitch here in an hour!"

He slammed the telephone into its cradle.

"I think Charley's mad about something," Chief Inspector Matt Lowenstein said drolly. "Doesn't he seem mad about something to you, Denny?"

"What was that all about, Charley?" Chief Inspector Coughlin asked, chuckling.

"The Army has the records of our guy—his name is Marion Claude, by the way, his first names—in the Depository in Kansas City," Larkin said. "So instead of calling Kansas City to get us a goddamn description and a picture, he calls me!"

"We have a man in Kansas City who does nothing but maintain liaison with the Army Records Depository," Mr. Frank F. Young of the FBI said. "Shall I give him a call, Charley?"

"So do we, Frank," Larkin said. "Don't take this the wrong way, but if we get your guy involved, that's liable to fuck things up even more than they are now."

"I think we can say," Young said, "that we're making progress."

"Yeah," Wohl said. "We now *know* that he has a lot of explosives, and from the way those burglar alarms were wired, even if he hadn't been in EOD, that he knows how to set them off. We don't know what he looks like, or where he is."

One of the telephones on the commissioner's conference table rang.

"Commissioner's conference room, Sergeant Washington," Jason said, grabbing it on the second ring. "Okay, let me have it!" He scribbled quickly on a pad of lined yellow paper, said "Thank you," and hung up.

The others at the table looked at him.

"Marion Claude Wheatley is employed as a petrochemicals market analyst at First Pennsylvania Bank & Trust, main office, on South Broad," Washington said. "A guy from Central Detectives just found out."

"Do they have a photograph of him?" Larkin asked.

"They're being difficult," Washington said. He looked at Peter Wohl. "You want me to go over there, Inspector?"

"You bet I do," Wohl said.

"Can I take Payne with me?"

"If you think you can keep him from playing Tarzan," Wohl said. "And jumping from roof to roof."

"Sergeant, would you mind if I went with you?" H. Charles Larkin asked. "If they're being difficult, I'll show them difficult."

"No, sir," Washington said. "Come along."

*Washington doesn't want him,* Wohl thought, *but there's nothing I can do to stop him.*

"Would four be a crowd?" Frank F. Young asked.

"No, sir," Washington said.

The four quickly left the room.

"What about that guy Young?" Denny Coughlin asked, when the door was closed.

"He either is very anxious to render whatever assistance the FBI can on this job," Lowenstein said, "or he wants to play detective."

"Now that we're alone," Wohl said. "It looks like Lanza, the corporal at the airport, *is* dirty."

"Oh, shit," Coughlin said. "What have you got, Peter?"

"He's been having middle of the night meetings with various Mafioso scumbags. Gian-Carlo Rosselli, Paulo Cassandro, and others. They have been talking about a fruit basket coming in."

"How do you know that, Peter? About the fruit basket?" Lowenstein asked.

"Please don't ask me that question, Chief," Wohl said.

Lowenstein and Coughlin exchanged glances.

"He's under surveillance?" Lowenstein asked.

"By Internal Affairs when he's off the job. And Dickinson Lowell, who's chief of security for Eastern at the airport, has people watching him when he's on the job. Chief Marchessi set that up. He and Lowell are old pals."

"Dickie Lowell is, was, a good cop," Coughlin said. "You have any idea when this 'fruit basket' is coming in?"

"Nine forty-five tonight," Wohl replied. "Eastern Flight 4302 from San Juan."

"You picked that information up, right, from ordinary, routine, legal surveillance of Corporal Lanza, right?" Chief Lowenstein asked.

Wohl hesitated a moment, and then did not reply directly.

"The surveillance of Corporal Lanza leads us to believe that he is spending a lot of time with a lady by the name of Antoinette Marie Wolinski Schermer," he said. "Spends his nights with her. We find this interesting because Organized Crime says Mrs. Schermer is ordinarily the squeeze of Ricco Baltazari, the well-known restaurateur."

"When you take Lanza, can you take any of the scumbags with him?" Coughlin asked.

"More important, are you sure you can take Lanza?" Lowenstein asked.

"We'll just have to see, Chief," Wohl said.

"You have good people doing the surveillance?" Lowenstein asked.

"Internal Affairs is providing most of it," Wohl replied. "And I loaned them Sergeant O'Dowd, but my priority, of course, is finding this Wheatley screwball before he hurts somebody."

"For all of us," Denny said.

"I want this dirty corporal, Peter," Lowenstein said. "Rather than blow it, I would just as soon let this 'fruit basket' tonight slip through. If there's one, there'll be others."

"I'll keep that in mind, Chief."

"We have a minute, with Larkin and Young gone, to talk about what we do now that we know who this Wheatley nut is, but not where he is," Coughlin said.

"Which means you've been thinking about it," Lowenstein said. "Go on, Denny."

"Worst case scenario," Coughlin said. "Despite one hell of an effort by everybody concerned to find this guy, and the only way I know to do that is by running down any and every lead we come across, ringing every other doorbell in the city, we don't find him. The odds are that Washington *will* turn up something at the bank, or from his neighbors. But let's say that doesn't happen."

"Worst case scenario, right?" Lowenstein said sarcastically.

Coughlin's face darkened, but he decided to let the sarcasm pass.

"When Peter said we have to catch Wheatley before he hurts somebody," he went on, "he wasn't talking about just the Vice President. This guy has the means, and I think is just crazy enough, to hurt a lot of people. You heard what Charley said his expert said, that he's probably going to set off his bomb, *bombs*, by radio?"

Both Wohl and Lowenstein nodded.

"That means he could be walking up Market Street with his bomb under his arm and *his* radio in Camden, and somebody turns on a shortwave radio, maybe in an RPC, and off the bomb goes."

"I don't know what we can do about that," Lowenstein said.

"Or he could be walking up Market Street with his bomb under one arm, and his radio under the other, and he spots somebody who looks like the Secret Service, or the FBI, and he pushes the button."

"I don't know where you're going, Denny," Lowenstein confessed.

"Well, I said, 'Market Street' but I don't think he's going to try to set his bomb off on Market Street. He may be a nut, but he's smart. And I don't think he plans to commit suicide when he— what did he say, *'disintegrates'*?—the Vice President. That means he has to put the bomb someplace where he can see it, and the Vice President, from someplace he'll be safe when it goes off."

"Okay," Lowenstein said after a moment.

"There aren't very many places he can do that on Market Street," Coughlin went on. "The only place you could hide a bomb would be, for example, an empty store or a trash can or a mailbox."

"The Post Office will send somebody to open all mailboxes an hour before the Vice President arrives," Wohl replied. "Then they'll chain them shut. Larkin set that up with the postal inspectors. And I, actually Jack Malone, arranged with the City to have every trash basket, et cetera, in which a bomb could be hidden, removed by nine A.M., two hours before the Vice President gets here. And we'll check the stores, empty and otherwise."

"I don't think he's thinking about Market Street anyway," Coughlin said. "He'd have only a second or two to set the bomb off. That's not much margin for error." He paused. "But I damned sure could be wrong. So we're going to have to have Market Street covered from the river to 30th Street Station."

"Which leaves Independence Square and 30th Street Station," Wohl said. "I don't think Independence Square. He knows that we're going to have people all over there, and that he will have a hard time getting close to the Vice President, close enough to hurt him with a bomb."

"That presumes Denny's right about him not wanting to commit suicide," Lowenstein said. "Maybe he likes the idea of being a martyr."

"I think we can let the Secret Service handle somebody rushing up to the Vice President," Coughlin said. "They're very good at that. I keep getting back to 30th Street Station."

"Okay. But tell me why?"

"Well, we can't close it off, for one thing. Trains are going to arrive and depart. They will be carrying people, and many, if not most, of those people will be carrying some kind of luggage, either a briefcase, if they're commuters, or suitcases. Are we going to stop everybody and search their luggage?"

"I don't suppose there's any chance, now that we know this guy is for real, that the Vice President can be talked out of this goddamned motorcade?" Lowenstein asked.

"None," Coughlin said. "I was there when Larkin called Washington."

Lowenstein shrugged and struck a wooden match and relit his cigar.

"We're listening, Denny," he said.

"And there's a lot of places in 30th Street Station to hide a bomb, half a dozen bombs," Coughlin went on. "Places our guy can see from half a dozen places he'd be hard to spot. You follow?"

"Not only do I follow, but I have been wondering if you think Larkin doesn't know all this."

"Larkin knows. We've talked."

"Ah *ha!* And I'll bet that you're about to tell us what you and the Secret Service have come up with, aren't you?"

"What *I* came up with, Matt," Coughlin said. "And what Larkin is willing to go along with."

"Inspector Wohl," Lowenstein said, "why do you think I think the genial Irishman here has just been sold the toll concession on the Benjamin Franklin Bridge?"

"Goddammit, do you always have to be such a cynical sonofabitch? You can be a real pain in the ass, Matt!" the genial Irishman flared. "There *are* some good feds, and Charley Larkin happens to be one of them. If you're too dumb to see that, I'm sorry."

"If I have in any way offended you, Chief Coughlin, please accept my most profound apologies," Lowenstein said innocently. "Please proceed."

"Goddammit, you won't quit, will you?"

They glared at each other for a moment.

Finally, Lowenstein said, "Okay. Sorry, Denny. Let's hear it."

"We are going to have police officers every twenty feet all along the motorcade route, and every ten feet, every five feet, in 30th Street Station and at Independence Hall."

Lowenstein looked at him with incredulity on his face, and then in his voice: "That's it? That's the brilliant plan you and the Secret Service came up with?"

"You have a better idea?"

"How many men is it going to take if we saturate that large an area for what, four hours?" Lowenstein asked.

"We figure six hours," Coughlin said.

"Has Charley Larkin offered to come up with the money to pay for all that overtime?" Lowenstein asked. "Or are we going to move cops in from all over the city, and pray that nothing happens elsewhere?"

"We are going to bring in every uniform in Special Operations," Coughlin began, and then stopped. "This is the idea, Peter. Subject, of course, to your approval."

*I know,* Wohl thought, *and he knows I know, that me arguing against this would be like me telling the pope he's wrong about the Virgin Mary.*

"Go on, please, Chief," Wohl said.

"That's the whole idea of Special Operations, the federal grants we got for it," Coughlin said. "To have police force available anywhere in the city. . . ."

"There's not that many people in Special Operations to put one every ten feet up and down Market Street," Lowenstein said. "The feds pay the bills, and then they tell us what to do, right?" Lowenstein said. "I was against those goddamn grants from the beginning."

*On the other hand,* Wohl thought, *we have the grants all the time, and they don't ask for our help all the time.*

"There will be men available from the districts, and I thought the Detective Bureau would make detectives available."

Lowenstein grunted.

"Plus undercover officers, primarily from Narcotics, but from anyplace else we can find them," Coughlin went on.

He looked at Lowenstein for his reply. Lowenstein grunted, and then looked at Wohl.

"Peter?"

"I don't have a better idea," Wohl said.

"Neither do I," Lowenstein said. "Okay. Next question. Do you think the commissioner will go along with this?"

"The commissioner, I think, is going to hide under his desk until this is all over," Coughlin said. "If we catch this guy, or at least keep him from disintegrating the Vice President, he will hold a press conference to modestly announce how pleased he is his plan worked. If the Vice President is disintegrated, it's Peter's fault. He was never in favor of Special Operations in the first place."

"Was that a crack at me, Denny?"

"If the shoe fits, Cinderella."

"Gentlemen," Mr. H. Logan Hammersmith of First Philadelphia Bank & Trust said, "while I don't mean to appear to be difficult, I'm simply unable to permit you access to our personnel records. The question of confidentiality . . ."

"Mr. Hammersmith," Jason Washington began softly. "I understand your position. But . . ."

"Fuck it, Jason," Mr. H. Charles Larkin interrupted. "I've had enough of this bastard's bullshit."

Mr. Hammersmith was obviously not used to being addressed in that tone of voice, or with such vulgarity and obscenity, which is precisely why Mr. Larkin had chosen that tone of voice and vocabulary.

"I want Marion Claude Wheatley's personnel records, all of them, on your desk in three minutes, or I'm going to take you out of here in handcuffs," Mr. Larkin continued.

"You can't do that!" Mr. Hammersmith said, without very much conviction. "I haven't done anything."

"You're interfering with a federal investigation," Mr. Frank F. Young said.

"Now, we can get a search warrant for this," Larkin said. "It'll take us about an hour. But to preclude the possibility that Mr. Hammerhead here . . ."

"Hammer*smith*," Hammersmith interjected.

". . . who, in my professional judgment, is acting very strangely, does not, in the meantime, conceal, destroy, or otherwise hinder our access to these records, I believe we should take him into custody."

"I agree," Frank F. Young said.

"May I borrow your handcuffs, please, Jason?" Larkin asked politely.

"Yes, sir."

"Would you please stand up, Mr. Hammerhead, and place your hands behind your back?"

"Now just a moment, please," Mr. Hammersmith said. He reached and picked up his telephone.

"Mrs. Berkowitz, will you please go to Personnel and get Mr. Wheatley's entire personnel file? And bring it to me, right away."

"We very much appreciate your cooperation, Mr. Hammersmith," Mr. Larkin said.

The personnel records of Marion Claude Wheatley included a photograph. But either the photographic paper was faulty, or the processing had been, for the photograph stapled to his records was entirely black.

Neither were his records of any help at all in suggesting where he might be found. He listed his parents as next of kin, and Mr. Hammersmith told them he was sure they had passed on.

Mr. Young arranged for FBI agents to go out to the University of Pennsylvania, to examine Wheatley's records there. They found a photograph, but it was stapled to Mr. Wheatley's application for admission, and showed him at age seventeen.

When Mr. Wheatley's records in Kansas City were finally exhumed and examined, the only photograph of Mr. Wheatley they contained, a Secret Service agent reported to Mr. Larkin, had been taken during his Army basic training. It was not a good photograph, and for all practical purposes, Army barbers had turned him bald.

"Wire it anyway," Mr. Larkin replied. "We're desperate."

# TWENTY-NINE

Supervisory Special Agent H. Charles Larkin, Chief Inspector (retired) Augustus Wohl, and Chief Inspector Dennis V. Coughlin were seated around Coughlin's dining-room table when Inspector Peter Wohl came into the apartment a few minutes before ten P.M.

On the table were two telephones, a bottle of Scotch, a bottle of bourbon, and clear evidence that the ordinance of the Commonwealth of Pennsylvania that prohibited gaming, such as poker, was being violated.

"Who's winning?"

"Your father, of course," Charley Larkin replied.

"Deal you in, Peter?" Chief Wohl asked.

"Why not?" Wohl said.

"You want a drink, Peter?" Coughlin asked.

"I better not," Wohl said. "I want to go back to the Schoolhouse before I go home. I hate to have whiskey on my breath."

His father ignored him. He made him a drink of Scotch and handed it to him.

"You look like you need this," he said.

"I corrupt easily," Peter said, taking it, and added, "In case any-body's been wondering, we have come up with zilch, zero."

"That include the airport too?" Coughlin asked.

"Yeah. I gave them this number, Chief, in case something does happen."

"What's going on at the airport?" Larkin asked.

Peter Wohl looked at Coughlin.

"I'm afraid we have a dirty cop out there," Coughlin said.

"I'm sorry," Larkin said.

"We're playing seven-card stud," Chief Wohl said. "Put your money on the table, Peter."

Peter had just taken two twenty-dollar bills and four singles from his wallet when one of the telephones rang.

Coughlin grabbed it on the second ring.

"Coughlin," he said. "Yes, just a moment, he's here." He started to hand the telephone to Peter and then changed his mind. "Is this Dickie Lowell? I thought I recognized your voice. This is Denny Coughlin, Dickie. How the hell are you?"

Then he handed the phone to Peter.

"Peter Wohl," he said, and then listened.

"Have you spoken with Captain Olsen?" he asked. There was a brief pause, and then: "Thank you very much. I owe you one."

He hung up.

"Dickie Lowell?" Chief Wohl asked as he dealt cards. "Retired out of Headquarters Division in the Detective Bureau?"

"He got a job running security for Eastern Airlines," Coughlin said. "He's got his people watching our dirty cop. Peter set it up."

"Chief Marchessi set it up," Peter said. "Lowell's people just saw our dirty cop take a suitcase off Eastern Flight 4302. Specifi-cally, remove a suitcase from a baggage trailer after it had been re-moved from Eastern 4302."

"So what are you going to do, Peter?" Coughlin asked.

Wohl hesitated, and then shrugged.

"Resist the temptation to get on my horse and charge out to the airport," he said. "Where I probably would fuck things up. I sent Sergeant Jerry O'Dowd . . . you know him?"

His father and Chief Coughlin shook their heads, no.

"He works for Dave Pekach. Good man. He's going to follow our dirty cop when he comes off duty. We already have people watching his house and his girlfriend's apartment."

"Sometimes the smartest thing to do is keep your nose out of the tent," Coughlin said. "I think they call that delegation of authority."

"And I think what we have there is the pot calling the kettle black," Chief Wohl said. "Denny was an inspector before he stopped turning off fire hydrants in the summer."

"Go to hell, Augie!"

"What's in the suitcase?" Larkin asked. "Drugs?"

"What else?" Coughlin said.

"I didn't know you handled drugs, Peter," Larkin said.

"Normally, I don't," Peter replied. "Drugs or dirty cops. Thank God. This was Commissioner Marshall's answer to the feds wanting to send their people out there masquerading as cops. He gave the job to me."

"Because you get along so well with we feds, right?" Larkin asked, chuckling.

"There's an exception to every rule, Charley," Coughlin said. "Just be grateful it's you."

"Are we going to play cards or what?" Chief Wohl asked.

Peter Wohl was surprised to find Detective Matthew M. Payne in the Special Investigations office at Special Operations when he walked in at quarter past midnight. He said nothing, however.

*Maybe Jack Malone called him in.*

"How are we doing?" he asked.

"Well," Lieutenant Malone said tiredly, "Mr. Wheatley is not registered in any of Philadelphia's many hotels, motels, or flop houses," Malone said. "Nor did anybody in the aforementioned remember seeing anyone who looked like either of the two artists' representations of Mr. Wheatley."

The Philadelphia Police Department had an artist whose ability to make a sketch of an individual from a description was uncanny. The Secret Service had an artist who Mr. H. Charles Larkin announced was the best he had ever seen. In the interest of getting a picture of Mr. Wheatley out on the street as quickly as possible, the Department artist had made a sketch of Wheatley based on his neighbor's, Mr. Crowne's, description of him, while the Secret Service artist had drawn a sketch of Mr. Wheatley based on Mr. Wheatley's boss, Mr. H. Logan Hammersmith's, description of him.

There was only a very vague similarity between the two sketches. Rather than try to come up with a third sketch that would be a compromise, Wohl had ordered that both sketches be distributed.

"Too bad," Wohl said.

"The sonofabitch apparently doesn't have any friends," Malone said. "The neighbor, two houses down, lived there fifteen years, couldn't ever remember seeing him."

"He's got to be somewhere, Jack," Wohl said.

"I sent Tony Harris to Vice," Malone said. "They went to all the fag bars with the pictures."

"We don't know he's homosexual."

"I thought maybe he's a closet queen, who has an apartment somewhere," Malone said.

"Good thought, Jack, I didn't think about that."

"They struck out too," Malone said.

"And how's your batting record, Detective Payne?"

It was intended as a joke. Payne looked very uncomfortable.

"I just thought maybe I could make myself useful, so I came in," Payne said.

*That's bullshit.*

The telephone rang. Malone grabbed it and handed it to Wohl.

"Jerry O'Dowd, Inspector," his caller said. "I'm calling from the tavern down the corner from our friend's house. He drove straight here, with the suitcase, and took it into the house."

"Good man," Wohl said.

"Oooops, there he comes."

"With the suitcase?"

"No. He doesn't have it. He's changed out of his uniform."

"You're going to stay there, right?"

"Right. He's walking back to his car. But Captain Olsen can see him. No problem."

"Olsen is on him?" Wohl asked, surprised.

"Yes, sir. Olsen won't lose him."

"If anything happens, call this number, they'll know where to get me."

"Yes, sir."

"I'm going to send somebody to back you up," Wohl said. "In case somebody interesting comes to pick up the suitcase."

"Yes, sir."

"Good job, Jerry," Wohl said, and hung up.

*If Olsen can work this job himself, why can't I? I'd love to catch Ricco Baltazari or one of his pals walking down Ritner Street with that suitcase in his hand.*

*Dangerous thought. No!*

"Jack, can we get our hands on Tony Harris?"

"Yes, sir."

"Get on the horn to him and tell him to go back up O'Dowd."

"Yes, sir."

"And then turn this over to the duty lieutenant and go home and get some sleep."

"Yes, sir."

"That applies to you too, Detective Payne. With all the jumping from roof to roof, and through windows, you've done today, I'm sure you're worn out. Go home and go to bed. I want you here at eight A.M., bright-eyed and bushy-tailed."

*That, to judge by the kicked puppy look in your eyes, was another failed attempt to be jocular.*

"Yes, sir."

*Or is there something else wrong with him? Something is wrong.*

"Jack, you want to go somewhere for a nightcap?" Wohl asked. "The reason I am being so generous is that I just took forty bucks from my father and Chief Coughlin, who don't play poker nearly as well as they think they do."

"I accept, Inspector. Thank you."

"The invitation includes you, Detective Payne, if you promise not to jump through a window or otherwise embarrass Lieutenant Malone and me."

"Thank you, I'll try to behave."

*The look of gratitude in your eyes now, Matt, is almost pathetic. What the hell is wrong with you?*


Jack Malone had two drinks, the second reluctantly, and then said he had to get to bed before he went to sleep at the bar.

"I'm going to call the Schoolhouse, and see what happened to Lanza," Wohl said. "And then I'm going home. Order one more, please, Matt."

Two minutes later, Wohl got back on the bar stool beside Payne.

"Lanza went to the Schermer woman's apartment. The lights went out, and Olsen figures he's in for the night," he reported.

"And you're hoping that somebody will show up at his house for the suitcase?" Payne asked.

Wohl nodded. "We may get lucky."

"Why didn't he take it with him? Isn't that woman involved?"

"I don't know how much she's involved, and I don't know why he left the suitcase at his house. These people are very careful."

Payne nodded.

"And now that Malone has gone home, and I don't have to be officially outraged—as opposed to personally admiring—at your roof-jumping escapade, are you going to tell me what's bothering you?"

"Jesus, does it show?"

"Yeah, it shows."

Matt looked at him for a moment, and then at his drink for a longer moment, before finally saying, "Penny Detweiler is in the psycho ward at University Hospital."

"I'm sorry to hear that," Wohl said.

*But not surprised. A junkie is a junkie is a junkie.*

"I put her there," Matt said.

"What do you mean, you put her there?"

"You really don't want to hear this."

*You're right. I really don't want to hear this.*

"I'm not trying to pry, Matt. But, hell, sometimes if you talk things over, when you're finished, they don't seem to be as bad."

It was quarter to two when Inspector Wohl, not without misgivings, installed Detective Payne behind the wheel of the unmarked Ford and sent him home with the admonition to try not to run any stoplights or into a station wagon full of nuns.

*I believed what I told him, that if it hadn't been the other woman showing up at his apartment, that it would have been something else. That being turned loose from a drug addiction program does not mean the addiction is cured, just that, so far as they can tell, it's on hold.*

*But clearly, if the horny little bastard wasn't fucking every woman in town, it would not have happened. Taking the Detweiler girl to bed was idiotic. He has earned every ounce of the weight of shameful regret he's carrying.*

*But his wallowing in guilt isn't going to do anybody any good.*

*Sometimes, Peter Wohl, you are so smart, so Solomon-like, I want to throw up.*

He started home to Chestnut Hill, then suddenly changed his mind, got on first Roosevelt Boulevard and then the Schuylkill Expressway and headed for Ritner Street.

*I don't want to go to bed. I don't want to delegate authority. I want to put that dirty cop and the Mafioso he's running around with away. And right now there's nobody who can tell me to butt out.*

Wohl drove slowly down Ritner Street, saw where Sergeant O'Dowd was parked, and made a left at the next corner and parked the car.

O'Dowd had been alone when he had driven past, but as he walked up to the car now, he first saw another head, and then recognized it as that of Detective Tony Harris, sitting beside O'Dowd.

Wohl opened the rear door and got in.

"I thought that was you driving by," O'Dowd said. "Something come up?"

"I got curious, is all," Wohl said. "I just happened to be in the neighborhood."

"There's somebody in the house," Tony Harris said. "I was out in back. You know how these houses are laid out, Inspector? With the bathroom at the back of the house?"

"Yeah, sure."

"First a dull light, which means a light on in one of the bedrooms, shining into the hall. Then a bright light. Somebody's in the bathroom. I figure it's his mother, taking a piss. Then the bright light goes out, and then the dim light, and I figure she's back in bed."

"Okay. So what?"

"So nothing. So that's what's been going on here."

"There's more, Tony. What are you thinking?"

"I don't think Paulo Cassandro or Ricco Baltazari or any other Mafioso is going to come waltzing down Ritner Street tonight to pick up that suitcase. Those bastards aren't stupid. There's been half a dozen cars come by here, any one of who could have been taking a look, and if they were, they saw us."

"Oh, ye of little faith!" Wohl said.

*Why did you say that? Jesus, that was dumb! Three drinks and your mouth gallops away with you!*

"You're the boss. You say sit on the house, we'll sit on the house."

"Tell me what you think is going to happen, Tony," Wohl said.

"I'll tell you what I *don't* think is going to happen," Harris said.

"Okay. Tell me what's not going to happen."

"I don't think we're going to catch anybody but this dirty cop. The Mob is going to come up with some pretty clever way to get their hands on that suitcase without us catching them at it."

"Okay. So what would you do if you were me?"

"Let's say we catch Lanza actually handling the suitcase to, say, Ricco Baltazari. We arrest them. They have the best lawyers around. They say we set them up. They ask all kinds of questions of how come we were watching Lanza in the first place. The guy has a spotless record, et cetera. And Lanza is not, I'll bet my ass on it, going to pass the suitcase to anybody. If they send somebody for it, or they tell Lanza to carry it someplace and give it to somebody, we arrest him, it will be some jerk we can't tie to Baltazari or anybody else. And Lanza pleads the Fifth and won't help either. He takes the fall. He pleads guilty to stealing a suitcase. He doesn't know anything about drugs, he just stole a suitcase. First offense, what'll he get?"

"What I asked, Tony, is what you would do if you were in charge?"

"You really want to know, or are we just sitting here killing time bullshitting?"

"I really want to know."

"I go up to the door, I say 'Sorry to bother you this time of night, Mrs. Lanza, but Vito brought my suitcase here, and I'm here to collect it.' She gives me the suitcase, while you and O'Dowd watch, and O'Dowd takes pictures, and then we bust her for possession of cocaine, or whatever shit is in the suitcase. And then we go get Vito out of his girlfriend's bed and tell him he better go down to Central lockup and see what he can do for his mother, who's charged with possession with the intent to distribute. And the Mob is out however much shit they was trying to ship in."

There was a long silence.

"Not you, Tony," Wohl said, finally. "Martinez. In uniform."

"Martinez, the little Spic? What's he got to do with this?"

"*Detective* Martinez, Detective Harris, has been working undercover at the airport, trying to catch whoever has been smuggling drugs."

"No shit?"

"If Mrs. Lanza asked him questions about the airport, he would know the answers," Wohl said.

"Yeah," Harris said thoughtfully.

"That saloon is closed," Wohl said, after looking out the rear window. "Where can I find a telephone around here?"

"There's a pay station on Broad Street. If somebody hasn't ripped it off the wall."

● ● ●

"Hello?"

"You awake, Matt?"

"Yes, sir. What's up?"

"You know Martinez's home phone and where he lives?"

"Yes, sir."

"Call him up. Tell him to put his uniform on, then pick him up, and meet me at Moyamensing and South Broad."

"Right now?"

"Right now."

The door to the apartment of Mrs. Antoinette Marie Wolinski Schermer opened just a crack. It was evident that she had the chain in place.

"What is it?" Mrs. Schermer asked, her tone mingled annoyance and concern.

"It's the police, Mrs. Schermer," Captain Swede Olsen said. "We're here to talk to Corporal Lanza."

When there was no immediate response, Captain Olsen added, "We know he's here, Tony. Open the door."

The door closed. It remained closed for about a minute, but it seemed much longer than that. And then it opened.

Vito, wearing a sleeveless undershirt and trousers, his hair mussed, stood inside the door.

"Corporal Lanza," Olsen said, "I'm Captain Olsen of Internal Affairs. These are Detectives Martinez and Payne. I think you can guess why we're here."

Vito looked at Martinez and Payne. His surprise registered in his eyes, but then they grew cold and wary.

"What's going on?"

"We want you to get dressed and come with us, Corporal," Olsen said conversationally.

"What for?"

"You know what for, Lanza," Olsen said.

"You got a warrant?"

"No. We don't have a warrant. We don't need a warrant."

"What's the charge?"

"That's going to depend in large part on you, Lanza. For the moment, you can consider yourself under arrest for theft of luggage from Eastern Airlines."

Lanza's face whitened.

"I don't know what you're talking about," Lanza said.

"Detective Martinez," Olsen said, "will you go with Corporal Lanza while he puts his clothes on? Take his pistol."

"Yes, sir."

"This is some kind of mistake," Vito Lanza said.

"Get your clothes on, Lanza," Olsen said.

"You're a detective?" Lanza asked Martinez.

"Yeah, I'm a detective."

"Get your clothes on," Captain Olsen repeated. "It's over, Lanza."

Lanza turned and went into the apartment. Martinez followed him.

"Mrs. Schermer," Captain Olsen said. "Detectives are going to want to talk to you later today. They will call you either here, or at work, and set up a time."

"I don't know what this is all about," Tony said.

"You can talk about that with the detectives," Captain Olsen said.

The three stood at the door for the two or three minutes it took Vito to put his shoes and socks and a shirt on.

Finally he came back to the door, followed by Jesus Martinez, who carried Vito's off-duty snub-nosed revolver and its holster in his hand.

"Give the pistol to Detective Payne," Captain Olsen ordered. "And put handcuffs on Corporal Lanza."

They walked down the corridor to the elevator, where Vito saw that the door was being held open by a Highway Patrolman. There was another Highway Patrolman in the lobby, and when they got to the street, there were two Highway RPCs, the lights on their bubble gum machines flashing. There were two unmarked cars on the street, their behind-the-grills blue lights flashing, and three or four people in plainclothes Vito had been a cop long enough to know were fellow police officers.

Vito Lanza, for a moment, thought he was going to throw up, then he felt hands on his arms, and a Highway Patrolman put his hand on the top of Vito's head, and pushed down, so that Vito wouldn't bang his head on the door as he got into the back seat of one of the Highway RPCs.

"Watch your fucking head, scumbag," the Highway officer said.

Ricco Baltazari's voice, when he answered the telephone, was sleepy and annoyed.

"Yeah?" he snarled.

"Ricco?" Tony asked.

He recognized the voice. His tone changed to concern and anger. "What are you doing, calling here?"

"Who is it?" Mrs. Baltazari asked, rolling over on her back.

"Ricco, the cops were just here. They arrested Vito."

"What?"

"A guy who said he was a captain, and two detectives, and they told him to get dressed, and they took his gun away and put hand-cuffs on him, and when I looked out the window, there was cop cars all over the street."

"Jesus, Mary, and Joseph!"

"What *is* it, honey?" Mrs. Baltazari asked. "Who is that?"

"Go back to sleep, for Christ's sake," Ricco said. "Okay. I'll take care of it. You just keep your mouth shut, Tony, you under-stand?"

"Ricco, I'm scared!"

"Just keep your goddamned mouth shut!" Ricco said, and hung up.

He got out of bed, and found a cigarette, but no matches.

He walked to the bedroom door.

"Where are you *going*?" Mrs. Baltazari demanded.

"Just, goddammit, go back to sleep."

Mr. Baltazari then went downstairs and into the kitchen and found a match for his cigarette, and lit it, and then banged his fist on the sink and said, "Shit!"

He then picked up the handset of the wall telephone and started to dial a number, but then hung up angrily.

*If the cops have the cop, they maybe have this line tapped. I can't call from here. I'm going to have to go to a pay phone.*

*But shit, if the cops have the cop, they're as likely to have Gian-Carlo's phone tapped as they are to have this one tapped.*

*I'm going to have to go to Gian-Carlo's house and wake him up and tell him the cops have the cop. And that means they have the shipment for the people in Baltimore!*

*Jesus Christ! He's not going to like this worth a fuck! And Mr. Savarese!*

*It's not my fucking fault! I don't know what happened, but it's not my fucking fault!*

*But they're not going to believe that!*

*Oh, Jesus Christ!*

• • •

Salvatore J. Riccuito, Esq., a slightly built, olive-skinned thirty-two-year-old, was a recent addition to the district attorney's staff. Prior to his admission to the bar, he had spent eleven years as a police officer, mostly in the 6th District, passing up opportunities to take examinations for promotion in order to find time to graduate from LaSalle College and then the Temple University School of Law, both at night.

Understandably, because he knew how cops thought and behaved, if he was available, he was assigned cases involving the prosecution of police officers. When this case had come up, via a 3:15 A.M. telephone call from Thomas J. "Tommy" Callis, the district attorney himself, Sal had pleaded unavailability. Callis has been unsympathetic.

"We'll rearrange your schedule. Get down to Narcotics and see Inspector Peter Wohl."

Sal knew there was no point in arguing. Wohl had been the investigator in the case that resulted in Judge Findermann taking a long-term lease in the Pennsylvania Penal System. Callis had prosecuted himself. The publicity would probably help him get reelected.

In a way, Sal thought as he drove to the Narcotics Unit, it was flattering. Wohl almost certainly had not asked for "an assistant DA." He had either asked for "a good assistant DA" or possibly even for him by name.

"Let me tell you how things are, Vito," Sal, who had grown up six blocks from Vito, but didn't know him personally, said.

Vito was sitting handcuffed to a steel captain's chair in one of the interview rooms in the headquarters of the Narcotics unit. He was slightly mussed, as it had been necessary to physically restrain him on his arrival at Narcotics, when he had seen his mother similarly handcuffed to a steel captain's chair.

"Tell me how things are," Vito said with a bluster that was almost pathetically transparent.

"You're dead. That's how things are. They saw you steal the suitcase. They saw you sneak it out to the parking lot. They have *photographs*."

"The sonsofbitches, fucking cocksuckers, had no right to do that to my mother!"

"Let's talk about your mother," Sal said. "She gave the suitcase to Detective Martinez. They have photographs. They have witnesses, a detective, a sergeant, *a staff inspector*. The chain of evidence, with your mother, is intact. The suitcase contained about twenty pounds of cocaine. Nine Ks. They just got the lab report. It's good stuff. If they decide to prosecute, she's going down. Simple possession is all it takes for a conviction."

"She didn't know anything about it," Lanza said. "They tricked her. Can they do that?"

"The little Mexican said, quote, Can I have the suitcase Vito brought? end quote, and she gave it to him. No illegal search and seizure, if that's what you're asking."

"Sonsofbitches!"

"They will not prosecute your mother if you cooperate."

"Fuck 'em!"

"You want your mother to ride downtown to Central Detention? You got the money to make her bail? You got ten thousand dollars to pay a bondsman? And that's what the bail will be for that much cocaine. Or do you want her to spend the next six months waiting for her trial in the House of Detention?"

"Why the fuck should I trust them after what they did to my mother?"

"You're not trusting them. You're trusting me. *I'm* the assistant DA. You cooperate, and I'll have your mother out of here in ten minutes. I'll even see she gets home safe."

"Okay, okay," Vito said. He tried to put his right hand to his eyes to stem the tears that were starting, but it was held fast by handcuffs. He put his left hand to his eyes.

Sal handed Vito a handkerchief.

"Take a minute," Sal said. "Then we'll get a steno in here."

At 8:45 A.M. Marion Claude Wheatley finished his breakfast of poached eggs on toast and milk, left a fifty-cent tip under his plate in the dining room of the Divine Lorraine Hotel, and rode the elevator up to his room.

He unlocked the closet, and took AWOL bag #4 of the three remaining AWOL bags—another one with *Souvenir of Asbury Park, N.J.* airbrushed on its sides—from the closet and locked the closet door again.

He was pleased that he had had the foresight to prepare all of the AWOL bags at once. Now all he had to do was take them from the closet as he began the delivery process.

He looked around the room, and, although he really didn't think it would do any good, walked to the Bible on the desk and read Haggai 2:17 again, seeking insight.

"I smote you with blasting and with mildew and with hail in all the labours of your hands; yet ye turned not to me, saith the Lord," made no more sense now than it ever had.

Marion picked up AWOL bag #4 and left his room, carefully locking the door after him, and went down in the elevator to the lobby.

He left his key with the colored lady behind the desk. He had learned that her name was Sister Fortitude, and he used it now.

"It looks, praise the Lord, as if we're going to have another fine day, doesn't it, Sister Fortitude?"

"Yes, it does," Sister Fortitude said.

*She doesn't seem very friendly,* Marion thought. *I wonder if that is because I'm not colored? Or am I just imagining it?*

Marion walked out onto North Broad Street and crossed it, and walked up half a block to the little fast-food place he'd found where he could get a cup of coffee and a Danish pastry to begin the day, and went in.

Sister Fortitude walked from behind the desk and went and stood by the door beside the revolving door and watched as Marion took a seat at the counter and ordered his coffee.

*I knew there was something about that man,* she thought.

She watched until Marion had finished a second cup of coffee and left the restaurant and walked, north, out of sight.

Then she went to the elevator and went up to Marion's room and unlocked the door and went inside. She knew what the room should contain, in terms of hotel property, and a quick look showed nothing missing.

But Sister Fortitude, who had read several magazine articles about how professional hotel thieves operated, knew that did not mean that he hadn't stolen whatever he was stealing from another room.

There was nothing in the closet that the white man could steal but wire hangers, but Sister Fortitude decided to check it anyway. When she found that it was locked, her suspicions grew. She went into the adjacent room, took the key from that closet door, and carried it back to Marion's room. It didn't work.

Sister Fortitude had to get, and try, four different closet keys from four different rooms before one operated the lock in the white man's room.

Two minutes later, Sister Fortitude ran out onto North Broad Street, looking for a policeman.

*You never could find one when you needed one,* she thought.

And then she saw one, in the coffee shop where the white man had gone to get the coffee he couldn't get in the Divine Lorraine Hotel Restaurant.

She walked quickly across Broad Street.

"I want you to come with me," Sister Fortitude said to the policeman. "I got something to show you."

At ten minutes past nine A.M., Sergeant Jerry O'Dowd and Detective Matt Payne were driving up North Broad Street in O'Dowd's unmarked car. They had finally been released at Internal Affairs, and although Matt thought he was about to fall asleep on his feet, he knew he had to go back to Northwest Detectives and get his Bug before all sorts of questions he didn't want to answer would be asked.

There was considerable police activity at the intersection of Broad and Ridge; Broad Street was blocked off, and a white cap was directing traffic in a detour.

When they finally got to the white cap, Jerry rolled the window down in idle curiosity to ask him what was going on.

And then he saw, at the same moment Matt Payne saw, the large blue and white Ordnance Disposal van, with the Explosive Containment trailer hitched to the rear of it.

Without exchanging a word, they both got out of the car and ran toward the Divine Lorraine Hotel.

"You can't just leave your car here!" the white cap called after them.

There was a uniformed lieutenant standing with a large black woman at the desk.

"What's going on here?" O'Dowd asked as he pinned his badge to his jacket.

"And who the hell are you, Sergeant?"

"Watch your mouth, we don't tolerate that sort of talk in here," Sister Fortitude said.

"I'm Sergeant O'Dowd, sir, of Special Operations. We're working on the bomb threat."

Matt took the artists' drawings of Marion Claude Wheatley from his pocket and gave them to Sister Fortitude.

"Ma'am, do you recognize these?"

Sister Fortitude studied both pictures carefully, and then held one out.

"This one, I do. I never saw the other one."

"This is the man who . . . what, rented a room?" Matt asked.

"Said he was about the Lord's work. Satan's work is more like it."

"Where is the bomb?" O'Dowd asked.

"Six-eighteen," Sister Fortitude said.

The elevators were not running. The hotel's electric service had been shut off to make sure no stray electric current would trigger the bomb's detonators.

Matt and O'Dowd were panting when they reached the sixth floor. O'Dowd pulled open the fire door on the landing, and they entered the dark corridor, now lit only by police portable flood-lights and what natural light there was.

Halfway down the corridor Matt saw two Bomb Squad men in their distinctive, almost black coveralls. He remembered hearing at the Academy that they were made of special material that did not generate static electricity.

O'Dowd shook hands with one of the Bomb Squad men.

"Hey, Bill. What have we got?"

"Enough C-4, wrapped with chain, to do a lot of damage."

"Bill Raybold, Matt Payne," O'Dowd said.

"Yeah, I know who you are," Raybold said, shaking Matt's hand.

*He knows me by reputation. Is that reputation that of the brave and heroic police officer who won the shootout in the alley, or that of the poor sonofabitch who's got a junkie for a girlfriend?*

"The lady at the desk downstairs says the guy who rented 618 is the guy we're looking for," Matt said. "I showed her the police artist's drawing."

"This guy knows what he's doing with explosives," Raybold replied. "The explosive is Composition C-4. It's military, and as safe as it gets. Your man may be crazy, but he's not stupid. He's got them all ready to go except for the detonators. It would take him no more than ten seconds to hook them up."

"Detonators?" O'Dowd asked.

"Not close to here. Jimmy Samuels was in here with his dog, and the only time the dog got happy was when he sniffed the closet. After we get the hotel cleared, we'll take a really good look."

"Bill," O'Dowd said. "If our guy sees the dog and pony show outside, he'll disappear again."

Raybold considered that for a moment.

"Yeah," he said, after a moment. "I don't see why we couldn't leave this stuff here for a while. It's safe. But that don't mean the district captain would go along. And it's his call."

"Sergeant, I don't know who you think you are," the district captain said, "But nobody tells me to throw the book away. We got a crime scene here, and we're going to work it."

"Captain," Detective Payne said, "sir, I've got Chief Coughlin on the line. He'd like to talk to you."

At fifteen minutes to eleven A.M., Marion Claude Wheatley got off the bus and walked across Ridge Avenue and into the lobby of the Divine Lorraine Hotel.

He smiled at Sister Fortitude but she didn't smile back, just nodded.

*I wonder if I have done, or said, something that has offended her?*

Marion got on the elevator and rode to his floor. He had bought a newspaper in 30th Street Station, and he planned to read it as he tried to move his bowels. He was suffering from constipation, and had decided it was a combination of his usual bowel movement schedule being disrupted and the food in the Divine Lorraine Hotel Restaurant. He had decided he would take the next several meals elsewhere to see if that would clear his elimination tract.

There was a man sitting in the upholstered chair in the room. He smiled.

"Hello, Marion," he said. "We've been waiting for you."

"Who are you? What do you want?"

"The Lord sent us, Marion. I'm Brother Jerome, and that is Brother Matthew," the man said.

Marion turned and saw another man, a younger one, almost a boy, nicely dressed, standing behind him, just inside the door.

"The Lord sent you?"

"Yes, He did," Brother Jerome said.

"Why?"

"You misunderstood the Lord's message, Marion," Brother Jerome said. "You have the Lord's method out of sequence."

"I don't understand," Marion said.

O'Dowd picked up the Bible from the desk and read aloud: " 'I smote you with blasting and with mildew and with hail in all the labours of your hands; yet ye turned not to me.' "

"Haggai 2:17," Marion said.

"Precisely," Brother Jerome said, adding kindly, "First mildew, Marion. Then hail, and only *finally* blasting."

"Oh," Marion said. "*Oh!* Now I understand."

"Marion, could I see your newspaper, please?" the younger man asked.

"Certainly," Marion said and gave it to him. Then he turned back to Brother Jerome. "I knew the Lord wanted to tell me something," he said.

Brother Matthew patted the newspaper as if he expected to find something in it. Brother Jerome gave him a dirty look. Brother Matthew shook his head, no, and shrugged.

"Well, the Lord understands, Marion," Brother Jerome said. "You were trying, and the Lord knows that."

"Marion, where's the transmitter?" Brother Matthew asked.

Brother Jerome closed his eyes.

"It's in the 30th Street Station," Marion said. "Why do you want to know?"

"The Lord wants us to take over from here, Marion," Brother Jerome said. "He knows how hard you've been working. Where's the transmitter in 30th Street Station?"

"In a locker," Marion said, and reached in his watch pocket and took out several keys. "I really can't tell you which of these keys . . ."

"It's all right, Marion," Brother Jerome said, taking the keys from him. "We'll find it."

At 7:45 P.M., Detective Matthew M. Payne got off the elevator in the Psychiatric Wing of the University of Pennsylvania Hospital.

One of the nurses at the Nursing Station, a formidable red-haired harridan, told him that Miss Detweiler was in 9023, but he couldn't see her because his name wasn't on the list, and anyway, her doctor was in there.

"Dr. Payne is expecting me," Matt said. "Ninety twenty-three, you said?"

Penny was sitting in a chrome, vinyl-upholstered chair by the window. She was wearing a hospital gown and, he could not help but notice, absolutely nothing else. Amelia Payne, M.D., was sitting on the bed.

"What are you doing here?" Dr. Payne snapped.

"I heard this is where the action is," Matt said.

"I don't think this is a good idea," Amy said. "I think you had better leave."

"Please, Amy!" Penny said.

"Take a walk, Amy," Matt said.

Dr. Payne considered that for a long moment, and then pushed herself off the bed and walked to the door, where she turned.

"Five minutes," she said, and left.

Matt walked over to Penny and handed her a grease-stained paper bag.

"Ribs," he said. "They're cold by now, but I'll bet they'll be better than what they serve in here."

"I don't suppose I could have eaten roses, but candy would have been nice," Penny said. "Matt, are you disgusted with me?"

"I was," he blurted. "Until just now. When I saw you."

"My parents blame you for the whole thing, you know," she said.

"I figured that would happen."

"Amy says it was my fault."

"Amy's right," Matt said. "If you had thrown something at me, even taken a shot at me, that would have been my fault. But what you did to yourself . . ."

Penny suddenly pushed herself out of the chair. She threw the bag of ribs at the garbage can and missed. She turned to the window. Matt could see her backbone and the crack of her buttocks. He looked away, then headed for the door.

"Amy's right. I shouldn't have come here."

Penny turned.

"Matt!"

He looked at her.

"Matt, don't leave me!"

After a long moment, he said, his voice on the edge of breaking, "Penny, I don't know what to do with you!"

"Give me a chance," she said. "Give *us* a chance!"

Then she walked, almost ran to him, stopped and looked up at him.

"Please, Matt," she said, and then his arms went around her.

*I love her.*

*A junkie is a junkie is a junkie.*

*Oh,* shit!

District Attorney Thomas J. Callis, after a psychiatric examination of Marion Claude Wheatley, petitioned the court for Mr. Wheatley's involuntary commitment to a psychiatric institution for the criminally insane. The petition was granted.

• • •

District Attorney Callis, after studying the available evidence, decided that it was insufficient to bring Mr. Paulo Cassandro, Mr. Ricco Baltazari, Mr. Gian-Carlo Rosselli, or any of the others mentioned in Mr. Vito Lanza's sworn statements to trial.

Mr. Vito Lanza, on a plea of guilty to charges of possession of controlled substances with the intention to distribute, was sentenced to two years imprisonment. At Mr. Callis's recommendation, no charges were brought against Mrs. Magdelana Lanza.

Inspector Peter Wohl retained command of the Special Operations Division of the Philadelphia Police Department.

Detective Matthew M. Payne was led to believe by Supervisory Special Agent H. Charles Larkin of the Secret Service that his application for appointment to the Secret Service would be favorably received. Detective Payne declined to make such an application.

Mr. Ricco Baltazari was found shot to death in a drainage ditch in the Tinnicum Swamps near Philadelphia International Airport. No arrests have been made to date in the case.